# Breathmoss

## and Other Exhalations

## IAN R. MACLEOD

GOLDEN GRYPHON PRESS · 2004

"Big Lies," copyright © 2004, by Ian R. MacLeod.
"Breathmoss," first published in *Asimov's Science Fiction*, May 2002.
"Verglas," first published in *The Magazine of Fantasy & Science Fiction*, October/November 1996.
"The Chop Girl," first published in *Asimov's Science Fiction*, December 1999.
"The Noonday Pool," first published in *The Magazine of Fantasy & Science Fiction*, May 1995.
"New Light on the Drake Equation," first published in SCI FICTION, May 2001.
"Isabel of the Fall," first published in *Interzone*, July 2001.
"The Summer Isles," first published in *Asimov's Science Fiction*, October/November 1998.

LIBRARY OF CONGRESS CATALOGING–IN–PUBLICATION DATA

MacLeod, Ian R., 1956–
    Breathmoss and other exhalations / Ian R. MacLeod. — 1st ed.
        p.        cm.
    ISBN 1-930846-26-6 (alk. paper)
        1. Fantasy fiction, English.    I. Title.
PR6063.A24996    B74        2004
823'.914—dc22                    2003026207

# CONTENTS

For Valda and Colin

With love

# Big Lies

WITH ALL THE TALK ABOUT THIS OR THAT KIND of writing, it's often easy to forget what fiction is really about. Yes, there can be badges, definitions, but they're always a cheap shorthand for the real thing, and not the thing itself. Fiction, at its heart, is about telling stories, and stories, in their essence, are interesting lies. The most realistic fiction, even the fiction which attempts to tell something resembling the truth, either thinly veiled or supposedly unveiled, is still made up. If we want reality, or what generally passes for it, we can seek it elsewhere. But it's a strange characteristic of us humans that we often find our curiosity more piqued by events that have never happened than by those which have.

If all stories are interesting lies, and if the whole genre of fantastic fiction were to be boiled down to one overriding principle, it might be: If we're going to tell lies, we might as well make them big ones. Why set your events in your version of a real city, for example, when you can make a whole city up? And then, once you've started inventing that city, it almost seems a shame, a poverty of the imagination, to stick entirely to ordinary architecture, road names, social habits, and shop fronts. Once you start in that direction, there is, I think, always a desire to go that little bit further. Perhaps it's born of nothing more unusual than the natural human tendency to exaggerate.

For me, first as a reader and then also as a writer, the paradox of the Big Lie has always been a source of fascination. Why should we often care more about the lives of made-up people than we do about our colleagues and neighbours? And then, why should that concern extend into impossible pasts and unknown futures? In essence, I think the reason is the same one that makes us want to read any kind of story. Stories, in their big or small lies, promise to make a better fist of cause and effect, happiness and sadness, love, hate, redemption, and all the other things we fear and crave, than we often experience in our own lives.

You'll find that some of the lies I tell in this book are about the future, and that some depict odd varieties of the present or past. There are cities, certainly, far odder and more remote than any we can reach today. There are also, I hope, wonders and glories and horrors. But there are also things, feelings and moments which are meant to lie close to where we are now, and what we felt yesterday, and will dream tonight, and see tomorrow when we awake.

Stories are complex lies. They stretch the imagination, and ask us to believe in and care about things which aren't. And the best kind of stories, to my mind, are the ones which tell the biggest lies and stretch us the furthest. Not because they make us jump implausible light years, or subject us to unremitting strangeness or horror, and especially not because they're quite like the tale we read last week. The best stories, the ones I strive to tell, are stories that make us think, stories which surprise us not because they're showing us something new, but because they're revealing through a lie's tilted mirror something we suddenly realise with that lovely rush of recognition we've known all along. So let's forget, at least for a while, about categories, and even about what is and what isn't real. Let's just enjoy some Big Lies.

Ian R. MacLeod
West Midlands, UK
October 2003

# Breathmoss
# And Other Exhalations

# Breathmoss

## 1.

IN HER TWELFTH STANDARD YEAR, WHICH ON HABARA was the Season of Soft Rains, Jalila moved across the mountains with her mothers from the high plains of Tabuthal to the coast. For all of them, the journey down was one of unhurried discovery, with the kamasheens long gone and the world freshly moist, and the hayawans rusting as they rode them, and the huge flat plates of their feet swishing through purplish-green undergrowth. She saw the cliffs and qasrs she'd only visited from her dreamtent, and sailed across the high ridges on ropewalks her distant ancestors had built, which had seemed frail and antique to her in her worried imaginings, but were in fact strong and subtle; huge dripping gantries heaving from the mist like wise giants, softly humming, and welcoming her and her hayawan, whom she called Robin, in cocoons of effortless embrace. Swaying over the drop beyond into grey-green nothing was almost like flying.

The strangest thing of all in this journey of discoveries was that the landscape actually seemed to rise higher as they descended and encamped and descended again; the sense of *up* increased, rather than that of down. The air on the high plains of Tabuthal was rarefied—Jalila knew that from her lessons in her dreamtent; they were so close to the stars that Pavo had had to clap a mask over her face from the moment of her birth until the breathmoss was embedded in her lungs. And it had been clear up there, it was always clear, and it was pleasantly cold. The sun shone all day hard and cold and white from the blue blackness, as did a billion stars at night, although Jalila had never thought of those things as she ran amid the crystal trees and her mothers smiled at her and occasionally warned her that, one day, all of this would have to change.

And now that day was upon her, and this landscape—as Robin, her hayawan, rounded the path through an urrearth forest of alien-looking trees with wrinkled brown trunks and soft green leaves, and the land fell away, and she caught her first glimpse of something far and flat on the horizon—had never seemed so high.

Down on the coast, the mountains reared behind them and around a bay. There were many people here—not the vast numbers, per-haps, of Jalila's dreamtent stories of the Ten Thousand and One Worlds, but so many that she was sure, as she first walked the streets of a town where the buildings huddled in ridiculous proximity, and tried not to stare at all the faces, that she would never know all their families.

Because of its position at the edge of the mountains, the town was called Al Janb, and, to Jalila's relief, their new haramlek was some distance away from it, up along a near-unnoticeable dirt track that meandered off from the blue-black serraplated coastal road. There was much to be done there by way of repair, after the long season that her bondmother Lya had left the place deserted. The walls were fused stone, but the structure of the roof had been mostly made from the stuff of the same strange urrearth trees that grew up the mountains, and in many places it had sagged and leaked and grown back toward the chaos that seemed to want to encompass everything here. The hayawans, too, needed much attention in their makeshift stables as they adapted to this new climate, and mother Pavo was long employed constructing the nec-essary potions to mend the bleeding bonds of rusty metal and flesh, and then to counteract the mold that grew like slow tears across their long, solemn faces. Jalila would normally have been in anguish to think of the sufferings that this new climate was visiting on Robin, but she was too busy feeling ill herself to care. Ri-diculously, seeing as there was so much more oxygen to breathe in this rich coastal air, every lungful became a conscious effort, a dreadful physical lunge. Inhaling the damp, salty, spore-laden atmosphere was like sucking soup through a straw. She grew feverish for a while, and suffered the attentions of similar molds to those that were growing over Robin, yet in even more irritating and embarrassing places. More irritating still was the fact that Ananke her birthmother and Lya her bondmother—even Pavo, who was still busily attending to the hayawans—treated her discomforts and fevers with airy disregard. They had, they all assured her vaguely, suffered similarly in their own youths. And the weather would soon change in any case. To Jalila, who had spent all her life in the cool, unvarying glare of Tabuthal, where the wind only ever blew from one direction and the trees jingled like ice, that last statement might as well have been spoken in another language.

If anything, Jalila was sure that she was getting worse. The rain drummed on what there was of the roof of their haramlek, and dripped down and pooled in the makeshift awnings, which burst in bucketloads down your neck if you bumped into them, and the mist drifted in from every direction through the paneless windows, and the mountains, most of the time, seemed to consist of cloud, or to have vanished entirely. She was coughing. Strange stuff was coming out on her hands, slippery and green as the slime that tried to grow everywhere here. One morning, she awoke, sure that part of her was bursting, and stumbled from her dreamtent and out through the scaffolding that had by then surrounded the haramlek, then barefoot down the mud track and across the quiet black road and down onto the beach, for no other reason than that she needed to *escape*.

She stood gasping amid the rockpools, her hair lank and her skin feverishly itching. There was something at the back of her throat. There was something in her lungs. She was sure that it had taken root and was growing. Then she started coughing as she had never coughed before, and more of the greenstuff came splattering over her hands and down her chin. She doubled over. Huge lumps of it came showering out, strung with blood. If it hadn't been mostly green, she'd have been sure that it *was* her lungs. She'd never imagined anything so agonizing. Finally, though, in heaves and starts and false dawns, the process dwindled. She wiped her hands on her night-dress. The rocks all around her were splattered green. It was breathmoss; the stuff that had sustained her on the high plains. And *now* look at it! Jalila took a slow, cautious breath. And then another. Her throat ached. Her head was throbbing. But still, the process was suddenly almost ridiculously easy. She picked her way back across the beach, up through the mists to her haramlek. Her mothers were eating breakfast. Jalila sat down with them, wordlessly, and started to eat.

That night, Ananke came and sat with Jalila as she lay in her dreamtent in plain darkness and tried not to listen to the sounds of the rain falling on and through the creaking, dripping building. Even now, her birthmother's hands smelled and felt like the high desert as they touched her face. Rough and clean and warm, like rocks in starlight, giving off their heat. A few months before, Jalila would probably have started crying.

"You'll understand now, perhaps, why we thought it better not to tell you about the breathmoss. . . ?"

There was a question mark at the end of the sentence, but Jalila ignored it. They'd known all along! She was still angry.

"And there are other things, too, which will soon start to happen to your body. Things that are nothing to do with this place. And I shall now tell you about them all, even though you'll say you knew it before. . . ."

The smooth, rough fingers stroked her hair. As Ananke's words unraveled, telling Jalila of changings and swellings and growths she'd never thought would really apply to *her*, and which these fetid lowlands really seemed to have brought closer, Jalila thought of the sound of the wind, tinkling through the crystal trees up on Tabuthal. She thought of the dry, cold wind in her face. The wet air here seemed to enclose her. She wished that she was running. She wanted to escape.

Small though Al Janb was, it was as big a town as Jalila had ever seen, and she soon came to volunteer to run all the various errands that her mothers required as they restored and repaired their haramlek. She was used to wide expanses, big horizons, the surprises of a giant landscape that crept upon you slowly, visible for miles. Yet here, every turn brought abrupt surprise and sudden change. The people had such varied faces and accents. They hung their washing across the streets, and bickered and smoked in public. Some ate with both hands. They stared at you as you went past, and didn't seem to mind if you stared back at them. There were unfamiliar sights and smells, markets that erupted on particular days to the workings of no calendar Jalila yet understood, and which sold, in glittering, shining, stinking, disgusting, fascinating arrays, the strangest and most wonderful things. There were fruits from off-planet, spices shaped like insects, and insects that you crushed for their spice. There were swarming vats of things Jalila couldn't possibly imagine any use for, and bright silks woven thin as starlit wind that she longed for with an acute physical thirst. And there were aliens, too, to be glimpsed sometimes wandering the streets of Al Janb, or looking down at you from its overhung top windows like odd pictures in old frames. Some of them carried their own atmosphere around with them in bubbling hookahs, and some rolled around in huge grey bits of the sea of their own planets, like babies in a birthsac. Some of them looked like huge versions of the spice insects, and the air around them buzzed angrily if you got too close. The only thing they had in common was that they seemed blithely unaware of Jalila as she stared and followed them, and then returned inexcusably late from whatever errand she'd supposedly been sent on. Sometimes, she forgot her errands entirely.

"You must learn to get *used* to things. . . ." Lya her bondmother said to her with genuine irritation late one afternoon, when she'd come back without the tool she'd been sent to get early that morning, or even any recollection of its name or function. "This or any other world will never be a home to you if you let every single thing *surprise* you. . . ." But Jalila didn't mind the surprises; in fact, she was coming to enjoy them, and the next time the need arose to visit Al Janb to buy a new growth-crystal for the scaffolding, she begged to be allowed to go, and her mothers finally relented, although with many a warning shake of the head.

The rain had stopped at last, or at least held back for a whole day, although everything still looked green and wet to Jalila as she walked along the coastal road toward the ragged tumble of Al Janb. She understood, at least in theory, that the rain would probably return, and then relent, and then come back again, but in a decreasing pattern, much as the heat was gradually *increasing*, although it still seemed ridiculous to her that no one could ever predict exactly how, or when, Habara's proper Season of Summers would arrive. Those boats she could see now, those fisherwomen out on their feluccas beyond the white bands of breaking waves, their whole lives were dictated by these uncertainties, and the habits of the shoals of whiteback that came and went on the oceans, and which could also only be guessed at in this same approximate way. The world down here on the coast was so *unpredictable* compared with Tabuthal! The markets, the people, the washing, the sun, the rain, the aliens. Even Hayam and Walah, Habara's moons, which Jalila was long used to watching, had to drag themselves through cloud like cannonballs through cotton as they pushed and pulled at this ocean. Yet today, as she clambered over the groynes of the long shingle beach that she took as a shortcut to the center of the town when the various tides were out, she saw a particular sight that surprised her more than any other.

There was a boat, hauled far up from the water, longer and

blacker and heavier-looking than the feluccas, with a sort-of ram-shackle house at the prow, and a winch at the stern that was so massive that Jalila wondered if it wouldn't tip the craft over if it ever actually entered the water. But, for all that, it wasn't the boat that first caught her eye, but the figure who was working on it. Even from a distance, as she struggled to heave some ropes, there was something different about her, and the way she was moving. Another alien? But she was plainly human. And barefoot, in ragged shorts, and bare-breasted. In fact, almost as flat-chested as Jalila still was, and probably of about her age and height. Jalila still wasn't used to introducing herself to strangers, but she decided that she could at least go over, and pretend an interest in—or an ignorance of—this odd boat.

The figure dropped another loop of rope over the gunwales with a grunt that carried on the smelly sea breeze. She was brown as tea, with her massy hair hooped back and hanging in a long tail down her back. She was broad-shouldered, and moved in a way that didn't quite seem wrong, but didn't seem entirely right either. As if, somewhere across her back, there was an extra joint. When she glanced up at the clatter of shingle as Jalila jumped the last groyne, Jalila got a proper full sight of her face, and saw that she was big-nosed, big-chinned, and that her features were oddly broad and flat. A child sculpting a person out of clay might have done better.

"Have you come to help me?"

Jalila shrugged. "I might have done."

"That's a funny accent you've got."

They were standing facing each other. She had grey eyes, which looked odd as well. Perhaps she was an off-worlder. That might explain it. Jalila had heard that there were people who had things done to themselves so they could live in different places. She sup-posed the breathmoss was like that, although she'd never thought of it that way. And she couldn't quite imagine why it would be a requirement for living on any world that you looked this ugly.

"Everyone talks oddly here," she replied. "But then your accent's funny as well."

"I'm Kalal. And that's just my *voice*. It's not an accent." Kalal looked down at her oily hands, perhaps thought about wiping one and offering it to shake, then decided not to bother.

"Oh. . . ?"

"You don't get it, do you?" That gruff voice. The odd way her features twisted when she smiled.

"What is there to get? You're just—"

"—I'm a man." Kalal picked up a coil of rope from the shingle, and nodded to another beside it. "Well? Are you going to help me with this, or aren't you?"

The rains came again, this time starting as a thing called *drizzle*, then working up the scale to *torrent*. The tides washed especially high. There were storms, and white crackles of lightening, and the boom of a wind that was so unlike the kamasheen. Jalila's mothers told her to be patient, to wait, and to remember—*please* remember this time, so you don't waste the day for us all, Jalilaneen—the things that they sent her down the serraplate road to get from Al Janb. She trudged under an umbrella, another new and useless coastal object, which turned itself inside out so many times that she ended up throwing it into the sea, where it floated off quite happily, as if that was the element for which it was intended in the first place. Almost all of the feluccas were drawn up on the far side of the roadway, safe from the madly bashing waves, but there was no sign of that bigger craft belonging to Kalal. Perhaps he—the antique genderative word *was* he, wasn't it?—was out there, where the clouds rumbled like boulders. Perhaps she'd imagined their whole encounter entirely.

Arriving back home at the haramlek surprisingly quickly, and carrying for once the things she'd been ordered to get, Jalila dried herself off and buried herself in her dreamtent, trying to find out from it all that she could about these creatures called *men*. Like so many things about life at this awkward, interesting, difficult time, men were something Jalila would have insisted she definitely already knew about a few months before up on Tabuthal. Now, she wasn't so sure. Kalal, despite his ugliness and his funny rough-squeaky voice and his slightly odd smell, looked little like the hairy-faced werewolf figures of her childhood stories, and seemed to have no particular need to shout or fight, to carry her off to his rancid cave, or to start collecting odd and pointless things that he would then try to give her. There had once, Jalila's dreamtent told her, for obscure biological reasons she didn't quite follow, been far more men in the universe; almost as many as there had been women. Obviously, they had dwindled. She then checked on the word *rape*, to make sure it really was the thing she'd imagined, shuddered, but nevertheless investigated in full holographic detail the bits of himself that Kalal had kept hidden beneath his shorts as she'd helped stow those ropes. She couldn't help feeling sorry for

him. It was all so pointless and ugly. Had his birth been an accident? A curse? She began to grow sleepy. The subject was starting
to bore her. The last thing she remembered learning was that Kalal
wasn't a proper man at all, but a *boy*—a half-formed thing; the
equivalent to girl—another old urrearth word. Then sleep drifted
over her, and she was back with the starlight and the crystal trees of
Tabuthal, and wondering as she danced with her own reflection
which of them was changing.

By next morning, the sun was shining as if she would never
stop. As Jalila stepped out onto the newly formed patio, she gave
the blazing light the same sort of an appraising *what-are-you-up-to-
now* glare that her mothers gave her when she returned from Al
Janb. The sun had done this trick before of seeming permanent,
then vanishing by lunchtime into sodden murk, but today her bril-
liance continued. As it did the day after. And the day after that. Half
a month later, even Jalila was convinced that the Season of Summers on Habara had finally arrived.

The flowers went mad, as did the insects. There were colors everywhere, pulsing before your eyes, swarming down the cliffs toward
the sea, which lay flat and placid and salt-rimed, like a huge animal, basking. It remained mostly cool in Jalila's dreamtent, and the
haramlek by now was a place of tall malqaf windtowers and flashing fans and well-like depths, but stepping outside beyond the
striped shade of the mashrabiyas at midday felt like being hit
repeatedly across the head with a hot iron pan. The horizons had
drawn back; the mountains, after a few last rumbles of thunder and
mist, as if they were clearing their throats, had finally announced
themselves to the coastline in all their majesty, and climbed up and
up in huge stretches of forest into stone limbs that rose and tangled
until your eyes grew tired of rising. Above them, finally, was the sky,
which was always blue in this season; the blue color of flame. Even
at midnight, you caught the flash and swirl of flame.

Jalila learned to follow the advice of her mothers, and to change
her daily habits to suit the imperious demands of this incredible,
fussy, and demanding weather. If you woke early, and then drank
lots of water, and bowed twice in the direction of Al'Toman while
she was still a pinprick in the west, you could catch the day by surprise, when dew lay on the stones and pillars, and the air felt soft
and silky as the arms of the ghostly women who sometimes visited
Jalila's nights. Then there was breakfast, and the time of work, and
the time of study, and Ananke and Pavo would quiz Jalila to ensure
that she was following the prescribed Orders of Knowledge. By

midday, though, the shadows had drawn back and every trace of moisture had evaporated, and your head swarmed with flies. You sought your own company, and didn't even want *that*, and wished, as you tossed and sweated in your dreamtent, for frost and darkness. Once or twice, just to prove to herself that it could be done, Jalila had tried walking to Al Janb at this time, although of course everything was shut and the whole place wobbled and stank in the heat like rancid jelly. She returned to the haramlek gritty and sweaty, almost crawling, and with a pounding ache in her head.

By evening, when the proper order of the world had righted itself, and Al'Toman would have hung in the east if the mountains hadn't swallowed her, and the heat, which never vanished, had assumed a smoother, more manageable quality, Jalila's mothers were once again hungry for company, and for food and for argument. These evenings, perhaps, were the best of all the times that Jalila could remember of her early life on the coast of Habara's single great ocean, at that stage in her development from child to adult when the only thing of permanence seemed to be the existence of endless, fascinating change. *How* they argued! Lya, her bondmother, and the oldest of her parents, who wore her grey hair loose as cobwebs with the pride of her age, and waved her arms as she talked and drank, wreathed in endless curls of smoke. Little Pavo, her face smooth as a carved nutmeg, with her small, precise hands, and who knew so much but rarely said anything with insistence. And Jalila's birthmother Ananke, for whom, of her three mothers, Jalila had always felt the deepest, simplest love, who would always touch you before she said anything, and then fix you with her sad and lovely eyes, as if touching and seeing were far more important than any words. Jalila was older now. She joined in with the arguments—of course, she had *always* joined in, but she cringed to think of the stumbling inanities to which her mothers had previously had to listen, while, now, at last, she had real, proper things to say about life, whole new philosophies that no one else on the Ten Thousand Worlds and One had ever thought of. . . . Most of the time, her mothers listened. Sometimes, they even acted as if they were persuaded by their daughter's wisdom.

Frequently, there were visitors to these evening gatherings. Up on Tabuthal, visitors had been rare animals, to be fussed over and cherished and only reluctantly released for their onward journey across the black, dazzling plains. Down here, where people were nearly as common as stones on the beach, a more relaxed attitude reigned. Sometimes, there were formal invitations that Lya would issue to someone who was *this* or *that* in the town, or more often

Pavo would come back with a person she had happened to meet as she poked around for lifeforms on the beach, or Ananke would softly suggest a *neighbor* (another new word and concept to Jalila) might like to *pop in* (ditto). But Al Janb was still a small town, and the dignitaries generally weren't that dignified, and Pavo's beach wanderers were often shy and slight as she was, while *neighbor* was frequently a synonym for *boring*. Still, Jalila came to enjoy most kinds of company, if only so that she could hold forth yet more devastatingly on whatever universal theory of life she was currently developing.

The flutter of lanterns and hands. The slow breath of the sea. Jalila ate stuffed breads and fuul and picked at the mountains of fruit and sucked lemons and sweet, blue rutta and waved her fingers. The heavy night insects, glowing with the pollen they had collected, came bumbling toward the lanterns or would alight in their hands. Sometimes, afterward, they walked the shore, and Pavo would show them strange creatures with blurring mouths like wheels, or point to the vast, distant beds of the tideflowers that rose at night to the changes of the tide; silver, crimson, or glowing, their fronds waving through the dark like the beckoning palm trees of islands from storybook seas.

One guestless night, when they were walking north away from the lights of the town, and Pavo was filling a silver bag for an aquarium she was ostensibly making for Jalila, but in reality for herself, the horizon suddenly cracked and rumbled. Instinctively by now, Jalila glanced overhead, expecting clouds to be covering the coastal haze of stars. But the air was still and clear; the hot, dark edge of that blue flame. Across the sea, the rumble and crackle was continuing, accompanied by a glowing pillar of smoke that slowly tottered over the horizon. The night pulsed and flickered. There was a breath of impossibly hot salt air. The pillar, a wobbly finger with a flame-tipped nail, continued climbing skyward. A few geelies rose and fell, clacking and cawing, on the far rocks; black shapes in the darkness.

"It's the start of the Season of Rockets," Lya said. "I wonder who'll be coming. . . ?"

## 2.

By now, Jalila had acquired many of her own acquaintances and friends. Young people were relatively scarce amid the long-lived human Habarans, and those who dwelt around Al Janb were continually drawn together and then repulsed from each other like spinning magnets. The elderly mahwagis, who had outlived the need for wives and the company of a haramlek and lived alone, were often more fun, and more reliably eccentric. It was a relief to visit their houses and escape the pettinesses and sexual jealousies that were starting to infect the other girls near to Jalila's own age. She regarded Kalal similarly—as an escape—and she relished helping him with his boat, and enjoyed their journeys out across the bay, where the wind finally tipped almost cool over the edge of the mountains and lapped the sweat from their faces.

Kalal took Jalila out to see the rocketport one still, hot afternoon. It lay just over the horizon, and was the longest journey they had undertaken. The sails filled with the wind, and the ocean grew almost black, yet somehow transparent, as they hurried over it. Looking down, Jalila believed that she could glimpse the white sliding shapes of the great sea-leviathans who had once dwelt, if local legend was to be believed, in the ruined rock palaces of the qasrs, which she had passed on her journey down from Tabuthal. Growing tired of sunlight, they had swarmed back to the sea that had birthed them, throwing away their jewels and riches, which bubbled below the surface, then rose again under Habara's twin moons to become the beds of tideflowers. She had gotten that part of the story from Kalal. Unlike most people who lived on the coast, Kalal was interested in Jalila's life in the starry darkness of Tabuthal, and repaid her with his own tales of the ocean.

The boat ploughed on, rising, frothing. Blissfully, it was almost cold. Just how far out at sea was this rocketport? Jalila had watched some of the arrivals and departures from the quays at Al Janb, but those journeys took place in sleek sail-less craft with silver doors that looked, as they turned out from the harbor and rose out on stilts from the water, as if they could travel halfway up to the stars on their own. Kalal was squatting at the prow, beyond that ramshackle hut that Jalila now knew contained the pheromones and grapplers that were needed to ensnare the tideflowers that this craft had been built to harvest. The boat bore no name on the prow, yet Kalal had many names for it, which he would occasionally mention without explaining. If there was one thing that was different about Kalal, Jalila had decided, it was this absence of proper talk or explanation. It put many people off, but she had found that most things became apparent if you just hung around him and didn't ask direct questions.

People generally pitied Kalal, or stared at him as Jalila still

stared at the aliens, or asked him questions that he wouldn't answer
with anything other than a shrug. Now that she knew him better,
Jalila was starting to understand just how much he hated such
treatment—almost as much, in fact, as he hated being thought of as
ordinary. I am a *man*, you know, he'd still remark sometimes—
whenever he felt that Jalila was forgetting. Jalila had never yet
risked pointing out that he was in fact a *boy*. Kalal could be prickly
and sensitive if you treated him as if things didn't matter. It was
hard to tell, really, just how much of how he acted was due to his
odd sexual identity, and how much was his personality.

To add to his freakishness, Kalal lived alone with another male
—in fact, the only other male in Al Janb—at the far end of the
shore cottages, in a birthing relationship that made Kalal term him
his *father*. His name was Ibra, and he looked much more like the
males of Jalila's dreamtent stories. He was taller than almost anyone, and wore a black beard and long, colorful robes or strode
about bare-chested, and always talked in a thunderously deep
voice, as if he were addressing a crowd through a megaphone. Ibra
laughed a lot and flashed his teeth through that hairy mask, and
clapped people on the back when he asked them how they were,
and then stood away and seemed to lose interest before they had
answered. He whistled and sang loudly and waved to passers-by
while he worked at repairing the feluccas for his living. Ibra had
come to this planet when Kalal was a baby, under circumstances
that remained perennially vague. He treated Jalila with the same
loud and grinning friendship with which he treated everyone, and
which seemed like a wall. He was at least as alien as the tubelike
creatures who had arrived from the stars with this new Season of
Rockets, which had had one of the larger buildings in Al Janb
encased in transparent plastics and flooded in a freezing grey goo
so they could live in it. Ibra had come around to their haramlek
once, on the strength of one of Ananke's *pop in* evening invitations.
Jalila, who was then nurturing the idea that no intelligence could
exist without the desire to acknowledge some higher deity, found
her propositions and examples drowned out in a flurry of counter-
questions and assertions and odd bits of information that she
half-suspected that Ibra, as he drank surprising amounts of virtually
undiluted zibib and freckled aniseed spit at her, was making up on
the spot. Afterward, as they walked the shore, he drew her apart and
laid a heavy hand on her shoulder and confided in his rambling
growl how much he'd enjoyed *fencing* with her. Jalila knew what
fencing was, but she didn't see what it had to do with talking. She

wasn't even sure if she liked Ibra. She certainly didn't pretend to understand him.

The sails thrummed and crackled as they headed toward the spaceport. Kalal was absorbed, staring ahead from the prow, the water splashing reflections across his lithe brown body. Jalila had almost grown used to the way he looked. After all, they were both slightly freakish: she, because she came from the mountains; he, because of his sex. And they both liked their own company, and could accept each other into it without distraction during these long periods of silence. One never asked the other what they were thinking. Neither really cared, and they cherished that privacy.

"Look—" Kalal scuttled to the rudder. Jalila hauled back the jib. In wind-crackling silence, they and their nameless and many-named boat tacked toward the spaceport.

The spaceport was almost like the mountains: when you were close up, it was too big to be seen properly. Yet, for all its size, the place was a disappointment; empty and messy, like a huge version of the docks of Al Janb, similarly reeking of oil and refuse, and essentially serving a similar function. The spaceships themselves— if indeed the vast cisternlike objects they saw forever in the distance as they furled the sails and rowed along the maze of oily canals were spaceships—were only a small part of this huge, floating complex of islands. Much more of it was taken up by looming berths for the tugs and tankers that placidly chugged from icy pole to equator across the watery expanses of Habara, taking or delivering the supplies that the settlements deemed necessary for civilized life, or collecting the returning bulk cargoes. The tankers were rust-streaked beasts, so huge that they hardly seemed to grow as you approached them, humming and eerily deserted, yet devoid of any apparent intelligence of their own. They didn't glimpse a single alien at the spaceport. They didn't even see a human being.

The journey there, Jalila decided as they finally got the sails up again, had been far more enjoyable and exciting than actually arriving. Heading back toward the sun-pink coastal mountains, which almost felt like home to her now, she was filled with an odd longing that only diminished when she began to make out the lighted, dusky buildings of Al Janb. Was this homesickness, she wondered? Or something else?

This was the time of Habara's long summer. This was the Season of Rockets. When she mentioned their trip, Jalila was severely warned by Pavo of the consequences of approaching the spaceport during periods of possible launch, but it went no further than that.

Each night now, and deep into the morning, the rockets rumbled at the horizon and climbed upward on those grumpy pillars, bringing to the shore a faint whiff of sulphur and roses, adding to the thunderous heat. And outside at night, if you looked up, you could sometimes see the blazing comet-trails of the returning capsules, which would crash somewhere in the distant seas.

The beds of tideflowers were growing bigger as well. If you climbed up the sides of the mountains before the morning heat flattened everything, you could look down on those huge, brilliant, and ever-changing carpets, where every pattern and swirl seemed gorgeous and unique. At night, in her dreamtent, Jalila sometimes imagined that she was floating up on them, just as in the oldest of the old stories. She was sailing over a different landscape on a magic carpet, with the cool night desert rising and falling beneath her like a soft sea. She saw distant palaces, and clusters of palms around small and tranquil lakes that flashed the silver of a single moon. And then yet more of this infinite sahara, airy and frosty, flowed through curves and undulations, and grew vast and pinkish in her dreams. Those curves, as she flew over them and began to touch herself, resolved into thighs and breasts. The winds stirring the peaks of the dunes resolved in shuddering breaths.

This was the time of Habara's long summer. This was the Season of Rockets.

Robin, Jalila's hayawan, had by now, under Pavo's attentions, fully recovered from the change to her environment. The rust had gone from her flanks, the melds with her thinly grey-furred flesh were bloodless and neat. She looked thinner and lighter. She even smelled different. Like the other hayawans, Robin was frisky and bright and brown-eyed now, and didn't seem to mind the heat, or even Jalila's forgetful neglect of her. Down on the coast, hayawans were regarded as expensive, uncomfortable, and unreliable, and Jalila and her mothers took a pride in riding across the beach into Al Janb on their huge, flat-footed, and loping mounts, enjoying the stares and the whispers, and the whispering space that opened around them as they hobbled the hayawans in a square. Kalal, typically, was one of the few coastal people who expressed an interest in trying to ride one of them, and Jalila was glad to teach him, showing him the clicks and calls and nudges, the way you took the undulations of the creature's back as you might the ups and downs of the sea, and when not to walk around their front and rear ends. After her experiences on his boat, the initial rope burns, the cracks on the head and the heaving sickness, she enjoyed the reversal of situations.

There was a Tabuthal saying about falling off a hayawan ninety-nine times before you learnt to ride, which Kalal disproved by falling off far into triple figures. Jalila chose Lya's mount Abu for him to ride, because she was the biggest, the most intelligent, and generally the most placid of the beasts unless she felt that something was threatening her, and because Lya, more conscious of looks and protocol down here than the other mothers, rarely rode her. Domestic animals, Jalila had noticed, often took oddly to Kalal when they first saw and scented him, but he had learned the ways of getting around them, and developed a bond and understanding with Abu even while she was still trying to bite his legs. Jalila had made a good choice of riding partners. Both of them, hayawan and human, while proud and aloof, were essentially playful, and never shirked a challenge. While all hayawans had been female throughout all recorded history, Jalila wondered if there wasn't a little of the male still embedded in Abu's imperious downward glance.

Now that summer was here, and the afternoons had vanished into the sun's blank blaze, the best time to go riding was the early morning. North, beyond Al Janb, there were shores and there were saltbeds and there were meadows, there were fences to be leapt, and barking feral dogs as male as Kalal to be taunted, but south, there were rocks and forests, there were tracks that led nowhere, and there were headlands and cliffs that you saw once and could never find again. South, mostly, was the way that they rode.

"What happens if we keep riding?"

They were taking their breath on a flatrock shore where a stream, from which they had all drunk, shone in pools on its way to the ocean. The hayawans had squatted down now in the shadows of the cliff and were nodding sleepily, one nictitating membrane after another slipping over their eyes. As soon as they had gotten here and dismounted, Kalal had walked straight down, arms outstretched, into the tideflower-bobbing ocean. Jalila had followed, whooping, feeling tendrils and petals bumping into her. It was like walking through floral soup. Kalal had sunk to his shoulders and started swimming, which was something Jalila still couldn't quite manage. He splashed around her, taunting, sending up sheets of colored light. They'd stripped from their clothes as they clambered out, and laid them on the hot rocks, where they now steamed like fresh bread.

"This whole continent's like a huge island," Jalila said in

delayed answer to Kalal's question. "We'd come back to where we started."

Kalal shook his head. "Oh, you can never do that. . . ."

"Where would we be, then?"

"Somewhere slightly different. The tideflowers would have changed, and we wouldn't be us, either." Kalal wet his finger, and wrote something in naskhi script on the hot, flat stone between them. Jalila thought she recognized the words of a poet, but the beginning had dissolved into the hot air before she could make proper sense of it. Funny, but at home with her mothers, and with their guests, and even with many of the people of her own age, such statements as they had just made would have been the beginning of a long debate. With Kalal, they just seemed to hang there. Kalal, he moved, he passed on. Nothing quite seemed to stick. There was something, somewhere, Jalila thought, lost and empty about him.

The way he was sitting, she could see most of his genitals, which looked quite jaunty in their little nest of hair; like a small animal. She'd almost gotten as used to the sight of them as she had to the other peculiarities of Kalal's features. Scratching her nose, picking off some of the petals that still clung to her skin like wet confetti, she felt no particular curiosity. Much more than Kalal's funny body, Jalila was conscious of her own—especially her growing breasts, which were still somewhat uneven. Would they ever come out right, she wondered, or would she forever be some unlovely oddity, just as Kalal seemingly was? Better not to think of such things. Better to just enjoy the feel of the sun baking her shoulders, loosening the curls of her hair.

"Should we turn back?" Kalal asked eventually. "It's getting hotter. . . ."

"Why bother with that—if we carry on, we'll get back to where we started."

Kalal stood up. "Do you want to bet?"

So they rode on, more slowly, uphill through the uncharted forest, where the urrearth trees tangled with the blue fronds of Habara fungus, and the birds were still, and the crackle of the dry undergrowth was the only sound in the air. Eventually, ducking boughs, then walking, dreamily lost and almost ready to turn back, they came to a path, and remounted. The trees fell away, and they found that they were on a clifftop, far, far higher above the winking sea than they could possibly have imagined. Midday heat clapped around them. Ahead, where the cliff stuck out over the ocean like a

cupped hand, shimmering and yet solid, was one of the ruined castles or geological features that the sea-leviathans had supposedly
deserted before the arrival of people on this planet—a qasr. They
rode slowly toward it, their hayawans' feet thocking in the dust. It
looked like a fairy place. Part natural, but roofed and buttressed,
with grey-black gables and huge and intricate windows, that flashed
with the colors of the sea. Kalal gestured for silence, dismounted
from Abu, led his mount back into the shadowed arms of the forest,
and flicked the switch in her back that hobbled her.

"You *know* where this is?"

Kalal beckoned.

Jalila, who knew him better than to ask questions, followed.

Close to, much of the qasr seemed to be made of a quartz-
speckled version of the same fused stone from which Jalila's
haramlek was constructed. But some other bits of it appeared to be
natural effusions of the rock. There was a big, arched door of sun-
bleached and iron-studded oak, reached by a path across the
narrowing cliff, but Kalal steered Jalila to the side, and then up and
around a bare angle of hot stone that seemed ready at any moment
to tilt them down into the distant sea. But the way never quite gave
out; there was always another handhold. From the confident manner in which he moved up this near-cliff face, then scrambled
across the blistering black tiles of the rooftop beyond, and dropped
down into the sudden cool of a narrow passageway, Jalila guessed
that Kalal had been to this qasr before. At first, there was little sense
of trespass. The place seemed old and empty—a little-visited mon-
ument. The ceilings were stained. The corridors were swept with
the litter of winter leaves. Here and there along the walls there
were friezes, and long strings of a script which made as little sense
to Jalila, in their age and dimness, as that which Kalal had written
on the hot rocks.

Then Kalal gestured for Jalila to stop, and she clustered beside
him, and they looked down through the intricate stone lattice of
a mashrabiya into sunlight. It was plain from the balcony drop
beneath them that they were still high up in this qasr. Below, in the
central courtyard, somehow shocking after this emptiness, a fountain played in a garden, and water lapped from its lip and ran in
steel fingers toward cloistered shadows.

"Someone *lives* here?"

Kalal mouthed the word *tariqua*. Somehow, Jalila instantly
understood. It all made sense, in this Season of Rockets, even the
dim scenes and hieroglyphs carved in the honeyed stones of this

fairy castle. Tariquas were merely human, after all, and the space-port was nearby; they had to live somewhere. Jalila glanced down at her scuffed sandals, suddenly conscious that she hadn't taken them off—but by then it was too late, and below them and through the mashrabiya a figure had detached herself from the shadows. The tariqua was tall and thin, and black and bent as a burnt-out match-stick. She walked with a cane. Jalila didn't know what she'd expected—she'd grown older since her first encounter with Kalal, and no longer imagined that she knew about things just because she'd learnt of them in her dreamtent. But still, this tariqua seemed a long way from someone who piloted the impossible distances between the stars, as she moved and clicked slowly around that courtyard fountain, and far older and frailer than anyone Jalila had ever seen. She tended a bush of blue flowers, she touched the foun-tain's bubbling stone lip. Her head was ebony bald. Her fingers were charcoal. Her eyes were as white and seemingly blind as the flecks of quartz in the fused stone of this building. Once, though, she seemed to look up toward them. Jalila went cold. Surely it wasn't possible that she could *see* them?—and in any event, there was something about the motion of looking up which seemed habitual. As if, like touching the lip of the fountain, and tending that bush, the tariqua always looked up at this moment of the day at that particular point in the stone walls that rose above her.

Jalila followed Kalal further along the corridors, and down stair-ways and across drops of beautifully clear glass, that hung on nothing far above the prismatic sea. Another glimpse of the tariqua, who was still slowly moving, her neck stretching like an old tortoise as she bent to sniff a flower. In this part of the qasr, there were more definite signs of habitation. Scattered cards and books. A moth-eaten tapestry that billowed from a windowless arch overlooking the sea. Empty coat hangers piled like the bones of insects. An active but clearly little-used chemical toilet. Now that the initial sense of surprise had gone, there was something funny about this mixture of the extraordinary and the everyday. Here, there was a kitchen, and a half-chewed lump of aish on a plate smeared with seeds. To imagine, that you could both travel between the stars *and* eat bread and tomatoes! Both Kalal and Jalila were red-faced and chuffing now from suppressed hilarity. Down now at the level of the cloisters, hunched in the shade, they studied the tariqua's stoop-ing back. She really did look like a scrawny tortoise, yanked out of its shell, moving between these bushes. Any moment now, you expected her to start chomping on the leaves. She moved more by touch than by sight. Amid the intricate colors of this courtyard, and the flashing glass windchimes that tinkled in the far archways, as she fumbled sightlessly but occasionally glanced at things with those odd, white eyes, it seemed yet more likely that she was blind, or at least terribly near-sighted. Slowly, Jalila's hilarity receded, and she began to feel sorry for this old creature who had been aged and withered and wrecked by the strange process of travel between the stars. *The Pain of Distance*—now, where had that phrase come from?

Kalal was still puffing his cheeks. His eyes were watering as he ground his fist against his mouth and silently thumped the nearest pillar in agonized hilarity. Then he let out a nasal grunt, which Jalila was sure that the tariqua must have heard. But her stance didn't alter. It wasn't so much as if she hadn't noticed them, but that she already *knew* that someone was there. There was a sadness and resignation about her movements, the tap of her cane . . . But Kalal had recovered his equilibrium, and Jalila watched his fingers snake out and enclose a flake of broken paving. Another moment, and it spun out into the sunlit courtyard in an arc so perfect that there was never any doubt that it was going to strike the tariqua smack between her birdlike shoulders. Which it did—but by then they were running, and the tariqua was straightening herself up with that same slow resignation. Just before they bundled themselves up the stairway, Jalila glanced back, and felt a hot bar of light from one of the qasr's high upper windows stream across her face. The tariqua was looking straight toward her with those blind white eyes. Then Kalal grabbed her hand. Once again, she was running.

Jalila was cross with herself, and cross with Kalal. It wasn't *like* her, a voice like a mingled chorus of her three mothers would say, to taunt some poor old mahwagi, even if that mahwagi happened also to be an aged tariqua. But Jalila was young, and life was busy. The voice soon faded. In any case, there was the coming moulid to prepare for.

The arrangement of festivals, locally, and on Habara as a whole, was always difficult. Habara's astronomical year was so long that it made no sense to fix the traditional cycle of moulids by it, but at the same time, no one felt comfortable celebrating the same saint or eid in conflicting seasons. Fasting, after all, properly belonged to winter, and no one could quite face their obligations toward the Almighty with quite the same sense of surrender and equanimity in the middle of spring. People's memories faded, as well, as to how

one *did* a particular saint in autumn, or revered a certain enlight-
enment in blasting heat that you had previously celebrated by
throwing snowballs. Added to this were the logistical problems of
catering for the needs of a small and scattered population across a
large planet. There were traveling players, fairs, wandering sufis
and priests, but they plainly couldn't be everywhere at once. The
end result was that each moulid was fixed locally on Habara,
according to a shifting timetable, and after much discussion and
many meetings, and rarely happened twice at exactly the same
time, or else occurred simultaneously in different places. Lya threw
herself into these discussions with the enthusiasm of one who had
long been missing such complexities in the lonelier life up on
Tabuthal. For the Moulid of First Habitation—which commemorated the time when the Blessed Joanna had arrived on Habara at a
site that several different towns claimed, and cast the first urrearth
seeds, and lived for five long Habaran years on nothing but tideflowers and starlight, and rode the sea-leviathans across the oceans
as if they were hayawans as she waited for her lover Pia—Lya was
the leading light in the local organizations at Al Janb, and the rest
of her haramlek were expected to follow suit.

The whole of Al Janb was to be transformed for a day and a
night. Jalila helped with the hammering and weaving, and tuning
Pavo's crystals and plants, which would supposedly transform the
serraplate road between their haramlek and the town into a glittering tunnel. More in the forefront of Jalila's mind were those
colored silks that came and went at a particular stall in the markets,
and which she was sure would look perfect on her. Between the
planning and the worries about this or that turning into a disaster,
she worked carefully on each of her three mothers in turn; a nudge
here, a suggestion there. Turning their thoughts toward accepting
this extravagance was a delicate matter, like training a new hayawan to bear the saddle. Of course, there were wild resistances and
buckings, but you were patient, you were stronger. You knew what
you wanted. You kept to your subject. You returned and returned
and returned to it.

On the day when Ananke finally relented, a worrying wind had
struck up, pushing at the soft, half-formed growths that now strag-
gled through the normal weeds along the road into Al Janb like
silvered mucus. Pavo was fretting about her creations. Lya's life was
one long meeting. Even Ananke was anxious as they walked into Al
Janb, where faulty fresh projections flickered across the buildings
and squares like an incipient headache as the sky greyed. Jalila,

urging her birthmother on as she paused frustratingly, was sure that the market wouldn't be there, or that if it was, the stall that sold the windsilks was sure to have sold out—or, even then, that the particular ones she'd set her mind on would have gone. . . .

But it was all there. In fact, a whole new supply of windsilks, even more marvelous and colorful, had been imported for this moulid. They blew and lifted like colored smoke. Jalila caught and admired them.

"I think this might be you. . . ."

Jalila turned at the voice. It was Nayra, a girl about a standard year and a half older than her, whose mothers were amongst the richest and most powerful in Al Janb. Nayra herself was both beautiful and intelligent; witty, and sometimes devastatingly cruel. She was generally at the center of things, surrounded by a bickering and admiring crowd of seemingly lesser mortals, which sometimes included Jalila. But today she was alone.

"You see, Jalila. That crimson. With your hair, your eyes . . ."

She held the windsilk across Jalila's face like a yashmak. It danced around her eyes. It blurred over her shoulders. Jalila would have thought the color too bold. But Nayra's gaze, which flickered without ever quite leaving Jalila's, her smoothing hands, told Jalila that it was right for her far better than any mirror could have. And then there was blue—that flame color of the summer night. There were silver clasps, too, to hold these windsilks, which Jalila had never noticed on sale before. The stallkeeper, sensing a desire to purchase that went beyond normal bargaining, drew out more surprises from a chest. *Feel! They can only be made in one place, on one planet, in one season. Look! The grubs, they only hatch when they hear the song of a particular bird, which sings only once in its life before it gives up its spirit to the Almighty. . . .* and so on. Ananke, seeing that Jalila had found a more interested and willing helper, palmed her far more cash than she'd promised, and left her with a smile and an oddly sad backward glance.

Jalila spend the rest of that grey and windy afternoon with Nayra, choosing clothes and ornaments for the moulid. Bangles for their wrists and ankles. Perhaps—no? yes?—even a small tiara. Bolts of cloth the color of today's sky bound across her hips to offset the windsilk's beauty. A jewel still filled with the sapphire light of a distant sun to twinkle at her belly. Nayra, with her dark blonde hair, her light brown eyes, her fine strong hands, which were pale pink beneath the fingernails like the inside of a shell, she hardly needed anything to augment her obvious beauty. But Jalila knew from her endless studies of herself in her dreamtent mirror that *she* needed to be more careful; the wrong angle, the wrong light, an incipient spot, and whatever effect she was striving for could be so easily ruined. Yet she'd never really cared as much about such things as she did on that windy afternoon, moving through stalls and shops amid the scent of patchouli. To be so much the focus of her own and someone else's attention! Nayra's hands, smoothing across her back and shoulders, lifting her hair, cool sweat at her shoulders, the cool slide and rattle of her bangles as she raised her arms. . . .

"We could be creatures from a story, Jalila. Let's imagine I'm Scheherazade." A toss of that lovely hair. Liquid gold. Nayra's seashell fingers, stirring. "You can be her sister, Dinarzade. . . ."

Jalila nodded enthusiastically, although Dinarzade had been an unspectacular creature as far as she remembered the tale; there only so that she might waken Scheherazade in the Sultana's chamber before the first cock crow of morning. But her limbs, her throat, felt strange and soft and heavy. She reminded herself, as she dressed and undressed, of the doll Tabatha she'd once so treasured up on Tabuthal, and had found again recently, and thought for some odd reason of burying. . . .

The lifting, the pulling, Nayra's appraising hands and glance and eyes. This unresisting heaviness. Jalila returned home to her haramlek dazed and drained and happy, and severely out of credit.

That night, there was another visitor for dinner. She must have taken some sort of carriage to get there, but she came toward their veranda as if she'd walked the entire distance. Jalila, whose head was filled with many things, was putting out the bowls when she heard the murmur of footsteps. The sound was so slow that eventually she noticed it consciously, looked up, and saw a thin, dark figure coming up the sandy path between Pavo's swaying and newly sculpted bushes. One arm leaned on a cane, and the other strained seekingly forward. In shock, Jalila dropped the bowl she was holding. It seemed to roll around and around on the table forever, slipping playfully out of reach of her fingers before spinning off the edge and shattering into several thousand white pieces.

"Oh dear," the tariqua said, finally climbing the steps beside the windy trellis, her cane tap-tapping. "Perhaps you'd better go and tell one of your mothers, Jalila."

Jalila felt breathless. All through that evening, the tariqua's trachoman white eyes, the scarred and tarry driftwood of her face, seemed to be studying her. Even apart from that odd business of her knowing her name, which she supposed could be explained, Jalila was more and more certain that the tariqua knew that it was she and Kalal who had spied on her and thrown a stone at her on that hot day in the qasr. As if that mattered. But somehow, it *did*, more than it should have done. Amid all this confused thinking, and the silky memories of her afternoon with Nayra, Jalila scarcely noticed the conversation. The weather remained gusty, spinning the lanterns, playing shapes with the shadows, making the tapestries breathe. The tariqua's voice was as thin as her frame. It carried on the spinning air like the croak of an insect.

"Perhaps we could walk on the beach, Jalila?"

"What?" She jerked as if she'd been abruptly awakened. Her mothers were already clearing things away, and casting odd glances at her. The voice had whispered inside her head, and the tariqua was sitting there, her burnt and splintery arm outstretched, in the hope, Jalila supposed, that she would be helped up from the table. The creature's robe had fallen back. Her arm looked like a picture Jalila had once seen of a dried cadaver. With an effort, nearly knocking over another bowl, Jalila moved around the billowing table. With an even bigger effort, she placed her own hand into that of the tariqua. She'd expected it to feel leathery, which it did. But it was also hot beyond fever. Terribly, the fingers closed around hers. There was a pause. Then the tariqua got up with surprising swiftness, and reached around for her cane, still holding Jalila's hand, but without having placed any weight on it. *She could have done all that on her own, the old witch,* Jalila thought. *And she can see, too—look at the way she's been stuffing herself with kofta all evening, reaching over for figs. . . .*

"What do you know of the stars, Jalila?" the tariqua asked as they walked beside the beach. Pavo's creations along the road behind them still looked stark and strange and half-formed as they swayed in the wind, like the wavering silver limbs of an upturned insect. The waves came and went, strewing tideflowers far up the strand. Like the tongue of a snake, the tariqua's cane darted ahead of her.

Jalila shrugged. There were these Gateways, she had always known that. There were these Gateways, and they were the only proper path between the stars, because no one could endure the eons of time that crossing even the tiniest fragment of the Ten Thousand and One Worlds would entail by the ordinary means of traveling from *there* to *here*.

"Not, of course," the tariqua was saying, "that people don't do such things. There are tales, there are always tales, of ghost-ships of sufis drifting for tens of centuries through the black and black. . . . But the wealth, the contact, the *community*, flows through the Gateways. The Almighty herself provided the means to make them in the Days of Creation, when everything that was and will ever be spilled out into a void so empty that it did not even exist as an emptiness. In those first moments, as warring elements collided, boundaries formed, dimensions were made and disappeared without ever quite dissolving, like the salt tidemarks on those rocks. . . ." As they walked, the tariqua waved her cane. ". . . which the sun and the eons can never quite bake away. These boundaries are called cosmic strings, Jalila, and they have no end. They must form either minute loops, or they must stretch from one end of this universe to the other, and then turn back again, and turn and turn without end."

Jalila glanced at the brooch the tariqua was wearing, which was of a worm consuming its tail. She knew that the physical distances between the stars were vast, but the tariqua somehow made the distances that she traversed to avoid that journey seem even vaster. . . .

"You must understand," the tariqua said, "that we tariquas pass through something worse than nothing to get from one side to the other of a Gateway."

Jalila nodded. She was young, and *nothing* didn't sound especially frightening. Still, she sensed that there were the answers to mysteries in this near-blind gaze and whispering voice that she would never get from her dreamtent or her mothers. "But, *hanim*, what could be worse," she asked dutifully, although she still couldn't think of the tariqua in terms of a name, and thus simply addressed her with the short honorific, "than sheer emptiness?"

"Ah, but emptiness is *nothing*. Imagine, Jalila, passing through *everything* instead!" The tariqua chuckled, and gazed up at the sky. "But the stars are beautiful, and so is this night. You come, I hear, from Tabuthal. There, the skies must all have been very different."

Jalila nodded. A brief vision flared over her. The way that up there, on the clearest, coldest nights, you felt as if the stars were all around you. Even now, much though she loved the fetors and astonishments of the coast, she still felt the odd pang of missing something. It was a *feeling* she missed, as much as the place itself, which she guessed would probably seem bleak and lonely if she returned to it now. It was partly to do, she suspected, with that sense that she was losing her childhood. It was like being on a ship, on Kalal's nameless boat, and watching the land recede, and half of you loving the loss, half of you hating it. A war seemed to be going on inside her between these two warring impulses. . . .

To her surprise, Jalila realized that she wasn't just thinking these thoughts, but speaking them, and that the tariqua, walking at her slow pace, the weight of her head bending her spine, her cane whispering a jagged line in the dust as the black rags of her djibbah flapped around her, was listening. Jalila supposed that she, too, had been young once, although that was hard to imagine. The sea frothed and swished. They were at the point in the road now where, gently buzzing and almost out of sight amid the forest, hidden there as if in shame, the tariqua's caleche lay waiting. It was a small filigree, a thing as old and black and ornate as her brooch. Jalila helped her toward it through the trees. The craft's door creaked open like an iron gate, then shut behind the tariqua. A few crickets sounded through the night's heat. Then, with a soft rush, and a static glow like the charge of windsilk brushing flesh, the caleche rose up through the treetops and wafted away.

The day of the moulid came. It was everything that Jalila expected, although she paid it little attention. The intricate, bowered pathway that Pavo had been working on finally shaped itself to her plans—in fact, it was better than that, and seemed like a beautiful accident. As the skies cleared, the sun shone through prismatic arches. The flowers, which had looked so stunted only the evening before, suddenly unfolded, with petals like beaten brass, and stamens shaped so that the continuing breeze, which Pavo had always claimed to have feared, laughed and whistled and tooted as it passed through them. Walking beneath the archways of flickering shadows, you were assailed by scents and the clashes of small orchestras. But Jalila's ears were blocked, her eyes were sightless. She, after all, was Dinarzade, and Nayra was Scheherazade of the Thousand and One Nights.

Swirling windsilks, her heart hammering, she strode into Al Janb. Everything seemed to be different today. There were too many sounds and colors. People tried to dance with her, or sell her things. Some of the aliens seemed to have dressed themselves as humans. Some of the humans were most definitely dressed as aliens. Her feet were already blistered and delicate from her new crimson slippers. And there was Nayra, dressed in a silvery serwal and blouse of such devastating simplicity that Jalila felt her heart kick and pause in its beating. Nayra was surrounded by a small storm of her usual admirers. Her eyes took in Jalila as she stood at their edge, then beckoned her to join them. The idea of Dinarzade and Scheherazade, which Jalila had thought was to be their secret, was now shared with everyone. The other girls laughed and clustered around, admiring, joking, touching and stroking bits of her as if she was a hayawan. *You of all people, Jalila! And such jewels, such silks* . . . Jalila stood half-frozen, her heart still kicking. *So, so marvelous! And not at all dowdy.* . . . She could have lived many a long and happy life without such compliments.

Thus the day continued. All of them in a crowd, and Jalila feeling both over-dressed and exposed, with these stirring, whispering windsilks that covered and yet mostly seemed to reveal her body. She felt like a child in a ribboned parade, and when one of the old mahwagis even came up and pressed a sticky lump of basbousa into her hand, it was the final indignity. She trudged off alone, and found Kalal and his father Ibra managing a seafront stall beside the swaying masts of the bigger trawlers, around which there was a fair level of purchase and interest. Ibra was enjoying himself, roaring out enticements and laughter in his big, belling voice. At last, they'd gotten around to harvesting some of the tideflowers for which their nameless boat had been designed, and they were selling every sort here, salt-fresh from the ocean.

"Try this one. . . ." Kalal drew Jalila away to the edge of the harbor, where the oiled water flashed below. He had just one tideflower in his hand. It was deep-banded the same crimson and blue as her windsilks. The interior was like the eye of an anemone.

Jalila was flattered. But she hesitated. "I'm not sure about wearing something dead." In any case, she knew she already looked ridiculous. That this would be more of the same.

"It isn't dead, it's as alive as you are." Kalal held it closer, against Jalila's shoulder, toward the top of her breast, smoothing out the windsilks in a way that briefly reminded her of Nayra. "And isn't this material the dead tissue of some creature or other. . . ?" Still, his hands were smoothing. Jalila thought again of Nayra. Being dressed like a doll. Her nipples started to rise. "And if we take it back to the tideflower beds tomorrow morning, place it down there carefully, it'll still survive. . . ." The tideflower had stuck itself to her now, anyway, beneath the shoulder, its adhesion passing through the thin windsilks, burning briefly as it bound to her flesh. And it *was* beautiful, even if she wasn't, and it would have been churlish to refuse. Jalila placed her finger into the tideflower's center, and felt a soft suction, like the mouth of a baby. Smiling, thanking

Kalal, feeling somehow better and more determined, she walked away.

The day went on. The night came. Fireworks crackled and rumpled, rippling down the slopes of the mountains. The whole of the center of Al Janb was transformed unrecognizably into the set of a play. Young Joanna herself walked the vast avenues of Ghezirah, the island city that lies at the center of all the Ten Thousand and One Worlds, and which grows in much the same way as Pavo's crystal scaffoldings, but on an inconceivable scale, filled with azure skies, glinting in the dark heavens like a vast diamond. The Blessed Joanna, she was supposedly thinking of a planet that had come to her in a vision as she wandered beside Ghezirah's palaces; it was a place of fine seas, lost giants, and mysterious natural castles, although Jalila, as she followed in the buffeting, cheering procession, and glanced around at the scale of the projections that briefly covered Al Janb's ordinary buildings, wondered why, even if this version of Ghezirah was fake and thin, Joanna would ever have wanted to leave *that* city to come to a place such as this.

There were more fireworks. As they rattled, a deeper sound swept over them in a moan from the sea, and everyone looked up as sunglow poured through the gaudy images of Ghezirah that still clad Al Janb's buildings. Not one rocket, or two, but three were all climbing up from the spaceport simultaneously, the vast white plumes of their energies fanning out across half the sky to form a billowy *fleur de lys*. At last, as she craned her neck and watched the last of those blazing tails diminish, Jalila felt exulted by this moulid. In the main square, the play continued. When she found a place on a bench and began to watch the more intimate parts of the drama unfold, as Joanna's lover Pia pleaded with her to remain amid the cerulean towers of Ghezirah, a figure moved to sit beside her. To Jalila's astonishment, it was Nayra.

"That's a lovely flower. I've been meaning to ask you all day . . ." Her fingers moved across Jalila's shoulder. There was a tug at her skin as she touched the petals.

"I got it from Kalal."

"Oh . . ." Nayra sought the right word. "*Him.* Can I smell it. . . ?" She was already bending down, her face close to Jalila's breast, the golden fall of her hair brushing her forearm, enclosing her in the sweet, slightly vanilla scent of her body. "That's nice. It smells like the sea—on a clear day, when you climb up and look down at it from the mountains. . . ."

The play continued. Would Joanna really go to this planet,

which kept appearing to her in these visions? Jalila didn't know. She didn't care. Nayra's hand slipped into her own and lay there upon her thigh with a weight and presence that seemed far heavier than the entire universe. She felt like that doll again. Her breath was pulling, dragging. The play continued, and then, somewhere, somehow, it came to an end. Jalila felt an aching sadness. She'd have been happy for Joanna to continue her will-I-won't-I agonizing and prayers throughout all of human history, just so that she and Nayra could continue to sit together like this, hand in hand, thigh to thigh, on this hard bench.

The projections flickered and faded. She stood up in wordless disappointment. The whole square suddenly looked like a wastetip, and she felt crumpled and used-up in these sweaty and ridiculous clothes. It was hardly worth looking back toward Nayra to say goodbye. She would, Jalila was sure, have already vanished to rejoin those clucking, chattering friends who surrounded her like a wall.

"Wait!" A hand on her arm. That same vanilla scent. "I've heard that your mother Pavo's displays along the south road are something quite fabulous. . . ." For once, Nayra's golden gaze as Jalila looked back at her was almost coy, nearly averted. "I was rather hoping you might show me. . . ."

The two of them. Walking hand in hand, just like all lovers throughout history. Like Pia and Joanna. Like Romana and Juliet. Like Isabel and Genya. Ghosts of smoke from the rocket plumes that had buttressed the sky hung around them, and the world seemed half-dissolved in the scent of sulphur and roses. An old woman they passed, who was sweeping up discarded kebab sticks and wrappers, made a sign as they passed, and gave them a weary, sad-happy smile. Jalila wasn't sure what had happened to her slippers, but they and her feet both seemed to have become weightless. If it hadn't been for the soft sway and pull of Nayra's arm, Jalila wouldn't even have been sure that she was moving. *People's feet really* don't *touch the ground when they are in love!* Here was something else that her dreamtent and her mothers hadn't told her.

Pavo's confections of plant and crystal looked marvelous in the hazed and doubled silver shadows of the rising moons. Jalila and Nayra wandered amid them, and the rest of the world felt withdrawn and empty. A breeze was still playing over the rocks and the waves, but the fluting sound had changed. It was one soft pitch, rising, falling. They kissed. Jalila closed her eyes—she couldn't help it—and trembled. Then they held both hands together and stared at each other, unflinching. Nayra's bare arms in the moonslight, the curve inside her elbow and the blue trace of a vein: Jalila had never seen anything as beautiful, here in this magical place.

The stables, where the hayawans were breathing. Jalila spoke to Robin, to Abu. The beasts were sleepy. Their flesh felt cold, their plates were warm, and Nayra seemed a little afraid. There, in the sighing darkness, the clean scent of feed and straw was overlaid with the heat of the hayawans' bodies and their dung. The place was no longer a ramshackle tent, but solid and dark, another of Pavo's creations; the stony catacombs of ages. Jalila led Nayra through it, her shoulders brushing pillars, her heart pounding, her slippered feet whispering through spills of straw. To the far corner, where the fine new white bedding lay like depths of cloud. They threw themselves onto it, half-expecting to fall through. But they were floating in straggles of windsilk, held in tangles of their own laughter and limbs.

"Remember." Nayra's palm on Jalila's right breast, scrolled like an old print in the geometric moonlight that fell from Walah, and then through the arched stone grid of a murqana that lay above their heads. "I'm Scheherazade. You're Dinarzade, my sister . . ." The pebble of Jalila's nipple rising through the windsilk. "That old, old story, Jalila. Can you remember how it went. . . ?"

*In the tide of yore and in the time of long gone before, there was a Queen of all the Queens of the Banu Sasan in the far islands of India and China, a Lady of armies and guards and servants and dependents . . .*

Again, they kissed.

*Handsome gifts, such as horses with saddles of gem-encrusted gold; mamelukes, or white slaves; beautiful handmaids, high-breasted virgins, and splendid stuffs and costly . . .*

Nayra's hand moved from Jalila's breast to encircle the tide-flower. She gave it a tug, pulled harder. Something held, gave, held, hurt, then gave entirely. The windsilks poured back. A small dark bead of blood welled at the curve between Jalila's breast and shoulder. Nayra licked it away.

*In one house was a girl weeping for the loss of her sister. In another, perhaps a mother trembling for the fate of her child; and instead of the blessings that had formerly been heaped on the Sultana's head, the air was now full of curses . . .*

Jalila was rising, floating, as Nayra's mouth traveled downward to suckle at her breast.

*Now the Wazir had two daughters, Scheherazade and Dinarzade, of whom the elder had perused the books, annals, and legends of preceding queens and empresses, and the stories, examples, and instances of bygone things. Scheherazade had read the works of the poets and she knew them by heart. She had studied philosophy, the sciences, the arts, and all accomplishments. And Scheherazade was pleasant and polite, wise and witty. Scheherazade, she was beautiful and well bred* . . .

Flying far over frost-glittering saharas, beneath the twin moons, soaring through the clouds. The falling, rising dunes. The minarets and domes of distant cities. The cries and shuddering sighs of the beloved. Patterned moonlight falling through the murqana in a white and dark tapestry across the curves and hollows of Nayra's belly.

*Alekum as-salal wa rahmatu allahi wa barakatuh.* . . .

Upon you, the peace and the mercy of God and all these blessings.

*Amen.*

There was no cock-crow when Jalila startled awake. But Walah had vanished, and so had Nayra, and the light of the morning sun came splintering down through the murqana's hot blue lattice. Sheltering her face with her hands, Jalila looked down at herself, and smiled. The jewel in her belly was all that was left of her costume. She smelled faintly of vanilla, and much of Nayra, and nothing about her flesh seemed quite her own. Moving through the dazzling drizzle, she gathered up the windsilks and other scraps of clothing that had settled into the fleece bedding. She found one of Nayra's earrings, which was twisted to right angles at the post, and had to smile again. And here was that tideflower, tossed upturned like an old cup into the corner. She touched the tiny scab on her shoulder, then lifted the flower up and inhaled, but caught on her palms only the scents of Nayra. She closed her eyes, feeling the diamond speckles of heat and cold across her body like the ripples of the sea.

The hayawans barely stirred as she moved out through their stables. Only Robin regarded her, and then incuriously, as she paused to touch the hard, grey melds of her flank that she had pressed against the bars of her enclosure. One eye, grey as rocket smoke, opened, then returned to its saharas of dreams. The hayawans, Jalila supposed for the first time, had their own passions, and these were not to be shared with some odd two-legged creatures of another race and planet.

The morning was still clinging to its freshness, and the road, as she crossed it, was barely warm beneath her feet. Wind-towered Al Janb and the haramlek behind her looked deserted. Even the limbs of the mountains seemed curled in sleepy haze. On this day after the moulid, no one but the geelies was yet stirring. Cawing, they rose and settled in flapping red flocks from the beds of the tide-flowers as Jalila scrunched across the hard stones of the beach. Her feet encountered the cool, slick water. She continued walking, wading, until the sea tickled her waist and what remained of the windsilks had spread about in spills of dye. From her cupped hands, she released the tideflower, and watched it float away. She splashed her face. She sunk down to her shoulders as the windsilks dissolved from her, and looked down between her breasts at the glowing jewel that was still stuck in her belly, and plucked it out, and watched it sink; the sea-lantern of a ship, drowning.

Walking back up the beach, wringing the wet from her hair, Jalila noticed a rich green growth standing out amid the sky-filled rockpools and the growths of lichen. Pricked by something re-sembling Pavo's curiosity, she scrambled over, and crouched to examine it as the gathering heat of the sun dried her back. She recognized this spot—albeit dimly—from the angle of a band of quartz that glittered and bled blue oxides. This was where she had coughed up her breathmoss in that early Season of Soft Rains. And here it still was, changed but unmistakable—and growing. A small patch here, several larger patches there. Tiny filaments of green, a minute forest, raising its boughs and branches to the sun.

She walked back up toward her haramlek, humming.

## 3.

The sky was no longer blue. It was no longer white. It had turned to mercury. The rockets rose and rose in dry crackles of summer lightening. The tubelike aliens fled, leaving their strange house of goo-filled windows and pipes still clicking and humming until something burst and the whole structure deflated, and the mess of it leaked across the nearby streets. There were warnings of poison-ings and strange epidemics. There were cloggings and stenches of the drains.

Jalila showed the breathmoss to her mothers, who were all intrigued and delighted, although Pavo had of course noticed and categorized the growth long before, while Ananke had to touch the stuff, and left a small brown mark there like the tips of her three fingers, which dried and turned golden over the days that followed.

But in this hot season, these evenings when the sun seemed as if it would never vanish, the breathmoss proved surprisingly hardy. . . .

After that night of the moulid, Jalila spent several happy days absorbed and alone, turning and smoothing the memory of her love-making with Nayra. Wandering above and beneath the unthinking routines of everyday life, she was like a fine craftsman, spinning silver, shaping sandalwood. The dimples of Nayra's back. Sweat glinting in the checkered moonslight. That sweet vein in the crook of her beloved's arm, and the pulse of the blood that had risen from it to the drumbeats of ecstasy. The memory seemed entirely enough to Jalila. She was barely living in the present day. When, perhaps six days after the end of the moulid, Nayra turned up at their doorstep with the ends of her hair chewed wet and her eyes red-rimmed, Jalila had been almost surprised to see her, and then to notice the differences between the real Nayra and the Scheherazade of her memories. Nayra smelled of tears and dust as they embraced; like someone who had arrived from a long, long journey.

"Why didn't you *call* me? I've been waiting, waiting. . . ."

Jalila kissed her hair. Her hand traveled beneath a summer shawl to caress Nayra's back, which felt damp and gritty. She had no idea how to answer her questions. They walked out together that afternoon in the shade of the woods behind the haramlek. The trees had changed in this long, hot season, departing from their urrearth habits to coat their leaves in a waxy substance that smelled medicinal. The shadows of their boughs were chalkmarks and charcoal. All was silent. The urrearth birds had retreated to their summer hibernations until the mists of autumn came to rouse them again. Climbing a scree of stones, they found clusters of them at the back of a cave; feathery bundles amid the dripping rock, seemingly without eyes or beak.

As they sat at the mouth of that cave, looking down across the heat-trembling bay, sucking the ice and eating the dates that Ananke had insisted they bring with them, Nayra had seemed like a different person to the one Jalila had thought she had known before the day of the moulid. Nayra, too, was human, and not the goddess she had seemed. She had her doubts and worries. She, too, thought that the girls who surrounded her were mostly crass and stupid. She didn't even believe in her own obvious beauty. She cried a little again, and Jalila hugged her. The hug became a kiss. Soon, dusty and greedy, they were tumbling amid the hot rocks. That evening, back at the haramlek, Nayra was welcomed for dinner by Jalila's mothers with mint tea and the best china. She was invited to bathe. Jalila sat beside her as they ate figs fresh from distant Ras and the year's second crop of oranges. She felt happy. At last, life seemed simple. Nayra was now officially her lover, and this love would form the pattern of her days.

Jalila's life now seemed complete; she believed that she was an adult, and that she talked and spoke and loved and worshipped in an adult way. She still rode out sometimes with Kalal on Robin and Abu, she still laughed or stole things or played games, but she was conscious now that these activities were the sweetmeats of life, pleasing but unnutritous, and the real glories and surprises lay with being with Nayra, and with her mothers, and the life of the haramlek that the two young women talked of founding together one day.

Nayra's mothers lived on the far side of Al Janb, in a fine, tall clifftop palace that was one of the oldest in the town, clad in white stone and filled with intricate courtyards, and a final beautiful tajo that looked down from gardens of tarragon across the whole bay. Jalila greatly enjoyed exploring this haramlek, deciphering the peeling scripts that wound along the cool vaults, and enjoying the company of Nayra's mothers who, in their wealth and grace and wisdom, often made her own mothers seem like the awkward and recent provincial arrivals that they plainly were. At home, in her own haramlek, the conversations and ideas seemed stale. An awful dream came to Jalila one night. She was her old doll Tabatha, and she really was being buried. The ground she lay in was moist and dank, as if it was still the Season of Soft Rains, and the faces of everyone she knew were clustered around the hole above her, muttering and sighing as her mouth and eyes were inexorably filled with soil.

"Tell me what it was like, when you first fell in love."

Jalila had chosen Pavo to ask this question of. Ananke would probably just hug her, while Lya would talk and talk until there was nothing to say.

"I don't know. Falling in love is like coming home. You can never quite do it for the first time."

"But in the stories—"

"—The stories are always written *afterward*, Jalila."

They were walking the luminous shore. It was near midnight, which was now by far the best time of the night or day. But what Pavo had just said sounded wrong; perhaps she hadn't been the right choice of mother to speak to, after all. Jalila was sure she'd loved Nayra since that day before the moulid of Joanna, although it was true she loved her now in a different way.

"You still don't think we really will form a haramlek together, do you?"

"I think that it's too early to say."

"You were the last of our three, weren't you? Lya and Ananke were already together."

"It was what drew me to them. They seemed so happy and complete. It was also what frightened me and nearly sent me away."

"But you stayed together, and then there was . . ." This was the part that Jalila still found hardest to acknowledge; the idea that her mothers had a physical, sexual relationship. Sometimes, deep at night, from someone else's dreamtent, she had heard muffled sighs, the wet slap of flesh. Just like the hayawans, she supposed, there were things about other people's lives that you could never fully understand, no matter how well you thought you knew them.

She chose a different tack. "So why did you choose to have me?"

"Because we wanted to fill the world with something that had never ever existed before. Because we felt selfish. Because we wanted to give ourselves away."

"Ananke, she actually gave birth to me, didn't she?"

"Down here at Al Janb, they'd say we were primitive and mad. Perhaps that was how we wanted to be. But all the machines at the clinics do is try to recreate the conditions of a real human womb— the voices, the movements, the sound of breathing. . . . Without first hearing that Song of Life, no human can ever be happy, so what better way could there be than to hear it naturally?"

A flash of that dream-image of herself being buried. "But the birth itself—"

"—I think that was something we all underestimated." The tone of Pavo's voice told Jalila that this was not a subject to be explored on the grounds of mere curiosity.

The tideflower beds had solidified. You could walk across them as if they were dry land. Kalal, after several postponements and broken promises, took Jalila and Nayra out one night to demonstrate.

Smoking lanterns at the prow and stern of his boat. The water slipping warm as blood through Jalila's trailing fingers. Al Janb receding beneath the hot thighs of the mountains. Kalal at the prow. Nayra sitting beside her, her arm around her shoulder, hand straying across her breast until Jalila shrugged it away because the heat of their two bodies was oppressive.

"This season'll end soon," Nayra said. "You've never known the winter here, have you?"

"I was *born* in the winter. Nothing here could be as cold as the lightest spring morning in the mountains of Tabuthal."

"Ah, the *mountains*. You must show me sometime. We should travel there together. . . ."

Jalila nodded, trying hard to picture that journey. She'd attempted to interest Nayra in riding a hayawan, but she grew frightened even in the presence of the beasts. In so many ways, in fact, Nayra surprised Jalila with her timidity. Jalila, in these moments of doubt, and as she lay alone in her dreamtent and wondered, would list to herself Nayra's many assets: her lithe and willing body; the beautiful haramlek of her beautiful mothers; the fact that so many of the other girls now envied and admired her. There were so many things that were good about Nayra.

Kalal, now that his boat had been set on course for the further tidebeds, came to sit with them, his face sweated lantern-red. He and Nayra shared many memories, and now, as the sails pushed on from the hot air off the mountains, they vied to tell Jalila of the surprises and delights of winters in Al Janb. The fogs when you couldn't see your hand. The intoxicating blue berries that appeared in special hollows through the crust of the snow. The special saint's days. . . . If Jalila hadn't known better, she'd have said that Nayra and Kalal were fighting over something more important.

The beds of tideflowers were vast, luminous, heavy-scented. Red-black clusters of geelies rose and fell here and there in the moonlight. Walking these gaudy carpets was a most strange sensation. The dense interlaces of leaves felt like rubber matting, but sank and bobbed. Jalila and Nayra lit more lanterns and dotted them around a field of huge primrose and orange petals. They sang and staggered and rolled and fell over. Nayra had brought a pipe of kif resin, and the sensation of smoking that and trying to dance was hilarious. Kalal declined, pleading that he had to control the boat on the way back, and picked his way out of sight, disturbing flocks of geelies.

And so the two girls danced as the twin moons rose. Nayra, twirling silks, her hair fanning, was graceful as Jalila still staggered amid the lapping flowers. As she lifted her arms and rose on tiptoe, bracelets glittering, she had never looked more desirable. Somewhat drunkenly—and slightly reluctantly, because Kalal might return at any moment—Jalila moved forward to embrace her. It was good to hold Nayra, and her mouth tasted like the tideflowers and sucked needily at her own. In fact, the moments of their love had never been sweeter and slower than they were on that night, although, even as Jalila marveled at the shape of Nayra's breasts and listened to the changed song of her breathing, she felt herself chilling, receding, drawing back, not just from Nayra's physical presence, but from this small bay beside the small town on the single continent beside Habara's great and lonely ocean. Jalila felt infinitely sorry for Nayra as she brought her to her little ecstasies and they kissed and rolled across the beds of flowers. She felt sorry for Nayra because she was beautiful, and sorry for her because of all her accomplishments, and sorry for her because she would always be happy here amid the slow seasons of this little planet.

Jalila felt sorry for herself as well; sorry because she had thought that she had known love, and because she knew now that it had only been a pretty illusion.

There was a shifting wind, dry and abrasive, briefly to be welcomed, until it became something to curse and cover your face and close your shutters against.

Of Jalila's mothers, only Lya seemed at all disappointed by her break from Nayra, no doubt because she had fostered hopes of their union forming a powerful bond between their haramleks, and even she did her best not to show it. Of the outside world, the other young women of Al Janb all professed total disbelief—*why if it had been me, I'd never have* . . . But soon, they were cherishing the new hope that it might indeed *be* them. Nayra, to her credit, maintained an extraordinary dignity in the face of the fact that she, of all people, had finally been rejected. She dressed in plain clothes. She spoke and ate simply. Of course, she looked more devastatingly beautiful than ever, and everyone's eyes were reddened by airborne grit in any case, so it was impossible to tell how much she had really been crying. Now, as the buildings of Al Janb creaked and the breakers rolled and the wind howled through the teeth of the mountains, Jalila saw the gaudy, seeking, and competing creatures who so often surrounded Nayra quite differently. Nayra was not, had never been, in control of them. She was more like the bloody carcass over which, flashing their teeth, their eyes, stretching their limbs, they endlessly fought. Often, riven by a sadness far deeper than she had ever experienced, missing something she couldn't explain, wandering alone or lying in her dreamtent, Jalila nearly went back to Nayra. . . . But she never did.

This was the Season of Winds, and Jalila was heartily sick of herself and Al Janb, and the girls and the mahwagis and the mothers, and of this changing, buffeting banshee weather that seemed to play with her moods. Sometimes now, the skies were entirely beautiful, strung by the curling multicolored banners of sand that the winds had lifted from distant corners of the continent. There was crimson and there was sapphire. The distant saharas of Jalila's dreams had come to haunt her. They fell—as the trees tore and the paint stripped from the shutters and what remained of Pavo's arches collapsed—in an irritating grit that worked its way into all the crevices of your body and every weave of your clothes.

The tariqua had spoken of the pain of *nothing*, and then of the pain of *everything*. At the time, Jalila had understood neither, but now, she felt that she understood the pain of nothing all too well. The product of the combined genes of her three mothers; loving Ananke, ever-curious Pavo, proud and talkative Lya, she had always felt glad to recognize these characteristics mingled in herself, but now she wondered if these traits hadn't canceled each other out. She was a null-point, a zero, clumsy and destructive and unloving. She was Jalila, and she walked alone and uncaring through this Season of Winds.

One morning, the weather was especially harsh. Jalila was alone in the haramlek, although she cared little where she or anyone else was. A shutter must have come loose somewhere. That often happened now. It had been banging and hammering so long that it began to irritate even her. She climbed stairs and slammed doors over jamming drifts of mica. She flapped back irritably at flapping curtains. Still, the banging went on. Yet all the windows and doors were now secure. She was sure of it. Unless. . . .

Someone was at the front door. She could see a swirling globular head through the greenish glass mullion. Even though they could surely see her as well, the banging went on. Jalila wondered if she wanted it to be Nayra; after all, this was how she had come to her after the moulid; a sweet and needy human being to drag her out from her dreams. But it was only Kalal. As the door shoved Jalila back, she tried not to look disappointed.

"You can't do this with your life!"

"Do what?"

"This—*nothing*. And then not answering the fucking door. . . ." Kalal prowled the hallway as the door banged back and forth and tapestries flailed, looking for clues as if he was a detective. "Let's go out."

Even in this weather, Jalila supposed that she owed it to Robin.

Then Kalal had wanted to go north, and she insisted on going south, and was not in any mood for arguing. It was an odd journey, so unlike the ones they'd undertaken in the summer. They wrapped their heads and faces in flapping howlis, and tried to ride mostly in the forest, but the trees whipped and flapped and the raw air still abraded their faces.

They took lunch down by a flatrock shore, in what amounted to shelter, although there was still little enough of it as the wind eddied about them. This could have been the same spot where they had stopped in summer, but it was hard to tell; the light was so changed, the sky so bruised. Kalal seemed changed, too. His face beneath his howli seemed older, as he tried to eat their aish before the sand-laden air got to it, and his chin looked prickled and abraded. Jalila supposed that this was the same facial growth that his father Ibra was so fond of sporting. She also supposed he must choose to shave his off in the way that some women on some decadent planets were said to shave their legs and armpits.

"Come a bit closer—" she half-shouted, working her way back into the lee of the bigger rock beside which she was sitting to make room for him. "I want you to tell me what you know about love, Kalal."

Kalal hunched beside her. For a while, he just continued tearing and chewing bits of aish, with his body pressed against hers as the winds boiled around them, the warmth of their flesh almost meeting. And Jalila wondered if men and women, when their lives and needs had been more closely intertwined, had perhaps known the answer to her question. What *was* love, after all? It would have been nice to think that, in those dim times of myth, men and women had whispered the answer to that question to each other. . . .

She thought then that Kalal hadn't properly heard her. He was telling her about his father, and a planet he barely remembered, but on which he was born. The sky there had been fractaled gold and turquoise—colors so strange and bright that they came as a delight and a shock each morning. It was a place of many islands, and one great city. His father had been a fisherman and boat-repairer of sorts there as well, although the boats had been much grander than anything you ever saw at Al Janb, and the fish had lived not as single organisms, but as complex shoals that were caught not for their meat, but for their joint minds. Ibra had been approached by a woman from off-world, who had wanted a ship on which she could sail alone around the whole lonely band of the northern oceans. She had told him that she was sick of human company. The planning and the making of the craft was a joy for Ibra, because such a lonely journey had been one that he had long dreamed of making, if ever he'd had the time and money. The ship was his finest-ever creation, and it turned out, as they worked on it, that neither he nor the woman were quite as sick of human company as they had imagined. They fell in love as the keel and the spars grew in the city dockyards and the ship's mind was nurtured, and as they did so, they slowly relearned the expressions of sexual need between the male and female.

"You mean he *raped* her?"

Kalal tossed his last nub of bread toward the waves. "I mean that they *made love*."

After the usual negotiations and contracts, and after the necessary insertions of the appropriate cells, Ibra and this woman (whom Kalal didn't name in his story, any more than he named the world) set sail together, fully intending to conceive a child in the fabled way of old.

"Which was *you?*"

Kalal scowled. It was impossible to ask him even simple questions on this subject without making him look annoyed. "Of *course* it was! How many of me do you think there are?" Then he lapsed into silence. The sands swirled in colored helixes before them.

"That woman—your birthmother. What happened to her?"

"She wanted to take me away, of course—to some haramlek on another world, just as she'd been planning all along. My father was just a toy to her. As soon as their ship returned, she started making plans, issuing contracts. There was a long legal dispute with my father. I was placed in a birthsac, in stasis."

"And your father won?"

Kalal scowled. "He took me here, anyway. Which is winning enough."

There were many other questions about this story that Jalila wanted to ask Kalal, if she hadn't already pressed too far. What, after all, did this tale of dispute and deception have to do with love? And were Kalal and Ibra really fugitives? It would explain quite a lot. Once more, in that familiar welling, she felt sorry for him. Men were such strange, sad creatures; forever fighting, angry, lost. . . .

"*I'm* glad you're here anyway," she said. Then, on impulse, one of those careless things you do, she took that rough and ugly chin in her hand, turned his face toward hers and kissed him lightly on the lips.

"What was that for?"

"*El-hamdu-l-Illah.* That was for thanks."

They plodded further on their hayawans. They came eventually to a cliff-edge so high that the sea and sky above and beneath vanished. Jalila already knew what they would see as they made their way along it, but still it was a shock; that qasr, thrust into these teeming ribbons of sand. The winds whooped and howled, and the hayawans raised their heads and howled back at it. In this grinding atmosphere, Jalila could see how the qasrs had been carved over long years from pure natural rock. They dismounted, and struggled bent-backed across the narrowing track toward the qasr's studded door. Jalila raised her fist and beat on it.

She glanced back at Kalal, but his face was entirely hidden beneath his hood. Had they always intended to come here? But they had traveled too far to do otherwise now; Robin and Abu were tired and near-blinded; they all needed rest and shelter. She beat on the door again, but the sound was lost in the booming storm. Perhaps the tariqua had left with the last of the Season of Rockets, just as had most of the aliens. Jalila was about to turn away when the door, as if thrown wide by the wind, blasted open. There was no one on the other side, and the hallway beyond was dark as the bottom of a dry well. Robin hoiked her head back and howled and resisted as Jalila hauled her in. Kalal with Abu followed. The door, with a massive drumbeat, hammered itself shut behind them. Of course, it was only some old mechanism of this house, but Jalila felt the hairs on the nape of her neck rise.

They hobbled the hayawans beside the largest of the scalloped arches, and walked on down the passageway beyond. The wind was still with them, and the shapes of the pillars were like the swirling helixes of sand made solid. It was hard to tell what parts of this place had been made by the hands of women and what was entirely natural. If the qasr had seemed deserted in the heat of summer, it was entirely abandoned now. A scatter of glass windchimes, torn apart by the wind. A few broken plates. Some flapping cobwebs of tapestry.

Kalal pulled Jalila's hand.

"Let's go back. . . ."

But there was greater light ahead, the shadows of the speeding sky. Here was the courtyard where they had glimpsed the tariqua. She had plainly gone now—the fountain was dry and clogged, the bushes were bare tangles of wire. They walked out beneath the tiled arches, looking around. The wind was like a million voices, rising in ululating chorus. This was a strange and empty place; somehow dangerous. . . . Jalila span around. The tariqua was standing there, her robes flapping. With insect fingers, she beckoned. "Are you leaving?" Jalila asked. "I mean, this place. . . ."

The tariqua had led them into the shelter of a tall, wind-echoing chamber set with blue and white tiles. There were a few rugs and cushions scattered on the floor, but still the sense of abandonment remained. As if, Jalila thought, as the tariqua folded herself on the floor and gestured that they join her, this was her last retreat.

"No, Jalila. I won't be leaving Habara. *Itfaddal*. . . . Do sit down."

They stepped from their sandals and obeyed. Jalila couldn't quite remember now whether Kalal had encountered the tariqua on her visit to their haramlek, although it seemed plain from his stares at her, and the way her grey-white gaze returned them, that they knew of each other in some way. Coffee was brewing in the corner, over a tiny, blue spirit flame, which, as it fluttered in the many drafts, must have taken hours to heat anything. Yet the spout of the brass pot was steaming. And there were dates, too, and nuts and seeds. The tariqua, apologizing for her inadequacy as a host, nevertheless insisted that they help themselves. And somewhere there was a trough of water, too, for their hayawans, and a basket of acram leaves.

Uneasily, they sipped from their cups, chewed the seeds. Kalal had picked up a chipped lump of old stone and was playing with it nervously. Jalila couldn't quite see what it was.

"So," he said, clearing his throat, "you've been to and from the stars, have you?"

"As have you. Perhaps you could name the planet? It may have been somewhere that we have both visited. . . ."

Kalal swallowed. His lump of old stone clicked the floor. A spindle of wind played chill on Jalila's neck. Then—she didn't know how it began—the tariqua was talking of Ghezirah, the great and fabled city that lay at the center of all the Ten Thousand and One Worlds. No one Jalila had ever met or heard of had ever visited Ghezirah, not even Nayra's mothers—yet this tariqua talked of it as if she knew it well. Before, Jalila had somehow imagined the tariqua trailing from planet to distant planet with dull cargoes of ore and biomass in her ship's holds. To her mind, Ghezirah had always been more than half-mythical—a place from which a dubious historical figure such as the Blessed Joanna might easily emanate, but certainly not a place composed of solid streets upon which the gnarled and bony feet of this old woman might once have walked. . . .

Ghezirah . . . she could see it now in her mind, smell the shadowy lobbies, see the ever-climbing curve of its mezzanines and rooftops vanishing into the impossible greens of the Floating Ocean. But every time Jalila's vision seemed about to solidify, the tariqua said something else that made it tremble and change. And then the tariqua said the strangest thing of all, which was that the City At The End Of All Roads was actually *alive*. Not alive in the meager sense in which every town has a sort of life, but truly living. The city thought. It grew. It responded. There was no central mind or focus to this consciousness, because Ghezirah *itself*, its teeming streets and minarets and rivers and caleches and its many millions of lives, was itself the mind. . . .

Jalila was awestruck, but Kalal seemed unimpressed, and was still playing with that old lump of stone.

## 4.

"Jalilaneen. . . ."

The way bondmother Lya said her name made Jalila look up. Somewhere in her throat, a wary nerve started ticking. They took their meals inside now, in the central courtyard of the haramlek, which Pavo had provided with a translucent roofing to let in a little of what light there was in the evenings' skies, and keep out most of the wind. Still, as Jalila took a sip of steaming hibiscus, she was sure that the sand had gotten into something.

"We've been talking. Things have come up—ideas about which we'd like to seek your opinion. . . ."

In other words, Jalila thought, her gaze traveling across her three mothers, you've decided something. And this is how you tell me—by pretending that you're consulting me. It had been the same with leaving Tabuthal. It was always the same. An old ghost of herself got up at that point, threw down her napkin, stalked off up to her room. But the new Jalila remained seated. She even smiled and tried to look encouraging.

"We've seen so little of this world," Lya continued. "All of us, really. And especially since we had you. It's been marvelous. But, of course, it's also been confining. . . . Oh *no*—" Lya waved the idea away quickly, before anyone could even begin to start thinking it. "—we won't be leaving our haramlek and Al Janb. There are many things to do. New bonds and friendships have been made. Ananke and I won't be leaving, anyway. . . . But Pavo . . ." And here Lya, who could never quite stop being the chair of a committee, gave a nod toward her mate. ". . . Pavo here has dec—expressed a *wish*—that she would like to travel."

"Travel?" Jalila leaned forward, her chin resting on her knuckles. "How?"

Pavo gave her plate a half turn. "By boat seems the best way to explore Habara. With such a big ocean . . ." She turned the plate again, as if to demonstrate.

"And not just a *boat*," Ananke put in encouragingly. "A brand new *ship*. We're having it built—"

"—But I thought you said you hadn't yet decided?"

"The contract, I think, is still being prepared," Lya explained. "And much of the craft will be to Pavo's own design."

"Will you be building it yourself?"

"Not alone." Pavo gave another of her flustered smiles. "I've asked Ibra to help me. He seems to be the best, the most knowledgeable—"

"—Ibra? Does he have any references?"

"This is *Al Janb*, Jalila," Lya said. "We know and trust people. I'd have thought that, with your friendship with Kalal. . . ."

"This certainly *is* Al Janb. . . ." Jalila sat back. "How can I ever forget it!" All of her mothers' eyes were on her. Then something broke. She got up and stormed off to her room.

The long ride to the tariqua's qasr, the swish of the wind, and banging three times on the old oak door. Then hobbling Robin and hurrying through dusty corridors to that tall tiled chamber, and somehow expecting no one to be there, even though Jalila had now come here several times alone.

But the tariqua was always there. Waiting.

Between them now, there was much to be said.

"This ant, Jalila, which crawls across this sheet of paper from *here* to *there*. She is much like us as we crawl across the surface of this planet. Even if she had the wings some of her kind sprout, just as I have my caleche, it would still be the same." The tiny creature, waving feelers, was plainly lost. A black dot. Jalila understood how it felt. "But say, if we were to fold both sides of the paper together. You see how she moves now. . . ?" The ant, antennae waving, hesitant, at last made the tiny jump. "We can move more quickly from one place to another by not traveling across the distance that separates us from it, but by folding space itself.

"Imagine now, Jalila, that this universe is not one thing alone, one solitary series of *this* following *that*, but an endless branching of potentialities. Such it has been since the Days of Creation, and such it is even now, in the shuffle of that leaf as the wind picks at it, in the rising steam of your coffee. Every moment goes in many ways. Most are poor, half-formed things, the passing thoughts and whims of the Almighty. They hang there and they die, never to be seen again. But others branch as strongly as this path that we find ourselves following. There are universes where you and I have never sat here in this qasr. There are universes where there is no Jalila. . . . Will you get that for me. . . ?"

The tariqua was pointing to an old book in a far corner. Its leather was cracked, the wind lifted its pages. As she took it from her, Jalila felt the hot brush of the old woman's hand.

"So now, you must imagine that there is not just one sheet of a single universe, but many, as in this book, heaped invisibly above and beside and below the page upon which we find ourselves crawling. In fact . . ." The ant recoiled briefly, sensing the strange heat of the tariqua's fingers, then settled on the open pages. "You must imagine shelf after shelf, floor upon floor of books, the aisles of an infinite library. And if we are to fold this one page, you see, we or the ant never quite knows what lies on the other side of it. And there may be a tear in that next page as well. It may even be that another version of ourselves has already torn it."

Despite its worn state, the book looked potentially valuable, hand-written in a beautiful flowing script. Jalila had to wince when the tariqua's fingers ripped through them. But the ant had vanished now. She was somewhere between the book's pages. . . .

"That, Jalila, is the Pain of Distance—the sense of every potentiality. So that womankind may pass over the spaces between the stars, every tariqua must experience it." The wind gave an extra lunge, flipping the book shut. Jalila reached forward, but the tariqua, quick for once, was ahead of her. Instead of opening the book to release the ant, she weighed it down with the same chipped old stone with which Kalal had played on his visit to this qasr.

"Now, perhaps, my Jalila, you begin to understand?"

The stone was old, chipped, grey-green. It was inscribed, and had been carved with the closed wings of a beetle. Here was something from a world so impossibly old and distant as to make the book upon which it rested seem fresh and new as an unbudded leaf —a scarab, shaped for the Queens of Egypt.

"See here, Jalila. See how it grows. The breathmoss?"

This was the beginning of the Season of Autumns. The trees were beautiful; the forests were on fire with their leaves. Jalila had been walking with Pavo, enjoying the return of the birdsong, and wondering why it was that this new season felt sad when everything around her seemed to be changing and growing.

"Look. . . ."

The breathmoss, too, had turned russet-gold. Leaning close to it beneath this tranquil sky, which was composed of a blue so pale it was as if the sea had been caught in reflection inside an upturned white bowl, was like looking into the arms of a miniature forest.

"Do you think it will die?"

Pavo leaned beside her. "Jalila, it should have died long ago. *Inshallah*, it is a small miracle." There were the three dead marks where Ananke had touched it in a Season of Long Ago. "You see how frail it is, and yet . . ."

"At least it won't spread and take over the planet."

"Not for a while, at least."

On another rock lay another small colony. Here, too, oddly enough, there were marks. Five large dead dots, as if made by the outspread of a hand, although the shape of it was too big to have been Ananke's. They walked on. Evening was coming. Their shadows were lengthening. Although the sun was shining and the waves sparkled, Jalila wished that she had put on something warmer than a shawl.

"That tariqua. You seem to enjoy her company. . . ."

Jalila nodded. When she was with the old woman, she felt at last as if she was escaping the confines of Al Janb. It was liberating, after the close life in this town and with her mothers in their haramlek, to know that interstellar space truly existed, and then to feel, as the tariqua spoke of Gateways, momentarily like that ant, infinitely small and yet somehow inching, crawling across the many universes' infinite pages. But how could she express this? Even Pavo wouldn't understand.

"How goes the boat?" she asked instead.

Pavo slipped her arm into the crook of Jalila's and hugged her. "You must come and *see!* I have the plan in my head, but I'd never realized quite how big it would be. And complex. Ibra's full of enthusiasm."

"I can imagine!"

The sea flashed. The two women chuckled.

"The way the ship's designed, Jalila, there's more than enough room for others. I never exactly planned to go alone, but then Lya's Lya. And Ananke's always—"

Jalila gave her mother's arm a squeeze. "I know what you're saying."

"I'd be happy if you came, Jalila. I'd understand if you didn't. This is such a beautiful, wonderful planet. The leviathans—we know so little about them, yet they plainly have intelligence, just as all those old myths say."

"You'll be telling me next about the qasrs. . . ."

"The ones we can see near here are *nothing*! There are islands on the ocean that are entirely made from them. And the wind pours through. They sing endlessly. A different song for every mood and season."

"Moods! If I'd said something like that when you were teaching me of the Pillars of Life, you'd have told me I was being unscientific!"

"Science is *about* wonder, Jalila. I was a poor teacher if I never told you that."

"You did." Jalila turned to kiss Pavo's forehead. "You did. . . ."

Pavo's ship was a fine thing. Between the slipways and the old mooring posts, where the red-flapping geelies quarreled over scraps of dying tideflower, it grew and grew. Golden-hulled. Far sleeker and bigger than even the ferries that had once borne Al Janb's visitors to and from the rocket port, and which now squatted on the shingle nearby, gently rusting. It was the talk of the Season. People came to admire its progress.

As Jalila watched the spars rise over the clustered roofs of the fisherwomen's houses, she was reminded of Kalal's tale of his father and his nameless mother, and that ship that they had made together in the teeming dockyards of that city. Her thoughts blurred. She saw the high balconies of a hotel far bigger than any of Al Janb's inns and boarding houses. She saw a darker, brighter ocean. Strange flesh upon flesh, with the windows open to the oil-and-salt breeze, the white lace curtains rising, falling. . . .

The boat grew, and Jalila visited the tariqa, although back in Al Janb, her thoughts sometimes trailed after Kalal as she wondered how it must be—to be male, like the last dodo, and trapped in some endless state of part-arousal, like a form of nagging worry. Poor Kalal. But his life certainly wasn't lonely. The first time Jalila noticed him at the center of the excited swarm of girls that once again surrounded Nayra, she'd almost thought that she was seeing things. But the gossip was loud and persistent. Kalal and Nayra were *a couple*—the phrase normally followed by a scandalized shriek, a hand-covered mouth. Jalila could only guess what the proud mothers of Nayra's haramlek thought of such a union, but, of course, no one could subscribe to outright prejudice. Kalal was, after all, just another human being. Lightly probing her own mothers' attitudes, she found the usual condescending tolerance. Having sexual relations with a male would be like smoking kif, or drinking alcohol, or any other form of slightly aberrant adolescent behavior; to be tolerated with easy smiles and sympathy, as long as it didn't go on for too long. To be treated, in fact, in much the same manner as her mothers were now treating her regular visits to the tariqua.

Jalila came to understand why people thought of the Season of Autumns as a sad time. The chill nights. The morning fogs that shrouded the bay. The leaves, finally falling, piled into rotting heaps. The tideflower beds, also, were dying as the waves pulled and dismantled what remained of their colors, and they drifted to the shores, the flowers bearing the same stench and texture and color as upturned clay. The geelies were dying as well. In the town, to compensate, there was much bunting and celebration for yet another moulid, but to Jalila the brightness seemed feeble—the flame of a match held against winter's gathering gale. Still, she sometimes wandered the old markets with some of her old curiosity, nostalgically touching the flapping windsilks, studying the faces and nodding at the many she now knew, although her thoughts were often literally light-years away. *The Pain of Distance*; she could feel it. Inwardly, she was thrilled and afraid. Her mothers and everyone else, caught up in the moulid and Pavo's coming departure, imagined from her mood that she had now decided to take that voyage with her. She deceived Kalal in much the same way.
  The nights became clearer. Riding back from the qasr one dark evening with the tariqua's slight voice ringing in her ears, the stars seemed to hover closer around her than at any time since she had left Tabuthal. She could feel the night blossoming, its emptiness and the possibilities spinning out to infinity. She felt both like crying, and like whooping for joy. She had dared to ask the tariqua the question she had long been formulating, and the answer, albeit not entirely yes, had not been no. She talked to Robin as they bobbed along, and the puny yellow smudge of Al Janb drew slowly closer. You must understand, she told her hayawan, that the core of the Almighty is like the empty place between these stars, around which they all revolve. It is *there*, we know it, but we can never *see* it. . . . She sang songs from the old saharas about the joy of loneliness, and the loneliness of joy. From here, high up on the gradually descending road that wound its way down toward her haramlek, the

horizon was still distant enough for her to see the lights of the rocketport. It was like a huge tidebed, holding out as the season changed. And there at the center of it, rising golden, no longer a stumpy silo-shaped object but somehow beautiful, was the last of the year's rockets. It would have to rise from Habara before the coming of the Season of Winters.

Her mothers' anxious faces hurried around her in the lamplight as she led Robin toward the stable.

"Where have you *been*, Jalilaneen?"

"Do you *know* what time it is?"

"We should be in the town *already!*"

For some reason, they were dressed in their best, most formal robes. Their palms were hennaed and scented. They bustled Jalila out of her gritty clothes, practically washed and dressed her, then flapped themselves down the serraplate road into town, where the processions had already started. Still, they were there in plenty of time to witness the blessing of Pavo's ship. It was to be called *Endeavor*, and Pavo and Jalila together smashed the bottle of wine across its prow before it rumbled into the nightblack waters of the harbor with an enormous white splash. Everyone cheered. Pavo hugged Jalila.

There were more bottles of the same frothy wine available at the party afterward. Lya, with her usual thoroughness, had ordered a huge case of the stuff, although many of the guests remembered the Prophet's old injunction and avoided imbibing. Ibra, though, was soon even more full of himself than usual, and went around the big marquee with a bottle in each hand, dancing clumsily with anyone who was foolish enough to come near him. Jalila drank a little of the stuff herself. The taste was sweet, but oddly hot and bitter. She filled up another glass.

"Wondered what you two mariners were going to call that boat. . . ."

It was Kalal. He'd been dancing with many of the girls, and he looked almost as red-faced as his father.

"Bet you don't even know what the first *Endeavor* was."

"You're wrong there," Jalila countered primly, although the simple words almost fell over each other as she tried to say them. "It was the spacecraft of Captain Cook. She was one of urrearth's most famous early explorers."

"I thought you were many things," Kalal countered, angry for no apparent reason. "But I never thought you were *stupid*."

Jalila watched him walk away. The dance had gathered up its

beat. Ibra had retreated to sit, foolishly glum, in a corner, and Nayra had moved to the middle of the floor, her arms raised, bracelets jingling, an opal jewel at her belly, windsilk-draped hips swaying. Jalila watched. Perhaps it was the drink, but for the first time in many a Season, she felt a slight return of that old erotic longing as she watched Nayra swaying. Desire was the strangest of all emotions. It seemed so trivial when you weren't possessed of it, and yet when you were possessed, it was as if all the secrets of the universe were waiting. . . . Nayra was the focus of all attention now as she swayed amid the crowd, her shoulders glistening. She danced before Jalila, and her languorous eyes fixed her for a moment before she danced on. Now she was dancing with Kalal, and he was swaying with her, her hands laid upon his shoulders, and everyone was clapping. They made a fine couple. But the music was getting louder, and so were people's voices. Her head was pounding. She left the marquee.

She welcomed the harshness of the night air, the clear presence of the stars. Even the stench of the rotting tideflowers seemed appropriate as she picked her way across the ropes and slipways of the beach. So much had changed since she had first come here—but mostly what had changed had been herself. Here, its shape unmistakable as rising Walah spread her faint blue light across the ocean, was Kalal's boat. She sat down on the gunwale. The cold wind bit into her. She heard the crunch of shingle, and imagined it was someone else who was in need of solitude. But the sound grew closer, and then whoever it was sat down on the boat beside her. She didn't need to look up now. Kalal's smell was always different, and now he was sweating from the dancing.

"I thought you were enjoying yourself," she muttered.

"Oh—I was . . ." The emphasis on the *was* was strong.

They sat there for a long time, in windy, wave-crashing silence. It was almost like being alone. It was like the old days of their being together.

"So you're going, are you?" Kalal asked eventually.

"Oh, yes."

"I'm pleased for you. It's a fine boat, and I like Pavo best of all your mothers. You haven't seemed quite so happy lately here in Al Janb. Spending all that time with that old witch in the qasr."

"She's not a witch. She's a tariqua. It's one of the greatest, oldest callings. Although I'm surprised you've had time to notice what I'm up to, anyway. You and Nayra . . ."

Kalal laughed, and the wind made the sound turn bitter.

"I'm sorry," Jalila continued. "I'm sounding just like those stupid gossips. I know you're not like that. Either of you. And I'm happy for you both. Nayra's sweet and talented and entirely lovely . . . I hope it lasts . . . I hope. . . ."

After another long pause, Kalal said, "Seeing as we're apologizing, I'm sorry I got cross with you about the name of that boat you'll be going on—the *Endeavor*. It's a good name."

"Thank you. *El-hamadu-l-illah*."

"In fact, I could only think of one better one, and I'm glad you and Pavo didn't use it. You know what they say. To have two ships with the same name confuses the spirits of the winds. . . ."

"What are you talking about, Kalal?"

"This boat. You're sitting right on it. I thought you might have noticed."

Jalila glanced down at the prow, which lay before her in the moonslight, pointing toward the silvered waves. From this angle, and in the old naskhi script that Kalal had used, it took her a moment to work out the craft's name. Something turned inside her.

*Breathmoss.*

In white, moonslit letters.

"I'm sure there are better names for a boat," she said carefully. "Still, I'm flattered."

"Flattered?" Kalal stood up. She couldn't really see his face, but she suddenly knew that she'd once again said the wrong thing. He waved his hands in an odd shrug, and he seemed for a moment almost ready to lean close to her—to do something unpredictable and violent—but instead, picking up stones and skimming them hard into the agitated waters, he walked away.

Pavo was right. If not about love—which Jalila knew now that she still waited to experience—then at least about the major decisions of your life. There was never quite a beginning to them, although your mind often sought for such a thing.

When the tariqa's caleche emerged out of the newly teeming rain one dark evening a week or so after the naming of the *Endeavor*, and settled itself before the lights of their haramlek, and the old woman herself emerged, somehow still dry, and splashed across the puddled garden while her three mothers flustered about to find the umbrella they should have thought to look for earlier, Jalila still didn't know what she should be thinking. The four women would, in any case, need to talk alone; Jalila recognized that. For once, after the initial greetings, she was happy to retreat to her dreamtent.

But her mind was still in turmoil. She was suddenly terrified that her mothers would actually agree to this strange proposition, and then that, out of little more than embarrassment and obligation, the rest of her life would be bound to something that the tariqua called the Church of the Gateway. She knew so little. The tariqua talked only in riddles. She could be a fraud, for all Jalila knew—or a witch, just as Kalal insisted. Thoughts swirled about her like the rain. To make the time disappear, she tried searching the knowledge of her dreamtent. Lying there, listening to the rising sound of her mothers' voices, which seemed to be studded endlessly with the syllables of her own name, Jalila let the personalities who had guided her through the many Pillars of Wisdom tell her what they knew about the Church of the Gateway.

She saw the blackness of planetary space, swirled with the mica dots of turning planets. Almost as big as those, as she zoomed close to it, yet looking disappointingly like a many-angled version of the rocketport, lay the spacestation, and, within it, the junction that could lead you from *here* to *there* without passing across the distance between. A huge rent in the Book of Life, composed of the trapped energies of those things the tariqua called cosmic strings, although they and the Gateway itself were visible as nothing more than a turning ring near to the center of the vast spacestation, where occasionally, as Jalila watched, crafts of all possible shapes would seem to hang, then vanish. The gap she glimpsed inside seemed no darker than that which hung between the stars behind it, but it somehow hurt to stare at it. This, then, was the core of the mystery; something both plain and extraordinary. We crawl across the surface of this universe like ants, and each of these craft, switching through the Gateway's moment of loss and endless potentiality, is piloted by the will of a tariqua's conscious intelligence, which must glimpse those choices, then somehow emerge sane and entire at the other end of everything. . . .

Jalila's mind returned to the familiar scents and shapes of her dreamtent, and the sounds of the rain. The moment seemed to belong with those of the long-ago Season of Soft Rains. Downstairs, there were no voices. As she climbed out from her dreamtent, warily expecting to find the haramlek leaking and half-finished, Jalila was struck by an idea that the tariqua hadn't quite made plain to her; that a Gateway must push through *time* just as easily as it pushes through every other dimension. . . ! But the rooms of the haramlek were finely furnished, and her three mothers and the tariqua were sitting in the rainswept candlelight of the courtyard, waiting.

With any lesser request, Lya always quizzed Jalila before she would even consider granting it. So as Jalila sat before her mothers and tried not to tremble in their presence, she wondered how she could possibly explain her ignorance of this pure, boundless mystery.

But Lya simply asked Jalila if this was what she wanted—to be an acolyte of the Church of the Gateway.

"Yes."

Jalila waited. Then, not even, *are you sure?* They'd trusted her less than this when they'd sent her on errands into Al Janb. . . . It was still raining. The evening was starless and dark. Her three mothers, having hugged her, but saying little else, retreated to their own dreamtents and silences, leaving Jalila to say farewell to the tariqua alone. The heat of the old woman's hand no longer came as a surprise to Jalila as she helped her up from her chair and away from the sheltered courtyard.

"Well," the tariqua croaked, "that didn't seem to go so badly."

"But I know so *little!*" They were standing on the patio at the dripping edge of the night. Wet streamers of wind tugged at them.

"I know you wish I could tell you more, Jalila—but then, would it make any difference?"

Jalila shook her head. "Will you come with me?"

"Habara is where I must stay, Jalila. It is written."

"But I'll be able to return?"

"Of course. But you must remember that you can never return to the place you have left." The tariqua fumbled with her clasp, the one of a worm consuming its tail. "I want you to have this." It was made of black ivory, and felt as hot as the old woman's flesh as Jalila took it. For once, not really caring whether she broke her bones, she gave the small, birdlike woman a hug. She smelled of dust and metal, like an antique box left forgotten on a sunny windowledge. Jalila helped her out down the steps into the rainswept garden.

"I'll come again soon," she said, "to the qasr."

"Of course . . . there are many arrangements." The tariqua opened the dripping filigree door of her caleche and peered at her with those half-blind eyes. Jalila waited. They had stood too long in the rain already.

"Yes?"

"Don't be too hard on Kalal."

Puzzled, Jalila watched the caleche rise and turn away from the lights of the haramlek.

✻      ✻      ✻

Jalila moved warily through the sharded glass of her own and her mothers' expectations. It was agreed that a message concerning her be sent, endorsed by the full, long, and ornate formal name of the tariqua, to the body that did indeed call itself the Church of the Gateway. It went by radio pulse to the spacestation in wide solar orbit that received Habara's rockets, and was then passed on inside a vessel from *here* to *there* that was piloted by a tariqua. Not only that, but the message was destined for Ghezirah! Riding Robin up to the cliffs where, in this newly clear autumn air, under grey skies and tearing wet wind, she could finally see the waiting fuselage of that last golden rocket, Jalila felt confused and tiny, huge and mythic. It was agreed though, that for the sake of everyone—and not least Jalila herself, should she change her mind—that the word should remain that she was traveling out around the planet with Pavo on board the *Endeavor.* In need of something to do when she wasn't brooding, and waiting for further word from (could it really be?) the sentient city of Ghezirah, Jalila threw herself into the listings and loadings and preparations with convincing enthusiasm.

"The hardest decisions, once made, are often the best ones."

"Compared to what you'll be doing, my little journey seems almost pointless."

"We love you so deeply."

Then the message finally came: an acknowledgment; an acceptance; a few (far too few, it seemed) particulars of the arrangements and permissions necessary for such a journey. All on less than half a sheet of plain, two-dimensional printout.

Even Lya had started touching and hugging her at every opportunity.

Jalila ate lunch with Kalal and Nayra. She surprised herself and talked gaily at first of singing islands and sea-leviathans, somehow feeling that she was hiding little from her two best friends but the particular details of the journey she was undertaking. But Jalila was struck by the coldness that seemed to lie between these two supposed lovers. Nayra, perhaps sensing from bitter experience that she was once again about to be rejected, seemed near-tearful behind her dazzling smiles and the flirtatious blonde tossings of her hair, while Kalal seemed . . . Jalila had no idea how he seemed, but she couldn't let it end like this, and concocted some queries about the *Endeavor* so that she could lead him off alone as they left the bar. Nayra, perhaps fearing something else entirely, was reluctant to leave them.

"I wonder what it is that we've both done to her?" Kalal sighed as they watched her give a final sideways wave, pause, and then turn reluctantly down a sidestreet with a most un-Nayran duck of her lovely head.

They walked toward the harbor through a pause in the rain, to where the *Endeavor* was waiting.

"Lovely, isn't she?" Kalal murmured as they stood looking down at the long deck, then up at the high forest of spars. Pavo, who was developing her acquaintance with the ship's mind, gave them a wave from the bubble of the forecastle. "How long do you think your journey will take? You should be back by early spring, I calculate, if you get ahead of the icebergs. . . ."

Jalila fingered the brooch that the tariqua had given her, and which she had taken to wearing at her shoulder in the place where she had once worn the tideflower. It was like black ivory, but set with tiny, white specks that loomed at your eyes if you held it close. She had no idea what world it was from, or of the substance of which it was made.

". . . You'll miss the winter here. But perhaps that's no bad thing. It's cold, and there'll be other Seasons on the ocean. And there'll be other winters. Well, to be honest, Jalila, I'd been hoping—"

"—Look!" Jalila interrupted, suddenly sick of the lie she'd been living. "I'm not going."

They turned and were facing each other by the harbor's edge. Kalal's strange face twisted into surprise, and then something like delight. Jalila thought that he was looking more and more like his father. "That's marvelous!" He clasped each of Jalila's arms and squeezed her hard enough to hurt. "It was rubbish, by the way, what I just said about winters here in Al Janb. They're the most magical, wonderful season. We'll have snowball fights together! And when Eid al-Fitr comes . . ."

His voice trailed off. His hands dropped from her. "What is it, Jalila?"

"I'm not going with Pavo on the *Endeavor*, but I'm going away. I'm going to Ghezirah. I'm going to study under the Church of the Gateway. I'm going to try to become a tariqua."

His face twisted again. "That witch—"

"—Don't keep calling her that! You have no idea!"

Kalal balled his fists, and Jalila stumbled back, fearing for a moment that this wild, odd creature might actually be about to strike her. But he turned instead, and ran off from the harbor.

Next morning, to no one's particular surprise, it was once again raining. Jalila felt restless and disturbed after her incomplete exchanges with Kalal. Some time had also passed since the message had been received from Ghezirah, and the few small details it had given of her journey had become vast and complicated and frustrating in their arranging. Despite the weather, she decided to ride out to see the tariqua.

Robin's mood had been almost as odd as her mothers' recently, and she moaned and snickered at Jalila when she entered the stables. Jalila called back to her, and stroked her long nose, trying to ease her agitation. It was only when she went to check the harnesses that she realized that Abu was missing. Lya was in the haramlek, still finishing breakfast. It had to be Kalal who had taken her.

The swirling serraplated road. The black, dripping trees. The agitated ocean. Robin was starting to rust again. She would need more of Pavo's attention. But Pavo would soon be gone too. . . . The whole planet was changing, and Jalila didn't know what to make of anything, least of all what Kalal was up to, although the unasked-for borrowing of a precious mount, even if Abu had been virtually Kalal's all summer, filled her with a foreboding that was an awkward load, not especially heavy, but difficult to carry or put down; awkward and jagged and painful. Twice, now, he had turned from her and walked away with something unsaid. It felt like the start of some prophecy. . . .

The qasr shone jet-black in the teeming rain. The studded door, straining to overcome the swelling damp, burst open more forcefully than usual at Jalila's third knock, and the air inside swirled dark and empty. No sign of Abu in the place beyond the porch where Kalal would probably have hobbled her, although the floor here seemed muddied and damp, and Robin was agitated. Jalila glanced back, but she and her hayawan had already obscured the possible signs of another's presence. Unlike Kalal, who seemed to notice many things, she decided that she made a poor detective.

Cold air stuttered down the passageways. Jalila, chilled and watchful, had grown so used to this qasr's sense of abandonment that it was impossible to tell whether the place was now finally empty. But she feared that it was. Her thoughts and footsteps whispered to her that the tariqua, after ruining her life and playing with her expectations, had simply vanished into a puff of lost potentialities. Already disappointed, angry, she hurried to the high-ceilinged room set with blue and white tiles and found, with no great surprise, that the strewn cushions were cold and damp, the coffee lamp was unlit, and that the book through which that patient ant had crawled was now sprawled in a damp-leafed scatter of torn pages. There was no sign of the scarab. Jalila sat down, and listened to the wind's howl, the rain's ticking, wondering for a long time when it was that she had lost the ability to cry.

Finally, she stood up and moved toward the courtyard. It was colder today than it had ever been, and the rain had greyed and thickened. It gelled and dripped from the gutters in the form of something she supposed was called *sleet*, and which she decided as it splattered down her neck that she would hate forever. It filled the bowl of the fountain with mucuslike slush, and trickled sluggishly along the lines of the drains. The air was full of weepings and howlings. In the corner of the courtyard, there lay a small black heap.

Sprawled half in, half out of the poor shelter of the arched cloisters, more than ever like a flightless bird, the tariqua lay dead. Her clothes were sodden. All the furnace heat had gone from her body, although, on a day such as this, that would take no more than a matter of moments. Jalila glanced up through the sleet toward the black wet stone of the latticed mashrabiya from which she and Kalal had first spied on the old woman, but she was sure now that she was alone. People shrank incredibly when they were dead—even a figure as frail and old as this creature had been. And yet, Jalila found as she tried to move the tariqua's remains out of the rain, their spiritless bodies grew uncompliant; heavier and stupider than clay. The tariqua's face rolled up toward her. One side was pushed in almost unrecognizably, and she saw that a nearby nest of ants were swarming over it, busily tunneling out the moisture and nutrition, bearing it across the smeared paving as they stored up for the long winter ahead.

There was no sign of the scarab.

## 5.

This, for Jalila and her mothers, was the Season of Farewells. It was the Season of Departures.

There was a small and pretty onion-domed mausoleum on a headland overlooking Al Janb, and the pastures around it were a popular place for picnics and lovers' trysts in the Season of Summers, although they were scattered with tombstones. It was the ever-reliable Lya who saw to the bathing and shrouding of the tariqua's body, which was something Jalila could not possibly face, and to the sending out through the null-space between the stars of all the necessary messages. Jalila, who had never been witness to the processes of death before, was astonished at the speed with which everything was arranged. As she stood with the other mourners on a day scarfed with cloud, beside the narrow rectangle of earth within which what remained of the tariqua now lay, she could still hear the wind booming over the empty qasr, feel the uncompliant weight of the old woman's body, the chill speckle of sleet on her face.

It seemed as if most of the population of Al Janb had made the journey with the cortege up the narrow road from the town. Hard-handed fisherwomen. Gaudily dressed merchants. Even the few remaining aliens. Nayra was there, too, a beautiful vision of sorrow surrounded by her lesser black acolytes. So was Ibra. So, even, was Kalal. Jalila, who was acknowledged to have known the old woman better than anyone, said a few words that she barely heard herself over the wind. Then a priestess who had flown in specially from Ras pronounced the usual prayers about the soul rising on the arms of Munkar and Nakir, the blue and the black angels. Looking down into the ground, trying hard to think of the Gardens of Delight that the Almighty always promised her stumbling faithful, Jalila could only remember that dream of her own burial: the soil pattering on her face, and everyone she knew looking down at her. The tariqua, in one of her many half-finished tales, had once spoken to her of a world upon which no sun had ever shone, but which was nevertheless warm and bounteous from the core of heat beneath its surface, and where the people were all blind, and moved by touch and sound alone; it was a joyous place, and they were forever singing. Perhaps, and despite all the words of the Prophet, Heaven, too, was a place of warmth and darkness.

The ceremony was finished. Everyone moved away, each pausing to toss in a damp clod of earth, but leaving the rest of the job to be completed by a dull-minded robotic creature, which Pavo had had to rescue from the attentions of the younger children, who, all through the long Habaran summer, had ridden around on it. Down at their haramlek, Jalila's mothers had organized a small feast. People wandered the courtyard, and commented admiringly on the many changes and improvements they had made to the place. Amid all this, Ibra seemed subdued—a reluctant presence in his own body—while Kalal was nowhere to be seen at all, although Jalila suspected that, if only for the reasons of penance, he couldn't be far away.

Of course, there had been shock at the news of the tariqua's death, and Lya, who had now become the person to whom the town most often turned to resolve its difficulties, had taken the lead in the inquiries that followed. A committee of wisewomen was organized even more quickly than the funeral, and Jalila had been summoned and interrogated. Waiting outside in the cold hallways of Al Janb's municipal buildings, she'd toyed with the idea of keeping Abu's disappearance and her suspicions of Kalal out of her story, but Lya and the others had already spoken to him, and he'd admitted to what sounded like everything. He'd ridden to the qasr on Abu to remonstrate with the tariqua. He'd been angry, and his mood had been bad. Somehow, but only lightly, he'd pushed the old woman, and she had fallen badly. Then, he panicked. Kalal bore responsibility for his acts, it was true, but it was accepted that the incident was essentially an accident. Jalila, who had imagined many versions of Kalal's confrontation with the tariqua, but not a single one that seemed entirely real, had been surprised at how easily the people of Al Janb were willing to absolve him. She wondered if they would have done so quite so easily if Kalal had not been a freak—a man. And then she also wondered, although no one had said a single word to suggest it, just how much she was to blame for all of this herself.

She left the haramlek from the funeral wake and crossed the road to the beach. Kalal was sitting on the rocks, his back turned to the shore and the mountains. He didn't look around when she approached and sat down beside him. It was the first time since before the tariqua's death that they'd been alone.

"I'll have to leave here," he said, still gazing out toward the clouds that trailed the horizon.

"There's no reason—"

"—No one's asked me and Ibra to *stay*. I think they would, don't you, if anyone had wanted us to? That's the way you women work."

"We're not *you women*, Kalal. We're people."

"So you always say. And all Al Janb's probably terrified about the report they've had to make to that thing you're joining—the Church of the Gateway. Some big, powerful body, and—whoops—we've killed one of your old employees. . . ."

"Please don't be bitter."

Kalal blinked and said nothing. His cheeks were shining.

"You and Ibra—where will you both go?"

"There are plenty of other towns around this coast. We can use our boat to take us there before the ice sets in. We can't afford to leave the planet. But maybe in the Season of False Springs, when

I'm a grown man and we've made some of the proper money we're always talking about making from harvesting the tideflowers—and when word's got around to everyone on this planet of what happened here—maybe then we'll leave Habara." He shook his head and sniffed. "I don't know why I bother to say *maybe*. . . ."

Jalila watched the waves. She wondered if this was the destiny of all men; to wander forever from place to place, planet to planet, pursued by the knowledge of vague crimes that they hadn't really committed.

"I suppose you want to know what happened?"

Jalila shook her head. "It's in the report, Kalal. I believe what you said."

He wiped his face with his palms, studied their wetness. "I'm not sure I believe it myself, Jalila. The way she was, that day. That old woman—she always seemed to be expecting you, didn't she? And then she seemed to know. I don't understand quite how it happened, and I was angry, I admit. But she almost *lunged* at me. . . . She seemed to want to die. . . ."

"You mustn't blame yourself. *I* brought you to this, Kalal. I never saw . . ." Jalila shook her head. She couldn't say. Not even now. Her eyes felt parched and cold.

"I loved you, Jalila."

The worlds branched in a million different ways. It could all have been different. The tariqua still alive. Jalila and Kalal together, instead of the half-formed thing that the love they had both felt for Nayra had briefly been. They could have taken the *Endeavor* together and sailed this planet's seas; Pavo would probably have let them—but when, but where, but how? None of it seemed real. Perhaps the tariqua was right; there are many worlds, but most of them are poor, half-formed things.

Jalila and Kalal sat there for a while longer. The breathmoss lay not far off, darkening and hardening into a carpet of stiff grey. Neither of them noticed it.

For no other reason than the shift of the tides and the rapidly coming winter, Pavo, Jalila, Kalal, and Ibra all left Al Janb on the same morning. The days before were chaotic in the haramlek. People shouted and looked around for things and grew cross and petty. Jalila was torn between bringing everything and nothing, and after many hours of bag-packing and lip-chewing, decided that it could all be thrown out, and that her time would be better spent down in the stables, with Robin. Abu was there too, of course, and she seemed to sense the imminence of change and departure even more than Jalila's own hayawan. She had become Kalal's mount far more than she had ever been Lya's, and he wouldn't come to say goodbye.

Jalila stroked the warm felt of the creatures' noses. Gazing into Abu's eyes as she gazed back at hers, she remembered their rides out in the heat of summer. Being with Kalal then, although she hadn't even noticed it, had been the closest she had ever come to loving anyone. On the last night before their departure, Ananke cooked one of her most extravagant dinners, and the four women sat around the heaped extravagance of the table that she'd spent all day preparing, each of them wondering what to say, and regretting how much of these precious last times together they'd wasted. They said a long prayer to the Almighty, and bowed in the direction of Al'Toman. It seemed that, tomorrow, even the two mothers who weren't leaving Al Janb would be setting out on a new and difficult journey.

Then there came the morning, and the weather obliged with chill sunlight and a wind that pushed hard at their cloaks and nudged the *Endeavor* away from the harbor even before her sails were set. They all watched her go, the whole town cheering and waving as Pavo waved back, looking smaller and neater and prettier than ever as she receded. Without ceremony, around the corner from the docks, out of sight and glad of the *Endeavor*'s distraction, Ibra and Kalal were also preparing to leave. At a run, Jalila caught them just as they were starting to shift the hull down the rubbled slipway into the waves. *Breathmoss*; she noticed that Kalal had kept the name, although she and he stood apart on that final beach and talked as two strangers.

She shook hands with Ibra. She kissed Kalal lightly on the cheek by leaning stiffly forward, and felt the roughness of his stubble. Then the craft got stuck on the slipway, and they were all heaving to get her moving the last few meters into the ocean, until, suddenly, she was afloat, and Ibra was raising the sails, and Kalal was at the prow, hidden behind the tarpaulined weight of their belongings. Jalila only glimpsed him once more, and by then *Breathmoss* had turned to meet the stronger currents that swept outside the grey bay. He could have been a figurehead.

Back at the dock, her mothers were pacing, anxious.

"Where have you *been?*"

"Do you *know* what *time* is?"

Jalila let them scold her. She *was* almost late for her own leaving. Although most of the crowds had departed, she'd half expected Nayra to be there. Jalila was momentarily saddened, and then she was glad for her. The silver craft that would take her to the rocketport smelled disappointingly of engine fumes as she clambered into it with the few other women and aliens who were leaving Habara. There was a loud bang as the hatches closed, and then a long wait while nothing seemed to happen, and she could only wave at Lya and Ananke through the thick porthole, smiling and mouthing stupid phrases until her face ached. The ferry bobbed loose, lurched, turned, and angled up. Al Janb was half gone in plumes of white spray already.

Then it came in a huge wave. That feeling of incompleteness, of something vital and unknown left irretrievably behind, which is the beginning of the Pain of Distance that Jalila, as a tariqua, would have to face throughout her long life. A sweat came over her. As she gazed out through the porthole at what little there was to see of Al Janb and the mountains, it slowly resolved itself into one thought. Immense and trivial. Vital and stupid. That scarab. She'd never asked Kalal about it, nor found it at the qasr, and the ancient object turned itself over in her head, sinking, spinning, filling her mind and then dwindling before rising up again as she climbed out, nauseous, from the ferry and crossed the clanging gantries of the spaceport toward the last huge golden craft, which stood steaming in the winter's air. A murder weapon?—but no, Kalal was no murderer. And, in any case, she was a poor detective. And yet . . .

The rockets thrust and rumbled. Pushing back, squeezing her eyeballs. There was no time now to think. Weight on weight, terrible seconds piled on her. Her blood seemed to leave her face. She was a clay-corpse. Vital elements of her senses departed. Then, there was a huge wash of silence. Jalila turned to look through the porthole beside her, and there it was. Mostly blue, and entirely beautiful: Habara, her birth planet. Jalila's hands rose up without her willing, and her fingers squealed as she touched the glass and tried to trace the shape of the greenish-brown coastline, the rising brown and white of the mountains of that huge single continent that already seemed so small, but of which she knew so little. Jewels seemed to be hanging close before her, twinkling and floating in and out of focus like the hazy stars she couldn't yet see. They puzzled her for a long time, did these jewels, and they were evasive as fish as she sought them with her weightlessly clumsy fingers. Then Jalila felt the salt break of moisture against her face, and realized what it was.

At long last, she was crying.

## 6.

Jalila had long been expecting the message when it finally came. At only one hundred and twenty standard years, Pavo was still relatively young to die, but she had used her life up at a frantic pace, as if she had always known that her time would be limited. Even though the custom for swift funerals remained on Habara, Jalila was able to use her position as a tariqua to ride the Gateways and return for the service. The weather on the planet of her birth was unpredictable as ever, raining one moment and then sunny the next, even as she took the ferry to Al Janb from the rocketport, and hot and cold winds seemed to strike her face as she stood on the dock's edge and looked about for her two remaining mothers. They embraced. They led her to their haramlek, which seemed smaller to Jalila each time she visited it, despite the many additions and extensions and improvements they had made, and far closer to Al Janb than the long walk she remembered once taking on those many errands. She wandered the shore after dinner, and searched the twilight for a particular shape and angle of quartz, and the signs of dark growth. But the heights of the Season of Storms on this coastline were ferocious, and nothing as fragile as breathmoss could have survived. She lay sleepless that night in her old room within her dreamtent, breathing the strong, dense, moist atmosphere with difficulty, listening to the sound of the wind and rain.

She recognized none of the faces but her mothers' of the people who stood around Pavo's grave the following morning. Al Janb had seemed so changeless, yet even Nayra had moved on—and Kalal was far away. Time was relentless. Far more than the wind that came in off the bay, it chilled Jalila to the bone. One mother dead, and her two others looking like the mahwagis she supposed they were becoming. *The Pain of Distance.* More than ever now, and hour by hour and day by day in this life that she had chosen, Jalila knew what the old tariqua had meant. She stepped forward to say a few words. Pavo's life had been beautiful and complete. She had passed on much knowledge about this planet to all womankind, just as she had once passed on her wisdom to Jalila. The people listened respectfully to Jalila, as if she were a priest. When the prayers were finished and the clods of earth had been tossed and the groups began to move back down the hillside, Jalila remained standing by Pavo's grave. What looked like the same old part-metal beast came lumbering up, and began to fill in the rest of the hole, lifting and

lowering the earth with reverent, childlike care. Just as Jalila had
insisted, and despite her mothers' puzzlement, Pavo's grave lay
right beside the old tariqua's whom they had buried so long ago.
This was a place that she had long avoided, but now that Jalila saw
the stone, once raw and brittle, but now smoothed and greyed by
rain and wind, she felt none of the expected agony. She traced the
complex name, scrolled in naskhi script, which she had once
found impossible to remember, but which she had now recited
countless times in the ceremonials that the Church of the Gateway demanded of its acolytes. Sometimes, especially in the High
Temple at Ghezirah, the damn things could go on for days. Yet not
one member of the whole Church had seen fit to come to the simple ceremony of this old woman's burial. It had hurt her, once, to
think that no one from offworld had come to her own funeral. But
now she understood.

About to walk away, Jalila paused, and peered around the back
of the gravestone. In the lee of the wind, a soft green patch of life
was thriving. She stooped to examine the growth, which was thick
and healthy, forming a patch more than the size of her two outstretched hands in this sheltered place. Breathmoss. It must have
been here for a long time. Yet who would have thought to bring it?
Only Pavo: only Pavo could possibly have known.

As the gathering of mourners at the haramlek started to thin,
Jalila excused herself and went to Pavo's quarters. Most of the stuff
up here was a mystery to her. There were machines and nutrients
and potions beyond anything you'd expect to encounter on such an
out-of-the way planet. Things were growing. Objects and data
needed developing, tending, cataloging, if Pavo's legacy was to be
maintained. Jalila would have to speak to her mothers. But, for
now, she found what she wanted, which was little more than a glass
tube with an open end. She pocketed it, and walked back up over
the hill to the cemetery, and said another few prayers, and bent
down in the lee of the wind behind the old gravestone beside
Pavo's new patch of earth, and managed to remove a small portion
of the breathmoss without damaging the rest of it.

That afternoon, she knew that she would have to ride out. The
stables seemed virtually unchanged, and Robin was waiting. She
even snickered in recognition of Jalila, and didn't try to bite her
when she came to introduce the saddle. It had been such a long
time that the animal's easy compliance seemed a small miracle.
But perhaps this was Pavo again; she could have done something to
preserve the recollection of her much-changed mistress in some

circuit or synapse of the hayawan's memory. Snuffling tears, feeling sad and exulted, and also somewhat uncomfortable, Jalila headed south on her hayawan along the old serraplate road, up over the cliffs and beneath the arms of the urrearth forest. The trees seemed different; thicker-leafed. And the birdsong cooed slower and deeper than she remembered. Perhaps, here in Habara, this was some Season other than all of those that she remembered. But the qasr reared as always—out there on the cliff face, and plainly deserted. No one came here now, but, like Robin, the door, at three beats of her fists, remembered.

Such neglect. Such decay. It seemed a dark and empty place. Even before Jalila came across the ancient signs of her own future presence—a twisted coathanger, a chipped plate, a few bleached and rotting cushions, some odd and scattered bits of Gateway technology that had passed beyond malfunction and looked like broken shells—she felt lost and afraid. Perhaps this, at last, was the final moment of knowing that she had warned herself she might have to face on Habara. *The Pain of Distance.* But at the same time, she knew that she was safe as she crawled across this particular page of her universe, and that when she did finally take a turn beyond the Gateways through which sanity itself could scarcely follow, it would be of her own volition, and as an impossibly old woman. The tariqua. Tending flowers like an old tortoise thrust out of its shell. Here, on a sunny, distant day. There were worse things. There were always worse things. And life was good. For all of this, pain was the price you paid.

Still, in the courtyard, Jalila felt the cold draft of prescience upon her neck from that lacy mashrabiya where she and Kalal would one day stand. The movement she made as she looked up toward it even reminded her of the old tariqua. Even her eyesight was not as sharp as it had once been. Of course, there were ways around that which could be purchased in the tiered and dizzy markets of Ghezirah, but sometimes it was better to accept a few things as the will of the Almighty. Bowing down, muttering the *shahada,* Jalila laid the breathmoss upon the shaded stone within the cloister. Sheltered here, she imagined that it would thrive. Mounting Robin, riding from the qasr, she paused once to look back. Perhaps her eyesight really was failing her, for she thought she saw the ancient structure shimmer and change. A beautiful green castle hung above the cliffs, coated entirely in breathmoss; a wonder from a far and distant age. She rode on, humming snatches of the old songs she'd once known so well about love and loss between the stars. Back at the haramlek, her mothers were as anxious as ever to know where she had been. Jalila tried not to smile as she endured their familiar scolding. She longed to hug them. She longed to cry.

That evening, her last evening before she left Habara, Jalila walked the shore alone again. Somehow, it seemed the place to her where Pavo's ghost was closest. Jalila could see her mother there now, as darkness welled up from between the rocks; a small, lithe body, always stooping, turning, looking. She tried going toward her; but Pavo's shadow always flickered shyly away. Still, it seemed to Jalila as if she had been led toward something, for here was the quartz-striped rock from that long-ago Season of the Soft Rains. Of course, there was no breathmoss left, the storms had seen to that, but nevertheless, as she bent down to examine it, Jalila was sure that she could see something beside it, twinkling clear from a rock-pool through the fading light. She plunged her hand in. It was a stone, almost as smooth and round as many millions of others on the beach, yet this one was worked and carved. And its color was greenish-grey.

The soapstone scarab, somehow thrust here to this beach by the storms of potentiality that the tariquas of the Church of the Gateway stirred up by their impossible journeyings, although Jalila was pleased to see that it looked considerably less damaged than the object she remembered Kalal turning over and over in his nervous hands as he spoke to her future self. Here at last was the link that would bind her through the pages of destiny, and, for a moment, she hitched her hand back and prepared to throw it so far out into the ocean that it would never be reclaimed. Then her arm relaxed. Out there, all the way across the darkness of the bay, the tideflowers of Habara were glowing.

She decided to keep it.

# Verglas

THE FIRST WEEK AFTER MARION AND THE KIDS
left I kept busy around the base, clearing tunnels, tidying up their
chambers, storing things away, taking in great gulps of memory.
But even then I felt restless. I spent a long afternoon digging their
graves by hand; trying to lose myself in working up a sweat, whack-
ing the hot blade of the shovel through grey-tufted tundra into the
course peat below. Then I went to seal up their bodies for the last
time. They looked so beautiful lying inside their half-open sleepsuits with the stillfield showing through their veins in tiny threads
of gold. I kissed Marion's mouth and her cool, white breasts. I
touched the bruise that still showed on Robbie's forehead from
when he fell chasing the silver-backed pseudocrabs on the day we
landed. I drew my fingers through Sarah's pale yellow hair. There
was a faint but palpable sense that, even though it was so slow as to
be undetectable, they were still breathing. And despite all I knew
and everything that we'd agreed, I felt that something of my family
remained with me here. It was hard to believe that the decay of
their bodies in Korai's acidic soil wouldn't destroy a lingering fragment. Not that I wanted to change things or go back, not that I
regretted the decision we'd jointly made, but I knew that I couldn't
bury them.

Next day as I walked out across the tundra to prepare the last quester for its journey across the mountains to explore Korai's far southern peninsula, I nearly stumbled into one of the long holes I'd cut. I spent that afternoon refilling all three, shovelling and then patting down and recompacting the ground until all that was left was a faint disturbance of the sod that the growth of the slow-gathering summer would obliterate.

That evening, as always, I lay out new slabs of meat along the fissured table of rock at the east end of the canyon, steaming hot from the processor so they'd show up well on infrared. I'd genuinely expected Marion, Robbie, and Sarah to return here the first few nights after they'd left. But with a week gone I'd decided that their staying away was really a positive sign; it showed they were managing to hunt and feed. By now I was just laying out the meat from habit. This deep and narrow rift between the mountains made a poor feeding ground, and Marion had always said that it made sense for them to start as they meant to go on, to get as far away as they could from their human bodies.

I sat on a rock with my powerpack set high to keep warm, as the wind from the vast eastern range poured down around me in the blue, gathering dark, waiting without much hope for Marion and Sarah and Robbie and thinking of the way things had been, enjoying the luxury of an undefined and unjustified melancholy. After all, it wasn't as though I was really losing them any more than I was losing myself. But there was Marion tossing Sarah in the clear spray of a forest rock pool back on Earth, her belly shining taut with Robbie who was yet to be born. And there was the night that we decided to make him, and the feel of snow and cold, marvellous starlight pouring down through the trees. Yes, even then, Marion had loved the mountains.

Korai's sun Deres, long set from my sight, had painted the tips of the furthest mountains red when I sensed the grey beat of wings. I stood up quickly, feeling reality tingle around me once more, the sharpness of the wind breaking through the mingled taste of love and snow on Marion's skin. Those days were gone now. I was here on this planet and my ears and eyes were telling me that three shapes were drifting down from the grainy, white cliffs that dropped from a desolate plateau. They seemed to shift and dance at the very edge of sight, drifting half shadows or mere flakes of soot swirling on the sparse thermals. Scale is nothing here. As I caught the beat of pinions and the near-ultrasonic keening—part sonar, part language—there came, hazy and unbidden, the image of Sarah on a white beach by the blue ocean, her hair falling in salt tangles as she stooped along the shore to collect fishbones and shells. I pushed it away, an unwanted comparison, and concentrated on those shapes in the blackening sky, clearer to me now against the red-edged mountains, and real. One large, and two smaller. Although I still knew little enough about species identifiers, it had to be Marion, Robbie, Sarah. They were the only ones.

I ran across the turf, trying to pull everything in, every sound and every sense, greedy to hold this moment—knowing that it would be soon gone. They swept over me once. Marion's larger shape darkened the already dark sky, then she slowed, circled, chittering to her offspring to keep aloft until she was sure that all was safe. There had to be an instinct for self-preservation, I supposed, and Marion was still Marion despite everything that had changed. She was always the one who had that extra sense of danger for our kids. That was why we'd decided she should go first.

I watched her finally settle on the table of rock. I saw her head pivot my way. I caught the faceted glint of her eyes. Then, with a lilting, hopping motion, she moved toward the meat. I could understand more easily now the point of that ugly, metallic-sheened fur, her looped and whorled skin, that greyish-black colouring; she was almost a part of the twilight. And her movements were so quick; the way her jointed arms shot out, and how she kept her balance, her wings still outstretched, pushing against the wind, ready to lift and flee at any moment. A bright, hot flash of fluid as her claws broke open the meat. Then, when she was finally sure that all was safe, she signalled to the children—*KAK KARR KIK KARR*—and they fluttered down with almost equal grace to join her. The wind beat and howled. They stooped and folded their wings. The glacier-strewn mountains shone in the distance.

It was over quickly, this moment that I'd almost given up hoping for. The fact was all—that they were here and surviving—and the mere sight of them feeding was nothing that I hadn't witnessed a thousand times before in the simulations we'd run back on Earth. *KI KIK KARR*; a sound like stones knocking, then beating wings again, and the brief, feral scent of fur and flesh. Marion the first to rise, to test—protective as ever—the return to their chosen element. Then Robbie and Sarah lifting as one, drawn by the wind. A mere process, it seemed to me, of letting go, a skyward falling. I tried to follow them with my eyes, but the sky between the mountains had brimmed with night, showing only a last hint in the east. Three specks, laughing, chattering, singing. Swooping.

I walked back down toward the base, calling on the lights as I did so, watching the string of tunnels and canopies blossom and fan like so many paper lanterns. Too big for me, this place, now that I was on my own. And I was sure that whatever remote chance there had been that the integration of the creatures that my family had become might fail was already long gone. Ducking the first of the air barriers, feeling the wind lessen, I sensed the smug emanations of the thought machines. They were already far into the next century, sniffing the wind, testing the air, communing with the questers, pushing things on and through, asking endless what-ifs, checking for implausible or non-existent ecological anomalies. But Marion and Robbie and Sarah would fit in. For us, Korai was perfect. There was a niche for a sky-borne predator that the indigenous species would never fill.

The nights on Korai are as long as the days. The planet sits upright in its axis to Deres and the seasonal shifts come from the passage and repassage of the dust belts that haze the space between. Somehow the local wildlife manage to keep track of the complex cycles of long and short winters, cold or savage summers, indeterminate half-autumns, endless springs. It caused, I remembered, one of the longest and most frustrating delays in configuring the new species. And the constant length of the periods of darkness was also a surprising barrier, even though the days are near as doesn't matter to Earth-standard. Night and day specialisations don't seem to work here; you need to be able to see and function in either. The pseudocrabs that scuttle across the tundra each morning possess smaller versions of the eyes that Marion flashed at me before she started to feed. Polyhedral, with each facet wired independently to the brain, alternately set with focusing and filtering layers of polarised cones. When a good design works, you carry on using it.

Marion came to me that night, as I'd half-expected she would. But it was hard to tell how much of it really was her, how much had been simply pushed through my sleepsuit by the thought machines, how much was my own pure imagination.

"I couldn't bury you," I said. "You're still here—your bodies, I mean. It seems gruesome, really, stupid. I know it was part of the deal we made."

"Did we?" she said, looking at me with her face smiling, forgetful. "Yes, I suppose we did. When you're in a body, it matters to you. But when you're not . . ."

"You don't mind?"

"Of course I don't mind. You'll know what to do when the time comes."

"It can't be long now," I said. "The projections I've seen are as good as anything we hoped for."

"I could tell," she said. "Right away. That first day as soon as I took flight. When I saw the mountains and felt the roaring air. I wonder now whether I was ever properly human. Perhaps I was an eagle or something in some other life. Not that I believe in mumbo jumbo . . ."

"No." I stared at her. Her face hovering there in the darkness. *Mumbo jumbo*. Would it be better if I willed the dream to gain more substance? Would it be worse? What did I want anyway? Marion sitting beside me at that cafe by the Spanish Steps? Marion swimming deep through the coral, drawing me to her from the flickering shoals, our silver bubbles joining? Or Marion now. Marion perched on a mountaintop with this entire world and the sky beneath her?

"What's it like?"

"I knew you'd ask that," she said. "I can't tell you really. But it's far more than the simulations. It's life. You'll just have to come and see."

"I mean—"

"Of course," she continued, wild dream-light in her eyes, "it feels scary. It was everything Robbie and Sarah ever wanted, and for me it was just the plain unknown. But it's harder still for you. Bound to be—that was why I hesitated to leave you. You've seen it now. Both sides. Don't you remember they said that it's always the most difficult for the one who stays behind. . . ?"

"How are they? I mean Robbie, Sarah."

"They're fine. We're all fine."

"I still love you."

She smiled. I watched the way her lips moved, the sharp clarity in her wide-set eyes. It all suddenly seemed like amusement at my quaint, human ways. But she said it anyway, the way she always had —*I love you*—and at that point the dream faded and the sleepsuit softened and refolded itself around me and the thought machines withdrew. I was drifting in deep, fathomless dark, alone.

I awoke the next morning feeling weary. Even after Marion had faded, I'd still been dreaming—unprompted and unaided—although whatever it was had gone too quickly for me to remember. Odd really, that so much of life slips by even as you live it. That was something Marion used to say. The thing about being human she most hated. Lying in my sleepsuit and with the taut canopy of my chamber gauzily lit with the grey Korain morning, I called up breakfast, then regretted doing so as my server stalked in. Another job that I should have done myself to help fill the long day I could feel stretching ahead of me. The prospect made me realise just how much, even though I'd ostensibly given up waiting, I'd actually been clinging to the hope that my wife and kids would show up one evening out of the sky. But although Marion hadn't said so specifically, the tone of her conversation had made it clear that she and Robbie and Sarah wouldn't come again. Not outside my dreams, anyway, and even inside them I knew that the warnings would soon be flashing, the thought machines trundling into my sleepy head in magnificent disguise to point out that I was in danger of starting to obsess. Not that I *was* starting to obsess. Not about Marion anyway. I believed every word she might have said. And believed, although she'd hardly mentioned them, that Robbie and Sarah were happy on this new planet also. They'd been elated at the prospect of changing from the start—more than eager to go— then puzzled and angry when Marion and I continued to worry over it. If we stay human, Sarah had said to me one evening when she was back from the shore barefoot with her rods and her nets, we're simply making the same decision in reverse. Can't you see that, Daddy? And look at us. It's not as though we humans are that exceptional. We can't fly, we can't swim very well, our limbs are weak, and we've only got four kinds of taste receptor on our tongues. Of course, Sarah really did look exceptional to me with the sun in her eyes and salt in her hair, but it seemed unjust to expect her and Robbie to spend all their lives as mere humans when a hundred different worlds beckoned.

After breakfast that morning I thought, briefly, of folding away all the extra chambers and tunnels to save on unnecessary power. But I realised that my motive was simply to make the base more right to my own scale, more long lasting, more homely. And I knew, anyway, looking back at the base from the flat, fissured rock that was quite astonishingly clean today (just a few shreds of skin and greasy stains marked with claw prints, a faint, ripe, ammoniac smell of something other than human), gazing down at the steel frames and the spun silver lines of fielding and the fluttering chambers and tunnels, that everything here would always be temporary.

Instead I spent the morning with the thought machines, hunched over a crystal emanator in a billowing chamber, where the wind broke intermittently through the last of the fields, drawing in images from the questers. The signals from the furthest one were bouncing off two satellites now, far over the horizon. Korai is a wide planet, larger than Earth, but with a cold core and no tectonic movement. There's just this one great, nameless continent; a world map in crystal. It's one of the main factors in the relative uniformity in life here. No marsupial freaks on Korai, no platypi or swimming birds or tree-climbing kangaroos or flying fish. No real intelligence either. Things might have been different if Korain life hadn't developed a replicating mode with enormous built-in redundancy, but the linked proteins even look chunky under a microscope, box shapes of squared-off links and arches, the kind of genes a Victorian engineer might have developed. A good planetary catastrophe like Earth's of sixty-five million years ago might still have pushed things on a different course. But Korai doesn't have comets or an asteroid belt. Funny, really, that we humans, with our tumbling-dice DNA, our fluctuating and meteorite-bombed planet, only realised how lucky we were when we found out what life was like on other worlds. Change and danger are the real stuff of species development.

I discovered that the furthest quester had now reached the lowlands on the coastal edge. It's mostly swampland in those mid-latitudes, but still dominated by the air currents tossed around by the mountains. Hot rain pours, trees swoop and sway, swathes of reddish-slimed bog shiver and glisten. Hurricanes all the year round, and the life that I pulled in from the quester's transmission was slick, stooped, hurrying. This creature here, as I gazed through the quester's main lens in rain-tossed real-time, even looked like a folded umbrella. I chased and caught it with the quester's claws, to see if it actually unfolded. But silvery-marbled blood burst from the rent I'd made, dribbling with the rain into the mud. The thing was dead, destroyed by my own long-distance curiosity. So I made the puzzled quester scoop out a deepish, brine-filled hole. And no, I didn't want ANALYSIS or PRESERVATION or AUTOPSY. When something is truly dead, I have no problem burying it.

I fixed lunch from the few remaining raw supplies, luxuries we'd brought with us from Earth. Picking out eggs and bread from the cooler, I noticed one last bottle of champagne at the back. What was it, I wondered, that we'd planned on celebrating? I opened out the flaps of the cooking chamber, set the fields to low and let the wind and the mountains roar. The sense of the mountains, anyway. I had to crane my neck up and out to see them. As the eggs thickened and the pan smoked and spat and the burner's blue fingers danced, I realised just how atavistic all this had become. I'd be making campfires next. But sitting outside afterward with a fork and a plate, making the most of Deres's brief appearance overhead through this strangely clouded sky, I still turned my powerpack up to keep warm—I mean, you can take these things too far.

I instructed the plate and the fork to destroy after finishing, and watched as they did that Dali-thing on a rock; drooping and fading. Another fragment of my supplies gone, slipping by like the hours and the days. Marion had been a little concerned about my being alone; how I'd cope with the isolation. I even guessed it was probably why she and the kids kept away once they'd changed—to give me the space I needed—although by now it was hard to read anything into their motives. The fact was, I was at least partly enjoying being alone. Sure, the days were hard to get through. But it was also nice, just being here, just being me.

I wandered down along the southern arm of the chambers, stepping through into the dome where the questers had been kept. I had a vague memory that there was also something else in there —and I saw it squatting in the dim canopy light now that all the packing had been cleared. It looked almost like another quester, and was certainly derived from the same design. I was surprised I hadn't noticed it on the inventory, but then there'd been so many other things on my mind before we left Earth.

Obviously complicated—no use in simply calling it to activate. So I summoned up its frequency instead, and spent the next few minutes studying the manual. Until then it had seemed almost menacing, but now I absorbed the phraseology and understood what those forward and rear-facing gunlike things were, the vicious studs on its belly, and long stinger sticking out from its abdomen, why it had even more legs than a quester. Questers, after all, always take the easiest route. But this was a climber. And it was designed, like we humans, to seek out adversity.

I stepped into it, calling the bracelets to curl around my torso and limbs. Clumsily ripping the fabric around the exit porthole, I lumbered out across the tundra. My position within the climber on level ground was tilted, almost sitting up. I could sense busy metal snapping around me, although the thing had been designed in such a way that the view was unrestricted. I strode faster, clattering over stones, squelching across bog the whole dim length of the canyon. I'd explored it all before, the narrow confines of this shadowed place of waiting where scree and ancient cliff rose high on all sides, holding me in. I skimmed the edge of the lifeless lake. I hopped with easy grace onto the fissured rock of the feeding table. *Tip tap. Scrape scrape.* The manual was good, quick, easily accessible. Help menus sprung up into my mind before I'd even decided I needed them. The trick was to use the climber's limbs without higher brain involvement. To think WALK as you would just think *walk* normally, or STOP or RUN or REACH or CRAWL. Even on that first afternoon I was running, jumping, leaping.

I felt happy and tired that night. I called up a meal from the processor in my chambers; chicken korma and nan bread followed by amaretti biscuits and coffee, the kind of good, rich, and uncomplicated food that I felt I deserved. Only a task-checking routine from the thought machines, just as I was sinking into the curry-dipped nan, finally reminded me that it was time to put out the meat. I compromised by contacting one of the outer sensors, and listened through the thought machines to the endless rustling howl of the wind. But that night my family didn't come.

I dreamed I was flying through bright clouds, feeling the wind—now a complex element, a rich, hidden tapestry woven with the taste of snow and air and sunlight. Everything was so sharp, so clear. I was lifting, falling, climbing. I was here at last. Truly *here*. And Marion was nearby, swooping over a great, greenish-rimed cornice, ice pluming from her wings as she caught the air that came in a deep-throated roar from the depths of a valley.

"This is it!" she shouted as we leapt and fell through the sky, her voice still human in my dream despite the beating pinions, the jaws, the claws. "This is everything. Look . . ."

We'd risen far higher than I'd imagined—borne aloft without trying. The air tasted thin, clear, and cool. I knew that the whole mountain range—all of Korai—was mine, spread out below me. I flexed my claws and tumbled, spinning and laughing. Dense, rainbow-threaded clouds fanned and shifted far below. Colours my poor human eyes had never seen. Senses I'd never imagined. Marion was close to me now, her wings slowing. Then I felt her claws on my back, the loose heat of her breath, the pulling weight of her body dragging me down through the bright sky.

"I love you," she said, her voice screaming as we fell.

I awoke and lay staring up from my sleepsuit at the canopy, listening to a sharp keening that was no more than the Korain wind howling down from the crystal peaks of the mountains. *This is everything. Look . . .* In the simulations, I'd always found that I needed some final leap of faith to see what she meant. In life, too.

But now Korai was becoming ever more marvellous, brighter. This planet, the great frozen peaks. Those mountains.

I set about using the climber in earnest the next day. After loading more detailed maps of the local area, and with the help of the climber's own intelligence, I selected a route to the southeast. It involved a scramble from the gorge up the white, crystalline scree beside the lake, then ten kils of lumbering along the dry bed of a meltwater stream to a five-hundred-metre peak. Five hundred metres doesn't seem like much in your head—not when you're three thousand up already—but looking at the sheer face of the mountain gleaming against the sky was another matter. The climber's lenses zoomed and scanned, searching for feasible routes across the fissured crystal then flashing them into my eyes. The difficulty grading was higher than I'd imagined from the satellite map, but at my command the climber began to work crossways toward the deep cleft of a chimney then boosting itself up through the crevices where the wind shrieked and eddied. The climber was methodical, working multi-pitch, shooting out spindles of wire ahead that buried and fused into the rock, testing the weight of the anchors, squatting to plant rivets beneath us, roping hexes into the cracks, taking the slack, testing, belaying, moving on. It finally hooked over onto a wide sheltered ledge where the light of Deres shone faint but warm, as if in reluctant benediction, through the hurrying clouds.

Something buzzed against me as I softened the climber's bracelets and clambered out onto the ledge. I batted at it unthinkingly. Through sheer luck I actually caught the thing and held it in my palm, feeling incredible lightness, brittle fur, puffed and trembling flight bladders. I reopened my hand, and watched smiling as it rose and fluttered, quickly gone with the wind against the swelling haze.

I could feel the cold, feel the wind. I was an explorer, a discoverer. I turned up my powerpack and reached inside the climber's harness for a pair of heated gloves. Then, grabbing an overhang, feeling an odd, tingling pull in my belly, I leaned out to look down at the drop. I quickly drew away, my boots pressed hard against the rock. Not that I was scared, not exactly. But the space. The blue, hurrying air. It just wasn't something I'd prepared for. I swallowed oxygen tablets, hauled myself back into the climber, blanked out its help manual, and prepared to move on.

Glinting flecks of opalescent light. Deres-blurring rainbows through the dust belts in a clear sky. LIFT. The climber straining, motors whining. BOLT. Sparks flinging from the rocks. PULL. Vertical, then an overhang, the wires spooling out and the ground distant as the sky: jagged, hazy. Moving the front right claw to JAM. Then up. And up, up. That solid perpetual moment of effort. I was in control now, my own muscles tensing as the climber tensed, my eyes searching each millimetre, each crack, each tiny chip of two billion years of frost erosion. Then a burst overhead, explosive as the detonation that had embedded the bolt, and the mountain tipped away from me in a cloudburst of shards. I was falling, then jerked and held; spinning. My vision swarmed over stone, peak, ground, horizon, sky. The line I'd strung across the mountain was still holding. I looked around, willing my mind to adjust, to find an up and a down, but even as I tried to move the climber's front mandibles and haul myself back, the machine's own defaults kicked into place, filling the air with smoke and sulphur, shooting out multiple ribbons of fresh bolts. Within a moment, without even having to will it, I was safely cradled.

I finally got back to my canyon in darkness and called up the base's homely lights. That night I didn't follow my usual practice of invoking a movie or a book from the thought machines. I just lay there, remembering the day; drawing myself up that mountain with the wind and the rock and the sun. The feeling of being astride the final ridge that led to the peak, and the timid, fluttering shoal of Korain flyers. Their tiny, blunt snouts, moist, faceted eyes, puffed, orange bladders, fluttering fins. Like the flashing coral fish that Marion and I had once swum through. . . .

"What you did was dangerous," Sarah told me in my dreams. "I can understand you wanting to use that climber, Daddy. But you're inexperienced, you mustn't suppress the defaults."

"I suppose it takes time to learn," I said. We were sitting in a high place. Some world or other, too beautiful and hazy to be truly seen, lay spread out in glory beneath us. I smiled at her. What was the point in arguing? Sarah was like all kids. She loved being superior, telling me the right and the wrong.

"Then come and join us, Daddy. Come and join us now."

I looked at her. I was sure the moment before that she'd been human. But now there were facets to her eyes. A grey membrane fluttered in her throat through which she somehow spoke.

"I thought I saw you today," I said. "When I was up on the last ridge. Three specks to the east. Those highest peaks. Would that be right? Is that where you are?"

"Are you looking for us, Daddy? Is that why you're climbing? You'll never get up there in that clumsy machine. You know how to find us. Just change. Look at me. It's easy. . . ."

I watched as Sarah's pinions unfurled and her wet jaws parted, wondering whether she could possibly understand my vague, human needs. But this was what we had wanted. This was it. The freedom of this clear, new planet, the joy of the hunt and the skies. This was it. To be here. To be real. So what was the matter with me now? Why was I holding on?

I set out again with the climber the next morning. The sole dissatisfaction of the day before had been that the peak, so real and majestic as I climbed, had finally revealed itself as but a doorstep to the range beyond—not even reaching the snow line.

With help from the climber and satellite projections, I was able to work out a three-day route that would take me deep into the range. I collapsed some spare chambers, ordered food and fluid and clothes from the processor, oxygen tablets, and an extra sling for the climber to hold it all. I wanted to go further, higher. It was a warm day, scented with metallic wafts of Korain sap. The dayflowers were unfolding, their glittering spinners catching the wind.

Up the scree slope, then along the dry riverbed, around the first day's mountain in the clear light of a dust-rainbowed sun. And on. I wasn't searching for another false triumph of some minor peak. All I wanted was that range, barely glimpsed through rearing, black facets of obsidian, but sensed already in the cold wind from the glaciers that ground the jewelled dust filling this riverbed.

I camped that night in shelter of a crag at the edge of the snow line. I swallowed oxygen tablets before I unfolded my sleepsuit, but still my throat was raw, my chest was tight, my limbs sore, my heart hammering. Was it the thinness of the air? Or was it fear? Cold? Excitement? But I was nearing, stone on stone, rock on rock, crest on crest, the living heart of this crystal planet, the great range that seen from space was a white diadem stretched around Korai's girth. Yes, on. Toward Marion, Robbie, Sarah. In my dreams, and already far from the thought machines, I willed them to come.

I saw Robbie slippery and new. I saw him at Marion's breast, and then creamy waves beating over coral. I saw a sunset through palm leaves.

"We've got to go," Marion said, sitting there in her sarong beside the shore. There were dancers on the beach beside the waves, and the throb of drums. The kids were like little savages out there

in the sudden tropic darkness, Robbie and Sarah amongst them.
"What's wrong with all this?" I asked.

Marion looked at me. The clear whites of her eyes. Her moon-
lit fingers moved impatient on the table, long and slim and lean.
I felt trim and relaxed from this endless holiday, although my
body was hardly my own; undeserved, really, after all I'd drunk and
eaten, and the age to which I was getting, the little that I had
done.

"What do you say we take a skimmer to Shell Island tomorrow?" I asked. "Sarah could bring her nets. You know how she loves
fishing. That guy I met on the quay says the mock-lobsters out there
are—"

Marion waved it away. "Sure. Tomorrow. But what about next
week? Next year?"

"It'll come."

She said, "That's it exactly," and a warm breath of sea wind
lifted the hair from her shoulders, and I thought of her already in
some ship, some spacecraft, sailing away from me. "I have just one
life. One Sarah, one Robbie. One *you*, goddamit. We die, you
know. We *die*. That's the one fact that still remains. I don't want to
waste what's left between just being simply . . ."

"Happy?"

"Happy." She nodded. "Yes. Happy. Is that all you want? Think
it over. Listen to what I've said."

In my dreams, I listened. But it was too late. That night by the
shore had gone, the decision had been made. Happy. Human. Not
happy. Not human. Death. Change. Time . . . Next morning as I
broke camp, as I ascended and searched, as the blue-black walls of
the glaciers grew around me and wind bit and chilled, I willed
Marion to show herself to me.

A ravine. Each time, another barrier, seemingly this whole
planet crisscrossed by fractures, tumbling narrow and dark yet easily forded by the little wire bridges made by the climber. By the end
of that second day I was finally up in Korai's main biosphere, amid
those marbled clouds that moved not quite as the wind pushed
them. The smaller grazers were a common sight now that I was up
on the snows of the great range; they hung fearless in the air, fluttering and drifting as I shot out ice screws and drew karabiners in
blinding flurries of spindrift. Red and blue, fat and thin, some with
barbed fins. I climbed through their pastures, great grey-odoured
clouds that suddenly billowed around me, tasting of new soil and
copper and mushrooms. Less often I saw bigger creatures etched

against the rainbowed whiteness. Mostly flyers the size of my out-stretched palms, although one I discovered was rockbound, a fronded mouth like a blue-lipped clam that puffed a steamy breath at me as I pulled over an overhang.

This was Korain high summer and the light of Deres was warm, dribbling water that formed extravagant cornices and pillars when it froze in solid sweeps of shadow. The higher I climbed, the less white the snow became. I thought at first that it was a trick of the marbled clouds, but scooping it in my hands I saw that almost every frozen crystal was alive, pricked with green, blue, amber.

On the long afternoon of that day's climb it became obvious that the climber was stretching its abilities. To get to a ridge that led upward in one jaggedly promising sweep, I had to traverse a long cliff that hung exposed in a thousand metres of space—not that nine hundred less or more would have made any difference had I fallen. Warmed then cooled by the wind that poured up from the glacier below, the rock had a thin coating of ice called verglas; something new to me—and not, if the warning flags in my head were anything to go by, greatly favoured by the climber. Huge plates of it came creaking off as I moved, shattering into blades that stung my face and hands. *Tip tap. Scrape scrape.* It was dangerous, frustrating work. Just millimetres beneath this ice crust, clearly visi-ble, lay good, solid rock. Nooks and jams and crevices that would have given technically easy climbing. For the first time, breathing hard, the outer reaches of my body beginning to slow and stiffen in this endless wind despite pulling on the powerpack's reserves, I was truly scared, shooting bolts into the half-cracked ice that the climber gave a 50% chance of holding. I glared at the cliff face, the thin patina holding me away from hard, solid rock, keeping me from everything real. I wanted to smash, destroy this treacherous barrier. But the verglas was my world—it was everything. *Tip tap. Scrape scrape.* I tested the surface again and was about to move on and up when I caught a movement at my back. I twisted my head and saw a Korain life form bigger than anything I'd seen before, a double-orange sphere bobbing on the wind like a fishing buoy, sucking and blowing its way along. A joke, really, that something so amiable and stupid should be free to wander the sky. . . .

Suddenly there was another movement. A shadow came over me, making me tense in expectation of an icefall. But it was too fast, too big, swooping like a black dart. The Korain creature didn't have time to react. Its twin spheres crumbled in a bright spray as the predator swept down, and then—barely slowed by the weight of its catch—was instantly rising, soaring up over the cliff and out of my sight.

I shook my head.

Marion, Robbie, Sarah.

*This is everything. Look* . . .

Slowly, still feeling the pull of the drop, I traversed the verglas cliff, and finally, gratefully, dug the climber's mandibles into the hard spine of the ridge on the far side. A few hundred metres up from there, tinted blood red, I could see a snow-scooped col that promised sheltered ground, and a route that the climber flashed up as EASY. Easy.

The fabric of my chamber was oddly dark when I awoke next morning. Outside, my feet sunk into soft crystal. The whole world seemed newly white—or almost. An opalescent mist hung in the air, veiling the snow-softened crags that I was planning to ascend.

I ate breakfast, collapsed and packed the chambers and shook the snow from the climber's limbs. Ascending the drifts to look over the edge of the col and take my bearings, I breathed the air, salt-tanged from the scatters of life that this morning seemed to have diffused over the whole mountainside. And overhead, enormous yet half-real, swarming in and out of the mists, there were glimpses of crags and flutings, ice cliffs and gullies. Eagerly, following the thin, red line across the rainbowed white that the climber laid before me, I began my crosswise ascent of the vast snow-slope that lay ahead of me.

After an hour of easy going, I came into sight of the mouth of a cave, a clear gap of shadow against the rainbowed incline. I traversed toward it, digging and hardening a bollard in a peak of snow to make a belay as a precaution. The mist had closed in when I glanced back toward it, but that hardly seemed to matter—and a cave was a rare formation on Korai.

I had climbed a few more steps when I saw claw prints in the snow. The outer digits were webbed and the inner claw made a deeper indentation. The climber made its own marks as I followed the prints up toward the cave, seeing how they skipped and faded as Marion and Sarah and Robbie took flight. I looked up again at the looming mouth as the snow slid in hissing plumes beneath me. The cave remained dark, but I knew from the simulations that they were unlikely to need shelter in the warm heart—to them, at least —of this Korain summer.

I called on the climber's lights as I entered the cave. *Tip tap.*

*Drip drip*, the mandibles touching bare, wet stone. It was warm in here, and a faint but definite fog seemed to emanate, something more than my own breath or condensation. Boulders and wet rock gleamed around me. It was a steep, upward climb. I saw crystalline shapes, metallic colours. I paused, tensing the limbs of the climber against the slippery drop, remembering the steaming mouth of the clamlike creature, wondering if some unexpected super-variant dwelled inside this cave. But that was absurd, and still I was curious.

The climber's front mandibles snagged on something dangling from the ceiling. Expecting a stalactite, I turned up the lights, but the substance broke loose in mucuslike strands that I saw also fronded from floor and walls and ceiling ahead. And what was this ball of threaded tissue, softly pulsing? There was something about all of this—the most bizarre thing of all, really—that made it seem familiar. I stared. *Ahhhh. Haaa.* A warm breeze was drawing me closer, pulling me away, and there was a muted thumping that sounded like a heart.

I took a step further, careful now with the climber's mandibles. The tunnel grew too narrow for it to get beyond here, but perhaps if I went unaided, got out . . . Then I heard a shrill screaming behind me; *KRREE KAARR* as if the wind had cracked open the mountain.

I lost footing as I spun the climber around. Scrabbling, trying to fire a steadying blot into the rock face, I tumbled over. Held tight within the climber's protective cage, my head spinning, I saw something large and black clamp itself over the two raised front mandibles. Multi-faceted eyes momentarily caught in the wash of the climber's lights, then were gone again.

The climber skidded and tumbled down the loose, wet rocks of the cave. My left leg snagged in a flare of pain. Then a burst of dazzling light and rainbowed plumes and the dry, mineral taste of Korain snow filling my mouth as I willed the climber to HOLD. But still there was nothing but tumbling whiteness. Then came the sudden tug of the belay.

I lay there. I could hear the climber's dented mandibles ticking and the soft plop of something—probably hydraulic fluid—dripping. Twisting my head, I saw that I was partly right. Some of it was yellow oil. The rest was blood, steaming and melting the snow. I looked up at the sky where a thousand black flecks seemed to be swarming. I blinked:—but Marion had gone. Just drifting, marbled clouds. And all I could hear was that soft drip, and the whistle of the wind, and the snow beneath me creaking.

I moved one of the inner claws LEFT then RIGHT, unsnagging the line. Slowly, discovering that the main mandibles on the right side hung useless, I hauled the climber back up the rope toward the belay, and saw when I reached it how the harness had almost worn through the pillar of ice.

The snow slope stretched wide and featureless above and below me until it dissolved in rainbowed mist. CUT, SCOOP, MOVE. I began to work my way back toward the col I had left that morning. I had to make a conscious effort not to move my left leg in sympathy when I issued a command; there was a surge of pain each time I forget. I checked the clock again. Four hours. Well past midday. Already the snow was darkening in long scoops and serrations. And there at last, suddenly picked out in clear outline by Deres's sinking flare, were the steps I'd made in the snow that morning.

I followed them and finally slid down into the col, shivering with relief and drawing great billows of warmth from my powerpack. The dull ache in my leg flared into something wildly brighter as I hauled myself out of the climber, unhooked the sling of supplies from its underside, and called up its still-functioning lights. It seemed ridiculous to put up the canopies by hand but I started work anyway, sucking in agonized breaths as I willed my powerpack to send out more opiates. Once the pain had reduced, my left leg was capable of holding me up. It was quite clever, really, the way that the blood had frozen around the leggings to make a kind of splint.

When I had finally dragged my body inside the warmth of my narrower-than-usual chamber, I took a knife and zipped it down the seam of my stiffened legging. There was a jagged gash across the outside of my calf, with glimpses of white inside that might or might not have been bone. But nothing seemed broken. I moulded artificial flesh and pressed it down over the wound. There was a brief agonizing flare at it stuck and welded—then nothing, bliss.

I forced myself to drink and eat, then gulped down oxygen tablets. I lay back. I could still feel commands running in my head, CUT SCOOP MOVE and the slow, reluctant motions of the climber. I thought back to the cave. I understood now why it had seemed familiar—I'd seen something similar in one of the simulations back on Earth. As a flighted predator, a complex, organised being, Marion could neither casually lay eggs like a bird nor carry the maturing weight of an embryo around inside her light-boned body. The compromise lay somewhere between the two; to create a mixture between womb and nest in some inaccessible spot. If I'd had the sense to recognise the cave for what it was and gone in alone, the human mechanisms that remained in her mind would probably have overridden her protective instincts more quickly. But clad in the climber—a great mechanical spider lumbering into her nest—what was I to expect?

I lay in my sleepsuit, shivering although I was no longer cold. Outside, rising slow and thunderous, drowning the wind, I heard the rumble of a distant avalanche. I remembered the dream I'd had of being in flight with Marion, her claws digging into me preparatory to some alien way of making love. The fact was, I'd avoided knowing too much about reproductive processes that were bound, from my human viewpoint, to appear strange—most certainly unerotic. I knew that the provision of the nest came soon after fertilisation. Fine. But Marion, Robbie, Sarah were supposed to be here alone—a mature female and two immature offspring. Or so I'd thought. It was ridiculous, really, here in this absurd situation I'd made out of my own confusion and vanity, to feel jealous. But that, as the avalanches sounded again, closer now, changing the wind, shaking the very crystal beneath me, was how I felt. And I felt cheated, too. I felt betrayed. I felt angry.

That night the snow crust covering the col grew thin filaments. It was like walking over hoar-frosted grass the next morning as I clambered across the drifts unaided to look at the horizon. I felt dreamless and rested. My leg was stiff but better, already healing. And there was so much light here, so much glory. Iridescent peaks, iridescent clouds. And no sign of three specks—or more—flying. My anger of the night before now seemed absurd, brought on by nothing but pain and worry. I just hoped that Marion hadn't been injured. And as to the peculiarities of making a new alien life, understanding would come to me soon enough.

As soon as I got back to the base, I'd bury those three empty bodies. I'd start the process of changing. My new shape was already waiting, a lump of Korain matter that needed only the will of the thought machines to precipitate it into life. That incident in the cave had been just what I had needed, a fortuitous accident—perhaps even something that Marion in her new alien wisdom had foreseen and planned. I ached to join her now. And Robbie. And Sarah.

I breathed the air. Salt and sap and snow and metal. From here, all I had to do was go down which, in climbing terms, surely had to be easier than up. It was like the process that had happened in my mind, giving way to the pull of this new world, a mere matter of accepting and adjusting. Hungry for breakfast, I skidded down the furred snow. The climber still sat where I had left it, coated like everything else in soft glitter. I called out to it with my mind. It just sat there. Puzzled, I stood beside it, brushing white from its limbs, noticing the congealed pool of oil that lay beneath its thorax and the deeper pelt of crystal that covered the rent from which the fluid had seeped. I flipped back a manual cover and gazed at the screens. But they too, were silvered with filaments. Stiff and cold and lifeless.

Food. Oxygen tablets. Ropes and karabiners, a harness. Sleepsuit. Water. The struts and fabrics of the chambers. Manual ice axes and bolts I'd never thought I'd have to use. Then food—enough to last for at least two days until I got within range of the thought machines. Heated boots and gloves. A first aid kit. It was bizarre, the weight we humans must carry just to stay alive. I packed it all into the extra pouch that the climber had carried, shortening the slings to fit across my shoulders.

I began to descend the ridge. My left leg was stiff but workable. Although the dead climber squatted uselessly in the col, I kept wondering what its help menu would have said about using a wind-driven ridge like this, so high that I could see nothing but garish cloud beneath, as a place to experiment in free climbing. Still, I kept going, resting and moving on, sticking to my rhythm and avoiding looking at anything but the step down. The task was doable if you split it into small components; and the climber, after all, had scooted up this ascent without even thinking, grading it as EASY. Easy, I thought, jamming a hex into a wedge of rock and using the harness to back down. Nothing to it, not so very different to those rocky shores I used to clamber over with Sarah. She had a knack of catching limpets, creeping up and banging them off the rocks with a swiftly wielded pebble—a trick I could never manage. And she was a huntress in the rock pools, too, was our Sarah. So poised with her bare hands waiting in the clear water like pink shell-less crabs. Then she'd catch something; hold it bright to the sun and then plop it into her bucket and then get the terminal to identify it back at the cottage. There was always one question Sarah would ask; could she cook it, eat it—no matter how tiny or gross— could she have it for her tea? Otherwise she lost interest. A little huntress, was—is—my—our—daughter. And Robbie was just the same, and looked up to his big sister, with her rods and her nets and her guns.

My left leg was becoming more awkward now, although there was still no pain. Sometimes I had to stoop and push it into position, and meanwhile had little enough purchase to hang on. I thought about using the bolts to pin myself to the rock but I kept climbing free, knowing that the going was still EASY, knowing that I should save my equipment for what was to come.

I reached the end of the ridge. From the height of Deres riding in over the peaks, it looked to be just past midday. Resting on a tilted rock, hunched against the wind, my breath pluming as I kneaded sore muscles, pulling all the extra heat and energy I could from my powerpack, I called up the time. But with the climber dead and far away from the thought machines, all I got was a cold space in my head. One thing I'd forgotten to bring was a manual timepiece.

After eating, and drinking what seemed like an absurdly large amount of fluid, I picked my way over the last of the ridge to look at the way ahead. The great verglas cliff face was gleaming half in shadow. It had taken the climber the larger part of an afternoon to get to the other side, and I had about five and a half, maybe six hours before darkness. I decided that it should be enough. The climber had been less than helpful during this part of the ascent anyway, and the alternative was just to wait here as the sweat began to chill and solidify in my outer garments, or to try some other route, possibly abseiling down into the jagged wasteland of crevasses below the verglas cliff. But the downward drop was too immense to be seriously contemplated, and even from here, picked out like some mad miniature fairyland, the crags and crevasses at the start of the glacier looked impassable.

Deres seemed to vanish in churning, purple clouds as soon I made my way onto the cliff face. The wind chilled, became a solid physical presence, pulling at me with icicle arms and driving up a sleet of pinkish flakes from the drop beneath. I realised that the morning's descent had used up more of my energy than I'd imagined. *Tip tap. Scrape scrape.* Creaking ice. The bang of each fresh bolt, the hot tensing of my arms, the sway of the verglas crust in the moment before it crumbled. Then, starting with a slow itch and rising notch by notch, my left leg began to hurt. But at least when the ice was hacked off there was rock beneath. Easy technical climbing, I reminded myself. EASY.

Verglas. I was hanging in five degrees of overhang on a wall of thin ice. My eyes searched, and my mind gave only 50% solidity in every direction; was hedging its bets as the climber had done.

Verglas. So clear, so slick and smooth to the touch. It was all I could see now. I looked around for Deres, no longer even tensing as fresh ice showered over me. The sky was dark. I tried to call up the time, but there was only the ice that held me and the pain in my trembling muscles and the thing that was working a hot dagger into my left leg. I looked down, truly expecting to see a grinning, fronded maw. But there was nothing, just the endless spinning of the drop.

LEFT, RIGHT, UP, DOWN. I was back now within the climber, cursing its stupidity although I knew I had no reason to expect more now that it was dead. I gazed at the ice-coated cliff through the weight of the darkness, willing it to dissolve, disappear. My whole life had been shielded by these walls, something smooth and thin and barely tangible that somehow managed to separate me from everything, from a chance to LIVE. *That's what this is about*, I could hear Marion whispering to me above the scream of the wind. *Us humans with our weak lives, our soft and cosy planet, our weak senses. You need to break the verglas, Darling. You need to get THROUGH.*

I leaned back, breathless, aching, sodden with freezing sweat. Somewhere in these mountains, the alien sun had finally set. The harness dug beneath my shoulders and crotch. The belay bolt creaked. This was pointless. I knew I'd still be hanging here when my powerpack and my heart gave out—slowly frozen, or eaten as some new morsel by the grazing Korain life. I looked LEFT, the way I was supposed to be going. I could see only verglas slipping further and further from the vertical. There was no way that I could traverse such an overhang, no way that I could simply hang here all night. And UP was out of the question too. So was RIGHT. Which left only DOWN, seeing if I could fly. The idea was appealing. The darkness below looked friendly. Cushions of black. And I could stretch out my arms as I fell. I could swoop and glide. Marion and kids would join me, shrieking, laughing. *KI KIK KARR KARR.* Lifting me up. It had to be the easiest way.

Feeling the trembling snap of weakened muscle, I reached for the remaining bolts strung in my harness. There was only one left. I unpeeled and dropped one of my gloves as I threaded the remaining length of rope through the loop of a descendeur. I twisted the descendeur, and the world slid by me as the rope hissed through. I dropped, slowed, then dropped again. The dark verglas cliff swung away, bounced back. I pushed off with my feet, yelping at a white flare of pain from my left leg. Down again, spinning. I thought of the fairyland of crevasses I'd seen below, the route I'd rather not have taken. How far up had I been from it? A thousand metres? But I'd gone DOWN as well as LEFT, and the beginnings of the glacier rose toward this end. The rope marker slipped through my hand. I slowed before I was jerked against the end knot. There was no change in the rock surface. It was still verglas; flat, iced, vertical. I fired in my last bolt, and looped it though. I snapped out the catch and the rope fell past me out of the darkness. I twisted the descendeur and abseiled down for what had to be the last time, wet blisters rising and bursting on my ungloved hand. How far had I gone? I felt the marker slide by, the jolt of the end-knot. I hung there, swinging in empty darkness. That was it. I had no more bolts, and this time I wasn't even close to the verglas cliff. I could go no further. Before I had time to think, I reached for the knife in my belt with my one good hand, and cut the rope.

Then I was flying.

Some kind of lunar morning. Grey-whiteness all around. Craters and mountain peaks. I leaned up on my elbows, breaking a stiff covering of snow. A greenish wall ￢f verglas loomed up into the mist.

I lay back again, surprised to be alive, wondering about all the pain and effort that implied. I drew on my powerpack. There was a brief flicker of warmth and energy. I called for my server. I searched for the thought machines. At least, I decided, lifting my good gloved hand up out of the snow, wondering at the odd absence of feeling in my other limbs, I still had the pouch. I some-how pulled it out of the snow. It was torn, empty. I lay back again, seeing the pretty amber flecks in the white, the way that, close to, they seemed to be moving. A few fell over me, glittering on my eyes. Feeling thirsty, I licked my lips. But the stuff was dry in my mouth. Salt, soil, and metal.

Some time after, I discovered that I was up on my knees and crawling around, looking for something. Even if the pouch was empty, the stuff inside must have fallen nearby. My left leg felt as though some livid mechanism was slicing within it, and the snow here was oddly light. Moving forward, it crumpled and my arms pushed through. Looking into the hole I had made, I saw that I was hanging over the bluish depths of a crevasse. I tumbled back and curled up in the snow, nursing my pain and willing the cold to take it from me, gazing at the stiffened grey fingers of my bare hand.

Hours passed. No sunlight got to me. There was little pain until something suddenly stabbed at me. Not my legs or arms, but at the side of my back that still stuck a little out of the snow. I ignored it but it came again, more insistent, and I turned, a grumbling sleeper. I saw a black shape now amid the white, and scratched the crust of ice from my eyes. I was having nightmares. A creature with black wings, grey fur, long jaws, triple-jointed limbs, squatted over me. It tilted its head, but said nothing. After all, what could it possibly have to say? But then it opened its jaws and something dropped. I gazed at it, steaming close to my own eye-level on the snow. A crumped sac of blood-silvered flesh almost like that hurrying umbrella I'd seen through the quester and so clumsily destroyed. It gave off an odd smell, more cinnamon than metal. I looked up at the creature that had brought it. Marion. Her faceted eyes. The pulsing membrane in her throat. Those thinly coated wings. What was she expecting me to do? Congratulate her on her kill?

KAK KARR KIK KARR

I shrank back at the sound, loud and sharp in this place of silence—the same noise Marion had made as she squatted on the stone table back at the base, a signal to Sarah and Robbie that it was safe for them to feed. Her head shot out, snakelike from her lengthening neck. She pushed the carcass closer to me. I touched the flesh with my good hand. Watched by Marion—afraid, in all honesty, about what she might do if I didn't—I pushed the threads of salty, coppery meat into my mouth, and chewed and swallowed.

She flew off in a quick burst of wings. I lay there, drowsier than ever, feeling whatever it was that she'd given me churn in my belly. Then she returned, hardly seeming to fly at all, just becoming there. Again, the dropped food. I marvelled at her simplicity, that she could think she could feed me alien meat. I wondered if I was simply dreaming, playing the same incident over and over. KAK KARR KIK KARR. Light bones, that snakelike neck, and already the day getting darker. Or perhaps it was my sight. The creature before me was smaller now anyway. Robbie or Sarah—I couldn't tell. The loose sac I was given burst moisture in my mouth. I drank it all, sucking greedily. Then I lay back. The problem was, the more I ate, the softer and wearier I became, the more comfortable grew the snow. I'd done everything right, really, to end up here. This place of understanding. Marion's voice now, as the pure wind began to rise, was a reassurance to me.

"It's not a question of *imagining*," she'd said that last day as we took the skimmer to Shell Island. Sweet sunlight and bright water.

So clear. "That's the whole point—can't you see?—it's everything we can't imagine."

I nodded, holding a tiller worn smooth by my own and other hands.

"You're too wrapped up in what you've seen in the simulations," she said. "It won't be like that. That's still all coming through these same minds we always use. We humans simply aren't equipped to be something else. Even as simple an action as looking, seeing, is routed in our heads down neural channels that are time-shared, jumbled up. The information's corrupted before it reaches our minds. Nothing is pure. . . ."

This crystal sea. The gulls and the frigate birds wheeling. In a way, she was right. Even as you saw things, tasted the breeze with the four meagre receptors on your tongue, it was slipping by, becoming memory. I searched around, thinking of a way to argue. But Marion, being Marion, was already ahead of me.

"I know all the things we humans have created. What we call civilisation. This skimmer. And I know about Paris, Venice, Acapulco. But think of the best times we've had. Think of Ayres Rock, think of Bhutan, and of Borrowdale. We've always sought out the pure and the natural. We don't want civilisation, we want *this*. This moment, uncorrupted. I mean look at them, there . . ."

She meant Sarah and Robbie, stooping over at the prow, untangling nets. Both brown and naked and weathered as the deck of this skimmer, Sarah's hair bleached whiter by the day, and Robbie's freckles blending into a mahogany stripe over his shoulders. When they came close to me now, my children smelled of the sea, and of sunlight and fishscale and sand, of woodsmoke and flowers and blood and palm trees. Already, they were halfway there.

We were nearing Shell Island. I could see the white blaze of sand.

"There!" said Marion, pointing to the water. "That's what it will be like!"

I left the tiller to its own devices and went to the rail where a school of dolphins, their wet backs shining, were leaping beside us. So fast. Astonishingly high. Masters of everything, who'd left the land long ago and returned to the freedom of the sea. . . .

Darkness was falling. There were heavy flakes lying over me, or a sense of high, beating wings. The odd thing was, as I turned my head, that the snow was alight, alive, glowing. Each twisting, amber fleck was the flame of a tiny candle. I hauled myself up on my arms. Truly this was some alien fairyland. Slowly, thinking MOVE,

LIFT, I got to my knees, and saw that my left leg had threaded a dark pool of moisture. I peeled away a little of my legging, expecting pain. My leg was clearly visible in the weak but all-pervading glow. The artificial skin had sloughed off. The lips of the wound were open again, and inside there was white fur, almost like the pelt that had formed over the rent in the dead climber's abdomen. I could feel nothing. There was no pain. I tried to pluck the stuff away. Then, suddenly, there *was* pain. Pain that rocketed out through all my senses. I lay back in the golden snow, feeling sick tremors running through me. Even when they had gone, the snow had lost its comfort. It was one thing to die from the slow loss of hypothermia, another to be consumed by some alien parasite. I felt stronger, anyway, than I had—sicker, too. I decided to start moving.

Some indeterminate time later, I was standing. All I had now was the pouch in which I'd carried my provisions—empty now, its contents dumped down the crevasse that had so nearly taken me. Still, I looped it around me and picked my vague and shambling way. At least, amid this candlelit snowfield, the deep mouths of the crevasses were easy to spot.

Morning and the darkening of the snows came simultaneously, one light fading as the other began. I could see the dawn-rain-bowed peaks that confined the glacier, even a hint of lowland beyond. I stopped without thinking, falling down, exhausted, dragging myself into the shelter of an overhang. My powerpack was totally dead now and my boots and the remaining glove had ceased to give off any heat. I held up my exposed hand in the blush of morning light, using the other to wiggle each finger tentatively. They were senseless and grey, still wetly indented from the burns of the rope, but by rights they should have been worse; frozen flesh that snapped off like icicles.

I dozed through the morning, missing my sleepsuit, hoping in moments of consciousness that Marion and Sarah and Robbie would find me again. I had a desire for the slick, coppery taste of the alien meat that I doubted was entirely healthy. But it was better than nothing, a sign of my determination for life. Dimly awake, I had to smile at the thought of being taken over by the crystal fur that had grown out along my leg now, trailing filaments. I could see me stumbling along the glacier like some mushroom-mantled log, yelling, See Marion! I've done it!—I've changed without even trying!

But there was no life here. No wingbeats. No glowing snow. Just me, the wind, cold aching silence. Despite the fluid I've been given the day before I was agonizingly thirsty. My tongue was swelling and sticking in my mouth. I knew I had to get going.

I was out of the worst of the crevasses now and my left leg, despite the worrying outward signs, was actually becoming easier to use. Crashing over splinters of ice and diamonded moraine, I stumbled my way down the glacier. I kept moving as darkness finally came and a dancing opalescence filled the night sky. Looking up, falling over, getting up again, I was reminded of the aurora borealis. But that hung as a curtain on Earth's horizon, and this was sky-encompassing. Pondering, I stumbled on, and was pleased with myself a few hours later when I realised that this glow probably came not from Korai but from the dust belts that swirled between it and Deres, casting off the cosmic rain that otherwise would have prevented life from ever beginning here.

Morning again. Another day. I'd got beyond the glittering moraine at the edge of the glacier—dry, when I'd been hoping for meltwater—and was now approaching the ravined foothills. I kept looking up to the sky, wishing Marion to bring down some more of the odd-tasting flesh, the sour water. But her ways were not mine —nor was her understanding. Her new brain was geared for the pure moment, the pure sensation, everything pouring in over an unimaginable bandwidth that would have burned my feeble human synapses in a moment.

I came to the ravines that the climber had crossed. The ropes that it had fired were still there, those rustless bands that had seemed on the way up to be an act of desecration were now my salvation. I karabinered my harness and slung myself over the first of them, slowly hauling with my good hand. It was wearying, agonizing work, and there was no sign of an end to the drop beneath me. It probably sunk deep into the planet, where all the meltwater went. And I felt sure that there was movement down there, some kind of flickering shoal.

The next ravine was wider. I had to stop many times, swaying and cursing myself as night began to fall. It was as bad as the verglas cliff face. I was sure I wouldn't make it. The flickering lights in the chasm below me seemed threatening, hallucinatory. Finally, I lay gasping on a rock on the far side, gazing up at the churning, starless sky. I knew there had to be a way around these chasms, but stuck with my own useless mind, my own useless memory, I had no idea how far I would have to go. I suspected, anyway, swallowing dry air over the boulder of my swollen tongue, gazing at the glow that came through my ripped and fungi-encrusted leggings, that I had only a day or so left. I reached over and unclipped the karabiner. A fissure of the ravine, deep but little wider than the reach of my arm, had split the rock beside me. There was no doubt, peering into it, that lights were moving down there, flickering goldfish shoals. I lay looking down as the wind swept over me. The movements were closer now, and the shapes more apparent, truly like little fish. I smiled, remembering Sarah, those rock pools, how she'd wait for hours with her bare hands. . . .

Deeper into the night, I felt two thoughts connect. I reached down with my good hand and saw the fish flicker close, near enough to throw their light onto my palm but always darting away as I grabbed toward them. Catching the little fish. It was a kind of dream-game, part nightmare. Then I remembered my empty pouch, and made the effort to unsling it, opening the mouth and I lowering it amid the dancing shapes so that it dangled like a net, then jerking it up. Running my hand down the fabric, I felt movement inside, and squeezed. My hand grew slippery wet. I lifted the creature out, and nibbled at its flesh. Still glowing, not fishy at all, but coppery like all Korain life, with the threadlike bones that were impossibly hard and sharp. Managing to chew a little, forcing the stuff back over my gums, I swallowed, then stooped over the life-filled crevice again.

I managed to catch six of the little fish that night, and to squeeze out and drink a fluid that probably came from their bladders. It tasted sweet enough; what for them was waste matter was for me the stuff of life. The prospect next morning of bridging more of the ravines, although grim, no longer seemed hopeless. Stuffing the two fish that I'd saved into my pouch, noting that they were translucent in daylight, their inner organs like the mechanism of an old analogue clock, I set out across the crystal landscape.

It was an hour or so later that my left leg, which I had done my best to ignore since it had stopped hurting, suddenly emitted a red shriek of pain. I rolled over on the rocks, gasping, and gazed down at my leg in agonized disbelief. The white fungus was moving, rippling. Then the mossy stuff parted, and a silvery eel about six centimetres long wriggled out from my flesh and sniffed the air. Too amazed to move, I watched it slide quickly across the rock beside me and bury itself out of sight. Then the fungus on my leg withered and shrank like melting snow. Within a few minutes all that was left was a sticky, grey residue, and a clean-looking scar. Still only half-believing, I touched it. It was so normal. So real.

I moved my leg, testing. Then my shoulders began to shake. I tilted my head up toward the rainbowed skies, and began to laugh.

I was sure that evening—crossing the last of the roped-over ravines, and even though any sense of the thought machines still evaded me—that I was within a day's reach of the base. As I sagged dangling on a rope or slithered over yet another fall of fractured crystal, I buoyed myself up with the knowledge of how far I had already come. I was immensely weary, but it would have seemed sinful to give up now. That night I fished for food in another narrow chasm—managing to catch five of the air fish, shyer and blue-banded here—then took shelter in a roofed-over rockfall.

The wind was quieter now, a thin shriek. And I no longer hoped that every sound might be Marion or Sarah or Robbie. I didn't even quite think of them by those names any longer. They had changed. And so, in a sense, had I. I was still hungry, thirsty, weary, but at least I no longer had to contend with the end of my existence. This planet, so strange, so hazardous, was also kind in a way that the mountain territories of Earth never were. Korai was truly a hopeful place, somewhere of fresh beginnings. I no longer felt scared here, or lonely. And when I go back to the base, when I got back . . . I winced in the darkness and shifted off a blade of rock, too tired to think by now, or sleep, or dream.

The last of the journey back to base was infinitely tedious. I kept looking back at the mountains, willing them to make the precise shape that I recognised from my days alone in the canyon. In near darkness, I reached the jewelled riverbed, and stumbled my way along it, heedless of the risk of falling. Every part of me ached and the thought machines, whose transmissions should have been vivid by now, remained vague. Finally, finally, I stumbled around a boulder and found that I was standing on top of the scree slope above a dead lake. Dim but definite, the whole territory of my confinement stood before me once again. I slid down to the tundra. Staggering toward the chambers, weaker than ever, I called for the lights, called for the server. Nothing happened. The chambers stayed dark. The thought machines murmured aimlessly. I ripped open my chamber, collapsed, and gazed up for a moment at the whipping, fieldless fabric before dropping into enormous caverns of sleep.

It was light when I awoke, then dark, then light again. I staggered out once to relieve myself and vomit up bile and silver-blue scales. I couldn't remember where the server kept the drinks.

Instead I dragged myself over to the lake. It tasted gritty, rank, familiar. I awoke again on what was probably the evening of my third day. I was sensible enough by now to understand that this odd failure of response had to do with my damaged powerpack. I hobbled along to the control chamber and manually turned up the lights, the heat. I also got the server working, and the processor. Fumbling with keys I was unused to handling, weak and suddenly ravenously hungry, I opted for the first item on the processor's menu. It was only after I'd eaten the grey slablike lumps that I realised what it was that I'd ordered.

By the next day I was in better control. My left leg seemed fine, and although my frost-bitten hand was still swollen I found that I could move the fingers tolerably well as long as I kept taking painkillers. The Korain sun was bright and warm. There was hardly any wind, or any need to set up the fields. I sat for timeless hours watching the pseudocrabs scuttling in their purposeful way, or gazing up at the warm, turquoise-streaked sky, remembering Robbie, and how he'd fallen and banged his head on that very first day. It was a chore to keep track of the thought machines without proper reception from my powerpack, but I grew used to keying in manual commands to the server—and many of the other distractions I'd once relied on seemed irrelevant. And my dreams were entirely my own now, even when I slept within a sleepsuit—and they were so vivid, and all about Earth.

I continued to live a kind of semi-detached existence from the normal goings-on at the base, watching the server scuttling on unexplained errands in much the same way that I watched the pseudocrabs. I had no warning when the first of the questers returned from its long journey. I even thought for a moment when the silver figure scuttled out of the twilight that the climber—or its ghost—had somehow returned.

Such were my days. A process of physical and mental healing. I no longer put out food for the creatures that Marion and Robbie and Sarah had become. I no longer scanned the skies in the hope that I might see them. And sometimes, although it seemed bizarre in view of all that had happened, I found myself clambering over the canyon with my feet and hands, traversing some gleaming stretch of cliff that seemed especially intriguing. I climbed unaided, just relishing the true, solid feel of the rock, the absence of any barrier between me and anything, the taste and the smell of this planet, the loss of verglas, the true sense of being here.

One day, perhaps three weeks after I'd returned, I was resting after a quick ascent of a greenish, fissured face above the white, scree slope, looking down at the canyon and the base and catching my breath in sunlight, thinking that tonight I would finally get around to drinking that last bottle of champagne, when I noticed a slight change in coloration of the tundra close to the base. Three long rectangles in the turf that I puzzled over for some minutes before realising.

I drank the champagne back inside the chambers that evening. It gave me the courage I needed to go and see the bodies of Marion, Robbie, Sarah. After all that had happened, it seemed wrong that they should still be here to remind me—even in my thoughts I'd been avoiding them. But I stood looking at those three beautiful bodies that once held the people I had loved. Now gone, leaving just slumbering golden-threaded flesh. . . .

I tossed and turned that night, experiencing insomnia for the first time in my life. Everything seemed grey, black. What, after all, was I doing here? What had I gained? I willed my Earth dreams to come, but there was nothing. My sleepsuit felt rough and unaccommodating. Somewhere in the higher reaches of this planet were alien beings I was too afraid to join, creatures that I could never understand or know. *Here. This is everything* . . . Marion's claws in me and the drop. *KI KIK KARR KARR.* And that cave. New life. Not even three circling figures, but more. More . . .

I could still taste the champagne—sweet and sharp, just the way it had been that last evening I'd spent here with my human family. I remembered how the kids had been so excited about the coming change that Marion had had to up-programme their sleepsuits to get them quiet for the night. Then she and I had sat outside the chambers around a real fire of apple-wood logs we'd brought with us for the occasion. I remembered the way she smiled and held her glass, the way the smoke was snatched as it drifted out of the fields. We didn't say much. There was nothing much left to say. A time of stillness here on this far planet that felt so much stranger to me then as the wind howled and the white mountains loomed. The silence of change, of resolution. I remembered Marion taking my hand and leading me to the chambers, stepping from her clothes, tossing away the sleepsuits. We slept naked and together that night, flesh on flesh. At some point, an act less of passion than of sharing, a remembrance of other times, we rocked slowly together, making love.

I sat up in the trembling dark and fumbled for the manual switch I'd rigged to turn on the lights. I stumbled down the chambers to the thought machines, and sat there for the rest of the night wrestling with the manual screens beside emanators I could no longer use, attempting to find my way into one programme amid the myriad. It took me until the light of Deres had began to show through the wind-fluttering fabric. And when I found it, that hidden blob that only senses stronger and stranger than my own could reveal, I had to keep checking, scanning and rescanning the cloudy images. Even then, I still couldn't quite believe.

The thought machines were grumpy and distant now. Perhaps it was just the difficulty they now had in dealing with me, this power-packless human—but I suspected that they would never have diagnosed Marion without my prompting, or have told me if they knew. It still seems likely to me that they would have simply allowed me to bury Marion. To their way of thinking, I suppose, she had carried the new life with her when she changed, to be reborn in that cave.

Summer faded and returned. I lived and breathed and walked and climbed. The sac of life nurtured within Marion's body continued to grow. I sat for hours beside the stillfield as the sky flickered green and red and blue outside, sometimes touching the swelling in the fold of her sleepsuit, sometimes lost in sorrow, or happy, or drifting with my mind almost clear of thought. Sometimes, too, I felt anguish at this thing that I was doing. What right had I, alone on this planet, to bring life? But the anguish faded with the touch of warm flesh and the scent and the nearness of the three loved bodies that surrounded me. I knew I couldn't destroy Marion now, knowing of the life that she was nurturing.

She grew big with the heat of summer, as the air turned truly warm and fresh water gurgled, too slick and fast for all the ravines between me and the mountains to swallow, into my swelling lake. There were new forms of life in there too. Coloured fronds and filaments. A slow, grey, mudlike wing that flapped and crawled along the bottom. The pseudocrabs brought out their young. Shell-less and pink like tiny, crawling hands, they dutifully studied their parents as they scuttled from rock to rock across the soggy tundra, clumsily stuffing berries into their own nascent pouches before getting lost, or falling over. A monitor satellite in deep solar orbit made contact with a starship that passed near Deres, and checked me out with a quick exchange of beams. I told them that I was well, making excuses for the clumsiness of my transmission, and worried for days after that they might still change route and visit me. But they didn't. And I was fine anyway. I felt safe being alone.

One evening as I was sitting outside of my chambers, studying the rock and the warm, ribboned glint of the skies, I heard, almost as I had expected to now that I'd given up hoping, the grey beat of wings. They came from a different angle this time, from another part of the sky. Who knew, after all, just how far across this planet Marion and Robbie and Sarah had been roaming? And now there were four shapes, not three; one large, another two only slightly smaller, then a smallest, a tiny fleck riding the slipstream of its mother. Marion settled first, cupping her new offspring inside the protective arch of her wings. She looked around as I ran over to her. I caught the faceted glint of her eyes.

"I'm fine!" I shouted. "Marion, it's great to see you!" But my voice sounded strange even to me after these months of silence and she backed away at the sound of it, her wings catching the air, ready for flight. Ugly as a gargoyle, the little creature beside her hissed and whimpered. Robbie and Sarah still circled. I looked again at Marion, willing her to call them down. But our children were nearly adult now, and would probably take little notice of her.

Moving slowly, I backed away from the rock table, then broke into a run, splashing through the puddled tundra. I stabbed breathlessly at the keys in a flapping chamber, grabbing the hot slabs as they emerged from the processor and running back out with them into the deepening twilight. But the shapes had already vanished from the rock table. There were no wingbeats in the air. I scanned the sky as darkness deepened until my eyes were nothing but thickened pools of black. But there was no sign of them. It was as if they had never been.

The first snows of winter came. I had seen the snow in patches here when we first arrived, and then of course up in the mountains, but none of it had ever been this green. The seasons here, I was coming to realise, were like the flash of light through a dozen different patterns of weave. Marion's belly grew taut. I saw the baby stirring on the scans, and felt it kicking with my own hands. Afraid to think of him growing alone and in silence, I began to talk and pace around the stillfield. And at night, as the wind howled and glowing plumes of ice curled over the canyon like beckoning hands, I even began to sing.

I ordered painkillers for Marion on the night she gave birth.

The thought machines couldn't understand why I didn't let them use the server's blades simply to cut the baby out—nor why her emptied synapses could be disturbed by the lost concept of pain. Anyway, the contractions came easily, thoughtlessly induced by the still-functioning ganglions in Marion's spine. I could even say the birth itself was easy, but then how can I ever know?—and for me, watching as Marion's eyes opened and her belly tensed and her jaw spasmed, as her whole body sweated and strained and came briefly to life, it was truly hard. I was in tears afterward as I washed the baby and cleaned and cut his cord, smiling and sobbing as I lay him in the crook of Marion's arms as she lay wrecked and drained amid the spreading pool of afterbirth and he sucked the clear, whitish fluid from her breasts.

I sat for many hours beside the stillfield, rocking my sleeping baby. He looked different as all babies look different. The red forehead, the huge thin-lidded eyes, those impossible toes and fingernails. It was so strange, that he should come here to me now. All so hard to believe—but then that's what it's like to be human, the way things slip away. It's what keeps us together and apart.

I let him suckle Marion for a few days, holding him against her in the crook of her warm, lifeless arms. But the golden veins of the stillfield threaded her breasts, and even with her body cleansed and refreshed, something had gone from her with the birth. The last vestige, I supposed, of the life that had held me back from burying her all those months before. And Robbie and Sarah, although I held the baby to them as well and whispered every secret I could imagine into their ears, seemed also to have lessened, changed. They were far brighter in my dreams and memories these days than they were in the flesh. I supposed they'd grown a little, become more of what they would never become. As with the true living sprits that soared the mountains with Marion, it was time for them to leave.

I worried as my baby cried when he wouldn't take to the milk the processor provided. I worried about his mind, the way he had grown within the stillfield, and how the air of this strange, new planet would affect him. I would sometimes take him out from the chambers when the wind died down, well-wrapped and held close against me. Then, in the blazing chill of these mountains, I knew that everything was safe. The way his face lit up at the sight of the glittering, multi-hued ice, those gorgeous, flooding skies. And even at two months old he was reaching out with his hands toward it all.

And the dream light that I remembered so well from Marion was there in his eyes.

Winter receded a little—although I knew enough about Korai by now not to think it would be followed by anything as mundane as spring. As the snows pooled and melted, blue mothlike creatures emerged from it and took flight. I was grateful for the new warmth —my food supplies had been stretched far longer than planned. Planning to replenish them, I set out one morning with my baby harnessed to my back, hiking up the scree slope and along the meltwater-threaded drifts to the first of the ravines. There were great shoals down there now, huge and plentiful. My baby watched and slept and smiled as I stooped into the roaring caverns. But when I hooked out the creatures twisting and flopping into my hands, when I had let my baby touch them with his plump-knuckled fingers, I simply let them slide back into the ravine. Now that my own life no longer depended on it, I couldn't bring myself to kill something that was living.

That was a year ago; I scrimped and survived. Another human family has now come to Korai. They contacted me via satellite when they arrived, and flew over the range a few days later in the big craft they'd brought with them. I watched it land, the howling engines flattening the tundra beside the table of rock. I held my baby close as he chuckled at this strange, new, sliver creature and at the smaller ones that emerged from it. But he frowned as they grew closer. Two boys, a man and a woman. I think he thought we were the only humans on this or any other world.

They treated us with courtesy. Their server unloaded fresh generators and chambers and supplies. As mine helped, I noticed how it had corroded to green in the near-on two Earth years I'd been here, and how the old chambers it was replacing had grown mottled and dark with Korain fungi. Before, I hadn't even noticed.

"What's his name?" the woman asked as we sat out in the cool lavender twilight. I'd let her hold my baby, which was a strange sensation in itself. He and I had become like parts of each other; it was like lending someone your arm. But my baby was uncomplaining after an initial squawk of surprise. He gazed up at her with fierce, blue, questioning eyes; he was that kind of kid.

She repeated her question. I blinked back at her. I hadn't thought of a name. With just the two of us here, there had never been any need.

Letting it pass, she smiled and looked around at where her boys

and her husband were wandering, calling to each other with
strange, loud voices as they peered under rocks and climbed up
slopes and made fresh discoveries. Even without asking, she'd know
my whole story anyway. She had her powerpack, access to my
thought machines.

"But this is such a beautiful planet," she said. "As soon as we
landed, everything else faded, all my worries and regrets. Even
. . ." she looked down. In her arms, my baby chuckled. "Him
. . . This . . ."

"I understand," I said, "why people want to change. I've
changed myself. That's the oddest thing of all. I've changed too. I
just didn't have to lose my humanity to do so."

"We'll all go together. I mean the kids. Me and Mark. It'll be
soon."

"That's probably the best way."

She held out her arms. I took my baby back from her. He said
*Ka-koo* and I breathed the salt-soapy scent of the crown of his
hair. Then she stood up, looking around. Those bright red peaks
behind which Deres had set long ago, even though the whole sky
was still glowing. "Those . . ." she pointed toward the mountains.
"That highest one there. What do you call it? Seeing it all this time,
you must have . . ."

I shook my head and followed her as she walked across the
tundra. Her youngest son ran up to her with something in his
hands. A pseudocrab that he'd tried to dismantle like a clockwork
toy was dribbling marbled Korain blood through his fingers.
Pseudocrab. A name of sorts. Dayflower. As for the rest, as for all
the life and the crags and ravines of this planet, as for that highest,
red-stained peak that I'd so nearly died on and the creatures that
Marion and Robbie and Sarah had become, I hadn't presumed to
give any of it a name. Things here are what they were, and ulti-
mately alien. No names could ever change that.

"Samuel," I said.

"What?"

"My baby. I call him Samuel."

"That's good. I once knew someone. . . ."

We wandered a little further. The wind was picking up. The sky
was showing threads of golden dark. The father was calling to his
eldest son to get down from the ridge above the lake that he was
trying to ascend. The servers had finished their work. Soon, the
family would be going.

The ground was a little softer here. Even folded over in this gathering gloom, the dayflowers beneath our feet seemed larger, brighter. She glanced down at the three darker rectangles they picked out in the sod, then back at me.

"You know the starship that brought us here will be out in stellar orbit for another month?"

"Yes." I nodded.

"I was wondering . . ."

"If I might be going? I'm not sure. I love this planet so much. But seeing you, realising about my—Samuel. I know I can't bring him up alone here. He has his own life."

"He has to learn how to deal with things," she said. "He'll need a powerpack—assessment and teaching, skills to understand the thought machines. How to work a sleepsuit. . . ."

"Not that I miss any of that."

"But you've got to let him make his own decisions. That's what we're all doing, here." She folded her arms and looked about her. "But you'll be going? You'll take that starship back to Earth?"

"Yes," I nodded, feeling the soft, Korain air flooding around me, the moments of my life slipping by. "I'll be going."

"Look." She smiled and touched my arm. She was pointing. "Up there." Her voice was shivering, expectant. Against the cliff, glimpsed and distant, four black specks were rising.

I held Samuel up to see. He chuckled—*Ka koo*—and pointed with his outstretched chubby hand.

# The Chop Girl

M E, I WAS THE CHOP GIRL — NOT THAT I SUPPOSE
that anyone knows what that means now. So much blood and
water under the bridge! I heard the lassies in the Post Office de-
bating how many world wars there had been last week when I
climbed up the hill to collect my pension, and who exactly it was
that had won them.

Volunteered for service, I did, because I thought it would get
me away from the stink of the frying pans at home in our Manchester tea room's back kitchen. And then the Air Force of all
things, and me thinking, lucky, lucky, lucky, because of the
glamour and the lads, the lovely lads, the best lads of all, who spoke
with BBC voices as I imagined them, and had played rugger and
footie for their posh schools and for their posh southern counties.
And a lot of it was true, even if I ended up typing in the annex to
the cookhouse, ordering mustard and HP on account of my, quote,
*considerable experience in the catering industry.*

So there I was — just eighteen and WRAF and lucky, lucky,
lucky. And I still didn't know what a chop girl was, which had nothing to do with lamb or bacon or the huge blocks of lard I ordered
for the chip pans. They were big and empty places, those bomber
airfields, and they had the wild and open and windy names of the
Fens that surrounded them. Wisbeach and Finneston and Witch-

ford. And there were drinks and there were dances and the money was never short because there was never any point in not spending it. Because you never knew, did you? You never knew. One day your bunk's still warm and the next someone else is complaining about not changing the sheets and the smell of you on it. Those big machines like ugly insects lumbering out in the dying hour to face the salt wind off the marshes and the lights and blue smoke of the paraffin lanterns drifting across the runways. Struggling up into the deepening sky in a mighty roaring, and the rest of us standing earthbound and watching. Word slipping out that tonight it would be Hamburg or Dortmund or Essen—some half-remembered place from a faded schoolroom map glowing out under no moon and through heavy cloud, the heavier the better, as the bombers droned over, and death fell from them in those long steel canisters onto people who were much like us when you got down to it, but for the chances of history. Then back, back, a looser run in twos and threes and searching for the seaflash of the coast after so many miles of darkness. Black specks at dawn on the big horizon that could have been clouds or crows or just your eyes' plain weariness. Noise and smoke and flame. Engines misfiring. An unsettled quiet would be lying over everything by the time the sun was properly up and the skylarks were singing. The tinny taste of fatigue. Then word on the wires of MG 3138, which had limped in at Brightlingsea. And of CZ 709, which had ploughed up a field down at Theddlethorpe. Word, too, of LK 452, which was last seen as a flaming cross over Brussels, and of Flight Sergeant Shanklin, who, hoisted bloody from his gun turret by the medics, had faded on the way to hospital. Word of the dead. Word of the lost. Word of the living.

Death was hanging all around you, behind the beer and the laughs and the bowls and the endless games of cards and darts and cricket. Knowing as they set out on a big mission that some planes would probably never get back. Knowing for sure that half the crews wouldn't make it through their twenty-mission tour. So of course we were all madly superstitious. It just happened—you didn't need anyone to make it up for you. Who bought the first round. Who climbed into the plane last. Not shaving or shaving only half your face. Kissing the ground, kissing the air, singing, not singing, pissing against the undercarriage, spitting. I saw a Flight Officer have a blue fit because the girl in the canteen gave him only two sausages on his lunchtime plate. That night, on a big raid over Dortmund, his Lancaster vanished in heavy flak, and I remember the sleepless nights because it was me who'd forgotten to requisition from the wholesale butcher. But everything was sharp and bright then. The feel of your feet in your shoes and your tongue in your mouth and your eyes in their sockets. That, and the sick-and-petrol smell of the bombers. So everything mattered. Every incident was marked and solid in the only time which counted, which was the time which lay between now and the next mission. So it was odd socks and counting sausages, spitting and not spitting, old hats and new hats worn backward and forward. It was pissing on the undercarriage, and whistling. And it was the girls you'd kissed.

Me, I was the chop girl, and word of it tangled and whispered around me like the sour morning news of a botched raid. I don't know how it began, because I'd been with enough lads at dances, and then outside afterward fumbling and giggling in the darkness. And sometimes, and because you loved them all and felt sorry for them, you'd let them go nearly all the way before pulling back with the starlight shivering between us. Going nearly all the way was a skill you had to learn then, like who wore what kind of brass buttons and marching in line. And I was lucky. I sang lucky, lucky, lucky to myself in the morning as I brushed my teeth, and I laughingly told the lads so in the evening NAFFI when they always beat me at cards.

It could have started with Flight Sergeant Martin Beezly, who just came into our smoky kitchen annex one hot summer afternoon and sat down on the edge of my desk, with his blonde hair sticking up, and told me he had a fancy to go picnicking and had got hold of two bikes. Me, I just unrolled my carbons and stood up and the other girls watched with the jaws of their typewriters dropped in astonishment as I walked out into the sunlight. Nothing much happened that afternoon, other than what Flight Sergeant Beezly said would happen. We cycled along the little dikes and bumped across the wooden bridges, and I sat on a rug eating custard creams as he told me about his home up in the northeast and the business he was planning to set up after the war, delivering lunchtime sandwiches to the factories. But all of that seemed as distant as the open, blue sky—as distant, given these clear and unsuitable weather conditions, as the possibility of a raid taking place that evening. We were just two young people enjoying the solid certainty of that moment—which the taste of custard creams still always brings back to me—and Flight Sergeant Beezly did no more than brush my cheek with his fingers before we climbed back onto the bikes, and then glance anxiously east toward the heavy clouds that were suddenly piling. It was fully overcast by the time we got back to the base, driven fast on our bikes by the cool and unsummery wind that was rustling the ditches. Already, orders had been posted and briefings were being staged and the groundcrews were working, their arclights flaring in the hangers. Another five minutes, a little less of that wind as we cycled, and they'd have been all hell to pay for me and for Flight Sergeant Beezly, who, as a navigator and vital to the task of getting one of those big machines across the dark sky, would have been shifted to standby and then probably court-martialed. But as it was, he just made it into the briefing room as the map was being unfolded and sat down, as I imagine him, on the schoolroom desk nearest the door, still a little breathless, and with the same smears of bike oil on his fingers that I later found on my cheek. That night, it was Amsterdam—a quick raid to make the most of this quick and filthy cloud that the weather boffins said wouldn't last. Amsterdam. One of those raids that somehow never sounded right even though it was enemy-occupied territory. That night GZ 3401, with Flight Sergeant Beezly navigating, was last seen labouring over the North Sea enemy coastal barrages with a full load of bombs, a slow and ugly butterfly pined on the needles of half a dozen searchlights.

So maybe that was the first whisper—me walking out of the annex before I should have with Flight Sergeant Beezly, although God knows it had happened to enough of the other girls. That, and worse. Broken engagements. Cancelled marriages. Visits to the burns unit, and up the stick for going all the way instead of just most of it. Wrecked, unmendable lives that you can still see drifting at every branch Post Office, if you know how and when to look. But then, a week after, there was Pilot Officer Charlie Dyson, who had a reputation as one of the lads, one for the lassies. All we did was dance and kiss at the Friday hall down in the village, although I suppose that particular night was the first time I was really drawn to him because something had changed about his eyes. That, and the fact that he'd shaved off the Clark Gable moustache that I'd always thought made him look vain and ridiculous. So we ended up kissing as we danced, and then sharing beers and laughs with the rest of his crew in their special corner. And after the band had gone and the village outside the hall stood stony dark, I let him lean me against the old oak that slipped its roots into the river and let him nuzzle my throat and touch my breasts and mutter words against my skin that were lost in the hissing of the water. I put my hand down between us then, touched him in the place I thought he wanted. But Pilot Officer Charlie Dyson was soft as smoke down there, as cool and empty as the night. So I just held him and rocked him as he began to weep, feeling faintly relieved that there wouldn't be the usual pressures for me to go the whole way. Looking up through the oak leaves, as the river whispered, I saw that the bright moon of the week before was thinning, and I knew from the chill air on my flesh that tomorrow the planes would be thundering out again. You didn't need to be a spy or a boffin. And not Amsterdam, but a long run. Hamburg. Dortmund. Essen. In fact, it turned out to be the longest of them all, Berlin. And somewhere on that journey Pilot Officer Charlie Dyson and his whole crew and his Lancaster simply fell out of the sky. Vanished into the darkness.

After that, the idea of my being bad luck seemed to settle around me, clinging like the smoke of the cookhouse. Although I was young, although I'd never really gone steady with anyone and had still never ventured every last inch of the way, and although no one dared to keep any proper score of these things, I was already well on my way to becoming the chop girl. I learned afterward that most bases had one; that—in the same way that Kitty from stores was like a mum to a lot of the crews, and Sally Morrison was the camp bicycle—it was a kind of necessity.

And I believed. With each day so blazingly bright and with the nights so dark and the crews wild-eyed and us few women grieving and sleepless, with good luck and bad luck teeming in the clouds and in the turning of the moon, we loved and lived in a world that had shifted beyond the realms of normality. So of course I believed.

I can't give you lists and statistics. I can't say when I first heard the word, or caught the first really odd look. But being the chop girl became a self-fulfilling prophecy. Empty wells of silence opened out when I entered the canteen. Chairs were weirdly re-arranged in the NAFFI. I was the chop, and the chop was Flight Sergeant Ronnie Fitfield and Flight Officer Jackie White and Pilot Officer Tim Reid, all of them in one bad, late summer month, men I can barely remember now except for their names and ranks and the look of loss in their eyes and the warm, bristle touch of their faces. Nights out at a pub; beating the locals at cribbage; a trip to the cinema at Lincoln, and the tight, cobbled streets afterward shining with rain. But I couldn't settle on these men because already I could feel the darkness edging in between us, and I knew even as I touched their shoulders and watched them turn away that they could feel it, too. At the dances and the endless booze-ups and the card schools, I became more than a wallflower: I was the petaled heart of death, its living embodiment. I was quivering with it like electricity. One touch, one kiss, one dance. Groundcrew messages were hard to deliver when they saw who it was coming across the tarmac. It got to the point when I stopped seeing out the planes, or watching them through the pane of my bunk window. And the other girls in the annex and the spinster WRAF officers and even the red-faced women from the village who came in to empty the bins—all of them knew I was the chop, all of them believed. The men who came up to me now were white-faced, already teetering. They barely needed my touch. Once you'd lost it, the luck, the edge, the nerve, it was gone anyway, and the black bomber's sky crunched you in its fists.

I can't tell you that it was terrible. I knew it wasn't *just*, but then justice was something we'd long given up even missing. Put within that picture, and of the falling bombs and the falling bombers, I understood that the chop girl was a little thing, and I learned to step back into the cold and empty space that it provided. After all, I hadn't *loved* any of the men—or only in a sweet, generalised, and heady way which faded on the walk from the fence against which we'd been leaning. And I reasoned—and this was probably the thing that kept me sane—that it wasn't *me* that was the chop. I reasoned that death lay somewhere else and was already waiting, that I was just a signpost that some crewmen had happened to pass on their way.

Me, I was the chop girl.

And I believed.

Such were the terrors and the pains of the life we were leading.

With the harvest came the thunderflies, evicted from the fields in sooty clouds that speckled the windows and came out like black dandruff when you combed your hair. And the moths and the craneflies were drawn for miles by the sparks and lights flaring from the hangers. Spiders prowled the communal baths, filled with their reek of bleach and wet towels. The sun rippled small and gold like a dropped coin on the horizon, winking as if through fathoms of ocean.

With harvest came Walt Williams. Chuttering up to the Strictly Reserved parking space outside the Squadron Leader's office in a once-red MG and climbing out with a swing of his legs and the heave of his battered carpetbag. Smiling with cold, blue eyes as he looked around him at the expanse of hangers as if he would never be surprised again. Walt had done training. Walt had done

Pathfinders. Walt had done three full tours, and most of another that had only ended when his plane had been shot from under him and he'd been hauled out of the Channel by a passing MTB. We'd all heard of Walt, or thought we had, or had certainly heard of people like him. Walt was one of the old-style pilots who'd been flying since before the War for sheer pleasure. Walt was an old man of thirty with age creases on his sun-browned face to go with those blue eyes. Walt had done it all and had finally exhausted every possibility of death that a bemused RAF could throw at him. Walt was the living embodiment of lucky.

We gathered around, we sought to touch and admire and gain advice about how one achieved this impossible feat—the *we* at the base that generally excluded me did, anyway. The other crew members who'd been selected to fly with him wandered about with the bemused air of a pools winner. Walt Williams stories suddenly abounded. Stuff about taking a dead cow up in a Lancaster and dropping it bang into the middle of a particularly disliked Squadron Leader's prized garden. Stuff about half a dozen top brass wives. Stuff about crash landing upside down on lakes. Stuff about flying for hundreds of miles on two engines or just the one or no engines at all. Stuff about plucking women's washing on his undercarriage and picking apples from passing trees. Amid all this excitement that fizzed around the airfield, like the rain on the concrete and the corrugated hangers as the autumn weather heaved in, we seemed to forget that we had told each other many of these stories before, and that they had only gained this new urgency because we could now settle them onto the gaunt face of a particular man who sat smiling and surrounded yet often seeming alone at the smoke-filled centre of the NAFFI bar.

Being older, being who he was, Walt needed to do little to enhance his reputation other than to climb up into his Lancaster and fly it. That, and parking that rattling sports car the way he did that first day, his loose cuffs and his other minor disregards for all the stupidities of uniform, his chilly gaze, his longer-than-regulation hair, the fact that he was almost ten years older than most of the rest of us, and had passed up the chance to be promoted to the positions of the men who were supposedly in charge of him, was more than enough. The fact that, in the flesh, he was surprisingly quiet, and that his long, brown hands trembled as he chain-smoked his Dunhill cigarettes, the fact that his smile barely ever wavered yet never reached his eyes, and that it was said, whispered, that the Pilot Officer in the billet next to his had asked to be moved out

on account of the sound of screaming, was as insignificant as Alan
Ladd having to stand on a box before he kissed his leading ladies.
We all had our own inner version of Walt Williams in those soar-
ingly bright days.

For me, the shadow in bars and dancehall corners, potent in
my own opposite way, yet now mostly pitied and ignored, Walt
Williams had an especial fascination. With little proper company,
immersed often enough between work shifts in doleful boredom, I
had plenty of time to watch and brood. The base and surrounding
countryside made a strange world that winter. I walked the dikes. I
saw blood on the frost where the farmers set traps to catch the foxes,
and felt my own blood turn and change with the ebb and flow of
the bomber's moon. Ice on the runways, ice hanging like fairy
socks on the radio spars as the messages came in each morning.
The smell of the sea blown in over the land. In my dreams, I saw
the figures of crewmen entering the NAAFI, charcoaled and blistered, riddled with bleeding wormholes or greyly bloated from the
ocean and seeping brine. Only Walt Williams, laughing for once,
his diamond eyes blazing, stood whole and immune.

Walt was already halfway through his tour by the time Christmas came, and the consensus amongst those who knew was that he
was an unfussy pilot, unshowy. Rather like the best kind of foot-
baller, he drifted in, found the right place, the right time, then
drifted out again. I stood and watched him from my own quiet corners in the barroom, nursing my quiet drinks. I even got to feel that
I knew Walt Williams better than any of the others, because I actually made it my business to study him, the man and not the legend.
He always seemed to be ahead of everything that was happening,
but I saw that there was a wariness in the way he watched people,
and a mirrored grace in how he responded, as if he'd learned the
delicate dance of being human, of making all the right moves, but,
offstage and in the darkness of his hut where that pilot who was
dead now had said he'd heard screaming, he was something else
entirely. And there were things—apart from never having to buy
drinks—which Walt Williams never did. Games, bets, cards. He
always slipped back then, so smoothly and easily you'd have to be
watching from as far away as I was to actually notice. It was as if he
was frightened to use his luck up on anything so trivial, whereas
most of the other crewmen, fired up and raw through these times of
waiting, were always chasing a ball, a winning hand, thunking in
the darts and throwing dice and making stupid bets on anything
that moved, including us girls.

Watching Walt as I did, I suppose he must have noticed me. And he must have heard about me, too, just as everyone else here at the base had. Sometimes, on the second or third port and lemon, I'd just stare at him from my empty corner and will him, dare him, to stare back at me. But he never did. Those sapphire eyes, quick as they were, never quite touched on me. He *must*, I thought. He must look *now*. But never, never. Except when I stood up and left, and I felt his presence behind me like the touch of cool fingers on my neck. So strong and sharp was that feeling one night, as I stepped down the wooden steps outside the NAFFI, that I almost turned and went straight back in to confront him through those admiring crowds. But loneliness had become a habit by now, and I almost clung to my reputation. I wandered off, away from the billets and into the empty darkness of the airfield. There was no moon, but a seemingly endless field of stars. Not a bomber's night, but the kind of night you see on Christmas cards. After a week's rain, and then this sudden frost, I could feel the ground crackling and sliding beneath me. The NAFFI door swung open again, and bodies tumbled out. As they turned from the steps and made to sway arm in arm off to bed, I heard the crash of fresh ice and the slosh of water as they broke into a huge puddle. They squelched off, laughing and cursing. Standing there in the darkness, I watched the same scene play itself out over and over again. The splash of cold, filthy water. One man even fell into it. Freezing though I was, I took an odd satisfaction in watching this little scene repeat itself. Now, I thought, if they could see me as well as I can see them, standing in the darkness watching the starlight shining on that filthy puddle, they really would know I'm strange. Chop girl. Witch. Death incarnate. They'd burn me at the stake. . . .

I'd almost forgotten about Walt Williams when he finally came out, although I knew it was him instantly. He paused on the steps and looked up at the sky as I'd seen other aircrew do, judging what the next night would bring. As he did so, his shadow seemed to quiver. But he still walked like Walt Williams when he stepped down onto the frozen turf, and his breath plumed like anyone else's, and I knew somehow, knew in a way that I had never had before, that this time he really didn't know that I was there, and that he was off-guard in a way I'd never seen him. The next event was stupid, really. A non-event. Walt Williams just walked off with the loose walk of his, his hands stuffed into his pockets. He was nearly gone from sight into his Nissan hut when I realised the one thing that hadn't happened. Even though he'd taken the same route as everyone else, he hadn't splashed into that wide, deep puddle. I walked over to it, disbelieving, and tried to recall whether I'd even heard the crackle of his footsteps on the ice. And the puddle was even darker, wider and filthier than I'd imagined. The kind of puddle you only get at places military. I was stooping at the edge of it, and my own ankles and boots were already filthy, when the NAFFI door swung open again, and a whole group of people suddenly came out. Somebody was holding the door, and the light flooded right toward me.

Even though I was sure they must all have seen me and knew who I was, I got up and scurried away.

All in all, it was a strange winter. We were getting used to Allied victories, and there'd even been talk of a summer invasion of France that had never happened. But we knew it would come next summer, now that the Yanks had thrown their weight into it, and that the Russians wouldn't give up advancing, that it was really a matter of time until the War ended. But for us that wasn't reassuring, because we knew that peace was still so far away, and we knew that the risks and the fatalities would grow even greater on the journey to it. Aircrews were scared in any case of thinking further than the next drink, the next girl, the next mission. Peace for them was a strange, white god they could worship only at the risk of incurring the wrath of the darker deity who still reigned over them. So there was an extra wildness to the jollification when the year's end drew near, and a dawning realisation that, whether we lived or died, whether we came out of it all maimed or ruined, or whole and happy, no one else would ever understand.

There was a big pre-Christmas bash in a barn of the great house of the family that had once owned most of the land you could see from the top of our windsock tower. Of course, the house itself had been requisitioned, although the windows were boarded or shattered and the place was empty as we drove past it, and I heard later that it was never reoccupied after the war and ended up being slowly vandalised until it finally burnt down in the fifties. The barn was next to the stables and faced into a wide, cobbled yard and for once, out here in the country darkness and a million miles from peace or war, no one gave a bugger about the blackout and there were smoking lanterns hanging by the pens where fine, white horses would once have nosed their heads. It was freezing, but you couldn't feel cold, not in that sweet, orange light, not once the music had started, and the Squadron Leader himself, looking ridiculous in a pinny, began ladling out the steaming jamjars of mulled wine. And I was happy to be there, too, happy to be part of this scene with the band striking up on a stage made of bales. When Walt arrived, alone as usual in his rusty MG, he parked in the best spot between the trucks and climbed out with that fragile grace of his. Walt Williams standing there in the flame light, a modern prince with the tumbling chimneys of that empty, old house looming behind him. A perfect, perfect scene.

I did dance, once or twice, with some of the other girls and a few of the older men who worked in the safety of accounts and stores and took pity on me. I even had a five-minute word—just like everyone else, kindly man that he was, and spectrally thin though the War had made him—with our Squadron Leader. As far away from everything as we were, people thought it was safe here to get in a bit closer to me. But it was hard for me to keep up my sense of jollity, mostly standing and sitting alone over such a long evening, and no chance of going back to base until far after midnight. So I did my usual trick of backing off, which was easier here than it was in the NAFFI. I could just drift out of the barn and across the cobbles, falling through layers of smoke and kicked-up dust until I became part of the night. I studied them all for a while, remembering a picture from Peter Pan which had showed the Indians and the Lost Boys dancing around a campfire.

Couples were drifting out now into the quiet behind the vans. I tried to remember what it was like, the way you could conjure up that urgency between flesh and flesh. But all I could think of was some man's male thing popping out like a dog's, and I walked further off into the dark, disgusted. I wandered around the walls of the big and empty house with its smell of damp and nettles, half-feeling my way down steps and along balustrades, moving at this late and early hour amid the pale shadows of huge statuary. It wasn't fully quiet here, this far away from the throb of the barn. Even in midwinter, there were things shuffling and creaking and breaking. Tiny sounds, and the bigger ones that came upon you just when you'd given up waiting. The hoot of an owl. The squeak of a mouse. The sound of a fox screaming. . . .

Perhaps I'd fallen asleep, for I didn't hear him coming, or at least didn't separate out the sound of his footsteps from my thoughts, which had grown as half-unreal as those dim statues, changing and drifting. So I simply waited in the darkness as one of the statues began to move, and knew without understanding that it was Walt Williams. He sat beside me on whatever kind of cold, stone bench I was sitting, and he still had the smell of the barn on him, the heat and the drink and the smoke and the firelight. The only thing he didn't carry with him was the perfume of a woman. I honestly hadn't realised until that moment that this was another item I should have added to my long list of the things Walt Williams avoided. But somehow that fact had been so obvious that even I hadn't noticed it. It wouldn't have seemed right, anyway. Walt and just one woman. Not with the whole base depending on him.

I watched the flare of the match, and saw the peaked outline of his face as he stooped to catch it with two cigarettes. Then I felt his touch as he passed one to me. One of those long, posh fags of his, which tasted fine and sweet, although it was odd to hold compared with the stubby NAFFI ones because the glow of it came from so far away. No one else, I thought, would ever do this for me—sit and smoke a fag like this. Only Walt.

He finally ground his cigarette out in a little shower of sparks beneath his shoe. I did the same, more by touch than anything.

"So you're the girl we're all supposed to avoid?"

Pointless though it was in this darkness, I nodded.

It was the first time I'd heard him laugh. Like his voice, the sound was fine and light. "The things people believe!"

"It's true, though, isn't it? It *is*, although I don't understand why. It may be that it's only because . . ." I trailed off. I'd never spoken about being the chop girl to anyone before. What I'd wanted to say was that it was our believing that had made it happen.

I heard the rustle of his packet as he took out another cigarette. "Another?"

I shook my head. "You of all people. You shouldn't be here with me."

The match flared. I felt smoke on my face, warm and invisible. "That's where you're wrong. You and me, we'd make the ideal couple. Don't bother to say otherwise. I've seen you night after night in the NAFFI. . . ."

"Not every night."

"But enough of them."

"And *I* saw you, that night. I saw you walk over that puddle."

"What night was that?"

So I explained—and in the process I gave up any pretence that I hadn't been watching him.

"I really don't remember," he said when I'd finished, although he didn't sound that surprised. This time, before he ground out his cigarette, he used it to light another. "But why should I? It was just a puddle. Lord knows, there are plenty around the base."

"But it was *there*. I was *watching*. You just walked over it."

He made a sound that wasn't quite a cough. "Hasn't everyone told you who I am? I'm Walt Williams. I'm lucky."

"But it's more than that, isn't it?"

Walt said nothing for a long while, and I watched the nervous arc of his cigarette rising and falling. And when he did begin to speak, it wasn't about the War, but about his childhood. Walt, he told me he'd come from a well-to-do family in the Home Counties, a place which always made me think of the BBC and pretty lanes with tall, flowering hedges. He was the only child, but a big investment, as was always made clear to him, of his mother's time, his father's money. At first, to hear Walt talk, he really was the image of those lads I'd imagined when I joined the RAF. He'd gone to the right schools. He really had played cricket—if only just the once when the usual wicket keeper was ill—for his county. His parents had him lined up to become an accountant. But Walt would have none of that, and my image of his kind of childhood, which was in all the variegated golds and greens of striped lawns and fine sunsets, changed as he talked like a film fading. His mother, he said, had a routine that she stuck to rigidly. Every afternoon, when she'd come back from whatever it was that she always did on that particular day, she'd sit in the drawing room with her glass and her sherry decanter beside her. She'd sit there, and she'd wait for the clock to chime five, and then she'd ring for the maid to come and pour her drink for her. Every afternoon, the same.

Walt Williams talked on in the darkness. And at some point, I began to hear the ticking rattle of something that I thought at first were his keys or his coins, the kind of nervous habit that most pilots end up getting. It didn't sound quite right, but by then I was too absorbed in what he was saying. Flying, once Walt had discovered it, had been his escape, although, because of the danger to their precious investment of time and good schools and money, his parents disapproved of it even as a hobby. They cut off his money, and what there was of their affection. Walt worked in garages and then on the airfields, and flew whenever he could. He even toured with a circus. The rattling sound continued as he spoke, and I sensed a repeated sweeping movement of his hand that he was making across the stone on which we were sitting, as if he was gently trying to scrub out some part of these memories.

Then the War came, and, even though the RAF's discipline,

and the regularity, were the same things that he detested in his parents, Walt was quick to volunteer. But he liked the people, or many of them, and he came to admire the big and often graceless military planes. From the kind of flying he'd done, often tricks and aerobatics, Walt was used to risk; he opted for bombers rather than fighters because, like anyone who's in a fundamentally dangerous profession, he looked for ways in which he thought, wrongly as it turned out, the risk could be minimised. And up in the skies and down on the ground, he sailed through his War. He dropped his bombs, and he wasn't touched by the world below him. Part of him knew that he was being even more heartless than the machines he was flying, but the rest of him knew that if he was to survive it was necessary to fly through cold, clear, and untroubled skies of his own making.

The faint sound of the band in the barn had long faded, and I could see the sweep and movement of Walt's hand more clearly now, and the clouds of our breath and his cigarette smoke hanging like the shapes of the statues around us. I had little difficulty in picturing Walt as he described the kind of pilot he'd once been; the kind who imagined, despite all the evidence, that nothing would ever happen to them. Not that Walt believed in luck back then—he said he only went along with the rituals so as not to unsettle his crew—but at a deeper and unadmitted level, and just like all the rest of us, luck had become fundamental to him.

In the big raids that were then starting, which were the revenge for the raids that the Germans had launched against us, so many bombers poured across their cities that they had to go over in layers. Some boffin must have worked out that the chance of a bomb landing on a plane flying beneath was small enough to be worth taking. But in a mass raid over Frankfurt, flying through dense darkness, there was a sudden jolt and a blaze of light, and Walt's top gunner reported that a falling incendiary had struck their starboard wing. Expecting a fuel line to catch at any moment, or for a nightfighter to home in on them now that they were shining like a beacon, they dropped their load and turned along the home flightpath. But the nightfighters didn't come, and the wind blasting across the airframe stopped the incendiary from fully igniting. Hours went by, and they crossed the coast of France into the Channel just as the night was paling. The whole crew were starting to believe that their luck would hold, and were silently wondering how to milk the most drama out of the incident in the bar that evening, when the whole plane was suddenly ripped apart as the wing, its spar damaged by the heat of that half-burning incendiary, tore off into the slipstream. In a fraction of a moment, the bomber became a lump of tumbling, flaming metal.

There was nothing then but the wild push of falling, and the sea, the sky, the sea flashing past them and the wind screaming as the bomber turned end over end and they tried to struggle from their harnesses and climb out through the doorways or the gaping hole that the lost wing had made. Walt said it was like being wedged in a nightmare fairground ride, and that all he could think of was having heard somewhere that the sea was hard as concrete when you hit it. That, and not wanting to die; that, and needing to be lucky. In a moment of weightlessness, globules of blood floated around him, and he saw his copilot with a spear of metal sticking right through him. There was no way Walt could help. He clambered up the huge height of the falling plane against a force that suddenly twisted and threw him down toward the opening. But he was wedged into it, stuck amid twisted piping and scarcely able to breathe as the tumbling forces gripped him. It was then that the thought came to him—the same thought that must have crossed the minds of thousands of airmen in moments such as these—that he would give anything, *anything* to get out. Anything to stay lucky. . . .

The darkness had grown thin and gauzy. Looking down now, I could see that Walt was throwing two white dice, scooping them up and throwing them again.

"So I was lucky," he said. "I got the parachute open before I hit the sea and my lifejacket went up and I wasn't killed by the flaming wreckage falling about me. But I still thought it was probably a cruel joke, to get this far and freeze to death in the filthy English Channel. Then I heard the sound of an engine over the waves, and I let off my flare. In twenty minutes, this MTB found me. One of ours, too. Of all the crew, I was the only one they found alive. The rest were just bodies. . . ."

I could see the outlines of the trees now through a dawn mist, and of the statues around us, which looked themselves like casualties wrapped in foggy strips of bandage. And I could see the numbers on the two dice that Walt was throwing.

A chill went through me, far deeper than this dawn cold. They went six, six, six. . . .

Walt made that sound again. More of a cough than a chuckle. "So that's how it is. I walk over puddles. I fly through tour after tour. I'm the living embodiment of lucky."

"Can't you throw some other number?"

He shook his head and threw again. Six and six. "It's not a trick. Not the kind of trick you might think it is anyway." Six and six, again. The sound of those rolling bones. The sound of my teeth chattering. "You can try if you like."

"You forget who I am, Walt. I don't need to try. I believe. . . ." Walt pocketed his dice and stood up and looked about him. With that gaze of his. Smiling but unsmiling. It was getting clearer now. The shoulders of my coat were clammy damp when I touched them. My hands were white and my fingertips were blue with the cold. And this place of statues, I finally realised, wasn't actually the garden of the house at all, but a churchyard. Our bench had been a tombstone. We were surrounded by angels.

"Come on. . . ." Walt held out his hand to help me up. I took it.

I expected him to head back to his battered MG, but instead he wandered amid the tombstones, hands in his pockets and half-whistling, inspecting the dates and the names, most of which belonged to the family which had lived in that big house beyond the treetops. Close beside us, there was a stone chapel, and Walt pushed at the door until something crumbled and gave, and beckoned me in.

Everything about the graveyard and this chapel was quiet and empty. That's the way it is in a war. There are either places with no people at all, or other places with far too many. The chapel roof was holed and there were pigeon droppings and feathers over the pews, but it still clung to its dignity. And it didn't seem a sad place to me even though it was decorated with other memorials, because there's a sadness about war that extinguishes the everyday sadnesses of people living and dying. Even the poor, brass woman surrounded by swaddled figures, whom Walt explained represented her lost babies, still had a sense of something strong and right about her face. At least she knew she'd given life a chance.

"What I don't understand," I said, crouching beside Walt as he fed odd bits of wood into an old iron stove in a corner, "is *why*. . . ?"

Walt struck a match and tossed it into the cobwebbed grate. The flames started licking and cracking. "It's the same with cards. It's the same with everything."

"Can't you. . . ?"

"Can't I *what*?" He looked straight at me, and I felt again a deeper chill even as the stove's faint heat touched me. I've never seen irises so blue, or pupils so dark, as his. Like a bomber's night. Like the summer sky. I had to look away.

He stood up and fumbled in his pockets for another cigarette. As he lit it, I noticed that once again his hands were shaking. "After the War, Walt, you could make a fortune. . . ."

He made that sound again, almost a cough; a sound that made me wish I could hear his proper laugh again. And he began to pace and to speak quickly, his footsteps snapping and echoing as the fire smoked and crackled and the pain of its warmth began to seep into me.

"What should I do? Go to a casino—me, the highest roller of them all? How long do you think *that* would last. . . ?"

Walt said then that you were never given anything for nothing. Not in life, not in war, not even in fairy tales. Before that night over Frankfurt, he'd sailed through everything. Up in those bomber's skies, you never heard the screams or the sound of falling masonry.

He slowed then, and crouched down again beside me, his whole body shivering as he gazed into the stove's tiny blaze. "I see it *all* now," he said, and the smile which never met his eyes was gone even from his lips. "Every bullet. Every bomb. Even in my dreams, it doesn't leave me. . . ."

"It won't last forever, Walt—"

His hand grabbed mine, hard and sharp, and the look in his eyes made me even more afraid. When he spoke, the words were barely a whisper, and his voice was like the voice of poor dead Pilot Officer Charlie Dyson as he pressed himself to me on that distant summer night under the oak tree.

When Walt said he saw it all, he truly meant he saw *everything*. It came to him in flashes and stabs—nightmare visions, I supposed, like those of the dead airmen that had sometimes troubled me. He saw the blood, heard the screams, and felt the terrible chaos of falling masonry. He'd been tormented for weeks, he muttered, by the screams of a woman as she was slowly choked by a ruptured sewer pipe flooding her forgotten basement. And it wasn't just Walt's own bombs, his own deeds, but flashes, terrible flashes that he still scarcely dared believe, of the war as a whole, what was happening now, and what would happen in the future. He muttered names I'd never heard. Belsen. Dachau. Hiro and Naga-something. And he told me that he'd tried walking into the sea to get rid of the terrors he was carrying, but that the tide wouldn't take him. He told me that he'd thought of driving his MG at a brick wall, only he didn't trust his luck—or trusted it too much—to be sure that any accident or deed would kill him. And yes, many of the stories of the things he'd done were true, but then the RAF would tolerate much from its best, its luckiest, pilots. For, at the end of the day, Walt still *was* a pilot—the sky still drew him, just as it always had. And he wanted the war to end like all the rest of us because he knew—far more than I could have then realised—about the evils we were fighting. So he still climbed into his bomber and ascended into those dark skies. . . .

Slowly, then, Walt let go of me. And he pushed back his hair, and ran his hand over his lined face, and then began stooping about collecting more bits of old wood and sticks for the fire. After a long time staring into the stove and with some of the cold finally gone from me, I stood up and walked amid the pews, touching the splintery dust and studying the bits of brass and marble from times long ago when people hadn't thought it odd to put a winged skull beside a puffy-cheeked cherub. . . .

Walt was walking up the church now. As I turned to him, I saw him make that effort that he always made, the dance of being the famous Walt Williams, of being human. From a figure made out of winter light and the fire's dull wood smoke, he gave a shiver and became a good-looking man again, still thinly graceful if no longer quite young, and with that smile and those eyes which were like ice and summer. He turned then, and put out his arms, and did a little Fred Astaire dance on the loose stones, his feet tap-tapping in echoes up to the angles and the cherubs and the skulls. I had to smile. And I went up to him and we met and hugged almost as couples do in films. But we were clumsy as kids as we kissed each other. It had been a long, long time for us both.

We went to the stove to stop ourselves shivering. Walt took off his jacket, and he spread it there before the glow, and there was never any doubt as we looked at each other. That we would go— stupid phrase—all the way.

So that was it. Me and Walt. And in a chapel—a *church*—of all places. And afterward, restless as he still was, still tormented, he pulled his things back on and smoked and wandered about. There was a kind of wooden balcony, a thing called a choir, at the back of the chapel. As I sat huddled by the stove, Walt climbed the steps that led up to it, and bits of dust and splinter fell as he looked down at me and gave a half-smiling wave. I could see that the whole structure was shot through with rot and woodworm, ridiculously unsafe. Then, of all things, he started to do that little Fred Astaire dance of his again, tip-tapping over the boards.

I was sure, as I stared up at Walt from the dying stove, that he danced over empty spaces where the floor had fallen though entirely.

*  *  *

Walt was due back at base that morning, and so was I; we all were. There had already been talk on the wire that tonight, hangover or no hangover, Christmas or no Christmas, there would be a big raid, one of the biggest. Leaving the chapel and walking back under the haggard trees toward the littered and empty barn which stank of piss and fag ends, we kept mostly silent. And Walt had to lever open the bonnet of his MG and fiddle with the engine before he could persuade it to turn over. He drove slowly, carefully, back along the flat roads between the ditches to the airfield where the Lancasters sat like dragonflies on the horizon. No one saw us as we came in through the gates.

Walt touched my cheek and gave that smile of his and I watched him go until he turned from sight between the Nissan huts and annexes, and then hurried off to get dressed and changed for my work. But for the smudge of oil left by his fingers, I could tell myself that none of it had happened, and get on with banging my typewriter keys, ordering mustard by the tub and jam by the barrel and currants by the sackload, as the ordnance trucks trundled their deadly trains of long steel canisters across the concrete and the groundcrews hauled fuel bousers and the aircrews watched the maps being unrolled and the pointers pointed at the name of a town in Europe that would mean death for some of them.

There was never long to wait for winter darkness, and the clouds were dense that day. The airfield seemed like the only place of brightness by the time the runway lanterns were lit and the aircrews, distant figures already, threw their last dart and played their last hand and put on their odd socks and whistled or didn't whistle and touched their charms and kissed their scented letters and pressed their fingers to the concrete and walked out to their waiting Lancasters. Standing away from where everyone else had gathered, I watched the impenetrable rituals and tried without success to figure out which dim silhouette was Walt as they clustered around their Lancasters. And I listened as the huge Merlin engines, one by one, then wave on wave on wave, began to fire up. You felt sorry, then, for the Germans. Just as the sound became unbearable, a green flare flickered and sparkled over the base. At this signal, the pitch of the engines changed as bombers lumbered up to face the wind and slowly, agonisingly, pregnant with explosives and petrol, they struggled up the runways to take flight.

That night, it was dark already. All we could do was listen—and wait—as the sound of the last Lancaster faded into that black bomber's sky without incident.

\*    \*    \*

The way things turned out—thanks to a secret war of homing beams and radar—it was a good, successful raid. But Walt Williams didn't come back from it, even though his Lancaster did, and the story of what had happened was slow to emerge, opposed as it was by most people's disbelief that anything could possibly have happened to him.

I made the cold journey across the airfield late that next afternoon to look at his Lancaster. The wind had picked up by then, was tearing at the clouds, and there was a stand-down after all the day's and the night before's activity. No one was about, and the machine had been drained of what remained of its ammunition, oil, and fuel, and parked in a distant corner with all the other scrap and wreckage.

It was always a surprise to be up close to one of these monsters, either whole or damaged; to feel just how big they were—and how fragile. I walked beneath the shadow of its wings as they sighed and creaked in the salt-tinged wind from across the Fens, and climbed as I had never climbed before up the crew's ladder, and squeezed through bulkheads and between wires and pipes toward the grey light of the main cabin amid the sickly oil-and-rubber reek.

The rest of the aircrew had reported a jolt and a huge inrush of air as they took the homeward flightpath, but what I saw up there, on that late and windy afternoon, told its own story. Most of the pilot's bubble and the side of the fuselage beside it had been ripped out—struck by a flying piece of debris from another plane, or a flak shell that refused to explode. Walt had been torn out, too, in the sudden blast, launched into the skies so instantly that no one else had really seen exactly what had happened. They'd all hoped, as the copilot had nursed the plane back home through the darkness, that Walt might still have survived, and, Walt being Walt, might even make it back through France instead of ending up as a German prisoner. But the morning had revealed that Walt, either intentionally or through some freak of the way the wind had hit him, had undone all the straps from his seat and had fallen without his parachute. Even now, it was still there, unclaimed, nestled in its well. I was able to bend down and touch it as the wind whistled through that ruined aircraft, and feel the hard inner burden of all those reams of silk that might have borne him.

Then, I believed.

I was transferred to another base in the spring when my section was reorganised in one of the strange bureaucratic spasms that you get in the military. They'd had their own chop girl there who'd committed suicide by hanging herself a few months before, and they mostly ignored the rumours that came with me. It was as if that poor girl's sacrifice had removed the burden from me. Her sacrifice —and that of Walt Williams.

Still, I was changed by what happened. There were other men with whom I had dates and longer-term romances, and there were other occasions when I went all instead of just part of the way. But Walt's ghost was always with me. That look of his. Those eyes. That lined, handsome face. I always found it hard to settle on someone else, to really believe that they might truly want to love me. And by the time the War had finally ended I was older, and, with my mother's arthritis and my father's stroke, I soon ended up having to cope with the demands of the tea room almost single-handed. Time's a funny thing. One moment you're eighteen, lucky, lucky, lucky, and enlisting and leaving Manchester forever. The next you're back there, your bones ache every morning, your face is red and puffy from the smoke and the heat of cooking and the people over the serving counter are calling you Mrs instead of Miss even though they probably know you aren't—and never will get—married. Still, I made a success of the business, even if it ruined my back, seared my hands, veined and purpled my face. Kept it going until ten years ago, I did, and the advent down the street of a McDonald's. Now, my life's my own, at least in the sense that it isn't anybody else's. And I keep active and make my way up the hill every week to collect my pension, although the climb seems to be getting steeper.

The dreams of the War still come, though, and thoughts about Walt Williams—in fact, they're brighter than this present dull and dusty day. I sometimes think, for instance, that if everyone saw what Walt saw, if everyone knew what was truly happening in wars and suffered something like his visions, the world would become more a peaceable place, and people would start to behave decently toward each other. But we have the telly now, don't we? We can all see starving children and bits of bodies in the street. So perhaps you need to be someone special to begin with, to have special gifts for the tasks you're given, and be in a strange and special time when you're performing them. You have to be as lucky and unlucky as Walt Williams was.

And I can tell myself now, as I dared not quite tell myself then, that Walt's life had become unbearable to him. Even though I treasure him for being the Walt who loved me for those few, short hours, I know that he sought me out because of what I was.

Chop girl.

Death flower.

Witch.

And I sometimes wonder what it was that hit Walt's Lancaster. Whether it really was some skyborne scrap of metal, or whether luck itself hadn't finally become a cold wall, the iron hand of that dark bomber's deity. And, in my darkest and brightest moments, when I can no longer tell if I'm feeling sad or desperately happy, I think of him walking across that foul puddle in the starlight as he came out of the NAFFI, and as I watched him in an old chapel after we'd made love, dancing across the choir above me on nothing but dust and sunlight. And I wonder if someone as lucky as Walt Williams could ever touch the ground without a parachute to save him, and if he isn't still out there in the skies that he loved. Still falling.

# The Noonday Pool

PEG COULD HEAR A TRAIN COMING. THE NIGHT express.

She pushed hair from her eyes and sank down on her knees to the earth. She was in the place between the reeds and the nettles, where steel tracks and the wandering river were drawn together by the hills. She could hear the dark beat emerging from the shimmering night, the stuttering engine breath. She waited. There were stars on the river, starlight on the rails.

The train was fast. The sound became a wall, blocking the hills. A long scarf of smoke, diamonded with sparks, trailed the sky. Carriage lights pearled the river. Peg reached down, pushing her fingers through a wet thatch of grass, curling them back around the mud.

The tracks wheezed and creaked. The train was upon her. Lights and wheels blasted by with the city reek of oil and coal. She fixed her moment, crouching on the trembling soil. She balled the mud tight until it began to worm through her fist. She held what was left and hitched back her arm. Biting her lip, she hurled it at the streaming carriage lights.

These were painful moments for Sir Edward. Just hours before, he'd been basking in waves of applause. Who, after all, would dare to criticise his own interpretation of his symphonies?—even if he had known in his heart that the orchestra had played the over-familiar work by rote, and that the second French horn had been disgracefully off-key in those vital, yearning opening bars of the slow movement.

Afterward, there had been hands to shake, and then the Trustees of the orchestra and some other worthies had taken him to Armando's, his favourite London restaurant where the maitre d' of twenty years standing knew all his foibles. Apart from the pre-dictably excellent food, dinner had been a bore. The worthies had laughed dutifully at his jokes and nodded seriously at his creakingly ancient stories of meeting Brahms and Joachim, even though he was sure that they must have heard them almost as many times as he had himself.

He left in time to catch the late express back to the Midlands. Even before the recent trouble with his lower back, which Doctor Walters in Harley Street still insisted was probably nothing more than sciatica, the great man had come to dislike sleeping away from home. And the guard—whom he'd known for almost as long as Armando's maitre d'—had kept a first-class compartment locked specifically for his use. The great man had sunk back into the plush seats, relishing the absence of company and the gentle pull of the train as it drew into darkness from the lighted cavern of the station.

But after an hour or so, his bladder, filled with the remains of several glasses of wine—and, he now remembered, at least three helpings of Armando's excellent coffee—began to feel like a dis-tended balloon. And the guard, ever conscious of the great man's desire for solitude, had thoughtfully locked the linking compart-ment doors, sealing him off from the toilets at both ends. Beyond pulling the communication cord, there was no way he could even talk with anyone else on the train.

So Sir Edward shifted in his seat and clenched his fists, the train rumbled through the night and the sensation in his bladder became a fiery ball of need. And his discomfort was worsened by the thought that it was *he*, he who had lunched at Balmoral and whose name had been mentioned in the same breath as the Ger-manic greats, should be dragged down to the level of an anxious, wriggling schoolchild. He checked his half hunter fob watch, heavy on the gold chain that Richter had given him: only twenty more minutes of this agony to go. But the thought brought little comfort. Nothing brought any comfort. He drummed his fingers on the cold glass. Faintly, beyond the spinning rails, he could see the grey gleam of the river in the carriage lights, that river whose moods and seasons he had portrayed in numerous songs, two quartets, and his one great tone poem. The river . . . the water . . . the . . . *no* . . . something lifeless and grey, tumbling end over ragged end out of the darkness toward him. In fear, he jerked his eyes away. A moment later, it struck the glass.

Brown tentacles crawled back and down. Only mud, and yet still the shock was almost too much. His bladder nearly gave way, and for a moment the pleasure of doing so almost overbalanced the terrible shame. But he held himself in, and crossed his legs tight as the mud spread into a lopsided star across the glass.

The minutes clawed by. The train began to slow: just for him, an unscheduled stop at the local station, for the great man alone. He hitched himself upright as the train halted, and moved with slow, painful steps toward the carriage door. The guard, who had run along the side of the train, opened the door for him and stepped to one side with an almost military salute. The great man eased himself down to the platform. The station, he saw, was closed. The first class waiting room was locked, and with it the toilets. As was (he was in no mood to be fussy) the second class waiting room: the last scheduled train would have departed several hours before. In the warm lights of the carriages, faces were pressed to the glass, straining for a glimpse. They would see him walking at an awkward shuffle, bent half double, and would remark how much older the great man had suddenly become, how the recent photographs in the newspapers couldn't be quite so recent after all.

Sir Edward's chauffeur was waiting at the far end of the platform. Home, he told himself, as the train pulled off through billows of steam, wasn't far off along these deep country lanes he knew so well. Somehow, clenching every muscle in his body, he climbed down the steps from the station and into the Bentley's leather interior. The pain was no longer localised in his bladder, but drove itching needles through his entire body, and burned like a brand over the ache in his lower back.

The Bentley started up. Headlights swung across hedgerows and trees before centring on the narrowed, rutted road. The chauffeur, with whom Sir Edward normally enjoyed a good repartee, slid back the communicating glass to ask how the concert had gone, but found his employer to be terse and uncommunicative. Used to these varying moods, the chauffeur dove on in silence. The great man, however, was swimming through agony. Unlike the train, the

Bentley rumbled unpredictably along the uneven roads, the soft swings bouncing this way and that.

About a mile from home, he knew he could last no longer. He growled instructions to stop through clenched teeth and managed to mutter something about walking the rest of the way as he levered his shrieking body out of the car into the night air. Shifting his feet from one foot to the other, clenching and unclenching his fists, he watched the Bentley pull slowly away before staggering like a drunk toward the dark hedgerow. The whole night seemed to be singing and swaying with his need.

The final actions were delicate. But somehow he managed without spillage or mishap . . . and gave way to blissful relief. Sparks fluttered before his eyes. A huge and airy rush of well being invaded his body.

And then, when it was far too late to stop, he heard someone approaching on light, unhurried feet.

Peg could feel that this night lay at the heart of summer. On all sides, almost forever, there was nothing but endless, blue avenues of leaf-shimmered sky, cuckoo cries and dove coos far into the green twilight; a circlet of warm days and nights like the stars that encircled the heavens.

The woodland curved and shimmered around her in the light of a rising, fattening moon. The air was palpable, dense. Scented moss and drooping white lanterns of nightshade made a pathway. And now, there were braids of dry undergrowth, and the smell of human spore and litter. She saw the watery glint of broken glass, and the flattened patch of grass beneath the boughs of the old white willow where she had watched a boy and a girl tumble and laugh. Bracken crackled beneath her feet. She could have moved silently if she wished, but she liked the snap and echo of her footsteps as she moved through the bowing, summer-heavy dark. . . .

Then there was another sound. She cocked her head, and smiled. The sound was one she recognised easily, although it differed slightly from the one she made herself. She picked her way around a dry snaggle of holly, toward the sound, and the shimmer of the roadway.

Sir Edward stood there stupidly, unable to stop—disguise, even— what he was doing. The nettles and brambles hissed and clattered in the dribbles of a low parabola, as (his bladder no longer furnishing the torrents of youth) he waited for nature to take its protracted course. He was glad at least that the darkness shrouded him with some little modesty; especially when the few details he could make out of the figure suggested that it was young and female. But for many long seconds, the sensation of release was too sharply bright for him to devote any real attention to his audience. It was only as the flow finally thinned that the proportions of the incident began to play alarming discords in his mind. What if she were one of the ghastly daughters of the local gentry whose abilities on the piano he was occasionally forced to admire? What if—worse still— she were just a maid at one of their houses. Girls of good breeding (unless, dear God, they went straight to the *Police*) could generally be expected to remain silent about incidents such as this, but the giggly females belowstairs . . . With their involvement, word would quickly spread across the entire neighbourhood.

"I, er, don't suppose you know who I am?" he asked hopefully, buttoning himself up.

To his pleasant surprise, the dim figure shook her head. Then spoiled the effect by saying, "But I've seen you about."

Still bathing, despite his embarrassment, in the absurdly rosy glow (how crisply wonderful the trees looked against the stars; the shimmer of the road like grey velvet!), Sir Edward straightened his shoulders and set off at what he hoped was a brisk and purposeful pace. The pace of one whom, above all, wished no other company than his own.

In a moment, he was past the girl. The dusky, open road beckoned. In another moment, she had fallen into step beside him.

"I know where you live," she said. "That big house beyond the greenwood with the copper beeches. When I sit on the hill above near the place where the fox brings her cubs in spring, I can see right into a room where you sit and stare at those blank pieces of paper. . . ."

So much for the anonymity. The girl was obviously ill-educated, but she knew more than enough about him to spread the word about tonight. Sir Edward's left hand went up to pull at the corner of his large moustache—a nervous habit he'd never quite been able to conquer. He forced it down to his side again and into a marching swing as he concentrated on setting a brisk, military pace. Pom pom, diddily-pom, and trying not to wince. Now that his bladder was empty, that confounded pain in his back was worse than ever.

"And where," he asked, "do you live?"

"Oh, I don't live anywhere."

He glanced at her. He doubted if she meant it literally, but it was obvious that she was some kind of waif or stray. In vague star-light through the overreaching trees, what little he could make out of her suggested greasily stringy hair, a face patched with grime, ragged clothes of uncertain grey. Someone who looked to be in need of a wash. No, he corrected himself as he caught a salty whiff of her skin, someone who *was* in need of a wash.

"What's your name?"

"Peg."

"Is it your custom to wander alone this late at night?"

"I don't know anything about custom."

"Where do you, ah, sleep?"

"Last night, it was under the big thorn bush near the river. Across the steel rails. I don't like sleeping too close to the Noonday Pool in case . . ." She gave a noisy shudder.

He nodded. Peg was obviously homeless and mad. That, at least, was a relief. No one would ever believe her story of seeing him relieving himself against a bush, even if she attempted to tell it.

They walked on in silence. Peg kept easily in step beside him, moving with a lightness that contrasted with the heavy rasp of his brogues. They seemed to be heading in the same direction, which —now that they had passed the last darkened farmhouse some way back along the road—the great man realised led only to his own dwelling.

They crested a hill, and the parlour lights glowed—a single ember in the deep bowl of the valley below. Mrs France his house-keeper would still be up, knitting and dozing, waiting for his return so she could lock up the house. Mrs France was a great one for waifs and strays. Cats and dogs, even squirrels—she was always taking them in. . . .

Waifs and strays. Sir Edward gave one of his notoriously rare smiles, secure in the knowledge that it wouldn't be seen in the darkness. He turned to Peg.

"If you have nowhere to sleep," he said, "I'm sure my house-keeper could find somewhere for you. Provided," he raised a stern finger, "that your honesty and propriety are beyond reproach."

"What's propriety?" Peg asked.

He chuckled. Together, they headed on toward the glowing beacon of the house.

Next morning, as he had done all his life, Sir Edward awoke early. He lay still for a moment, gazing at the play of dawn light on his curtains, listening to the liquid song of a blackbird in the garden. It was the same blackbird that he heard on every fair morning, and it sang another version of its usual song—although, as always, the exact particulars of the tune were slightly different. Those four ascending notes that lay somewhere close to A-B-C-A and followed by a scattering trill were still there, but the creature was ornamenting it now with a kind of backward coda—still A-B-C-A, yet almost in the minor. Of course, the sound was nothing more than a dumb animal proclaiming its territory, and as artless as a child in a garden piping on a whistle. But it was clear, pure, filled with variety, invention. Life.

He swung his legs over the side of his bed, and sat rubbing his lower back. Then, as the pain lessened to a dull murmur and he slid his bare feet into his slippers, the events of the previous evening returned to him. The girl Peg would be somewhere in the house at this very moment—doubtless still asleep. At this moment, the whole house was asleep. Even the undermaids didn't start work on the fires until well past five. The great man dressed and performed his ablutions, relishing as he always did the chill of the water on his hands and face, the pull of the razor, the coolness of a clean, white vest, the ticking silence of the house that surrounded him. He could, of course, have arranged things so that there was bustle and warmth, banging of grates and the smell of breakfast even at this early hour—he was, after all, the master—but, a habitual early riser, he had always enjoyed the sensation of being the first to be up and about.

He set out along the corridor and down the wide, carpeted stairs toward the kitchen, where his dog Mina leapt up from the rug to greet him. He scratched the spaniel's ears and, knowing that he was unobserved, briefly kissed her wet nose. The fire in the range was low, but still warm, and the kettle was filled and ready. Humming A-B-C-A ascending, he placed it on the hob, cut himself a thick slice of bread and spread it with dripping, then sat down before the glow on a three-legged stool. He treasured these early moments in the kitchen, surrounded by the dull gleam of copper and the scents of soot, laundry starch, and yesterday's cooking as, watched by Mina's adoring eyes, he listened for the kettle's soft rattle as it prepared to steam and whistle. It reminded him of his parent's little house in Worcester—long since bulldozed for some ghastly development—and of the long years of his marriage when, once the watched kettle had finally boiled, he would warm and fill the teapot, place it on a tray with the daisy-yellow cup and saucer, and carry it upstairs through the dim and peaceful house. Not, he sometimes thought, that Caroline had always welcomed being woken, but the early mornings were indeed beautiful, and it had become part of the ritual of their life together.

The kettle started to boil. Little gobbets of water jumped from the spout, leaping about on the hob like dervishes before disappearing in wafts of grey. Then the whistle screeched, and the great man snatched a dishcloth to hold the braided iron handle, warmed the pot, and spooned in the tea. Just enough for himself now, of course. It had been that way for many years.

With Mina trotting in his wake, Sir Edward walked along the tiled hall, up the narrow sidestairs and through the door that led to the upper study. Placing the teacup on his desk, he pulled the tassels that opened the velvet curtains, and long beams of early summer sunlight flooded in.

There, outside. The moist, shadowed garden, the soft woodland and hills beyond still half-unreal with dawn. In a sense, it was his life's work—all that he had ever sought to portray. The great man turned back toward the study, whose walls were covered with his framed awards, decorations, honours: those polished squares of glass which, such was the angle of the dawn sun, were now filled only with the reflected images of blue dawn and mullioned windows.

He sat down at his desk. It was already nearing five o'clock, and, as always, it was time for him to commence work. The routine went back fifty years to when he'd first been married and the money had been damnably short. In those days, he'd have maybe an hour to spare on composition before putting on his coat and setting out on a day of teaching a series of rich, dumb, and uninterested children the rudiments of harmony. His last appointments, where he was expected to enlighten the leisure of tone-deaf lawyers and malodorous bank managers, often went on until nine or ten at night. He'd come back home to Caroline with the muscles on his face tense from smiling, his hands trembling, his ears still ringing with the screech of badly made music—but glad at least that the precious time in the early morning had been his own. Now, for many years, the great man had until lunchtime—all day if he wished—to entice the muse. But he was a morning worker. Even in the darkest days of winter, there was still that promise in the air.

Sir Edward unlocked and opened a drawer at the side of the desk, and lifted out one of the dozen small card-covered notebooks that lay there. On the front there was a year and a date, written in his own hand. The book was—what?—fifty years old now. He fanned the yellowed pages, breathing the dusty aroma. His hand-writing had been neater then, clearer. Like everything else—like his ability to urinate—it had become crabbed and constricted over the years. But there; *that* was what he was looking for. He pressed the page flat, and reached for a fresh, white sheet of staved paper from the pile he kept ready on the corner of his desk.

There, in the notebook, was the motif he'd been after. He could even remember writing it. It had been soon after the first decent performance of one of his oratorios at the cathedral festival, when the reviews had been ecstatic, and his confidence was high. He'd been in love, too, and the money was starting to come. A wet morning in a steamy Worcester coffee house with the pretty, yellow-haired waitress fluttering around him and a view through the window of the bright, swollen river. It had come to him just like that, in the moment between one sip of coffee and the next. Flashing by too quickly to be truly heard, yet there, undoubtedly there, ready to be snatched into this world from whatever place it had come, to be captured in this notebook before the rents of time closed around it again. He looked at it now. That long, loping melody. Rising and falling, meandering, yet always sure. True to itself. Like the brown river he had seen through the condensation of that coffee house window. Flowing onward, never lost. Dah, dah, dee . . .

He unscrewed the top of his fountain pen. Yes, it was truly as good and vivid as he remembered. Exactly right for the developmental theme in the second movement of his long-awaited third symphony. Dah, dah, dee . . . start with the violoncellos to give it some depth. Keep it simple, yet overlay triads from the second strings. But his pen still hovered over the paper. He snapped at himself to get on with it, and quickly drew the clef, and sketched down abbreviations for the main instruments. There, the page was ready now. Nothing fancy, no need for detail. The orchestra. Poised. Waiting. Dah, dah, dee . . .

Sir Edward looked up for a moment. Again, he could hear the song of the blackbird in the garden. A-B-C-A. That simple rising quadruplet, robust yet innocent, followed by a trill. And the rising sun was stretching shadows across the lawn, kindling a white fire in the beads of dew that had formed in the heavy throats of the flowers. And the blackbird was singing. Laughing.

He shook his head, trying to regain concentration. But somehow, he knew that the theme from the notebook wasn't yet right. He was sure the tune was a good one—after all, hadn't the pages of this particular notebook furnished the material he'd used for the slow movement of his cello concerto, the Judas theme for his last (but unfinished) great oratorio?—yet he wasn't sure that it would blend with the other theme that he was intending to employ in the second movement. For a start, the two tunes came from different notebooks, different years. Not that that should matter. But it did. He'd grown increasingly superstitious about these notebooks.

Dah dee dee . . . but, yes, the problem of combining the themes lay in that lift toward the tonic. It came too early in the melody, drew the listener one way, then pulled him another. It would surely be a simple task to put that right. To re-draw the phrase. . . .

Finally, his lips pursed, the great man put pen to paper. Dah, dee, *dee* . . .

Peg knew from the sound of bird song in the trees, coming in through the open window, that she was up near the roof of the house. It was already long past dawn—already late morning by her standards—and her body felt stiff and odd, encased in all this white linen. And they'd insisted last night that she wash, too. Still, it was nice to be here in this room with the human smells of dust, dead wood, old cobwebs, and some odd kind of lavender, pressed up close to the roof and the sky.

She got up, and wriggled and pulled at the cloth of her nightgown until something gave. Then, stepping out of it, she gazed down at her reflection in the bowl of water on the table by the window. A clean, white face and shoulders, clean red-yellow hair. She bent down until her lips touched those of her reflection, and lapped at the water. Then, wiping her nose and mouth on the back of her hand, she opened the bedroom door, and skipped down the crooked stairs.

And there was Mrs France again in the hall below. All red face and bluster under a comical white bonnet, trying to shoo her back up the stairs. *Whatever your game is, Young Lady*, Mrs France hissed, *I can tell you're not so daft as to go around like Eve . . . .*

Of course, Peg knew about clothes—you wore them to look pretty, or keep out the chill—and she even acquiesced when Mrs France summoned a young girl called Maid to help her dress. You're about my size, Maid said, which was true enough, although she looked at Peg as though she'd never seen a pink, whole body before in her entire life. Once she was dressed, Maid took Peg down the hall to a mirror, and she saw a young human woman like those she had often watched climbing out of carriages and cars.

Dressed in blue and white, her legs and her arms entirely hidden. She had to laugh.

The door of the upper study opened, and Mrs France carried in a tray containing Sir Edward's breakfast of bacon, coffee, marmalade, and toast. He wouldn't eat that much of it—he never did—but the fact that he flinched a meal of bread and dripping from the kitchen every morning was a shared but unacknowledged secret between them.

Mrs France remained standing there after she had placed the tray on the desk beside him and removed his teacup. She cleared her throat.

Fighting back the premonition that something odd or bad was about to happen, the great man looked up from the blank staved sheet he'd been staring at.

"What is it Mrs France? Has the post been?"

"Yes. But nothing from Doctor Walters."

He nodded, unsure whether he felt disappointed or relieved. Letters of any kind were a distraction when he was working, but he'd given orders that anything from Harley Street was to be carried straight to him.

"That, ah, young lady you, ah . . ." Mrs France blinked, her face even redder than usual. ". . . brought in with you last night."

"Oh, you mean Peg." So that was all. "And I suppose you want to know what to do with her?"

"Sir, I'm not sure that she's quite right in the head. She seems very—well, *wild's* the word I'd use. I don't think there's any harm in her, but her ways are like a young animal's. She hasn't been brought up at all."

He slowly nodded. A young animal. He had half a mind to ask Mrs France for details but, thinking of the things that young animals did—and sparing her blushes—he decided against it.

"Does she say she has a home?"

Mrs France gave the great man one of her famous looks. Over the many years that she had worked for him, he'd become an expert in the subtle and often alarming intricacies of Mrs France's facial language. This particular look, he interpreted to mean; *You're the one who brought the creature here—and you're the one who should be answering any questions.*

"She says not sir," Mrs France said eventually. "She says she lives in the woods, and I'm inclined to believe her, although we've never seen her hereabouts before."

"You've fed her?"

"And washed her. I can tell you that she's causing a fair commotion and delay in the kitchen. And I can't just let her wander around the premises, now can I? We all of us have things to do."

"Alright." The great man steepled his fingers and nodded. "I can see that you—" Mrs France glared "—I mean, *we* have a problem. But I would like to speak to this girl. The trouble of it is . . ." he glanced over Mrs France's shoulder at the ormolu clock above the bookshelves. Quarter to six already. ". . . I can't do so until noon at the earliest. I must stick to my routine."

"Of course."

Then he had an idea. "Why not put her out in the garden until then? She can't do much damage there, now can she? Give her a coat or whatever. Something more to eat. I'll see her there as soon as I've finished work."

"The garden." Mrs France gave him another of her looks. "And I suppose you'll want me to speak to Mister Groves and tell him she'll be wandering at will amongst his plantings?"

"If you would, Mrs France." To avoid another glare, he returned his eyes to the blank paper before him. "If you would."

Mrs France stood there above him for a moment longer. Then, in eloquent silence, she turned and left the room.

Stepping out into the sunlit garden, Peg pulled off the boots and stockings she'd been given, leaving them side by side on the doorstep as she had seen shoes left outside other human dwellings. Beyond the shadows thrown by the house, the wide expanse of stone paving was already dry and warm beneath her bare feet, and the high, redbrick wall that reached toward the greenhouses glowed in patches of fire between the quivering strands of honeysuckle, sweet pea, and climbing ivy.

The air was in chaos with bird song. Up along the path, hidden in the green, heavy boughs of an oak tree, a blackbird was shouting out his territory. Dum dee dee . . . and there, the quicker, lighter song of a thrush. She turned this way and that. Dizzy, marvelling. It truly was another wonderful summer morning.

Skipping from the pavement to the lawn, crouching down, she ran her hands through the wet grass and raised her fingers to her lips, licking the jewels of dew that dangled there. They tasted dark and green and earthy, still tangled up with the star-bound secrets of the night. Even after all the jam and butter that Maid and Mrs France had given her, it made her feel hungry.

*      *      *

More than six hours after he had started work, Sir Edward finally put down his pen. On one side of his desk, the pile of blank staved paper had gone down a little. On the other, the waste bin was full. And between, on the leather-cornered blotter, lay the sheet that he'd just finished working on.

He gazed at the changed melody. It limped up and down the clefs, shifted direction, tone, three or four times in the space of a few bars. And the original, that long, loping, pristine tune that he'd extracted from his notebook . . . Looking at it now, he was no longer sure. The wrong tune? Perhaps that had always been the problem.

It was all gone now, anyway—another morning was finished, wasted. And, although this room was still cool, outside in the garden even the birds had been silenced by the noonday heat. And his third symphony still awaited. Unstarted. Unsung. He glanced up at the wall where, in the late morning sunlight, the frames no longer mirrored the scene beyond the window. There. The certificate of his knighthood. There. A programme that consisted entirely of his work, in the presence of her late Majesty, the Queen. There. An honourary degree (one of many) from Oxford. There. He was shaking hands for the camera with his one-time friend and admirer Richard Strauss (who was now squandering his gifts on pompous, grubby music for that pompous and grubby new German Chancellor). There. An impressive-looking gold medal from the Royal Philharmonic Society (although for what, he could no longer remember). There. The first review in the *Times* of what they were describing as his first great masterpiece (and now often enough said was his only one) and even then they were puzzling over the enigma, the origin of the theme. There. There. That. He'd have swapped them all for one good, new tune. Another enigma. For a moment like that moment on that long-ago, rainy morning in that Worcester coffee house.

He turned the pages of the notebook. Months and years flew by. Here was something he'd written in Venice, the slow, stately march that formed the basis of his first symphony. He remembered the play of sunlight on ancient water as he sat on his hotel balcony at the Danieli. He remembered the campanile bells that carved the watery golden air. And here, over the page in just two bars of faded ink, he saw Scotch pines on a Scottish hilltop, bowing in the warm breath of a summer wind. And here, the scented candle-darkness of Worcester Cathedral. The tunes and the themes were all hurried,

sketched with not a semiquaver more than necessary, the page balanced by a hand or a knee, yet the music was always captured with
ease and precision. It had all been there, whole years of music simply waiting to be expanded and unravelled. He turned the page
again and saw a dark winter's twilight. The frozen river. And that,
too, had been used. The cello concerto—the last real and decent
thing that he'd finished. Every decent fragment and moment in the
notebook. It had all been used.

He closed the notebook, and looked out of the window. He saw
that the girl Peg was out on the lawn. The foundling. Twirling in a
blue dress. Her red-yellow hair fanning out in the sunlight. Her
face uplifted.


Mrs France, having finished her noontime tour of the house to
check that the maids had performed their duties before His
Grouch finally emerged from his study, took the backstairs on the
way out to see to her foundlings. Emerging into the stable yard, she
paused a moment, struck by the heat that came in waves off the
cobbles, and by a return of her anger at His Grouch's nerve in
bringing that creature Peg to the house.

*She's just like your foundlings Mrs France*, he'd wheedled last
night in the hall as that dog of his barked and growled and the
Peg-creature stood right there beside him, grinning as-you-please
and stinking the place out. As though *that* young lady could in any
way, shape, or form be compared to the poor, motherless hedge-
hogs, broken-winged birds, and injured rabbits she tended in the
hutches beside the walled garden. . . .

Puffing her cheeks, Mrs France strode across the stable yard,
turning swiftly right under the archway that led past the cloches
and the potato store. Well, at least the brazen little hussy was somewhere out in the garden now, where she could do little harm. She
could only hope that His Grouch would see sense by this evening,
and send her smartly off the premises. After all, it wasn't like him to
show much interest in anyone or anything these days—apart, of
course, from that dog—and surely he wasn't so daft as to have his
head turned by the pretty face and figure of some cheap, little village runaway? No, Mrs France decided, that was most unlikely. He
was far too much of a snob for that. But, whatever happened, she
most certainly wasn't prepared to put up with another scene like
that in the kitchen at breakfast. Scooping up bits of butter and jam
with her fingers, and then spitting out fried kidneys like a two-year-
old, complaining that they were *cooked*, would you believe?

As Mrs France walked along the gravel path that ran by the main garden, His Grouch's dog ran up her. She crouched down and briefly rubbed behind the creature's ears, mimicking affection as she usually did because the presence of the dog generally meant that He himself wasn't far behind. But, looking back along the path toward the house, then across the shimmering lawn, she decided that there was no sign of anyone, and pushed the whining, slobbering animal away.

It ran off toward the house with its tail stuck between its legs, and Mrs France straightened herself up. Just as she was about to walk on, she saw two figures beyond the line of copper beeches at the far end of the garden. They wavered like ghosts in the heat, but there was no mistaking His Grouch with his hat and walking stick —and that girl Peg. Walking together. As Mrs France watched, they passed through the picket gate that led into the woods and disappeared from sight. Entirely into shadow.

Sighing, shaking her head, Mrs France headed on along the hot, gravel path. What did it matter what His Grouch got up to? He'd be in a foul enough mood this evening anyway when he read the review of last night's performance in the copy of the *Times* she'd just ironed for him. *Laboured. Confused. Dated.* Not that she knew anything about his music—most of it went on far too long—but she'd always liked that marching tune, and a few bits of what he called his coffee-house music. Some of it, you could almost sing along to.

But this time of the day was her own, and Mrs France resolved to think no more about His Grouch, or things to do with the house. Beyond the yew hedges lay the walled garden, and there, in a sheltered corner beside the thyme and the mint, were the hutches for her foundlings that kind Mister Groves had made for her.

Turning into the walled garden, she knew instantly that something was wrong. The hutch doors hung open, and, along with the mint and the thyme, a familiar, salt-sour smell hung in the warm air—the same aroma that pervaded the kitchen on days when she'd been busy gutting and hanging. As she crouched down over ragged lumps that lay in the loose grass before the hutches, the air was filled with the drone of disturbed flies.

Her foundlings were roughly gutted and skinned. Half eaten. Dead.

Sir Edward closed the latch on the gate, and followed Peg into the dappled woodland.

"You're very famous, aren't you?" she said.

He shrugged and smiled. "Some people might say that." Which was true. Some still did.

"And rich?"

"That too. By many standards."

"How many rooms have you got in that house of yours?"

"I don't know. I doubt if I've even been in all of them."

"If I had a big house," Peg said, "I'd be going into them all the time, just to make sure they were still there."

The great man chuckled, swinging his silver-top cane, looking up through the canopy at the flashing sun. He'd come this way often enough with Mina—who today, quite unaccountably, had run off—but walking with this girl Peg made it all seem a little different, a mite more real. He glanced over at her. Her eyes were startling blue, her lips incredibly red. Yet she wore no powder or paint, employed no artifice. And her long hair was neither blonde nor auburn nor red, but threaded with the russet of the shadows, the blaze of the sun. . . .

The great man pulled at the tip of his moustache, and gazed along the soft, green pathway. No fool, he reminded himself, like an old fool. And this girl Peg was just another well-made face and body, briefly blessed with health and youth. After all, and to his wife Caroline's occasional chagrin, he'd been a connoisseur of such things all his life—an appreciator of beauty. Beauty in music. Beauty in nature. Beauty in a woman. It had always been so; even, as he now recalled, long ago in that steamy, Worcester coffee house as he sat with a newspaper and a cup of coffee. Yes, he'd been watching the pretty, yellow-haired waitress in the moment before the long, soft, lovely melody had passed by. Yes. She'd turned and smiled at him with her eyes through the bustle of the tables, and the tune had been there at that very instant. Had touched him with fingers both warm and chill.

"What are you famous for?" Peg asked.

"Music," he said, stepping over a tree root, rubbing at his back, trying to recall the last time he's actually had to introduce or explain himself to someone in this way. "I compose tunes."

"Can you sing one for me?"

It wasn't quite impossible—he almost wanted to risk using his parched and cracked voice—but the only snippet that lodged in his head at that moment was *Jesu Maria, I am close to death*—a difficult, neglected piece at the best of times and, here in the noonday heart of this greenwood summer, hardly appropriate.

"Perhaps when we get back to the house, I'll play you something on the piano—you do know about the piano?"

"It's a big harp."

Again, he was laughing, nodding. Everything this girl said was
so intrinsically right—yet totally unexpected. A big harp! Perhaps
if he started thinking of the instrument in that way, he might even
be able to compose for the clumsy, clanking thing as his publishers at Booseys had always advised him. But the idea just hung
there before him, out of reach in the shadowed heat. Decades too
late.

The great man looked around him. The path had branched at
some point without his noticing. There was no bird song. The air
was hot, still, but the light shifted and danced on leaf-patterned
ground in whatever breeze ruffled the treetops. Along the avenue
ahead, everything seemed to dissolve and lose substance. It was
like, he decided, looking into the heart of a green fire.

"Does this lead to where you live?" he asked.

"I told you. This wood's where I live."

"In this wood? Isn't it, ah . . . private property? I mean, I know
Lord Shrewsbury—he's a friend, you know—permits me to wander
on his at will. But still, that's rather different from living here, isn't
it?" And why hadn't he ever seen her here before? But that was too
many questions at once. She probably meant woodlands or out-of-
doors in general.

Peg simply shrugged. "I've never seen this Lord you mention."

"No. I suppose not."

"But I'll show you my favourite place."

"I'd like that."

"But it doesn't belong to me," Peg added—unnecessarily.

"Of course."

"It's the Noonday Pool, and it belongs to nobody."

"As you wish," Sir Edward chuckled, twiddled the left tip of his
moustache. "I'll tell Lord Shrewsbury next time I see him."

They walked on. Beneath boughs and branches, the claws of
hawthorn were fluffed in white, and deep green patches of fern
were ornate as ironwork. But, after all his years of wandering, this
particular route was unfamiliar to him. He found the discovery to
be pleasing rather than alarming. It was always the way with woodland—you never quite got to know it the way you did open land.
But this plot was still only a few acres: all they'd have to do was walk
in any direction, and they'd soon come to a fence.

This way. He followed Peg where the ground sloped down, and

the trees made a stairway of sorts. The roots were thick and knarled, overlapping into moss-filled hollows, and the trees themselves, he now saw as he paused to catch his breath where the slope deepened and narrowed into some kind of glen, were very ancient, knobbled and veined with parasitic growths. There were no newcomers like sycamore, walnut, sweet chestnut. Only oak. Bowed with age.

"Come on!"

Peg was some way below him already. Calling, waving to him from out of the green fire. Her white hands, her white face, the shimmering gold of her hair. Levering his stick into the crotch of a tree for balance, feeling another surge of pain in his lower back, the great man pushed on, down.

When he finally caught up with Peg, she was standing on the lip of some kind of pool, although for some time his senses were too fogged for him to fully absorb the scene. He sat down on a convenient rock, and fished for a handkerchief to wipe his brow. Down here in this greenwood bowl the silence was intense, and it was even stiller, hotter. Yes, he must take off his jacket. He gathered his will for the exertion, undid the buttons and pulled the rapidly dampening cloth away from his chest and arms. Ah. Better . . .

"You're not used to this, are you?"

"No. Not for many years. When I was a lad, I'd go for miles. But . . ."

Fringed with foxglove, meadowsweet, bright yellow iris, the massive branches of oaks leaned over the pool in the centre of the clearing. Leaving his coat, his cane, Sir Edward pushed himself up from his rock and waddled across a carpet of moss to stand on the stone lip, and peer in. The pool was as still as the day itself. Not a murmur, not a ripple. The water had an intense clarity. Beyond the reflections of his own face and the outstretched boughs that strained to touch and enclose the sky, he could see right through the surface. Down and down. Where translucent green gave to blue gave to silver-grey, and finally to darkness. There was no sign of a stream or source or spring. Wherever it came from must be somewhere deep, far out of sight.

He sat down again. This time, on the moss. It was soft enough, and not at all damp. In fact, surprisingly comfortable. Peg sat down beside him.

"I'm glad you took me here," he said. "You know, I'd never have guessed there was such a place."

He looked around again, took a breath of the deep summer air. The peppery scent of water elder. Cool, still water. Mint forest darkness. Tansy and bindweed. And something feral, unidentifiable.

"This site could quite possibly repay serious academic investigation," he heard himself saying. "Now the Druids, the Romans, the Celts would all have sought out a place such as this. I must write to Lord Shrewsbury and tell him of the possibilities. Of course, there's Malvern Camp, and the springs that are there, as mentioned in the writings of Julius Caesar. There could well be a link. I'm sure that if a dredging could be arranged there would be a strong likelihood of finding . . ."

Peg was watching him, cross-legged like an Indian, her bare feet tucked under, her sleeves rolled up.

". . . of finding . . ."

The rusty golden fall of her hair. Eyes the colour of the sky in that pool, blue with the shimmer of some far darkness.

". . . ah, discovering . . ."

The vein inside the crook of her arm. The ripe-apple curve of her bare knees.

"Look," she said, reaching close by him. Again, he caught the feral scent as she plucked something from the tangles of undergrowth. He saw it was red in her hand, and that there were other drops of red amid the green, bright as scattered rubies. He saw her put it to her mouth, he saw scarlet juice break on her lips and teeth, and the movement of her throat as she swallowed.

"Wild strawberries?"

She nodded and wiped her lips. A smear of the juice was on her hand as she stretched out again. There were red crescents under her nails.

"Are they sweet?"

"Try."

He held out his hand, but she reached past it, toward his mouth. He felt heavy, warm, and numb. Like the air. He parted his lips, and felt her fingers brush against his moustache, then move on to touch his teeth, his tongue. He took the small fruit, and the taste of it was there in his mouth, and with it was the scent of her fingers, the fur and the salt and the hay and the linen. He closed his mouth and his eyes. The strawberry was tart and sweet. A drop of summer's blood.

"Is it good?"

He nodded, and felt himself blushing heavily; embarrassed by the intimacy of the moment, yet also somehow close to tears. Peg picked and ate another strawberry, then passed one to him. The juice, the scent on her fingers, the silent dell . . .

It was, for all its strangeness, a magical moment, and the great man could already feel part of his mind madly scurrying, searching. Hard at work. Another string serenade, perhaps? *Wild Strawberries? The Dell?* He might even risk dedicating it to this girl, as long as it wasn't made too obvious. Something cryptic that would get the critics wondering. And he could see them already, sitting in Albert Hall, amazed at the hot, young flood of this piece.

Peg lay back, her hair fanning out over the moss. The great man gazed down at her. Where the skirt had fallen away from her right leg, he could see the lovely curve of her bare thigh. He tried to think of it in terms of marble perfection, classical beauty—the kind of thing an artist might express—although he knew that it was more.

"Sometimes, you can see the stars like this at midday," she said. "Up through the trees. But you have to lie still. You have to be silent. . . ."

He nodded. He could feel the weight of the day pressing on his chest and shoulders. Carefully, crooking his elbows, he lay his head down beside Peg on the soft moss and looked up through the ancient branches, trying to see the midday stars. What she'd said was, he thought, just possible. An optical effect created by this shadowed dell. Writers since classical times, his mind, unasked, gambolled ahead to tell him, had recorded a similar effect when the sky was seen on a clear day from the bottom of a mine or well shaft. . . .

Giving up, seeing only branches and midday blue, hearing nothing but the useless babble of facts in his head, and feeling only the dull, burning pain in his back, the great man closed his eyes. And, oh, how he longed to create, to cut through whatever was inside him. Sometimes, for days and even weeks, there would be the illusion of progress. In the drawer below the one where he kept his notebooks, he had sketches and outlines galore. He'd even fully orchestrated one or two passages, although he'd known even at the time he was doing them that he was simply playing at composition, producing something that he could show visitors and extemporise around on the piano.

Not that the music had ever been easy—but it had always been there. Even in these many years that he'd had to rely on the sketches in those notepads, there had been always something beyond the silence on which he could draw. And now, in his late years, in the time when he'd always imagined there'd be some kind of peace and fulfilment, the need to create burned more fiercely than ever. Hot and bright as this noonday sun, an all-consuming fire in his bones. Often, he'd just sit motionless at his desk for hours, tense with fear and anger and envy as he remembered days in the past when the music had poured past him, free and lucid as the flood of his beloved river. And he had taken it, trapped it, his pen had danced over the paper. It had spilled over, sang in his head as he sat waiting for trains, danced with moth wings as he talked with friends and strangers, played through the breeze as he walked with his Caroline, had flowed from the waitress's eyes as he sat with a newspaper in the warm steam of a Worcester coffee house.

His whole life, since an age too young to be clearly remembered, had been governed by this need to create, compose. Everything, every sound, every sight, every emotion, had been perceived through the filter of that desire. Even at his wedding, he'd conquered his nervousness by listening for an off-pitch middle C in the church organ to sound again. And, later, his time with the children had been governed by the disciplines of work. There were always the early risings, the mornings, the work that must be done before noon, and the letters and the books that had to be studied after. Every sensation, every blink and breath and heartbeat, had been absorbed and churned in the cogs of this great musical engine. He'd once thought that God was kind, to provide both the gift to create and the need to do so in roughly equal proportions. But now the engine still churned, and the third symphony waited, and the motion of it racked him, tore at him. And God, if there was a God, was laughing, cackling.

The great man reopened his eyes to the sun and the sky and the bowing, ancient trees and the golden-haired girl that lay beside him, trying to remember the days when the audiences had actually listened before they applauded, when the reviews had been good, and the concert halls had been more than half-full. But, even at the time, there had been a sense of unreality, disbelief—above all, there had been the knowledge that it wouldn't last. What was it about his nature, the great man wondered? Why was it that when he reached something, he always felt as though he was already looking back?

The question hung, unanswered, in the hot noonday air. In the sky beyond the trees, and in the stars that for a flickering moment he thought he saw there. But then he blinked, and the stars became motes in his eyes, and there was no longer silence in the dell, but the patter of Peg's feet, followed by a hissing trickle.

Crouching to relieve herself on the stone lip beside the Noonday

Pool, Peg watched the old man as he awoke from his brief slumber. She liked his big moustache, and his eyes, and his great hook of a nose. He reminded her of some uncreated heraldic animal. But he was sad, she could see that as well, and she guessed that that was part of the reason why she'd been drawn to him, although she still had no idea of exactly why.

There he was now, levering himself up on those rickety bones, looking toward her, seeing what she was doing, looking away. This was the thing about humans that puzzled her more than anything, their constant desire to be somewhere other than where they were. And, even for her, even when she'd flown on the gossamer wings the fireside tales of this old man's forefathers had once allowed her, such a thing was quite impossible. Your body was changeable, disposable, but your spirit, ah!—that could only ever be in one place.

Now, the greenwood was shrinking—dying—and Peg knew that soon it would all be fields, and then, not long after, a green expanse in which humans with sticks would chase a small, white ball. And after that, the green would turn to brown, and things would happen that even her own prescience forbade her to witness. But she regarded the prospect without sadness. The stillness of the Noonday Pool would always be there, inside her, and there were bound to be other creatures that she could shape herself into, other myths to absorb. . . .

Surprised and embarrassed by what he saw, the great man heaved himself up from his bed of moss, and turned away. The pain clawed at his spine. His vision was prickled by odd blotches and patches of light. The boughs of the trees seemed to shimmer and sway with the heat.

"There." He heard Peg's voice, and her bare feet behind him. Stiffly, he turned.

"How long have I been asleep?"

She shrugged. "What does it matter?" Her eyes, shimmering like the greenwood, were filled with darkness and light.

He looked around for his coat, his cane. Pressing past the girl, he noticed the rivulet that curled over the stone lip toward the pool, and the faint yellow cloud that hung in the water. Otherwise, the Noonday Pool was even darker now, clearer. Yet there was something else. . . .

He leaned across to look into the depths. Far below, something grey and lifeless stirred, elongated, tumbled end over ragged end upon itself, prepared to rise. He shuddered and stepped back.

"What do you see?" she asked.

"Nothing. Absolutely nothing."

Peg chuckled and skipped over to him. "You're lying."

There were threads of moss in her hair now. He felt her arm entwine and tighten around his, and heard the soft, vulpine rustle of her breath. He was too tired to resist.

"Lean over again," she said, drawing him forward toward the lip of the Noonday Pool. He tottered. Almost lost balance. "Look into the water. Tell me what you see."

The great man hung there, teetering like a swimmer in the instant before the dive. He saw the mirrored sky, the boughs and branches of the trees. He saw an old, lonely man. Then he felt a wind pass through him and ripple the water, and the images quivered, multiplied, and dissolved.

"What can you see?"

Peg's voice was still beside him, but he was no longer sure whether she was pushing him on or holding him back.

"What do you see?"

The wind was still blowing through him, rippling the Noonday Pool. And the scent of it was familiar—not feral, or even the green darkness of ancient woodland, but dust, dry ink, and cheap paper. The pages of his notebooks, turning.

"What do you see?"

He strained his eyes. The pool was still shimmering, darkening. The eyes of the waitress in that Worcester coffee house? No . . .

"What do you see?"

The question came from the darkness below him.

"What do you see?"

Not some serpent or sea monster. No, not some creature from the depths. It was worse than that. The thing he feared most of all. . . .

"What do you see?"

He shook his head, pushed back and away.

Nothing. He saw nothing.

Recovering her composure in the servant's parlour, watched by Mister Groves's kind eyes as she sipped at her second cup of sweet tea, Mrs France tried once again to explain to him the whirl of feelings that were in her head. On the one hand, she was certain that the girl Peg had something to do with the destruction of her foundlings. Yet on the other, she couldn't imagine that it was anything other than a fox. . . .

"Perhaps you should ring the police," Mister Groves suggested.

Mrs France shook her head. "You know what that daft bunch in the village are like."

"But you say he's with the girl now?"

"The little strumpet. I caught her coming down the stairs this morning, naked as a plucked chicken. And I'm sure she'd have gone straight in to see His Grouch. . . ."

Mrs France shuddered at the recollection, and sipped her tea. But Mister Groves, she saw, was smiling—or, rather, was trying not to—trying to keep that stupid glint out of his eyes. He was just another man, after all. And men were all fools when it came to anything pretty and young.

"Tell you what," he said. "When I finish this cup, I'll go—" He stopped in mid-sentence as one of the service bells above the door began to ring.

"That'll be the front door," Mrs France said without looking. She knew the sound of every service bell by heart. His Grouch might have his music, but *she* knew about noises that really mattered.

"Sally'll get it."

"No," Mrs France said, standing up. "I will."

Even when Lady Caroline had been alive, Mrs France had always made a point of answering the front door so she could keep her finger on the pulse of the house. She passed from the servant's lobby into the main hall, fragrant with the warm scent of beeswax polish and from a fresh display of white lilies. She opened the front door just as the bell rang again, and was presented with the spectacle of the local postman, breathless and hot from the long, hot cycle ride up from the village. He had an envelope in his hand. She snatched it from him, wrinkling her nose at its crumpled state. No, not simply an envelope. A telegram.

"Will you sign for this?"

The postman offered her a pen. Disgustingly warm and slippery, but she took it and signed. *P.P.*, as always, His Grouch.

"This is thirsty work," he continued, "on a—"

"Thank you," Mrs France said, swiftly closing the door.

She walked over to the southwest side window beside the bowl of lilies where the early afternoon sun now poured in. Squinting with a practised eye, she held the telegram up to the light. No need to get the steam to this one. The message was visible, typed in block capitals—and short. It was from that posh quack in Harley Street that His Grouch was seeing. About TEST RESULTS and CONCERN and NEED FOR EARLY APPOINTMENT.

Meditatively, Mrs France smoothed out the crumpled envelope

on the table, then slipped it into her apron pocket. In her experience, they never did tell you straight if it was bad—not even a knighthood made any difference to that. All you ever got were sidelong smiles, requests like this one for early appointments and rubbish about not building up hopes. It had certainly been that way with her Arthur—and even with Her Grouch, for that matter, poor Lady Caroline.

It was all very sad, but then life had to go on. Pausing only to pat at her hair in the mirror, she headed back toward the servant's doorway, where that kind Mister Groves and her unfinished second cup of sweet tea awaited.

When the great man opened his eyes, he was alone. The trees of the dell still reached above him, but they no longer framed Peg's lovely face.

"I dreamed . . ." he croaked, to no one. He stared up at the deepening sky. Then: "What time is it?"

He levered himself up from the mossy ground. The dell was no longer silent. The trees were stirring, and the sun was falling into a cluster of evening clouds. He smelled still water and ancient, dying wood. There was a faint chill in the air. Everywhere, the shadows were thickening, stirring, growing. The girl, gone. Another day, already passing. And the music. The music . . .

"Why did you take me here? What was the point?" he shouted. "To give me nothing. . . ?"

He turned around. For a moment it seemed as though Peg had returned—then he saw the flash of red-golden hair was really only the last glimmer of the greenwood's noonday fire, now entangled with vines of shadow. Or even the padding dark-eyed shift of some stealthy animal. . . .

Sir Edward shivered. Glancing back at the Noonday Pool, which was now veined with the swirling ink-black reflections of the trees, he began to clamber up from the dell. Over the roots and fallen branches, through the leaf-drifts of dead summers, his hands and feet skidding on a slime of wet moss and lichen. A leaf stuck to his chin. The claws of a dead bush snagged at his jacket, ripped, tried to detain him.

When the ground finally began to level, the great man looked back and saw that the dell had already disappeared from sight. He felt a faint sadness, the loss of something already long lost. Galleries of trees receded into shade, brightened only by gaudy shelves of faintly luminous fungi and the glitter of cartridge cases left from Lord Shrewsbury's autumn shoot of the year before.

He trudged on through the wood, finding a path he recognised, a way off this land. And there was the fence, the gate. The lawns of his own house. Staid redbrick walls and yew hedges transformed by the deepening light. And in the pool of shade beneath a copper beech lay the white, wooden bench where he often rested his legs on returning from his afternoon walks. Sir Edward hobbled across the lawn toward it. He slumped down.

Now that her duties for the day had ended, Mrs France set out toward the walled garden again where Mister Groves had now kindly cleared out the hutches for her. She knew that it was important that she revisit the scene of the carnage now—on the same day. Otherwise, the sad image would inevitably stay with her.

But still, it was a pleasant evening. The air had grown lustrous, the birds were still wildly in song. She walked past the yew hedges, along the glimmering white gravel path, pausing only a moment to take a deep breath before turning under the arch into the walled garden. She saw that Mister Groves had sensibly left the hutch doors open so that they might air, and swept and cleaned the bare earth before them so that there was no trace of what had happened.

She crouched down before the hutches and breathed the faint, animal smell that somehow still lingered. Then, something seemed to move inside. She leaned forward, too surprised to be shocked. Was it possible that, unnoticed by herself and Mister Groves, one of her foundlings had survived the onslaught? Hardly possible, it seemed. Yet undoubtedly, at the back of the hutch, there was the shuffle of claws, the glint of an eye. Something there. Something alive . . .

After barely a moment's hesitation, she reached inside. Feeling warm fur, her hands closed, and she lifted the creature out, holding it up toward the light of the gloriously dimming sky. A fox cub. A poor abandoned fox cub. She stroked its silvered head, marvelling as she always marvelled at the perfection of nature, and at the rightness of the fact that—on this evening of all evenings—the creature should seek shelter in one of her empty hutches. For a moment, the thought crossed her mind that she might be holding a culprit rather than a victim, but, breathing the rich, feral scent, gazing into those dark, almost bluish eyes, she knew that that was impossible.

Holding the creature up, she kissed it softly on the nose, and was about to start preparing its bed for the night when she felt the crackle of the telegram in her apron. Kissing the creature again, setting it down, closing the door of the hutch, she peered out through the archway of the walled garden across the dim lawns, and saw that His Grouch had returned.

The birds were still singing in the branches, quarrelling and clattering their wings as the greenwood softened and dissolved. Here was the same blackbird he'd heard this morning, still singing A-B-C-A ascending. Those notes had been at the edge of his mind all day. He could even hear the trickling, racing play of the strings that followed the short opening phrase. A-B-C-A, then a fast interplay of invention. The waters of twilight entering the pools of the night. Not his own music. The music was Mendelssohn's—the opening of *A Midsummer Night's Dream*. And, of course, this blackbird's.

He felt the touch of something on his hand. Looking down, smiling, half-imagining that Peg's fingers were entwined once more around his own, he saw that a small spider had dropped down from one of the branches. It crawled away from his mottled flesh, spinning a faintly gleaming thread, and the blackbird ceased singing.

And there was silence.

The great man gazed out through the dusk where, in the final moment between light and darkness, faint, living shapes seemed to leap and play. This bench was still comparatively warm, but the damnable ache in his back was starting to grow worse; he couldn't stay out here forever. . . .

He glanced back toward the house, where the lights in the windows were now showing. As he watched, he saw that, such was the thickness of the night air and the residual summer heat, a lifeless, grey shape seemed to be forming across the lawns. And, yes, it truly seemed to writhe and dissolve, to tumble end over ragged end out of the darkness toward him. Sir Edward remembered the Noonday Pool, and felt a chill pass over him. But then the figure coalesced, and he saw that it was nothing more than Mrs France in her navy-blue apron, walking swiftly across the lawn, waving something in her hand.

Next morning, Mrs France woke earlier than her accustomed time, and well before her alarm. But still, the trees were whispering, the birds were in song, the sun was already up and out. Far better, at least, than the cold, damp darkness of mornings in December and January. She gazed up at the wood-panelled ceiling, recollecting all that had happened the previous day. The girl Peg (now gone, and good riddance), the telegram that His Grouch had so long been dreading, the senseless destruction of her foundlings. And, of course, the fox cub. The new fox cub . . .

In a pleasant lethargy, Mrs France stretched out on smooth, white sheets she herself had ironed. A lace of leaf shadows played over the pale yellow curtains. And could that be a cuckoo she heard? Normally, and not being a natural early riser, the clanging bell of the alarm clock set her bolt upright and tumbling out of bed, in a rush to get dressed and be down and cleared and well organised in the kitchen before any of the maids appeared. But today . . .

Slowly, she climbed out of bed. Warmed by a patch of golden sunlight, the bare wooden floor was pleasant beneath her bare feet. She twiddled her toes, yawned, pulled the big, blue-handled chamber pot out from beneath her bed, and stooped down. Then she rinsed her hands and her face. Then she dressed. She was still a little premature, but on a day like this, you could almost understand why His Grouch always got up so early. Remembering to turn off her alarm, she descended the narrow stairway to the kitchen.

Ah. The usual smell of Brasso and soot. The usual mess of dripping and bread left by His Grouch on the table. A half-eaten lump on the floor that that pampered dog of His was too well stuffed to even bother with eating. A waste. She picked it up, tidied, brushed up the clinker and coal dust from the grate, hung the kettle back where if belonged, cleared and restoked the rapidly failing fire. You'd think, after yesterday, after the telegram, that He would give it a rest. But no, he'd arisen as early as ever, and would be up there in his study right now. Grinding away. Getting nowhere.

Oh, well. Now that she was down here herself, and feeling slightly at a loss, she decided to set about preparing His proper breakfast—he could have it a bit early for a change. The poor man, really. And perhaps she should say something after yesterday evening. Touch that stooped and stiffened shoulder as she'd been unable to do as she stood beside him in the twilit lawn, spelling out the words of the telegram that his weakening eyes had been unable to read.

Mrs France whisked the toast out from the hotplate before it burned, flipped over the bacon, and finished laying out His Grouch's tray. He'd taken it oddly, really. Oddly for him. With uncharacteristic resignation—almost a kind of humility. But he'd probably be back in one of his usual moods this morning, blaming God and all the world. Worse, if anything. He was, after all, in some pain. Poor man, really. She backed out of the kitchen door, and ascended the stairs. Leaning on the handle, pushing with a practised hand, she managed her usual feat of opening the

baize-lined door to the upper study without putting down the tray.
Inside, the curtains were open, the sun was streaming. But as
for His Grouch . . . There was no sign. Mrs France checked around
the bookcases. The little alcove. But, no. No. She put down the
tray. Pens and paper lay out on His Grouch's desk but, although it
was obvious that he'd been at work this morning, the look of it
seemed different; oddly tidy.

He'd left the drawer that contained those old notebooks of his
unopened for a start, and there were none of the usual scraps and
squigglings and doodlings and crossings-out. Peering more closely,
briefly even forgetting the tantrumic consequences of Him catching her even glancing at his work, she saw that, framed by a square
of sunlight, a neat pile of staved sheets lay on the leather blotter in
the middle of the desk. He'd even threaded a red ribbon through
the edge to bind them, the way she remembered he always did
when he was ready to send something off to his publishers at
Booseys. But that hadn't happened for several years now. A new,
finished work? And it looked so fat. How on Earth had he managed
that, when only yesterday he'd been. . . ?

The top page was titled. She turned it around on the blotter to
read.

*The Noonday Pool*
*For Peg? (another enigma)*

The words were written out in a big hand, with all the flourish
and deliberation he reserved for his final copies. And how nice, Mrs
France couldn't help thinking, that he'd finally got something down
at last. The title was a bit odd, but perhaps it was actually some
fancy name for the third symphony he was always muttering about.
But there was something else about the look of the paper. . . .

Glancing over her shoulder, checking that the room was still
empty, Mrs France picked up the manuscript. On the first page,
below the title, there was nothing but blank staves. She turned over
to the next. Again, blank. Turned again. Page after page of it.
Empty, unwritten sheets, right through to the end. Which even
Mrs France knew signified only silence.

Well . . . Puzzled, yet skilfully as always, she rearranged the desk
as she had found it. Yesterday's news had obviously taken a big toll.
The poor man. And where had he got to, anyway? Even if he *had*
actually finished something, she knew that it was hardly like Him
to take the rest of the morning off. And as for this. He'd surely be
back by now if he'd just gone out and down the corridor to answer
the call. And as for this . . .

Filled with the beginnings of a greater foreboding, Mrs France glanced over the desk and out through the mullioned windows, across the long-shadowed lawn. Her hand went up to her bosom, and she drew in a surprised breath. There was a figure with outstretched arms, standing on the grass, with head raised to the deep blue midsummer. So strange and uncharacteristic was the posture, so unlike the person she thought she knew, that it was some moments before she realised who it was.

Then, skirts and pinny flying, she was out and down the backstairs, through the kitchen and the stillness of the shadowed yard, around the side of the house to the main garden. And there he was: His Grouch, still just standing in the middle of the garden.

In a panic, fearing that his brain might already have gone—that she'd already lost him as she lost Lady Caroline and her own Arthur—she ran up to him across warm paving and cool, wet grass.

"Sir Edward! I'm . . . I'm just . . ."

But he simply blinked and turned as though awoken, smiling one of his rare smiles.

"Yes?" he said, cheerful as you please.

Mrs France gazed at him, her buxom heaving. She felt oddly angry: Him giving her such a turn. And yet . . .

"Your breakfast is waiting up in your study, Sir Edward. As always."

He nodded. A hand went up to twiddle the left tip of the moustache, thought better of it, and went down again.

"I was just thinking," he said, "it is *such* a fine morning . . . Now, Mrs France, wouldn't you say so?"

She looked around, squinting, half-dazzled by the soft, long rays of sunlight that were falling through the trees, her head filling like some deep, empty pool with the wind-chatter of leaves, the song of thrush and blackbird and cuckoo.

"I suppose . . ." she conceded, taking a long breath, dabbing at a bead of sweat on her cheek. "That you could say so."

"Such a fine morning," he continued, "that I might as well stay out here and make the most of it. . . ."

He gazed around, still smiling. Even with the telegram, his shoulders seemed less stooped today. And the nostrils of his big nose flared as he breathed, his eyes sparkled. Mrs France reflected that, after a whole lifetime of early rising, it was almost as if he'd never actually seen an early summer's morning before.

"But, Sir Edward, you must at least sit down."

The great man nodded. He pointed across the lawns to a bench over by the trees, and began to walk toward it, the old man's shuffle of his feet leaving a dark trail on the bright grass. For some moments, Mrs France stood watching him, thinking of the many things as yet undone in her kitchen, the near-state it was in, and the ironing she couldn't trust anyone else to make a decent job of, and the bread that needed baking, and of course her new fox cub, and the maids who would soon be rising: of all the clamouring duties of her busy life. But then the great man stumbled slightly on a mole-hill, and she hurried across the lawn to join him.

"I was thinking, Mrs France," he said, taking her arm, "that there was something I might one day show you and Lady Caroline . . . But then again," he continued, looking about him, and toward the bench in a patch of sun beneath the tree where the blackbird sang, "it can wait. . . ."

They walked on through the endless morning light of summer.

Peg could hear the train coming, the night express.

The breath of her muzzle clouded the air as she pushed her way through the sharply frosted undergrowth. She halted, and sniffed. The berries had withered on the bushes now, and last season's incautious young had grown too quick and wise to be easy prey for her. But it was a clear, fine night, and her belly was still plump from long, pampered months. She had nothing to fear from the winter.

The train was fast approaching, trailing a long scarf of smoke diamonded with sparks. This time, the lights of the carriage that the guard always reserved for the great man no longer shone over the sweet, endless flow of his beloved river. The windows were black, and inside there was only rocking, creaking silence, the gleam of long mahogany, the white-scented gloom of tributes and flowers.

Tumbling out of the night, ragged beat of engine-breath echoing over the hills, the night express bore on, carrying the great man home for the last time, and on the start of the longest journey of all.

The tracks wheezed and creaked. The sound became a wall. Peg sank down onto the bare, giving earth, and waited.

**Author's note:** This story reflects some aspects of the life of the greatest of all English composers, Sir Edward Elgar. *My* Sir Edward, however—and Peg, and Mrs France, and Mr Groves, and the Noonday Pool—live only through you, the reader; and on these pages.

# New Light on the Drake Equation

A S HE DID ON THE FIRST WEDNESDAY OF EVERY month, after first finishing off the bottle of wine he'd fallen asleep with, then drinking three bleary fingers of absinthe, and with an extra slug for good measure, Tom Kelly drove down into St. Hilaire to collect his mail and provisions. The little town was red-brown, shimmering in the depths of the valley, flecked with olive trees, as he slewed the old Citröen around the hairpins from his mountain. Up to the east, where the karst rose in a mighty crag, he could just make out the flyers circling against the sheer, white drop if he rubbed his eyes and squinted, and the glint of their wings as they caught the morning thermals. But Tom felt like a flyer of sorts himself, now that the absinthe was fully in his bloodstream. He let the Citröen's piebald tyres, the skid of the grit, and the pull of the mountain take him endlessly downward. Spinning around the bends blind and wrong-side with the old canvas roof flapping, in and out of the shadows, scattering sheep in the sweet, hot roar of the antique motor, Tom Kelly drove down from his mountain toward the valley.

In the *Bureau de poste*, Madame Brissac gave him a smile that seemed even more patronising than usual.

"Any messages?" he croaked.

She blinked slowly. "One maybe two." Bluebottles circled the close air, which smelled of boiled sweets and Gitanes and Madame

Brissac. Tom swayed slightly in his boots. He wiped off some of the road grit, which had clung to the stubble on his face. He picked a stain from his T-shirt, and noticed as he did so that a fresh age spot was developing on the back of his right hand. It would disappoint her, really, if he took a language vial and started speaking fluent French after all these years—or even if he worked at it the old way, using bookplates and audio samples, just as he'd always been promising himself. It would deprive her of their small monthly battle.

"Then, ah, *je voudrais* . . ." He tried waving his arms.

"You would like to have?"

"Yes please. *Oui.* Ah—*s'il vous plaît* . . ."

Still the tepid pause, the droning bluebottles. Or Madame Brissac could acquire English, Tom thought, although she was hardly likely to do it for his sake.

"You late." She said eventually.

"You mean—"

Then the door banged open in a crowded slab of shadows and noise and a cluster of flyers, back from their early morning spin on the thermals, bustled up behind Tom with skinsuits squealing, the folded tips of their wings bumping against the brown curls of sticky flypaper which the bluebottles had been scrupulously avoiding. These young people, Tom decided as he glanced back at them, truly were like bright, alien insects in their gaudy skinsuits, their thin bodies garishly striped with the twisting logos of sports companies and their wings, a flesh of fine silk stretched between feathery bones, folded up behind their backs like delicate umbrellas. And they were speaking French, too; speaking it in loud, high voices, but overdoing every phrase and gesture and emphasis in the way that people always did when they were new to a language. They thought that just because they could understand each other and talk sensibly to their flying instructor and follow the tour guide and order a drink at the bar that they were jabbering away like natives, but then they hadn't yet come up against Madame Brissac, who would be bound to devise some bureaucratic twist or incomprehension which would send them away from here without whatever particular form or permission it was that they were expecting. Tom turned back to Madame Brissac and gave her a grin from around the edges of his gathering absinthe headache. She didn't bother to return it. Instead, she muttered something that sounded like *I'm Judy.*

"What? *Voulez-vous repeter?*"

"Is Thursday."

"Ah. *Je comprends.* I see . . ." Not that he did quite, but the flyers were getting impatient and crowding closer to him, wings
rustling with echoes of the morning air that had recently been filling them and the smell of fresh sweat, clean endeavour. How was
it, Tom wondered, that they could look so beautiful from a distance, and so stupid and ugly close up? But *Thursday*—and he'd
imagined it was Wednesday. Of course he'd thought that it was
Wednesday, otherwise he wouldn't be here in St. Hilaire, would
he? He was a creature of habit, worn in by the years like the grain
of the old wood of Madame Brissac's counter. So he must have lost
track, or not bothered to check his calendar back up on the mountain, or both. An easy enough mistake to make, living the way he
did. Although . . .

"You require them? Yes?"

"*S'il vous plait . . .*"

At long last, Madame Brissac was turning to the pigeonholes
where she kept his and a few other message cards filed according to
her own alchemic system. Putting them in one place, labelled
under Kelly, Tom—or American, Drunk; Elderly, Stupid—was too
simple for her. Neither had Tom ever been able to see a particular
pattern that would relate to the source of the cards, which were
generally from one or another of his various academic sponsors and
came in drips and drabs and rushes, but mostly drabs. Those old,
brown lines of wooden boxes, which looked as if they had probably
once held proper, old-fashioned letters and telegrams, and perhaps
messages and condolences from the World Wars, and the revolu-
tionary proclamations of the *sans-culottes,* and decrees from the
Sun King, and quite possibly even the odd pigeon, disgorged their
contents to Madame Brissac's quick hands in no way that Tom
could ever figure. He could always ask, of course, but that would
just be an excuse for a raising of Gallic eyebrows and shoulders in
mimed incomprehension. After all, Madame Brissac was Madame
Brissac, and the flyers behind him were whispering, fluttering,
trembling like young egrets, and it was none of his business.

There were market stalls lined across the Place de Revolution,
which had puzzled Tom on his way into the *Bureau de poste,* but
no longer. The world was right and he was wrong. This was Thursday. And his habitual café was busier than usual, although the
couple who were occupying his table got up at his approach and
strolled off, hand in hand, past the heaped and shadowed displays
of breads and fruits and cheeses. The girl had gone for an Audrey

Hepburn look, but the lad had the muscles of a paratrooper beneath his sleeveless T-shirt, and his flesh was green and lightly scaled. To Tom, it looked like a skin disease. He wondered, as lonely men gazing at young couples from café tables have wondered since time immemorial, what the hell she saw in him.

The waiter Jean-Benoît was busier than usual, and, after giving Tom a glance that almost registered surprise, took his time coming over. Tom, after all, would be going nowhere in any hurry. And he had his cards—all six of them—to read. They lay there, face down on the plastic tablecloth; a hand of poker he had to play. But he knew already what the deal was likely to be. One was blue and almost plain, with a pattern like rippled water, which was probably some kind of junk mail, and another looked suspiciously like a bill for some cyber-utility he probably wasn't even using, and the rest, most undoubtedly, were from his few remaining sponsors. Beside them on the table, like part of a fine still life into which he and these cards were an unnecessary intrusion, lay the empty carafe and the wineglasses from which the lovers had been drinking. Wine at ten in the morning! That was France for you. *This* was France. And he could do with a drink himself, could Tom Kelly. Maybe just a *pastis*, which would sit nicely with the absinthe he'd had earlier—just as a bracer, mind. Tom sighed and rubbed his temples and looked about him in the morning brightness. Up at the spire of St. Marie rising over the awnings of the market, then down at the people, gaudily, gorgeously fashionable in their clothes, their skins, their faces. France, this real France of the living, was a place he sometimes felt he only visited on these Wednesday—this Thursday—mornings. He could have been anywhere for the rest of the time, up with the stars there on his mountain, combing his way through eternity on the increasing off chance of an odd blip. That was why he was who he was—some old gook whom people like Madame Brissac and Jean-Benoît patronised without ever really knowing. That was why he'd never really got around to mastering this language which was washing all around him in persibilant waves. Jean-Benoît was still busy, flipping his towel and serving up crepes with an on-off smile of his regulation-handsome features, his wings so well tucked away that no one would ever really know he had them. Like a lot of the people who worked here, he did the job so he could take to the air in his free time. Tom, with his *trois diget pastis merci*, was never going to be much of a priority.

Tom lifted one of the cards and tried to suppress a burp as the bitter residue of absinthe flooded his mouth. The card was from the

University of Aston, in Birmingham, England, of all places. Now, he'd forgotten *they* were even sponsoring him. He ran his finger down the playline, and half-closed his eyes to witness a young man he'd never seen before in his life sitting at the kind of impressively wide desk that only people, in Tom's experience, who never did any real work possessed.

"Mister Kelly, it's a real pleasure to make your acquaintance . . ." The young man paused. He was clearly new to whatever it was he was doing, and gripping that desk as if it was perched at the top of a roller-coaster ride. "As you may have seen in the academic press, I've now taken over from Doctor Sally Normanton. I didn't know her personally, but I know that all of you who did valued her greatly, and I, too, feel saddened by the loss of a fine person and physicist . . ."

Tom withdrew his finger from the card for a moment, and dropped back into France. He'd only ever met the woman once. She'd been warm and lively and sympathetic, he remembered, and had moved about on autolegs because of the advanced arthritis which, in those days at least, the vials hadn't been able to counteract. They'd sat under the mossy trees and statues in Birmingham's Centenary Square, which for him had held other memories, and she'd sighed and smiled and explained how the basic policy of her institution had gone firmly against any positive figure to the Drake Equation several decades before, but Sally Normanton herself had always kept a soft spot for that kind of stuff, and she'd really got into physics in the first place on the back of reading Clarke and Asimov. Not that she imagined Tom had heard of them? But Tom had, of course. They were almost of the same generation. He'd developed a dust allergy from hunching over those thrilling, musty, analogue pages as a kid. They chatted merrily, and on the walk back to the campus Sally Normanton had confided, as she heaved and clicked on her legs, that she had control of a smallish fund. It was left over from some government work, and was his to have for as long as it took the accountants to notice. And that was more than twenty years ago. And now she was dead.

". . . physicist. But in clearing out and revising her responsibilities, it's come to my attention that monies have been allocated to your project which, I regret to say . . ."

Tom spun the thing forward until he came to the bit at the end when the young man, who had one eye green and one eye blue—and nails like talons, so perhaps he too was a flyer, although he didn't look quite thin enough and seemed too easily scared—

announced that he'd left a simulacrum AI of his business self on the card, which would be happy to answer any pertinent questions, although the decision to withdraw funds was, regrettably, quite irrevocable. The AI was there, of course, to save the chance that Tom might try to bother this man of business with feeble pleas. But Tom knew he was lucky to have got what he got from that source, and even luckier that they weren't talking about suing him to take it all back.

Aston University. England. The smell of different air. Different trees. If there was one season that matched the place, a mood that always seemed to be hanging there in the background, even on the coldest or hottest or wettest of days, it had to be fall, autumn. How long had it been now? Tom tried not to think—that was one equation which even to him always came back as a recurring nothing. He noticed instead that the wineglass that the pretty, young girl had been drinking bore the red imprint of her lipstick, and was almost sad to see it go, and with it the better memories he'd been trying to conjure, when Jean-Benoît finally bustled up and plonked a glass of cloudy, yellow liquid, which Tom wasn't really sure that he wanted any longer, down in front of him. *Voilà. Merci.* Pidgin French as he stared at the cards from Madame Brissac's incomprehensible pigeonholes. But he drank it anyway, the *pastis*. Back in one. At least it got rid of the taste of the absinthe.

And the day was fine, the market was bustling. It would be a pity to spoil this frail, good mood he was building with messages which probably included the words *regret, withdraw,* or at the very least, *must query* . . . This square, it was baguettes and Edith Piaf writ large, it was the Eiffel Tower in miniature. The warm smells of garlic and slightly dodgy drains and fine, dark coffee. And those ridiculous little poodles dragged along by those long-legged women. The shouts and the gestures, the black, old widows, who by now were probably younger than he was, muttering to themselves and barging along with their stripy shopping bags like extras from the wrong film and scowling at this or that vial-induced wonder. And a priest in his cassock stepping from the church, pausing in the sunlight at the top of the steps to take in the scene, although he had wings behind him which he stretched as if to yawn, and his hair was scarlet. Another flyer. Tom smiled to think how he got on with his congregation, which was mostly those scowling old women, and thought about ordering—why not?—another *pastis*. . . .

Then he noticed a particular figure wandering beside the stalls at the edge of the market where displays of lace billowed in the wind, which blew off the karst and squeezed in a warm, light breeze down between the washing-strung tenements. It couldn't be, of course. Couldn't be. It was just that lipstick on the edge of that glass which had prickled that particular memory. That, and getting a message from England, and that woman dying, and losing another income source, all of which, if he'd have let them, would have stirred up a happy-sad melange of memories. She was wearing a dark blue, sleeveless dress and was standing in a bright patch of sunlight which flamed on her blonde hair and made it hard for him to see her face. She could have been anyone, but in that moment, she could have been Terr, and Tom felt the strangely conflicting sensations of wanting to run over and embrace her, and also to dig a hole for himself where he could hide forever right here beneath this café paving. He blinked. His head swam. By the time he'd refocused, the girl, the woman, had moved on. A turn of bare arm, a flash of lovely calf. Why *did* they have to change themselves like they did now? Women were perfect as they were. Always had been, as far as Tom was concerned—or as best he could remember. Especially Terr. But then perhaps that had been an illusion, too.

Tom stood up and dropped a few francs on the table and blundered off between the market stalls. That dark blue, sleeveless dress, those legs, that hair. His heart was pounding as it hadn't done in years from some strange inner exertion of memory. Even if it *wasn't* her, which it obviously wasn't, he still wanted to know, to see. But St. Hilaire was Thursday-busy. The teeming market swallowed him up and spat him out again downhill where the steps ran beside the old battlements and the river flashed under the willow trees, then uphill by the bright, expensive shops along the Rue de Commerce, which offered in their windows designer clothes, designer vials, designer lives. Fifteen different brands of colloquial French in bottles like costly perfumes and prices to match. Only you crushed them between your teeth and the glass tasted like spun sugar and tiny miracles of lavish engineering poured down your throat and through the walls of your belly and into your bloodstream where they shed their protective coating and made friends with your immune system and hitched a ride up to your brain. Lessons were still necessary (they played that down on the packaging) but only one or two, and they involved little more than sitting in flashing darkness in a Zenlike state of calm induced by various drug suppositories (this being France) whilst nanomolecules fiddled with your sites of language and cognition until you started *parlez vous*-ing like a native. Or you could grow wings, although the vials in the sports shops were even more expensive. But the dummies beyond the plateglass whispered and beckoned to Tom and fluttered about excitedly; Day-Glo fairies, urging him to make the investment in a fortnight's experience that would last a lifetime.

Tom came to an old square at the far end of the shops. The Musée de Masque was just opening, and a group of people who looked like late revellers from the night before were sitting on its steps and sharing a bottle of neat Pernod. The women had decorated their wings with silks and jewels; although by now they looked like tired hatstands. The men, but for the pulsing tattoo-like adornments they'd woven into their flesh and the pouchlike g-strings around their crotches which spoke, so to speak, volumes, were virtually naked. Their skin was heliotrope. Tom guessed it was the colour for this season. To him, though, they looked like a clutch of malnourished, crash-landed gargoyles. He turned back along the street, and found his Citröen pretty much where he thought he'd left it by the *alimentation générale* where he'd already purchased next month's supplies, and turned the old analogue key he'd left in the ignition, and puttered slowly out across the cobbles, supplies swishing and jingling in their boxes, then gave the throttle an angry shove, and roared out toward midday, the heat, the scattered olive trees, and the grey-white bulk of his mountain.

Dusk. The coming stars. His time. His mountain. Tom stood outside his sparse wooden hut, sipping coffee and willing the sun to unravel the last of her glowing clouds from the horizon. Around him on the large, flat, mile-wide, slightly west-tilted slab of pavement limestone glittered the silver spiderweb of his tripwires, which were sheening with dew as the warmth of the day evaporated, catching the dying light as they and he waited for the stars.

He amazed himself sometimes, the fact that he was up here doing this, the fact that he was still searching for anything at all at the ripe, nearly old age of near-seventy, let alone for something as wild and extravagant as intelligent extra-terrestrial life. Where had it began? What had started him on this quest of his? Had it really been those SF stories—dropping through the Stargate with Dave Bowman, or staggering across the sandworm deserts of Arrakis with Paul Atreides? Was it under rocks in Eastport when he was a kid raising the tiny translucent crabs to the light, or was it down the wires on the few remaining SETI websites when he wasn't that much older? Was it pouring through the library screens at college, or was it now as he stood looking up at the gathering stars from his lonely hut on this lonely French mountain? Or was it somewhere else? Somewhere out there, sweet and glorious and imponderable?

Most of the people he still knew, or at least maintained a sort of long-distance touch with, had given up with whatever had once bugged them some time ago; the ones, in fact, who seemed the happiest, the most settled, the most at ease with their lives—and thus generally had the least to do with him—had never really started worrying about such things in the first place. They took vacations in places like St. Hilaire, they grew wings or gills just like the kids did, and acquired fresh languages and outlooks as they swallowed their vials and flew or dived in their new element. He put down his cup of coffee, which was already skinned and cold, and then he smiled to himself—he still couldn't help it—as he watched more of the night come in. Maybe it was that scene in *Fantasia*, watching it on video when he was little more than a baby. The one set to the music he recognised later as Beethoven's *Pastoral*. Those cavorting cherubs and centaurs, and then at the end, after Zeus has packed away his thunderbolts, the sun sets, and over comes Morpheus in a glorious cloak of night. The idea of life amid the stars had already been with him then, filling him as he squatted entranced before the screen and the Baltimore traffic buzzed by outside unnoticed, filled with something that was like a sweet sickness, like his mother's embrace when she thought he was sleeping, like the ache of cola and ice cream. That sweet ache had been with him, he decided as he looked up and smiled as the stars twinkled on and goosebumps rose on his flesh, ever since.

So Tom had become a nocturnal beast, a creature of twilights and dawns. He supposed that he'd become so used to his solitary life up here on this wide and empty mountain that he'd grown a little agora—or was it claustro?—phobic. Hence the need for the absinthe this morning—or at least the extra slug of it. The Wednesdays, the bustle of the town, had become quite incredible to him, a blast of light and smell and sound and contact, almost like those VR suites where you tumbled through huge fortresses on strange planets and fought and cannon-blasted those ever-imaginary aliens. Not that Tom had ever managed to bring himself to do such a thing. As the monsters glowered over him, jaws agape and fangs dripping, all he'd wanted to do was make friends and ask them about their customs and religions and mating habits. He'd never got through many levels on those VR games, the few times he'd tried them. Now he thought about it, he really hadn't got through so very many levels of the huge VR game known as life, either.

Almost dark. A time for secrets and lovers and messages. A time for the clink of wineglasses and the soft *puck* of opening bottles. The west was a faint, red blush of clouds and mountains, which caught glimmering in a pool on the fading slope of the mountain. Faint, grey shapes were moving down there; from the little Tom could see now from up here, they could have been stray flares and impulses from the failing remaining rods and cones in his weary eyes—random scraps of data—but he knew from other nights and mornings that they were the shy ibex which grazed this plateau, and were drawn here from miles around along with many other creatures simply because most of the moisture that fell here in the winter rains and summer storms drained straight through the cave-riddled limestone. Sometimes, looking that way on especially clear nights, Tom would catch the glimmer of stars as if a few had fallen there, although on the rare occasions he'd trekked to the pool down across difficult slopes, he'd found that, close to, it was a disappointment. A foul, brown oval of thick amoebic fluid surrounded by cracked and caked mud, it was far away from the sweet oasis he'd imagined, where bright birds and predators and ruminants all bowed their heads to sip the silver, cool liquid and forget, in the brief moments of their parched and mutual need, their normal animosities. But it was undeniably a waterhole, and as such important to the local fauna. It had even been there on the map all those years ago, when he'd been looking for somewhere to begin what he was sure was to be the remainder of his life's work. A blue full stop, a small ripple of hope and life. He'd taken it as a sign.

Tom went inside his hut and spun the metal cap off one of the cheap but decent bottles of *vin de table* with which he generally started the evenings. He took a swig from it, looked around without much hope for a clean glass, then took another swig. One handed, he tapped up the keys of one of his bank of machines. Lights stuttered, cooling fans chirruped like crickets or groaned like wounded bears. It was hot in here from all this straining antique circuitry. There was the strong smell of singed dust and warm wires, and a new, dim, fizzing sound which could have been a spark which, although he turned his head this way and that, as sensitive to the changes in this room's topography as a shepherd to the moods of his flock, Tom couldn't quite locate. But no matter. He'd wasted most of last night fiddling and tweaking to deal with the results of a wine spillage, and didn't want to waste this one doing the same.

There was something about today, this not-Wednesday known as Thursday, which filled Tom with an extra sense of urgency. He'd grounded himself far too firmly on the side of science and logic to believe in such rubbish as premonitions, but still he couldn't help but wonder if this wasn't how they felt, the Hawkings and the Einsteins and the Newtons—the Cooks and the Columbuses, for that matter—in the moment before they made their Big Discovery, their final break. Of course, any such project, viewed with hindsight, could be no more than a gradual accumulation of knowledge, a hunch that a particular area of absent knowledge might be fruitfully explored, followed generally by years of arse-licking and fund-searching and peer-group head shaking and rejected papers and hard work during which a few extra scraps of information made that hunch seem more and more like a reasonably intelligent guess, even if everyone else was heading in the opposite direction and thought that you were, to coin a phrase once used by Tom's cosmology professor, barking up the wrong fucking tree in the wrong fucking forest. In his bleaker moments, Tom sometimes wondered if there was a tree there at all.

But not now. The data, of course, was processed automatically, collected day and night according to parameters and wavelengths he'd predetermined but at a speed which, even with these processors, sieved and reamed out information by the gigabyte per second. He'd set up the search systems to flash and bleep and make whatever kind of electronic racket they were capable of if they ever came upon any kind of anomaly. Although he was routinely dragged from his bleary daytime slumbers by a surge in power or a speck of fly dirt or a rabbit gnawing the tripwires or a stray cosmic ray, it was still his greatest nightmare that they would blithely ignore the one spike, the one regularity or irregularity, that might actually mean something—or that he'd be so comatose he'd sleep through it. And then of course the computers couldn't look everywhere. By definition, with the universe being as big as it was, they and Tom were always missing something. The something, in fact, was so large it was close to almost everything. Not only was there all the data collected for numerous other astronomical and non-astronomical purposes which he regularly downloaded from his satellite link and stored on the disks which, piled and waiting in one corner, made a silvery pillar almost to the ceiling, but the stars themselves were always out there, the stars and their inhabitants. Beaming down in real-time. Endlessly.

So how to sort, where to begin? Where was the best place on all the possible radio wavelengths to start looking for messages from little green men? It was a question which had first been asked more than a century before, and to which, of all the many, many guesses, one still stood out as the most reasonable. Tom turned to that frequency now, live through the tripwires out on the karst, and powered up the speakers and took another slug of *vin de table* and switched on the monitor and sat there listening, watching, drinking. That dim hissing of microwaves, the cool dip of interstellar quietude amid the babble of the stars and the gas clouds and the growl of the big bang and the spluttering quasars, not to mention all the racket that all the other humans on Earth and around the solar system put out. The space between the emissions of interstellar hydrogen and hydroxyl radical at round about 1420 MHz, which was known as the waterhole; a phrase which reflected not only the chemical composition of water, but also the idea of a place where, just as the shy ibex clustered to quench themselves at dusk and dawn, all the varied species of the universe might gather after a weary day to exchange wondrous tales.

Tom listened to the sound of the waterhole. What were the chances, with him sitting here, of anything happening right now? Bleep, bleep. Bip, bip. Greetings from the planet Zarg. Quite, quite impossible. But then, given all the possibilities in the universe, what were the chances of him, Tom Kelly, sitting here on this particular mountain at this particular moment with this particular bank of equipment and this particular near-empty bottle of *vin de table* listening to this frequency in the first place? That was pretty wild in itself. Wild enough, in fact—he still couldn't help it —to give him goosebumps. Life itself was such an incredible miracle. In fact, probably unique, if one was to believe the figure of which was assigned to it by the few eccentric souls who still bothered to tinker with the Drake Equation. That was the problem.

He forced himself to stand up, stretch, leave the room, the speakers still hissing with a soft sea-roar, the monitor flickering and jumping. The moment when the transmission finally came through was bound to be when you turned your back. It stood to reason. A watched kettle, after all . . . And not that he was superstitious. So he wandered out into the night again, which was now starry and marvellous and moonless and complete, and he tossed the evening's first empty into the big skip and looked up at the heavens, and felt that swell in his chest and belly he'd felt those more than sixty years ago, which was still like the ache of cola and ice cream. And had he eaten? He really couldn't remember, although he was pretty sure he'd fixed some coffee. This darkness was food enough for him, all the pouring might of the stars. Odd to say, but on nights like this the darkness had a glow to it like something finely wrought, finally polished, a lustre and a sheen. You could believe in God. You could believe in anything. And the trip-wires were still just visible, the vanishing trails like tiny shooting stars crisscrossing this arid, limestone plain as they absorbed the endless transmission. They flowed toward the bowl of darkness that was the hidden valley, the quiet waterhole, the flyers sleeping in their beds in St. Hilaire, dreaming of thermals, twitching their wings. Tom wondered if Madame Brissac slept. It was hard to imagine her anywhere other than standing before her pigeonholes in the *Bureau de poste*, waiting for the next poor sod she could make life difficult for. The pigeonholes themselves, whatever code it was that she arranged them in, really would be worth making the effort to find out about on the remote chance that, Madame Brissac being Madame Brissac, the information was sorted in a way that Tom's computers, endlessly searching the roar of chaos for order, might have overlooked. And he also wondered if it wasn't time already for another bottle, one of the plastic litre ones, which tasted like shit if you started on them, but were fine if you had something half-decent first to take off the edge. . . .

A something—a figure—was walking up the track toward him. No, not a fluke, and not random data, and certainly not an ibex. Not Madame Brissac either, come to explain her pigeonholes and apologise for her years of rudeness. Part of Tom was watching the rest of Tom in quiet amazement as his addled mind and tired eyes slowly processed the fact that he wasn't alone, and that the figure was probably female, and could almost have been, no looked like, in fact was, the woman in the dark blue dress he'd glimpsed down by the lace stalls in the market that morning. And she really did bear a remarkable resemblance to Terr, at least in the sole dim light, which emanated from the monitors inside his hut. The way she walked. The way she was padding across the bare patch of ground in front of the tripwires. That same lightness. And then her face. And her voice.

"Why do you have to live so bloody far up here Tom? The woman I asked in the post office said it was just up the road. . . ."

He shrugged. He was floating. His arms felt light, his hands empty. "That would be Madame Brissac."

"Would it? Anyway, she was talking rubbish."

"You should have tried asking in French."

"I *was* speaking French. My poor feet. It's taken me bloody hours."

Tom had to smile. The stars were behind Terr, and they were shining on her once-blonde hair, which the years had silvered to the gleam of those tripwires, and touched the lines around her mouth as she smiled. He felt like crying and laughing. Terr. "Well, that's Madame Brissac for you."

"So? Are you going to invite me inside?"

"There isn't much of an inside."

Terr took another step forward on her bare feet. She was real. So close to him. He could smell the dust on her salt flesh. Feel and hear her breathing. She was Terr alright. He wasn't drunk or dreaming, or at least not that drunk yet; he'd only had—what?—two bottles of wine so far all evening. And she had and hadn't changed.

"Well," she said, "that's Tom Kelly for you, too, isn't it?"

The idea of sitting in the hut was ridiculous on a night like this. And the place, as Tom stumbled around in it and slewed bottles off the table and shook rubbish off the chairs, was a dreadful, terrible mess. So he hauled two chairs out into the night for them to sit on, and the table to go between, and found unchipped glasses from somewhere, and gave them a wipe to get rid of the mould, and ferreted around in the depths of his boxes until he found the solitary bottle of Santernay le Chenay 2058 he'd been saving for First Contact—or at least until he felt too depressed—and lit one of the candles he kept for when the generator went down. Then he went searching for a corkscrew, ransacking cupboards and drawers and cursing under his breath at the ridiculousness of someone who goes through as much wine as he did not being able to lay his hands upon one—but then the cheaper bottles were all screw-capped, and the really cheap plastic things had tops a blind child could pop off one-handed. He was breathless when he finally sat down. His heart ached. His face throbbed. His ears were singing.

"How did you find me, Terr?"

"I told you, I asked that woman in the post office. Madame Brissac."

"I mean . . ." He used both hands to still the shaking as he sloshed wine from the bottle. ". . . here in France, in St. Hilaire, on this mountain."

She chuckled. She sounded like the Terr of old speaking to him down the distance of an antique telephone line. "I did a search for you. One of those virtual things, where you send an AI out like a genie from a bottle. But would you believe I had to explain to it that SETI meant the Search for Extra-Terrestrial Intelligence? It didn't have the phrase in its standard vocabulary. But it found you anyway, once I'd sorted that out. You have this old-fashioned web-site-thingy giving information on your project here and inviting new sponsors. You say it will be a day-by-day record of setbacks, surprises, and achievements. You even offer T-shirts. By the look of it, it was last updated about twenty years ago. You can virtually see the dust on it through the screen. . . ."

Tom laughed. Sometimes, you have to. "The T-shirts never really took off . . ." He studied his glass, which also had a scum of dust floating on it, like most of his life. The taste of this good wine —sitting here—everything—was strange to him.

"Oh, and she sent me across the square to speak to this incredibly handsome waiter who works in this café. Apparently, you forgot these . . ." Terr reached into the top of her dress, and produced the cards he must have left on the table. They were warm when he took them, filled with a sense of life and vibrancy he doubted was contained in any of the messages. Terr. And her own personal filing system.

"And what about you, Terr?"

"What do you mean?"

"All these years, I mean I guess it's pretty obvious what *I've* been doing—"

"— which was what you always said . . ."

"Yes. But you, Terr. I've thought about you once or twice. Just occasionally . . ."

"Mmmm." She smiled at him over her glass, through the candlelight. "Let's just talk about *now* for a while, shall we, Tom? That is, if you'll put up with me?"

"Fine." His belly ached. His hands, as he took another long slug of this rich, good wine, were still trembling.

"Tom, you haven't said the obvious thing yet."

"Which is?"

"That I've changed. Although we both have, I suppose. Time being time."

"You look great."

"You were always good at compliments."

"That was because I always meant them."

"And you're practical at the bottom of it, Tom. Or at least you were. I used to like that about you, too. Even if we didn't always agree about it. . . ."

With Tom it had always been one thing, one obsession. With

Terr, it had to be everything. She'd wanted the whole world, the universe. And it was there even now, Tom could feel it quivering in the night between them, that division of objectives, a loss of contact, as if they were edging back toward the windy precipice which had driven them apart in the first place.

"Anyway," he said stupidly, just to fill the silence, "if you don't like how you look these days, all you do is take a vial."

"What? And be ridiculous—like those women you see along Oxford Street and Fifth Avenue, with their fake furs, their fake smiles, their fake skins? Youth is for the young, Tom. Always was, and always will be. Give them their chance, is what I say. After all, we had ours. And they're so much better at it than we are."

Terr put down her glass on the rough table, leaned back, and stretched on the rickety chair. Her hair sheened back from her shoulders, and looked almost blonde for a moment. Darkness hollowed in her throat. "When you get to my age, Tom—*our* age. It just seems . . . Looking back is more important than looking forward. . . ."

"Is that why you're here?"

A more minor stretch and shrug. Her flesh whispered and seemed to congeal around her throat in stringy clumps. Her eyes hollowed, and the candlelight went out in them. Her arms thinned. Tom found himself wishing there were either more illumination, or less. He wanted to see Terr as she was, or cloaked in total darkness; not like this, twisting and changing like the ibex at the twilight waterhole. So perhaps candlelight was another thing that the young should reserve for themselves, like the vials, like flying, like love and faith and enthusiasm. Forget about romance—what you needed at his, at their, ages, was to *know*. You wanted certainty. And Tom himself looked, he knew, from his occasional forays in front of a mirror, like a particularly vicious cartoon caricature of the Tom Kelly that Terr remembered; the sort of thing that Gerald Scarfe had done to Reagan and Thatcher in the last century. The ruined veins in his cheeks and eyes. The bruises and swellings. Those damn age spots that had recently started appearing—gravestone marks, his grandmother had once called them. He was like Tom Kelly hungover after a fight in a bar, with a bout of influenza on top of that, and then a bad case of sunburn, and struggling against the influence of the gravity of a much larger planet. That was pretty much what ageing felt like, too, come to think of it.

Flu, and too much gravity.

✣       ✣       ✣

He'd never been one for chat-up lines. He'd had the kind of natural, not-quite regular looks when he was young which really didn't need enhancing—which was good, because he'd never have bothered, or been able to afford it—but he had a shyness which came out mostly like vague disinterest when he talked to girls. The lovelier they were, the more vague and disinterested Tom became. But this woman or girl he happened to find himself walking beside along the canals of this old and once-industrial city called Birmingham after one of those parties when the new exchange students were supposed to meet up, she was different. She was English for a start, which to Tom, a little-traveled American on this foreign shore, seemed both familiar and alien. Everything she said, every gesture, had a slightly different slant to it, which he found strange, intriguing . . .

She'd taken him around the canals to Gas Street Basin, the slick waters sheened with antique petrol, antique fog, and along the towpath to the Sealife Centre, where deepsea creatures out of Lovecraft mouthed close to the tripleglass of their pressurised tanks. Then across the iron bridges of the Worcester and Birmingham Canal to a pub. Over her glass of wine, Terr had explained that an American president had once sat here in this pub and surprised the locals and drunk a pint of bitter during some world conference. Her hair was fine blonde. Her eyes were stormy green. She'd shrugged off the woollen coat with a collar that had brushed the exquisite line of her neck and jaw as she walked in a way that had made Tom envy it. Underneath, she was wearing a sleeveless, dark blue dress, which was tight around her hips and smallish breasts, and showed her fine legs. Of course, he envied that dress as well. There was a smudged red crescent at the rim of the glass made by her lipstick. Terr was studying literature then, an arcane enough subject in itself, and for good measure she'd chosen as her special field the kind of stories of the imaginary future which had been popular for decades, until the real and often quite hard to believe present had finally extinguished them. Tom, who'd been immersed in such stuff for much of his teenage years, almost forgot his reticence as he recommended John Varley, of whom she hadn't even heard, and that she avoid the late-period Heinlein, and then to list his own particular favourites, which had mostly been Golden Age writers (yes, yes, she knew the phrase) like Simak and Van Vogt and Wyndham and Sheckley. And then there was Lafferty, and Cordwainer Smith. . . .

Eventually, sitting at a table in the top room in that bar where an American president might once have sat and overlooking the canal where the long boats puttered past with their antique, petrol motors, bleeding their colours into the mist, Terr had steered Tom away from science fiction, and nudged him into talking about himself. He found out later that the whole genre of SF was already starting to bore her in any case. And he discovered that Terr had already worked her way through half a dozen courses, and had grown bored with all of them. She was bright enough to get a feel of any subject very quickly, and in the process to convince some new senior lecturer that, contrary to all the evidence on file, she finally had found her true focus in medieval history or classics or economics. And she was quick—incredibly so, by Tom's standards —at languages. That would have given her a decent career in any other age; even as she sat there in her blue dress in that Birmingham pub, he could picture her beside that faceless American president, whispering words in his ears. But by then it was already possible for any normally intelligent human to acquire any new language in a matter of days. Deep therapy. Bio-feedback. Nano-enhancement. Out in the real world, those technologies that Tom had spent his teenage years simply dreaming about, as he wondered over those dusty, analogue pages, had been growing at an exponential rate.

But Terr, she fluttered from enthusiasm to enthusiasm, flower to flower, sipping its nectar, then once again spreading her wings and wafting off to some other faculty. And people, too. Terr brought that same incredible focus to bear on everyone she met as well—or at least those who interested her—understanding, absorbing, taking everything in.

She was even doing it now, Tom decided as they sat outside all these years later together by his hut on this starlit French mountain. This Terr who changed and unchanged in the soft flood of candlelight across this battered table was reading him like a book. Every word, every gesture: the way this bottle of wine, good though it was, wouldn't be anything like enough to see him through the rest of this night. She was feeling the tides of the world which had borne him here with all his hopes still somehow intact like Noah in his Ark, and then withdrawn and left him waiting, beached, dry, and drowning.

"What are you thinking?"

He shrugged. But for once, the truth seemed easy. "That pub you took me to, the first time we met."

"You mean the Malt House?"

Terr was bright, quick. Even now. Of course she remembered. "And you went on and on about SF," she added.

"Did I? I suppose I did. . . ."

"Not really, Tom, but I'd sat through a whole bloody lecture of the stuff that morning, and I'd decided I'd had enough of it—of any kind of fiction. I realised I wanted something that was fabulous, but real."

"That's always been a tall order . . ." Terr had been so lovely back then. That blue dress, the shape of her lips on the wineglass she'd been drinking. Those stormy green eyes. Fabulous, but real. But it was like the couple he'd seen that morning. What had she ever seen in him?

"But then you told me you planned to prove that there was other intelligent life in the universe, Tom. Just like that. I don't know why, but it just sounded so wonderful. Your dream, and then the way you could be so matter-of-fact about it. . . ."

Tom gripped his glass a little tighter, and drank the last of it. His dream. He could feel it coming, the next obvious question.

"So did it ever happen?" Terr was now asking. "Did you ever find your little, green men, Tom? But then I suppose I'd have heard. Remember, how you promised to tell me? Or at least it might have roused you to post some news on that poor, old website of yours." She chuckled with her changed voice, slightly slurring the words. But Terr, Tom remembered, could get drunk on half a glass of wine. She could get drunk on nothing. Anything. "I'm sorry, Tom. It's your life, isn't it? And what the hell do I know? It was one of the things I always liked about you, your ability to dream in that practical way of yours. Loved . . ."

*Loved?* Had she said that? Or was that another blip, stray data?

"So you must tell me, Tom. How's it going? After I've come all this way. You and your dream."

The candle was sinking. The stars were pouring down on him. And the wine wasn't enough, he needed absinthe—but his dream. And where to begin? *Where* to begin?

"D'you remember the Drake Equation?" Tom asked.

"Yes, I remember," Terr said. "I remember the Drake Equation. You told me all about the Drake Equation that first day on our walk from that pub . . ." She tilted her head to one side, studying the glimmer of Aries in the west as if she was trying to remember the words of some song they'd once shared. "Now, how exactly did it go?"

Until that moment, none of it had yet seemed quite real to

Tom. This night, and Terr being here. And, as the candle flickered, she still seemed to twist and change from Terr as he remembered to the Terr she was now in each quickening pulse of the flame. But with the Drake Equation, with that Tom Kelly was anchored. And how *did* it go, in any case?

That long and misty afternoon. Walking beside the canal towpaths from that pub and beneath the dripping tunnels and bridges all the way past the old factories and the smart houses to the city's other university out in Edgbaston as the streetlights came on. He'd told Terr about a radio astronomer named Frank Drake who—after all the usual false alarms and funding problems which, even in its embryonic stage back in the middle of the last century, had beset SETI—had tried to narrow the whole question down to a logical series of parameters, which could then be brought together in an equation which, if calculated accurately, would neatly reveal a figure N which would represent a good estimate for the number of intelligent and communicating species currently in our galaxy. If the figure was found to be high, then space would be aswarm with the signals of sentient species anxious to talk to each other. If the figure was found to be one, then we were, to all intents and purposes, alone in the universe. Drake's equation involved the number of stars in our galaxy, and chances of those stars having habitable planets, and then those planets actually bearing life, and of that life evolving into intelligence, and of that intelligence wanting to communicate with other intelligences, and of that communication happening in an era in human history when we humans were capable of listening—which amounted to a microscopic *now*.

And they *had* listened, at least those who believed, those who wanted that number N at the end of the Drake Equation to be up in the tens or hundreds or thousands. They skived spare radiotelescopy and mainframe processing time and nagged their college principals and senators and fellow dreamers for SETI funding. Some, like a project at Arecibo, had even beamed out messages, although the message was going out in any cause, the whole babble of radio communications had been spreading out into space from Earth at the speed of light since Marconi's first transmission . . . *We are here. Earth is alive.* And they listened. They listened for a reply. Back then, when he had met Terr, Tom had still believed in the Drake Equation with a near-religious vehemence, even if many others were beginning to doubt it and funding was getting harder to maintain. As he walked with her beneath the clocktower through the foggy lights of Birmingham's other campus, his PC at his college digs in Erdington was chewing through the data he'd downloaded from a SETI website whilst his landlord's cat slept on it. Tom was sure that, what with the processing technology that was becoming available, and then the wide-array radio satellites, it was only a matter of time and persistence before that first wonderful spike of First Contact came through. And it had stood him in good stead, now that he came to think of it, had the Drake Equation, as he walked with Terr on that misty English autumn afternoon. One of the most convoluted chat-up lines in history. But, at least that once, it had worked.

They took the train back to the city and emerged onto New Street as the lights and the traffic fogged the evening, and at some point on their return back past the big shops and the law courts to the campus Terr had leaned against him and he had put his arm around her. First contact, and the tension between them grew sweet and electric and a wonderful ache had swelled in his throat and belly, until they stopped and kissed in the dank quietude of one of the old subways whilst the traffic swept overhead like a distant sea. Terr. The taste of her mouth, and at last he got to touch that space between her jaw and throat that he had been longing to touch all afternoon. Terr, who was dark and alive in his arms and womanly and English and alien. Terr, who closed her stormy eyes as he kissed her and then opened them again and looked at him with a thrilling candour. After that, everything was different.

Terr had a zest for life, an enthusiasm for everything. And she had an old car, a nondescript Japanese thing with leaky sills, a corrupted GPS, and a badly botched hydrogen conversion. Tom often fiddled under the bonnet to get the thing started before they set out on one of their ambitious weekend trips across the cool and misty country of love and life called England he suddenly found himself in. South to the biscuit-coloured villages of the Cotswolds, north to the grey hills of the Peak District, and then further, further up the map as autumn—he could no longer think of it as fall—rattled her leaves and curled up her smoky clouds and faded and winter set in, juddering for hours along the old public lanes of the motorways as the sleek, new transports swept past outside them with their occupants teleconferencing or asleep. But Tom liked the sense of effort, the sense of getting there, the rumble of the tyres and the off-centre pull of the steering, swapping over with Terr every hour or two, and the way the hills rose and fell but always got bigger as they headed north. And finally stepping out, and seeing the snow and the sunlight on the high flanks, and feeling the clean bite of the wind. They climbed fells where the tracks had long vanished and the sheep looked surprised at these humans who had invaded their territory. Hot and panting, they stopped in the lee of cols, and looked down at all the tiny details of the vast world they had made. By then, Terr had changed options from SF to the early romantics, poets such as Wordsworth and Coleridge, and she would chant from the *Prelude* in her lovely voice as they clambered up Scarfell and the snow and the lakes gleamed around them and Tom struggled, breathless, to keep up until they finally rested, sweating and freezing, and Terr sat down and smiled at him and pulled off her top layers of fleece and Gore-Tex and began to unlace her boots. It was ridiculous, the feel of snow and her body intermingled, and the chant of her breath in his ear, urging him on as the wind and her fingers and the shadows of the clouds swept over his naked back. Dangerous, too, in the mid of winter—you'd probably die from exposure here if you lapsed into a post-coital sleep. But it was worth it. Everything. He'd never felt more alive.

Terr huddled against him in a col. Her skin was taut, freezing, as the sweat evaporated from between them. Another hour, and the sun would start to set. Already, it was sinking down through the clouds over Helvellyn with a beauty that Tom reckoned even old Wordsworth would have been hard put to describe. His fingers played over the hardness of Terr's right nipple, another lovely peak Wordsworth might have struggled to get over in words. It was totally, absolutely cold, but, to his pleasant surprise, Tom found that he, too, was getting hard. He pressed his mouth against Terr's shoulder, ran his tongue around that lovely hollow beneath her ear. She was shivering already, but he felt her give a shiver within the shiver, and traced his fingers down her belly, and thought of the stars which would soon be coming, and perhaps of finding one of those abandoned farmhouses where they could spend the night, and of Terr's sweet moisture, and of licking her there. She tensed and shivered again, which he took as encouragement, even though he was sure, as the coat slid a few inches from his shoulder, that he felt a snowflake settle on his bare back. Then, almost abruptly, she drew away.

"Look over there, Tom. Can you see them—those specks, those colours?"

Tom looked, and sure enough, across in the last, blazing patch of sunlight, a few people were turning like birds. They could have been using microlites, but on a day like this, the sound of their engines would have cut through the frozen air. But Tom had a dim recollection of reading of a new craze, still regarded as incredibly dangerous, both physically and mentally, whereby you took a gene-twist in a vial, and grew wings, just like in a fairy tale, or an SF story.

Tom had dreamed, experienced, all the possibilities. He'd loved those creatures in *Fantasia*, half-human, half-faun; those beautiful, winged horses. And not much later, he'd willed the green-eyed monsters and robots that the cartoon superheroes battled to put their evil plans into practise at least once. Then there were the old episodes of *Star Trek*—the older, the better—and all those other series where the crews of warp-driven starships calmly conversed around long florescent-lit tables with computer-generated aliens and men with rubber masks. By the age of eight, he'd seen galaxy-wide empires rise and fall, and tunnelled through ice planets, he'd battled with the vast and still-sentient relics of ancient conflicts . . . And he found the pictures he could make in his head from the dusty books he discovered for sale in an old apple box when they were closing down the local library were better than anything bil-lion-dollar Hollywood could generate. And it seemed to him that the real technology which he had started to study at school and to mug up on in his spare time was always just a breakthrough or two away from achieving one or other of the technological feats which would get the future, the real future for which he felt an almost physical craving, up and spinning. The starships would soon be ready to launch, even if NASA was running out of funding. The photon sails were spreading, although most of the satellites spin-ning around the Earth seemed to be broadcasting virtual shopping and porn. The wormholes through time and dimension were just a quantum leap away. And the marvellous worlds, teeming with emerald clouds and sentient crimson oceans, the vast diamond cities and the slow beasts of the gas clouds with their gaping mouths spanning fractions of a light year, were out there waiting to be found. So, bright kid that he was, walking the salt harbours of Baltimore with his mother and gazing at the strange star-creatures in their luminous tanks at the National Aquarium long before he met Terr, he'd gone to sleep at nights with the radio on, but tuned between the station to the billowing hiss of those radio waves, spreading out. *We are here. Earth is alive.* Tom was listening, and waiting for a reply.

Doing well enough at exams and aptitudes at school to get to the next level without really bothering, he toyed with the cool physics of cosmology and the logic of the stars, and followed the tangled paths of life through chemistry and biology, and listened to the radio waves, and tinkered with things mechanical and electrical and gained a competence at computing and engineering, and took his degree in Applied Physics at New Colombia, where he had an on-off thing with a psychology undergrad, during which he'd finally got around to losing his virginity before—as she herself put it the morning after; as if, despite all the endearments and promises, she was really just doing him a favour—*it* lost him.

Postgrad time, and the cosmology weirdoes went one way, and the maths bods another, and the computer nerds went thataway, and physics freaks like Tom got jobs in the nano-technology companies which were then creating such a buzz on the World Stock Exchange. But Tom found the same problem at the interviews he went to that he still often found with girls, at least when he was sober—which was that people thought him vague and disinterested. But it was true in any case. His heart really wasn't in it— whatever *it* was. So he did what most shiftless, young academics with a good degree do when they can't think of anything else. He took a postgrad course in another country, which, pin in a map time, really, happened to be at Aston in Birmingham, England. And there he got involved for the first time in the local SETI project, which of course was shoestring and voluntary, but had hooked on to some spare radio time that a fellow-sympathiser had made available down the wire from Jodrell Bank. Of course, he'd known about SETI for ages; his memory of the Drake Equation went so far back into his childhood that, like Snow White or the songs of the Beatles, he couldn't recall when he had first stumbled across it. But to be involved at last, to be one of the ones who were listening. And then persuading his tutor that he could twist around his work on phase-shift data filtering to incorporate SETI work into his dissertation. He was with fellow dreamers at last. It all fitted. What Tom Kelly could do on this particular planet orbiting this common-or-garden sun, and what was actually possible. Even though people had already been listening for a message from the stars for more than fifty years and the politicians and the bureaucrats and the funding bodies—even Tom's ever-patient tutor—were shaking their heads and frowning, he was sure it was just a matter of time. One final push to get there.

*    *    *

There was a shop in Kendal, at the edge of the Lake District. It was on a corner where the cobbled road sloped back and down, and it had, not so many years before, specialised in selling rock-climbing and fell-walking gear, along with the mint cake for which the town was justly famous and which tasted, as Terr had memorably said to Tom when she'd first got him to try it, like frozen toothpaste. You still just about see the old name of the shop—Peak and Fell, with a picture of a couple of hikers—beneath the garish orange paintwork of the new name that had replaced it. EXTREME LAKES.

There were people going in and out, and stylish couples outside posing beneath the bubble hoods of their pristine, lime-green, balloon-tyred off-roaders. Even on this day of freezing rain, but there was no doubt that the new, bodily enhanced sports for which this shop was now catering were good for business. Stood to reason, really. Nobody simply looked up at one of those rounded, snowy peaks and consulted an old edition of Wainwright and then put one booted foot in front of another and walked up them any longer. Nobody except Tom and Terr, scattering those surprised, black-legged sheep across the frozen landscape, finding abandoned farmhouses, making sweet, freezing love which was ice cream and agony on the crackling ice of those frozen cols. Until that moment, Tom had been entirely grateful for it.

The people themselves had an odd look about them. Tom, who had rarely done more than take the autotram to and from the campus and his digs in England until he met Terr, and since had noticed little other than her, was seeing things here he'd only read about; and barely that, seeing as he had little time for newspapers. Facial enhancements, not just the subtle kind that made you look handsomer or prettier, but things, which turned your eyebrows into blue ridges, or widened your lips into pillowy creations, which would had surprised Salvador Dali, let alone Mick Jagger. Breasts on the women like airbags, or nothing but roseate nipples, which of course they displayed teasingly beneath outfits which changed transparency according to the pheromones the smart fabrics detected. One creature, Tom was almost sure, had a threesome, a double-cleavage, although it was hard to tell just by glancing, and he really didn't want to give her the full-bloodied stare she so obviously craved. But most of them were so *thin*. That was the thing, which struck him the most strongly. They were thin as birds, and had stumpy, quill-like appendages sticking from their backs. They were angels or devils, these people, creatures of myth whose wings God had clipped after they had committed some terrible, theological crime, although the wings themselves could be purchased once you went inside the shop. Nike and Reebok and Shark and Microsoft and Honda at quite incredible prices. Stacked in steel racks like ski poles.

The assistant swooped on them from behind her glass counter. She had green hair, which even to Tom seemed reasonable enough, nothing more than a playful use of hair dye, but close-up it didn't actually appear to be hair at all, but some sort of sleek curtain which reminded him of cellophane. It crackled when she touched it, which she did often, as if she couldn't quite believe it was there, the way men do when they have just grown a moustache or beard. She and Terr were soon gabbling about brands and tensile strength and power-to-weight ratios and cold-down and thrillbiting and brute thermals and cloud virgins—which Tom guessed was them. But Terr was soaking it all up in the way that she soaked up anything that was new and fresh and exciting. He watched her in the mirror behind the counter, and caught the amazing flash of those storm green eyes. She looked so beautiful when she was like this; intent and surprised. And he longed to touch that meeting of her throat and jaw just beneath her ear, which was still damp from the rain and desperately needed kissing, although this was hardly the appropriate time. And those eyes. He loved the way Terr gazed right back at him when she was about to come; that look itself was enough to send him tumbling, falling into those gorgeous, green nebulae, down into the spreading dark core of her pupils which were like forming stars.

"Of course, it'll take several weeks, just to make the basic bodily adjustments . . ."

Was the assistant talking to him? Tom didn't know or care. He edged slightly closer to the counter to hide the awkward bulge of his erection, and studied the Kendal Mint Cake, which they still had for sale. The brown and the chocolate-coated, and the standard white blocks, which did indeed taste like frozen toothpaste, but much, much sweeter. A man with jade skin and dreadfully thin arms excused-me past Tom to select a big bar, and then another. Tom found it encouraging, to think that Kendal Mint Cake was still thriving in this new age. There were medals and awards on the old-fashioned wrapping, which commemorated expeditions and treks from back in the times when people surmounted physical challenges with their unaided bodies because, as Mallory had said before he disappeared into the mists of the last ridge of Everest, they were there. But it stood to reason that you needed a lot of carbohydrate if your body was to fuel the changes which would allow you to, as the adverts claimed, fly like a bird. Or at least flap around like a kite. Pretty much, anyway.

This was the new world of extreme sports, where, if you wanted to do something that your body wasn't up to, you simply had your body changed. Buzzing between channels awhile back in search of a site which offered Carl Sagan's *Cosmos*, which to Tom, when he was feeling a bit down, was the equivalent of a warm malt whisky, he'd stumbled across a basketball match, and had paused the search engine, imagining for a moment he'd stumbled across a new version of *Fantasia*, then wondering at the extraordinary sight of these ten- and twelve-foot giants swaying between each other on their spindly legs, clumsy and graceful as new-born fawns. But this, after all, was the future. It was the world he was in. And Terr was right when she urged him to accept it, and with it this whole idea of flying, and then offered to help with the money, which Tom declined, ridiculously excessive though the cost of it was. He lived cheaply enough most of the time, and the bank was always happy to add more to his student loan so that he could spend the rest of his life repaying it. And not that he and Terr were going the whole way, in any case. They were on the nursery slopes, they were ugly chicks still trembling in their nest, they were Dumbo teetering atop that huge ladder in the circus tent. They were cloud virgins. So the heart and circulatory enhancements, and the bone-thinning and the flesh-wasting and the new growth crystals which sent spider-webs of carbon fibre teasing their way through your bone marrow, the Kevlar skin which the rapids surfers used, all the stuff which came stacked with health warnings and disclaimers which would have made the Surgeon General's warning on a packet of full-strength Camels look like a nursery tale: all of that they passed on. They simply went for the bog-standard Honda starter kits of vials and Classic (*Classic* meant boring and ordinary; even Tom had seen enough adverts to know that) wings. That would do—at least for a beginning, Terr said ominously, between humming to herself and swinging the elegant, little bag which contained the first installment of their vials as they headed out from the shop into the driving, winter rain.

It was January already, and the weather remained consistently foul for weeks in its own unsettled English way, which was cold and damp, and billows and squalls, and chortling gutters and rainswept parks, and old leaves and dog mess on the slippery Birmingham pavements. The Nissan packed up again too, but in a way which was beyond Tom's skill to repair, and a part was sent off for which might as well have been borne over from China on a none-too-fast sea clipper, the time it took to come. Days and weekends, they were grounded, and sort-of living together in Tom's digs, or in the pounding, smoky, Rastafarian fug of Terr's shared house in Handsworth. But Tom liked the Rastas; they took old-fashioned chemicals, they worshipped an old-fashioned God, and talked in their blurred and rambling way of a mythic Africa which would never exist beyond the haze of their dreams. Tom did a little ganja himself, and he did a fair amount of wine, and he lay in bed with Terr back in his digs in Erdington one night when the first men landed on Mars, and they watched the big screen on the wall from the rucked and damp sheets whilst the landlord's cat slept on the purring computer.

"Hey, look . . ." Terr squirmed closer to him. "Roll over. I want to see. I was *sure* I could feel something just then . . ."

"I should hope so."

Terr chuckled, and Tom rolled over. He stared at the face in the woodgrain of the old mahogany headboard. She drew back the sheets from him. The cold air. The rain at the window. The murmuring of the astronauts as they undocked and began the last, slow glide. Her fingers on his bare shoulders, then on his spine. It hurt there. It felt as if her nails were digging.

"Hey!!!"

"No no no no no . . ." She pressed him there, her fingers tracing the source of the pain. A definite lump was rising. An outgrowth which, in another age, would have sent you haring to the doctor thinking, *cancer*. . . .

"I'm jealous Tom. I thought I was going to be the first. It's like when I was a kid, and I concentrated hard on growing breasts."

"And it happened?"

"Obviously . . . cheeky sod . . . a bit, anyway . . ." Slim and warm and womanly, she pressed a little closer. He felt her breath, her lips, down on his back where the quills were growing. She kissed him there. "I check in the mirror every morning. I try to feel there . . ." he felt her murmur. "It's like a magic spell, isn't it? Waiting for the vials to work. You haven't noticed anything on me yet, have you, Tom?"

"No." He turned his head and looked at Terr. She was lying on her front too, and the red light of rising Mars on the screen was shining on the perfect skin of her thighs, her buttocks, her spine, her shoulders.

"You must have been waiting for this to happen for a long time," she said.

"What?"

Her blonde hair swayed as she tipped her head toward the screen. "Men landing on Mars."

He nodded.

"Will it take much longer before they actually touch down?"

"I suppose a few minutes."

"Well, that's good news . . ." Terr's hand traveled down his spine. Her knuckles brushed his buttocks, raising the goosebumps. Her fingers explored him there. "Isn't it . . . ?"

So they missed the actual instant when the lander kicked up the rusty dust of the surface, but were sharing a celebratory bottle of Asti Spumante an hour or so later when, after an interminable string of adverts, the first ever human being stepped onto the surface of another planet and claimed all its ores and energies and secrets for the benefit of the mission's various sponsors. Another figure climbed out. Amid the many logos on this one's suit there was a Honda one, which sent Tom's mind skittering back toward the growing lump on his back, which he could feel like a bad spot no matter how he laid the pillows now that Terr had mentioned it. How would he *sleep* from now on? How would they make *love*? Terr on top, fluttering her Honda wings like a predator as she bowed down to eat him? It was almost a nice idea, but not quite. And the Mars astronauts, even in their suits, didn't look quite right to Tom either. The suits themselves were okay—they were grey-white, and even had the sort of longer-at-top faceplates he associated with 2001 and Hal and Dave Poole and Kubrick's incredible journey toward the alien monolith—but they were the wrong shape in the body; too long and thin. It was more like those bad, old films; you half expected something horrible and inhuman to slither out of them once they got back into the lander, where it turned out to have crossed light years driven by nothing more than a simple desire to eat people's brains. . . .

Tom poured out the rest of the Asti into his glass.

"Hey!" Terr gave him a playful push. He slopped some of it. "What about me? You've had almost all of that. . . ."

He ambled off into the cupboard, which passed for his kitchen to get another bottle of something, and stroked the landlord's cat and gave the keyboard of his PC a tweak on the way. It was processing a search in the region of Cygnus, and not on the usual waterhole wavelength. Somebody's hunch. Not that the PC had found anything; even in those days, he had the bells and whistles rigged for *that* event. But what *was* the problem with him, he wondered, as he raked back the door of the fridge and studied its sparse contents? He was watching the first Mars landing, in bed with a naked, beautiful, and sexually adventurous woman, whilst his PC diligently searched the stars for the crucial first sign of intelligent life. If this wasn't his dream of the future, what on Earth was? And even this flying gimmick which Terr was insisting they try together —that fitted in as well, didn't it? In many ways, the technology that was causing his back to grow spines was a whole lot more impressive than the brute force and money and Newtonian physics which had driven that Martian lander from one planet to another across local space.

The problem with this manned Mars landing, as Tom had recently overheard someone remark in the university refectory, was that it had come at least four decades too late. Probably more, really. NASA could have gone pretty much straight from Apollo to a Mars project, back at the end of the delirious 1960s. Even then, the problems had been more of money than of science. Compared to politics, compared to getting the right spin and grip on the public's attention and then seeing the whole thing through Congress before something else took the headlines or the next recession or election came bounding along, the science and the engineering had been almost easy. But a first landing by 1995 at the latest, which had once seemed reasonable—just a few years after establishing the first permanent moonbase. And there really had been Mariner and Viking back in those days of hope and big-budget NASA: technically successful robot probes which had nevertheless demystified Mars and finished off H. G. Wells's Martians and Edgar Rice Burrows's princesses and Lowell's canals in the popular mind, and which, despite Sagan's brave talk about Martian giraffes wandering by when the camera wasn't looking, had scuppered any realistic sense that there might be large and complex Martian lifeforms waiting to be fought against, interviewed, studied, dissected, argued over by theologians, or fallen in love with. Still, there were hints that life might exist on Mars at a microscopic level; those tantalisingly contradictory results from the early Viking landers, and the micro-bacteria supposedly found on Martian meteorites back on Earth. But, as the probes had got more advanced and the organic tests more accurate, even those possibilities had faded. Tom, he'd watched Mars become a dead planet both in the real world, and in the books he loved reading. The bulge-foreheaded Martians faded to primitive cave-dwellers, then to shy kangaroo-like creatures of the arid plains, until finally they became bugs dwelling around vents deep in the hostile Martian soil, then anaerobic algae, until they died out entirely.

Mars was a dead planet.

Tom unscrewed the bottle of slivovitz that was the only thing he could find, and went back to bed with Terr, and they watched the figures moving about on the Martian landscape between messages from their sponsors. They were half Martians already. Not that they could breathe the emaciated atmosphere, or survive without their suits on, but nevertheless they had been radically transformed before the launch. Up in space, in null gravity, their bones and their flesh and their nutritional requirements had been thinned down to reduce the payload, then boosted up just a little as they approached Mars a year and a half later so they could cope with the planet's lesser pull. They were near-sexless creatures with the narrow heads and bulging eyes of a thyroid complaint, fingers as long and bony as ET's. The way they looked, far worse than any flyers, Tom figured that you really didn't need to search further than these telecasts to find aliens to Mars. Or Belsen victims.

The slivovitz and the whole thing got to him. He had a dim recollection of turning off the screen at some point, and of making love to Terr, and touching the hollow of her back and feeling a tiny, sharp edge there sliding beneath her skin; although he wasn't quite sure about that, or whether he'd said anything to her afterward about growing bigger breasts, which had been a joke in any case. In the morning, when she had gone, he also discovered that he had broken up the Honda vials and flushed them down the communal toilet. Bits of the spun glass stuff were still floating there. He nearly forgot his slivovitz headache as he pissed them down. This was one thing he'd done when he was drunk he was sure he'd never regret.

The winter faded. Terr went flying. Tom didn't. The spines on her back really weren't so bad; the wings themselves were still inorganic in those days, carbon fibre and smart fabric, almost like the old microlites, except you bonded them to the quills with organic superglue just before you took the leap, and unbonded them again and stacked them on the roof rack of your car at the end of the day. Terr's were sensitive enough when Tom touched them, licked them, risked brushing their sharp edges against his penis to briefly add a new and surprising spice to their love making, although if he grew too rough, too energetic, both he and they were prone to bleed.

Terr was unbothered about his decision to stop taking the vials. After all, it was his life. *And why do something you don't want to do just to please me?* she'd said with her characteristic logic. But Terr was moving with a different set now, with the flyers, and their relationship, as spring began and the clean thermals started to rise on the flanks of Skiddaw and Helvellyn and Ben Nevis, began to have that ease and forgetfulness which Tom, little versed though he was in the ways of love, still recognised as signaling the beginning of the end. Terr had always been one for changing enthusiasms in any case. At university, she was now talking of studying creative writing, or perhaps dropping the literature thing entirely and swapping over to cultural studies, whatever the hell that was. It would be another one of Terr's enthusiasms, just, as Tom was coming to realise, had been Tom Kelly.

He still saw plenty of Terr for a while, although it was more often in groups. He enjoyed the jazz with her at Ronnie Scott's and sat around florescent tables in the smart bars along Broad Street with people whose faces often reminded him of those rubber-masked creatures you used to get in *Star Trek*. The world was changing—just like Terr, it didn't feel like it was quite *his* any longer, even though he could reach out and touch it, taste it, smell it. He drove up with her once or twice to the Lakes, and watched her make that first incredible leap from above the pines on Skiddaw and across the wind-rippled, grey expanse of Bassenthwaite Lake. He felt nothing but joy and pride at that moment, and almost wished that he, too, could take to the air, but soon, Terr was just another coloured dot, swooping and circling in the lemony, spring sunlight on her Honda-logoed wings, and no longer a cloud virgin. He could block her out with the finger of one hand.

So they drifted apart, Tom and Terr, and part of Tom accepted this fact—it seemed like a natural and organic process; you meet, you exchange signals of mutual interest, you fall in love and fuck each other brainless for a while and live in each other's skin and hair, then you get to know your partner's friends and foibles and settle into a warmer and easier affection as you explore new hobbies and positions and fetishes until the whole thing becomes just a little stale—and part of Tom screamed and hollered against the loss, and felt as if he was drowning as the sounds, the desperate, pleading signals he wanted to make, never quite seemed to reach the surface. He had, after all, always been shy and diffident with women. Especially the pretty ones. Especially, now, Terr.

At the end of the summer term, Tom got his postgrad diploma based around his SETI work and Terr didn't get anything. Just as she'd done with Tom, she'd worn Aston University out as she explored its highways and byways and possibilities with that determination that was so uniquely Terr. Next year, if any would take her and she could gather up the money, she'd have to try another enthusiasm at another university. They hadn't been lovers for months, which seemed to Tom like years, and had lost regular contact at the time, by pure chance, he last saw her. Tom, he needed to get on with his life, and had already booked a flight to spend some time at home with his parents in the States whilst he decided what *getting on with life* might actually involve for him.

It was after the last, official day of term, and the wine bars around the top of the city were busy with departing students and the restaurants contained the oddly sombre family groups who had come up to bear a sibling and their possessions back home. The exams had been and gone, the fuss over the assessments and dissertations and oral hearings had faded. There was both a sense of excitement and anticlimax, and beneath that an edge of sorrow and bone-aching tiredness which came from too many—or not enough—nights spent revising, screwing, drinking . . . Many, many people had already left, and hallways in the North Wing rang hollow and the offices were mostly empty as Tom called in to pick up his provisional certificate, seeing as he wouldn't be here for the award ceremonies in the autumn, and he didn't attend such pompous occasions in any case.

There was no obvious reason for Terr to be around. Her friends by now were mostly flyers, non-students, and she hadn't sat anything remotely resembling an exam. The season wasn't a Terr season in Tom's mind, either. A late afternoon, warm and humid as a dishrag, uncomfortable and un-English, when the T-shirt clung to his back and a bluish smog, which even the switch from petrol to hydrogen hadn't been able to dissolve, hung over the city. Put this many people together, he supposed, holding his brown envelope by the tips of this fingers so that he didn't get sweat onto it, this much brick and industry, and you'd always get city air. Even now. In this future world. He caught a whiff of curry-house cooking, and of beer-infused carpets from the open doorways of the stifling Yate's Wine Lodge, and of hot pavements, and of warm tar and of dog mess and rank canals, and thought of the packing he'd left half finished in his room, and of the midnight flight he was taking back to the States, and of the last SETI download his PC would by now have probably finished processing, and decided he would probably miss this place.

Characteristically, Terr was walking one way up New Street as

Tom was heading the other. Characteristically, Terr was with a group of gaudy fashion victims; frail waifs and wasp-waisted freaks. Many of them looked Japanese, although Tom knew not to read too much into that, when a racial look was as easy to change as last season's shoes if you had the inclination and the money. In fact, Terr rather stood out, in that she really hadn't done anything that freakish to herself, although the clothes she wore—and sensibly enough, really, in this weather—were barebacked and scanty, to display the quills of those wings. And her hair was red; not the red of a natural redhead, or even the red of someone who had dyed it that colour in the old-fashioned way. But crimson; for a moment, she almost looked to Tom as if her head was bleeding. But he recognised her instantly. And Terr, Tom being Tom and thus unchanged, probably even down to his T-shirt, instantly recognised him.

She peeled off from the arm-in-arm group she was swaying along with, and he stopped and faced her as they stood in the shadow of the law courts whilst the pigeons cluttered up around them and the bypass traffic swept by beyond the tall buildings like the roar of the sea. He'd given a moment such as this much thought and preparation. He could have been sitting an exam. A thousand different scenarios, but none of them now quite seemed to fit. Terr had always been hard to keep up with, the things she talked about, the way she dressed. And those storm green eyes, which were the one thing about her that he hoped she would never change, they were a shock to him now as well.

They always had been.

"I thought you weren't going to notice, Tom. You looked in such a hurry. . . ."

"Just this . . ." He waved the limp, brown envelope as if it was the reason for everything. "And I've got a plane to catch."

She nodded, gazing at him. Tom gazed back—those green nebulae—and instantly he was falling. "I'd heard that you were leaving."

"What about you, Terr?"

She shrugged. The people behind her were chattering in a language Tom didn't recognise. His eyes traveled quickly over them, wondering which of them was now screwing Terr, and which were male—as if that would matter, Terr being Terr. . . .

"Well, actually, it's a bit of a secret, and quite illegal probably, but we're going to try to get onto the roof of one of the big halls of residence and—"

"—fly?"

She grinned. Her irises were wide. Those dark stars. She was high on something. Perhaps it was life. "Obviously. Can you imagine what the drift will be like, up there, with all these cliff-face buildings, on an afternoon like this?"

"Drift?"

"The thermals."

He smiled. "Sounds great."

One of those pauses, a slow, roaring beat of city silence, as one human being gazes at another and wonders what to say to them next. How to make contact—or how to regain it. That was always the secret, the thing for which Tom was searching. And he had a vision, ridiculous in these circumstances, of clear, winter daylight on a high fell. He and Terr . . .

"That dress you used to wear," he heard himself saying, "the blue one—"

"—Have you had any luck yet, Tom?" It was a relief, really, that she cut across his rambling. "With that SETI work you were doing? All that stuff about . . ." She paused. Her hands touched her hair, which didn't seem like hair at all, not curtains of blood, but of cellophane. It whispered and rustled in her fingers, and then parted, and he glimpsed in the crimson shade beneath that space at the join of her jaw and neck, just beneath her ear, before she lowered her hand and it was gone again. He wondered if he would ever see it again; that place which—of all the glories in the universe, the dark light years and the sentient oceans and the ice planets and the great beasts of the stellar void—was the one he now most longed to visit. Then she remembered the phrase for which she'd been searching, which was one Tom had explained, when they'd walked that first day by the canals in fall, in English autumn. ". . . the Drake Equation."

"I'm still looking."

"That's good." She nodded and smiled at him in a different way, as if taking in the full implications of this particular that's-goodness, and what it might mean one great day to all of mankind. "You're not going to give up on it, are you?"

"No."

"You're going to keep looking?"

"Of course I will. It's my life."

As he said it, he wondered if it was. But the creatures, the flyers, behind Tom and Terr, were twitching and twittering; getting restless. And one or two of the things they were saying Tom now recognised as having the cadence of English. There was just so much jargon thrown in there.

"And you'll let me know, won't you? You'll let me know as soon as you get that first message." Terr's tongue moistened her lower lip. "And I don't mean ages later, Tom. I want you to call me the moment it happens, wherever you are, up in whatever observatory. Will you do that for me? I want to be the first to hear. . . ."

Tom hesitated, then nodded. Hesitated not because of the promise itself, which seemed sweet and wonderful, but because of the way that she'd somehow made this chance meeting, this short conversation, into an almost final parting. Or entirely final. It all now really depended on the outcome of the Drake Equation. Life out there, or endless barren emptiness. Terr, or no Terr.

"And I'll let you know, too, Tom," she said, and gave him a kiss that was half on his cheek, half on the side of his mouth, "I'll let you know if I hear anything as well . . ." But it was too quick for him to really pay attention to this strange thing she was saying. He was just left with a fading impression of her lips, her scent, the coolly different feel of her hair.

"You'd better be going," he said.

"Yes! While we've still got the air. Or before the Provost finds us. And you've got that plane to catch. . . ."

Terr gave him a last smile, and touched the side of his face with her knuckles almost where she'd kissed it, and traced the line of his jaw with fingernails which were now crimson. Then she turned and rejoined the people she was with. Tom thought she looked thinner as he watched the departing sway of her hips, and the way a satyrlike oaf put his arm around her in what might or might not have been a normally friendly manner. And narrower around the shoulders, too. Almost a waif. Not quite the fully rounded Terr he'd loved through the autumn and winter, although her breasts seemed to be bigger. Another few months, and he'd probably barely recognise her, which was a comfort of sorts. Things changed. You moved on. Like it or not, the tide of the future was always rushing over you.

Determined not to look back, Tom headed briskly on down New Street. Then, when he did stop and swallow the thick choking in his throat, which was like gritty phlegm and acid, and turn around for a last, anguished glimpse of Terr, she and her friends had already gone from sight beyond the law courts. *I'll let you know if I hear anything, Tom . . .* What a strange, ridiculous idea! But at least the incident had helped him refine his own feelings, and put aside that hopeful longing which he realised had been dogging him like a cloud in a cartoon. As he strode down New Street to catch the autotram back to Erdington and finish his packing, Tom had a clear, almost Biblical certainty about his life, and the direction in which it would lead him. It was—how could he ever have doubted it?—the Drake Equation.

"So how does it work out?" Terr said to him now, up on his mountain. "That Drake fellow must have been around more than a century ago. So much has changed—even in the time since we were . . . since England, since Birmingham. We've progressed as a race, haven't we, us humans? The world hasn't quite disintegrated. The sun hasn't gone out. So surely you must have a better idea by now, surely you must know?"

"Nobody knows for sure, Terr. I wouldn't be here if I did. The Drake Equation is still just a series of guesses."

"But *we're* here on Earth, aren't we, Tom? Us humans and apes and bugs and cockroaches and dolphins. We must have somehow got started."

He nodded. Even now. Terr was so right. "Exactly."

"And we're still listening, and we want to hear . . ." She chuckled. "Or at least *you're* still listening, Tom. So all you have to hope for is another Tom Kelly out in space, up there amid all those stars. It's that simple, isn't it?"

"Can you imagine that?"

Terr thought for a moment. She thought for a long time. The wine bottle was empty. The candle was guttering. "Does he have to have the same colour skin, this alien Tom Kelly? Does he have to have four purple eyes and wings like a flyer?"

"That's up to you, Terr."

Then she stood up, and the waft of her passage toward him blew out the candle and brightened the stars and brought her scent, which was sweet and dusty and as utterly unchanged as the taste of her mouth, as she leaned down out of the swarming night and kissed him.

"I think you'll do as you are," she said, and traced her finger around his chin, just as she'd used to do, and down his nose and across his lips, as if he was clay, earth, and she was sculpting him. "One Tom Kelly. . . ."

In the years after he left Aston and split with Terr, Tom had found that he was able to put aside his inherent shyness, and go out in the big, bad world of academic science, and smile and press the flesh with administrators and business suits and dinosaur heads-of-department, and develop a specialisation of sorts which combined data

analysis with radio astronomy. He knew he was able enough—
somehow, his ability was the only thing about himself that he rarely
doubted—and he found to his surprise that he was able to move
from commercial development contracts to theoretical work to
pure research without many of the problems of job security and
unemployment which seemed to plague his colleagues. Or perhaps
he just didn't care. He was prepared to go anywhere, do anything.
He lived entirely in his head, as a brief womanfriend had said to
him. Which was probably true, for Tom knew that he was never
that sociable. Like the essential insecurity of research work, he simply didn't let it worry him. It helped, often, that there was a ready
supply of drinks at many of the conferences and seminars he
attended—not perhaps in the actual lecture halls and conference
suites, but afterward, in the bars and rooms where the serious science of self-promotion went on. It helped, too, that at the back of it
all, behind all the blind alleys and government cuts and flurries of
spending, he had one goal.

It had surprised Tom that that first Martian landing should have
had such a depressing effect on SETI research, when any sensible
interpretation of the Drake Equation had always allowed for the
fact that Earth was the only planet likely to harbour life in this
particular solar system. Even he was disappointed, though, when
the Girouard probe finally put the kibosh on any idea of life exist-
ing in what had once seemed like the potentially warm and
habitable waters of Jupiter's satellite Europa. Still, the Principal of
Mediocrity, which is that this sun, this solar system, this planet, and
even the creatures which dwell upon it, are all common-or-garden
phenomena, and thus likely to be repeated in similar form all over
the galaxy, remained entirely undamaged by such discoveries, at
least in Tom's mind. But in the mind of the general public (in that
the general public has a mind to care about such things) and in the
minds of the politicians and administrators who controlled scien-
tific funding (ditto), it was a turning point, and began to confirm
the idea that there really wasn't much out there in space apart from
an endless vacuum punctuated a few aggregations of rocks, searing
temperatures, hostile chemicals.

Funnily enough, this recession of the tides in SETI funding
worked in Tom's favour. Like a collector of a type of objet d'art
which was suddenly no longer fashionable, he was able to mop up
the data, airtime, and hardware of several abandoned projects at
bargain prices, sometimes using his own money, sometimes by tapping the enthusiasm of the few remaining SETI-freaks, sometimes

by esoteric tricks of funding. Now that the big satellite telescopes could view and analyse stars and their orbital perturbation with a previously unheard-of accuracy, a few other solar systems had come out of the woodwork, but they were astonishingly rare, and mostly seemed to consist either of swarms of asteroids and dust clouds or huge near-stella aggregations of matter, which would fuse and crush anything resembling organic life. So $f_p$ in the Drake Equation—the fraction of stars to likely have a planetary system—went down to something like 0.0001, and $n_e$—the number of those planets which could bear life—fell to the even lower 0.0000-somethings unless you happened to think that life was capable of developing using a different chemical basis to carbon, as Tom, reared as he was on a diet of incredible starbeasts, of course did. $f_l$—the probability that life would then develop on a suitable planet—also took a downturn, thanks to lifeless Mars and dead Europa, and then as every other potential niche in the solar system that some hopeful scientist had posited was probed and explored and spectrum analysed out of existence. The stock of SETI was as low as it had ever been, and Tom really didn't care. In fact, he relished it.

He wrote a paper entitled "New Light on the Drake Equation," and submitted it to *Nature*, and then, as the last SETI journal had recently folded, to the *Radio Astronomy Bulletin* and, without any more success, and with several gratuitously sneering remarks from referees, to all the other obvious and then the less obvious journals. In the paper, he analysed each element of the equation in turn, and explained why what had become accepted as the average interpretation of it was in fact deeply pessimistic. Taking what he viewed as the true middle course of balance and reason, and pausing only to take a few telling swipes at the ridiculous idea that computer simulations could provide serious data on the likelihood of life spontaneously developing, and thus on $f_l$, he concluded that the final N figure in the Drake Equation was, by any balanced interpretation, still in the region 1,000–10,000, and that it was thus really only a matter of time before contact was made. That was, as long as people were still listening. . . .

He didn't add it to the versions of the paper he submitted, but he also planned to ask whoever finally published the thing to place a dedication when it was printed: *For Terr*. That, at least, was the simplest variant of a text he spent many wall-staring hours expanding, cutting, revising. But the paper never did get published, although a much shortened work, stripped of its maths by Tom and then of a lot of its sense by the copy editor, finally did come out in a popular science comic, beside an article about a man who was growing a skein of his own nerve tissue to a length of several hundred feet so that he could bungee jump with it from the Victoria Falls. Still, the response was good, even if many of the people who contacted Tom were of a kind he felt reluctant to give out his e-mail, let alone his home, address to.

The years passed. Through a slow process of hard work, networking, and less-than-self-aggrandisement, Tom became Mr SETI. There always was, he tended to find, at least one member of the astronomy or the physics or even the biology faculty of most institutes of learning who harboured a soft spot for his topic. Just as Sally Normanton had done when he returned to Aston on that autumn, when the air had smelled cleaner and different and yet was in so many ways the same, they found ways of getting him small amounts of funding. Slowly, Tom was able to bow out of his other commitments, although he couldn't help noticing how few attempts were made to dissuade him. Perhaps he'd lost his youthful zest, perhaps it was the smell on his breath of whatever he'd drank the night before, which now seemed to carry over to the morning. He was getting suprisingly near to retirement age, in any case. And the thought, the ridiculous idea that he'd suddenly been on the planet for *this long*, scared him, and he needed something that would carry him through the years ahead. What scared him even more, though, like a lottery addict who's terrified that their number will come up on exactly the week that they stop buying the tickets, was what would happen to SETI if he stopped listening. Sometimes, looking up at the night sky as the computers at whatever faculty he was now at pounded their way through the small hours with his latest batch of star data, gazing at those taunting pinpricks with all their mystery and promise, he felt as if he was bearing the whole universe up by the effort of his mind, and that the stars themselves would go out, just as they did in that famous Clarke story, the moment he turned his back on them. It was about then that he generally thought about having another drink, just to see him through the night, just to keep up his spirits. It was no big deal. A drink was a drink. Everyone he knew did it.

So Tom finally got sufficient funds and bluff together to set up his own specialised SETI project, and then settled on France for reasons he couldn't now quite remember, except that it was a place he hadn't been to where they still spoke a language which wasn't English, and then chose the karst area of the Massif Central because it gave the sort of wide, flat planes which fitted with the technology of his tripwire receivers, and was high up and well away from the radio babble of the cities. The choice was semi-symbolic —as well as the tripwires, he planned to borrow and buy-in as much useful data as he could from all possible sources, and process it there with whatever equipment he could borrow or cannibalise. Then he saw the waterhole, a tiny, blue dot on the map of this otherwise desolate mountain plateau above a small place called St. Hilaire, and that settled it. He hadn't even known that the place was a flying resort, until he'd signed all the necessary legal papers and hitched his life to it. And even that, in its way—those rainbow butterflies and beetles, those prismatic famine victims clustering around their smart bars and expensive shops, queuing with their wings whispering to take the cable lifts to the high peaks in the sun-struck south each morning—seemed appropriate. It made him think of Terr, and how her life had been, and it reminded him—as if he'd ever forgotten—of his, of *their* promise.

But it had never happened. There'd never been a reason to let her know.

Tom wrestled with the memories, the feelings, as Terr touched him, and closed her hands around his with fingers that seemed to have lost all their flesh. She was tunneling down the years to him, kissing him from the wide sweep of some incredible distance. He tried closing his eyes, and felt the jagged rim of teeth and bone beneath her lips. He tried opening them, and he saw her flesh streaked and lined against the stars, as if the Terr of old was wearing a mask made of paper. And her eyes had gone out. All the storms had faded. She touched him, briefly, intimately, but he knew that it was useless.

She stood back from him and sighed, scarecrow figure in her scarecrow dress, long hair in cobwebs around her thin and witchy face.

"I'm sorry, Tom—"

"No, it isn't—"

"—I was making presumptions."

But Tom knew who and what was to blame. Too many years of searching, too many years of drink. He sat outside his hut, frozen in his chair with his tripwires glimmering, and watched as Terr wandered off. He heard the clink of bottles as she inspected his skip. He heard the shuffle of rubbish as she picked her way around indoors. He should have felt ashamed, but he didn't. He was past that, just as he was past, he realised, any approximation of the act of love.

When Terr came out again into the starlight, she was carrying a bottle. It was the absinthe.

"Is this what you want?" she said, and unstoppered it. She poured a slug of the stuff into her own empty wineglass, and raised it to her thin lips, and sipped. Even under this starlight, her face grew wrinkled, ugly. "God, it's so *bitter.* . . ."

"Perhaps that's why I like it."

"You know, you could get rid of this habit, Tom. It's like you said to me—if there's something about yourself you don't like, all you need do is take a vial."

Tom shrugged, wondering whether she was going to pour some absinthe out into his glass or just stand there, waving the bottle at him. Was he being deliberately taunted? But Terr was right, of course. You took a vial, and you were clean. The addiction was gone. Everything about you was renewed, apart from the fact that you were who you were, and still driven by the same needs and contradictions that had given you the craving in the first place. So you went back to the odd drink, because you knew you were clean now, you were safe. And the odd drink became a regular habit again, and you were back where you started again, only poorer and older, and filled with an even deeper self-contempt. And worse headaches. Yes, Tom had been there.

"It's like you say, Terr. We are as we are. A few clever chemicals won't change that."

"You're going to be telling me next that you're an addictive personality."

"I wouldn't be here otherwise would I, doing this?"

She nodded and sat down again. She tipped some absinthe into his glass, and Tom stared at it, and at the faintly glowing message cards which he still hadn't read which lay beside it on the table, allowing a slight pause to elapse before he drank the absinthe, just to show her that he could wait. Then the taste of anise and wormwood, which was the name of the star, as he recalled, which had fallen from the heavens and seared the rivers and fountains in the Book of Revelation. It had all just been a matter of belief, back then.

"You still haven't told me how things have been for you, Terr."

"They've been okay. On and off . . ." Terr considered, her head in shade and edged with starlight. Tom told himself that the skull he could now see had always been there, down beneath Terr's skin that he had once so loved to touch and taste. Nothing was really that different. "With a few regrets."

"Did you really get into flying? That was how I always pictured you, up in the skies. Like the kids you see now down in this valley."

"Yes! I was a flyer, Tom. Not quite the way they are now—I'm sure they'd think the stuff we used then was uselessly heavy and clumsy. But it was great while it lasted. I made a lot of friends."

"Did you ever go back to your studies?"

She gave that dry chuckle again; the rustle of wind through old telephone wires. "I don't think I ever had *studies*, Tom. No, I got a job. Worked in public relations. Built up this company I was involved in very well for a while, sold other people's projects and ideas, covered up other people's mistakes—"

"—We could have used you for SETI."

"I thought of that, Tom—or of you, at least. But you had your own life. I didn't want to seem patronising. And then I got sick of being slick and enthusiastic about other people's stuff, and I got involved in this project of my own. Basically, it was a gallery, a sort of art gallery, except the exhibits were people. I was . . ."

"You were one of them?"

"Of course I was, Tom! What do you expect? But it plays havoc with your immune system after a while. You hurt and ache and bleed. It's something for the very fit, the very young, or the very dedicated. And then I tried being normal and got married and unmarried, and then married again."

"Not to the same person?"

"Oh no. Although they made friends, funnily enough, did my two ex's. Last time I heard from one of them, they were both still keeping in touch. Probably still are. Then I got interested in religion. *Religions*, being me . . ."

"Any kids?"

"Now never quite seemed the time. I wish there had been a *now*, though, but on the other hand perhaps I was always too selfish."

"You were never selfish, Terr."

"Too unfocussed then."

"You weren't that either." Tom took another slug of absinthe, and topped up the glass. He could feel the bitter ease of it seeping into him. It was pleasant to sit talking like this. Sad, but pleasant. He realised he hadn't just missed Terr. These last few years up on his mountain, he'd missed most kinds of human company. "But I know what you mean. Even when I used to dream about us staying together, I could never quite manage the idea of kids. . . ."

"How can two people be so different, and so right for each other?"

"Is that what you really think?"

"I loved you more than I loved anyone, Tom. All the time since, I often got this feeling you were watching, listening. Like that afternoon when I jumped with my wings from that tower in Aston and then got arrested. And the body art. You were like a missing guest at the weddings. I was either going for or against you in whatever I did —and sort of wondering how you'd react. And then I went to the Moon, and your ghost seemed to follow me there, too. Have you ever been off-planet?"

He shook his head. He hadn't—or at least not in the obvious physical sense, although he'd traveled with Kubrick over the Moon's craters a thousand times to the thrilling music of Ligeti.

"Thought not. It was the most expensive thing I ever did."

"What's it like?"

"That's just about it with the moon, Tom—it's expensive. The place you stay in is like one of those cheap, old, Japanese hotels. Your room's a pod you can't even sit up in. Who'd ever have thought space could be so claustrophobic!"

"All these things you've done, Terr. They sound so fascinating."

"Do, don't they—saying them like I'm saying them now? But it was always like someone else's life that I seemed to be stuck in. Like wearing the wrong clothes. I was always looking for my own. And then you get older—God, you know what it's like! And there are so many *choices* nowadays. So many different ways of stretching things out, extending the years, but the more you stretch them, the thinner they get. I always knew that I never wanted to live to some great age. These one-and-a-half centenarians you see, they seem to be there just to prove a point. Tortoises in an endless race. Or animals in a grotty zoo. Minds in twisted rusty cages . . ."

"I'd never really thought—"

"—You'll just go on until the bang, won't you Tom? Until the booze finally wreaks some crucial organ or busts a capillary in your head. Or until the Vesuvians land over there, on those funny wires, in a flying saucer and take you away with them. Although you'd probably say no because they aren't quite the aliens you expected."

"What do you mean?"

"Nothing, Tom. It's just the way you are. And you've been lucky, really, to have managed to keep your dream intact, despite all the evidence. I read that article you did, years ago in that funny little paper with all the flashing adverts for body-changing. 'New Light on the Drake Equation.' I had to smile. You still sounded so positive. But don't you think we'd have heard from them by now, if they really were out there? Think of all the millions of stars, all these millions of years, and all those galactic civilisations you used to read about. It wouldn't be a whisper, would it, Tom, something you needed all this fiddly technology to pick up on? It would be all around us, and unavoidable. If the aliens wanted us to hear from them, it would be an almighty roar. . . ."

The stars were just starting to fade now at the edge of the east; winking out one by one in the way that Tom had always feared. Taurus, Orion . . . the first hint of light as this part of the planet edged its face toward the sun was always grey up here on the karst, oddly wan and depressing. It was the colour, he often felt as the night diluted and the optimism that the booze inspired drained out of him in torrents of piss and the occasional worrying hawk of bloody vomit, that his whole world would become—if he lost SETI. And the argument which Terr had so cannily absorbed, was, he knew, the most damning of all the arguments against his dream. The odd thing was, it lay outside the Drake Equation entirely, which was probably why that dumb article of his had avoided mentioning it. What Terr was saying was a version of a question that the founding father of the nuclear chain reaction Enrico Fermi had once asked in the course of a debate about the existence of extra-terrestrial intelligence nearly a century and half—and how time flew!—ago. The question was simply this: "Where are they?"

There were these things called von Neumann machines; perhaps Terr knew that as well. They'd once been a theory, and stalwarts of the old tales of the future Tom had loved reading, but now they were out working in the asteroid belt and on Jupiter's lesser moons, and down in deep mines on Earth and the sea trenches and on Terr's moon and any other place where mankind wanted something but didn't want to risk its own skin getting it. They were robots, really, but they were able to manufacture new versions of themselves—reproduce, if you wanted to make the obvious biological comparison—using the available local materials. They were smart, too. They could travel and adapt to new environments. They could do pretty much anything you wanted of them. So surely, went the argument, which sometimes crept along with the depression and the morning hangover into Tom's head, any other intelligent lifeform would have come up with a similar invention? Even with the staggering distance involved in travel between the stars, all you had to do was launch some into space, wait a few million years—a mere twitch of God's eye, by any cosmological timescale—and the things would be colonising this entire galaxy. So where were they?

The answer was as simple as Fermi's question: *They aren't here.*

And mankind was a freak; he and his planet were a fascinating out-rage against all the laws of probability. The rest of the universe was either empty, or any other dim glimmerings of life were so distant and faint as to be unreachable in all the time remaining until the whole shebang collapsed again. Better luck next time, perhaps. Or the time after that. By one calculation of the Drake Equation Tom had read, life of some kind was likely to appear somewhere in the entire universe once in every $10^{10}$ big bangs, and even that was assuming the physical laws remained unchanged. The guy hadn't bothered to put the extra spin on the figure, which would involve two communicating intelligences arising at the same time and in the same corner of the same galaxy. Probably hadn't wanted to wreck his computer.

Half the sky was greying out now. Star by star by star. At least he'd soon get a proper look at Terr, and she'd get a proper look at him, although he wasn't sure that that was what either of them wanted. Perhaps there was something to be said for the grey mists of uncertainty, after all.

"I always said—didn't I, Tom?—that I'd bring you a message."

"And *this* is it? You saying I should give up on the one thing that means something to me?"

"Don't look at it like that, Tom. Think of it as . . ." A faint breeze had sprung up, the start of the wind that would soon lift the flyers as the temperature gradients hit the valley. Tom thought for a moment that they must still have a candle burning on the table between them, the way Terr seemed to flicker and sway beyond it. She was like smoke. Her hair, her face. He poured him-self some more absinthe, which he decided against drinking. "The thing is, Tom, that you've got yourself into this state where you imagine that whether or not you listen in itself proves something. It doesn't, Tom. They're out there—they're not out there. Either way, it's a fact already isn't it? It's just one we don't happen to know the answer to . . . and wouldn't it be a pity, if we knew the answer to everything? Where would your dreams be then?"

"Science is all about finding out the truth—"

"—And this life of yours Tom! I mean, why on Earth do you have to go down to the village to pick up those messages? Can't you communicate with people from up here? It looks like you've got enough equipment in that hut to speak to the entire world if you wanted to. But I suppose that doesn't interest you."

"I find personal messages . . ." He gazed as the hills in the east as a questing spear of light rose over them, then down at the cards she'd brought up to him. "I find them distracting."

"I'm sorry, Tom. I don't want to distract you."

"I didn't mean . . ." There he went again. Terr in tears, just the way she'd been, in a memory he'd suppressed for so long, in his bed in Erdington on that night of the Mars landing when the booze first started to get the better of him. But this was different. Terr was different. She was twisting, writhing. And the wind, the dawn, was rising.

"And I always felt responsible for you in a way, Tom. It was probably just a sort of vanity, but I felt as if I'd given you some final push along a path down which you might not otherwise have taken. You were charming, Tom. You were handsome and intelligent. You could have made a fortune and had a happy life doing anything other than SETI. Is that true Tom? Does that make any sense to you?"

He didn't reply, which he knew in itself was a positive answer. The truth was always out there in any case, with or without him. What was the point in denying anything?

"And that promise I made you make, that last day when we were standing outside the law courts with all those stupid flyer friends of mine. It seemed clever, somehow. I knew how much you still loved me and I wanted to leave my mark on you, just to prove it. I'm sorry, Tom. It was another one of my stupid, stupid projects. . . ."

"You can't hold yourself responsible for someone else's life, Terr."

"I know, Tom. It didn't even feel like I was responsible for my own."

Tom looked away from Terr, and back at his ragged hut. But for the fine-spun silver of his field of tripwires, but for the faint glow of his computers, but for the bottle-filled skip and the old Citroën beside it, it could have been the dwelling of a medieval hermit. He sighed and looked down the slope of his mountain. In this gathering light, the whole world looked frail as a spiderweb. And down there—he could just see it—lay his waterhole, and the flickering movement of the shy mountain ibex who gathered dawn and dusk to drink there.

"The sun's coming up, Tom. I'll have to be going soon. . . ."

"But you haven't . . ." The words froze in his mouth as he looked back at Terr. Even as the light strengthened, the substance was draining from her. ". . . can't you stay. . . ?"

"I'm sorry, Tom. I've said all there is to be said. . . ."

She stood up and moved, floated, toward him. Changed and not changed. Terr and not Terr. What few stars remained in the west were now shining right through her. But Tom felt no fear as she approached him. All he felt, welling up in his heart, was that childhood ache, that dark sweetness which was cola and ice cream and his mother's embrace. All he felt was a glorious, exquisite sense of wonder.

The rim of the sun gilded the edge of those ranged peaks. Terr broke and shimmered. She was like her eyes now; a beautiful, swarming nebula. But the sun was brightening, the wind was still rising. She was fading, fading. Tom stretched out a hand to touch whatever it was she had become, and found only morning coolness, the air on his flesh.

*Remember, Tom.*

Terr had no voice now, no substance. She was just a feeling, little more than the sad and happy memory he had carried with him through all these years into this dim and distant age. But he felt also that she was moving, turning away from him, and he smiled as he watched her in that dark blue dress, as beautiful as she had always been, walking away down the silvered turf of his mountain toward the waterhole. Terr with her blonde hair. Terr with her beautiful eyes. Terr with the mist on her flesh in that place where her jaw met her throat beneath her earlobe. She turned and gave him a smile and a wave as the sun sent a clear spine of light up from the cleft between two mountains. Terr in her dark blue dress, heading down toward that waterhole where all the shy creatures of the universe might gather at the beginning or end of the longest of days. Then she was gone.

Tom sat there for a long while. It was, after all, his time of day for doing nothing. And the sun rose up, brightening the world, corkscrewing the spirals beside the limestone crags. He thought he caught the flash of wings, but the light, his whole world and mountain, was smeared and rainbowed. He thought that he had probably been crying.

The cards on the table before him had lost most of their glow. And they were cold and slickly damp when he turned them over. He selected the one card he didn't recognise, the one that was blue and almost plain, with a pattern on its surface like rippled water. He was sure now that it was more than just spam, junk mail. He ran his finger across the message strip to activate it, and closed his eyes, and saw a man standing before him in a fountained garden which was warm and afternoon-bright and almost Moorish; it could have been Morocco, Los Angeles, Spain. The man was good looking, but no longer young. He had allowed the wrinkles to spread over his face, his hair to grey and recede. There was something, Tom found himself thinking, about himself, about his face, or at least the self he thought he remembered once seeing in a mirror. But the man was standing with the fixedness of someone preparing for a difficult moment. His face was beyond ordinary sadness. His eyes were grave.

Tom waited patiently through the you-don't-know-me-and-I-don't-know-you part of the message, and the birds sang and the bees fumbled for pollen amid deep red and purple tropic flowers as the man gave Tom his name, and explained the one thing about their backgrounds which they had in common, which was that they had both loved Terr. They'd loved Terr, and then of course they'd lost her, because Terr was impossible to keep—it was in her nature; it was why they'd made the glorious leap of loving her in the first place. But this man was aware of Tom Kelly in a way that Tom wasn't aware of him. Not that Terr had ever said much about her past because she lived so much in the present, but he'd known that Tom was there, and in a way he'd envied him, because love for Terr was a first and only thing, glorious in its moment, then impossible to ever quite recapture in the same way. So he and Terr had eventually parted, and their marriage—which was her second, in any case—had ended as, although he'd hoped against hope, he'd always known it would. And Terr had gone on with her life, and he'd got on with his, and he'd followed her sometimes through the ether, her new friends, her new discoveries, and fresh obsessions, until he heard this recent news, which was terrible, and yet for him, not quite unexpected, Terr being Terr.

There was a ridge on a peak in the Andes known as Catayatauri. It sounded like a newly discovered star to Tom, and was almost as distant and as hostile. The ridge leading up to it was incredible; in the east, it dropped nearly ten thousand sheer feet, and it took a week of hard walking and another week of hard climbing to reach it, that was, if the winds and the treacherous séracs let you get there at all. But it had acquired a near-mythic reputation amongst a certain kind of flyer, a reputation which went back to the time of the Incas, when human sacrifices were thrown from that ridge to placate Viracocha, the old man of the sky.

So picture Terr making that climb alone in the brutal cold, no longer as young or as fit as she might once have been, but still as determined. She left messages in the village, which lay in Catayatauri's permanent shadow. If she didn't come back, she didn't want anyone risking their lives trying to find her. The Incas had held Catayatauri with a deep, religious intensity, and so had the climbers who came after, and so must Terr, alone up in those godly mountains. She climbed unaided; no wings, no muscle or lung enhancements, no crampon claws on her feet or hands, no ropes, and no oxygen. The fact that she made it there at all was incredible, clinging to that ridge at the roof of the world. From Catayatauri, from that drop, nothing else was comparable. And Terr had stood there alone, a nearly old woman at the edge of everything. She'd bought vials at a shop in Lima. She'd emptied what little she had left in her accounts to get hold of them. These weren't like the vials they sold along the Rue de Commerce in St. Hilaire. Scarcely legal, they were the quickest acting, the most radical, the most expensive. They tore through your blood and veins by the nanosecond, they burned you up and twisted your body inside out like a storm-wrecked umbrella. And Terr had purchased three times the usual dosage.

And she probably did get there, and make the leap from the ridge on Catayatauri. It seemed like the most likely explanation, even though her body hadn't been found. Terr had thrown herself from the precipice with the vials singing in her body, her bones twisting, the wings breaking out from her like a butterfly emerging from a chrysalis, although they would have been too damp and frail to do more than be torn to shreds in the brutal torrents of air. And then, finally, finally, she would have been buffeted on the rocks. Terr, it seemed, had chosen the most extreme of all possible ways of dying. . . .

Was it like her, to do this, Tom wondered? Terr plummeting, twisting and writhing? Had she meant to kill herself, or just wanted to take the risk, and lived the moment, and not really cared about the next? The man in the Moorish garden was as lost and puzzled by all these questions as Tom was himself. But the thing about Terr, as they both realised, was that she had always changed moment by moment, hour by hour, year by year. The thing about Terr was that you could never really know her. Tom, he had always been steady and purposeful; long ago, he had laid down the tracks of his life. Terr was different. Terr was always different. She'd never been troubled as Tom had been most of his life by that sense of missed appointments, unfinished business, time slipping by; of a vital message which he had never quite heard. Terr had always leapt without looking back.

The man gave a smile and signed off. The Moorish garden, the dense scent of the flowers, faded. Tom Kelly was back in the morning as the shadows raced the clouds over his mountain; and he was wondering, like a character in a fairy story, just where he had been this previous night, and exactly what it was that he had witnessed. And if he could have been granted one wish—which was something that Terr, whatever she had been, hadn't even offered to him —it would still be the thing for which he had always been hoping. He was nearly seventy, after all. He was Tom Kelly; Mr SETI. No matter what happened to you, no matter what wonders you witnessed, people his age didn't change. He was still sure of that, at least.

Tom Kelly, speeding down his mountain. The sun is blazing and the chairlifts are still and the flyers are resting as shadow lies down next to shadow for the long, slumberous afternoon. He parks in the near-empty Place de Revolution, and climbs out from his Citröen, and waves to Jean-Benoît wiping his tables, and then bangs on the door of the *Bureau de poste*. The sign says *fermé*, but Madame Brissac slides back the bolts. She seems almost pleased to see him. She nearly gives him a smile. Then they spend their hour together, seated beside the counter as bluebottles buzz and circle by her pigeonholes in the warm, intensely odorous air. Tom's got as far as transitive verbs, and here he's struggling. But after all, French is a foreign language, and you don't learn such things in a day—at least, not the way Tom's learning. It will be some months, he reckons late autumn at least—*l'automne*, and perhaps even winter, whatever that's called—before he's got enough of a grip to ask her about how she sorts the mail in those pigeonholes. And he suspects she'll think it's a stupid question in any case. Madame Brissac is, after all, Madame Brissac. But who'd have thought that she was once a teacher, back in the days when people still actually needed to be taught things? For every person, it seems to Tom, who gains something in this future age, there's someone else who makes a loss from it.

Things are just starting to reawaken when he emerges into the blazing Place de Revolution, and he has to move his Citröen and park it round the corner to make room for the evening's festivities. It's the *Foire aux Sorcières* tonight, which a few months ago would have meant nothing to him, and still means little enough. But the French like a good festival, he knows that much now at least. They have them here in St. Hilaire regularly—in fact, almost every week, seeing as there's such a regular throughput of new flyers needing to have their francs taken from them. But this festival is special. Tom knows that, too.

Drinking sweet, hot coffee at his usual table, he passes the necessary hour whilst the market stalls and the stage for the evening pageant assemble themselves to the attentions of robot crabs and the clang of poles and the shouts of a few, largely unnecessary artisans. The town, meanwhile, stretches itself and scratches its belly, emerges from its long meals and lovers' slumbers. The girl with that Audrey Hepburn look, whom he now knows is called Jeannette, gives him a smile and goes over to say hi, *boujour*. She thinks it's sweet, that a mad, old mountain goat like Tom should take the long way around to learning her language. And so does Michel, her boyfriend, who is as urbane and charming as anyone can be who's got the muscles of a cartoon god and the green, scaly skin of a reptile. They even help Tom carry his few boxes of stuff from the boot of his Citröen to the stall he's booked, and wish him luck, and promise to come back and buy something later on in the evening, although Tom suspects they'll be having too much fun by then to remember him.

But it turns out that business at his stall is surprisingly brisk in any case. It's been this way for a couple of weeks now, and if it continues, Tom reckons he'll have to order some new SETI T-shirts and tea towels to replace his lost stock, although the tea towels in particular will be hard to replace after all these years, seeing as people don't seem to have any proper use for them any longer. They ask him what they're for, these big SETI handkerchiefs, and then tie them around their necks like flags. Who'd have thought it —that tea towels would be a casualty of this future he finds himself in? But bargaining, setting a price for something and then dropping it to make the sale; that's no problem for Tom. The numbers of another language come almost easily to him; he supposes his brain dimly remembers it once had an aptitude for maths.

The *Foire aux Sorcières* seems an odd festival for summer, but, even before the darkness has settled, the children are out, dressed as witches, ghosts, goblins, and waving lanterns that cast, through some technical trick Tom can't even guess at, a night-murk across their faces. Still, the whole occasion, with those sweet and ghastly faces, the trailing sheets with cut eye-holes, the shrieking, cackling devices, has a pleasantly old-fashioned feel about it to Tom. Even the flyers, when they emerge, have done nothing more to change themselves than put on weird costumes and make-ups, although, to Tom's mind at least, many of them had looked the part already.

The scene, as the sun finally sinks behind the tenements and a semblance of cool settles over the hot and frenzied square, is incredible. Some of the people wandering the stalls have even dressed themselves up as old-fashioned aliens. He spots a bulge-headed Martian, then a cluster of those slim things with slanted eyes which were always abducting people in the Midwest, and even someone dressed as that slippery grey thing that used to explode out of people's stomachs in the films, although the guy's taken the head off and is mopping his face with one of Tom's SETI tea towels because he's so hot inside it. If you half closed your eyes, Tom thinks, it really could be market day on the planet Zarg, or any-where else of a million places in this universe which he suspects that humanity will eventually get around to colonising, when it stops having so much fun here on Earth. Look at Columbus, look at Cook, look at Einstein, look at NASA. Look at Terr. We are, in the depths of our hearts, a questing, dreaming race.

Small demons, imps, and several ghosts cluster around him now, and ask him *quel est SETI?* which Tom attempts to explain in French. They nod and listen and gaze up at him with grave faces. He's almost thinking he's starting to get somewhere, when they all dissolve into gales of laughter and scatter off through the crowds. He watches them go, smiling, those ghosts, those flapping sheets. When he returns his gaze, Madame Brissac has materialised before him. She is dressed as an old-fashioned witch. But she seems awk-ward beneath her stick-on warts and green make-up, shorn of the usual wooden counter which, even now that they're attempting to talk to each other in the same language, still separates Tom and her. Still, she politely asks the price of his SETI paperweights, and rummages in her witchy bag and purchases one from him, and then comments on the warmth and the beauty of this evening, and how pretty and amusing the children are. And Tom agrees with her in French, and offers Madame Brissac a SETI tea towel at no extra cost, which she declines. Wishing him a good evening, she turns and walks away. But Tom still feels proud of himself, and he knows that she's proud of him to. It's an achievement for them both, that they can talk to each other now in the same language, although, being Madame Brissac, she'll never quite let it show.

The music rides over him. The crowds whoop and sing. The lanterns sway. Down the slope toward the river, the lace-draped stalls look almost cool in the soft breeze, which plays down from the hills and over the tenements as Tom sweats in his SETI T-shirt. Jean-Benoît's down there, dressed red as fallen Lucifer and surrounded by lesser demons, and looking most strange and splendid for his evening off. There's no sign, though, of the woman in the dark blue dress whom Tom glimpsed standing in the sunlight all those weeks ago. He knows that Terr's dead now, although the thought still comes as a cold, blunt shock to him. So how could there ever be any sign of Terr?

Tom's got his days better sorted now. He's never got so drunk as to lose one whole day and imagine Thursday is Wednesday. In fact, nowadays, Tom never has a drink at all. It would be nice to say that he's managed it through pure willpower. But he's old, and a creature of habit, even when the habits are the wrong ones. And this *is* the future, after all. So Tom's taken a vial, just as he had done several times before, and the need, the desire, the welling emptiness, faded so completely that he found himself wondering for the first few days what all the trouble and fuss had been about. But that was two months ago, and he still rarely entertains the previous stupid thoughts about how a social drink, a sip and a glass here and there, would be quite safe for someone like him. Even on a night such as this, when the air smells of wine and sweat and Pernod and coffee and Gitanes, and he can hear bottles popping and glasses clinking and liquid choruses of laughter all around the square, he doesn't feel the usual emptiness. Or barely. Or at least he's stopped kidding himself that it's something the alcohol will ever fill, and decided to get on with the rest of his life unaided.

He sometimes wonders during the long, hot afternoons of his lessons with Madame Brissac whether a woman in a blue dress and grey or blonde hair really did enter the *Bureau de poste* to enquire about an elderly American called Tom Kelly on that magical Thursday. Sometimes, he's almost on the brink of interrupting her as she forces him through the endless twists and turns of French grammar, although he knows she'd probably regard it as an unnecessary distraction. He's thought of asking Jean-Benoît, too—at least, when he's not dressed up as Lucifer—if he remembers a woman who could have been old or might have been young coming to his café, and who undertook to pass on the message cards he'd forgotten to take with him. Would they remember Terr? Would they deny that they'd ever seen her at all? More likely, Tom has decided, they'll have long forgotten such a trivial incident amid the stream of faces and incidents that populate their lives.

Tom glances up from the bright Place de Revolution at the few, faint stars which have managed to gather over the rooftops and spires of St. Hilaire. Like Terr—or the ghost of her—he suspects they'll remain a mystery that he'll have to carry to his grave. But there's nothing so terrible about mysteries. It was mystery, after all, which drew him to the stars in the first place. Wonder and mystery. He smiles to himself, and waves to Jeannette and Michel as they pass through the crowds. Then Jean-Benoît, amid great cheers, flaps his crimson wings and rises over the stalls and hovers floodlit above the church spire to announce the real beginning of the night's festivities, which will involve fireworks, amazing pageants, dancing. . . .

This *Foire aux Sorcières* will probably still be going on at sunrise, but Tom Kelly knows it will be too much for him. He's getting too old for this world he finds himself in. He can barely keep pace. But he permits himself another smile as he starts to pack up his stall of SETI memorabilia, the T-shirts and paperweights, the lapel pins embossed with a tiny representations of the Drake Equation which not a single person who's bought one of the things has ever asked him to explain. He's looking forward to the midnight drive back up his mountain in his old Citröen, and the way the stars will blossom on when he finally turns off the headlights and steps into the cool darkness outside his hut, with the glitter of his tripwires, the hum and glow of his machines. Who knows what messages might be up there?

He's Tom Kelly, after all.

And this might be the night.

He's still listening, waiting.

---

# Isabel of the Fall

ONCE, IN THE TIME WHICH WAS ALWAYS LONG AGO, there lived a girl. She was called Isabel and—in some versions of this tale—you will hear of the beauty of her eyes, the sigh of her hair, the falling of her gaze which was like the dark glitter of a thousand wells, but Isabel wasn't like that. In other tellings, you will learn that her mouth stuck out like a seapug's, that she had a voice like the dawn-shriek of a geelie. But that wasn't Isabel, either. Isabel was plain. Her hair was brown, and so, probably, were her eyes, although that fact remains forever unrecorded. She was of medium height for the women who then lived. She walked without stoop or any obvious deformity, and she was of less-than-average wisdom. Isabel was unbeautiful and unintelligent, but she was also unstupid and unugly. Amid all the many faces of the races and species which populate these many universes, hers was one of the last you would ever notice.

Isabel was born and died in Ghezirah, the great City of Islands which lies at the meeting of all the Ten Thousand and One Worlds. Ghezirah was different then, and in the time that was always long ago, it is often said that the animals routinely conversed, gods walked the night, and fountains filled with ghosts. But, for Isabel, this was the time of the end of the War of the Lilies.

Her origins are obscure. She may have been a child of one of the beggars who, then as now, seek alms amid the great crystal concourses. She may have been daughter of one of the priestess soldiers who fought for their Church. She may even have been the lost daughter of some great matriarch, as is often the way in these tales. All that is certain is that, when Isabel was born in Ghezirah, the many uneasy alliances which always bind the Churches had boiled into war. There were also more men then, and many of them were warriors, so it is even possible that Isabel was born as a result of rape rather than conscious decision. Isabel never knew. All that she ever remembered, in the earliest of the fragmentary records that are attributed to her, is the swarming of a vast crowd, things broken underfoot, and the swoop and blast overhead of what might have been some kind of military aircraft. In this atmosphere of panic and danger, she was one moment holding onto a hand. Next, the sky seemed to ignite, and the hand slipped from hers.

Many people died or went mad in the War of the Lilies. Ghezirah itself was badly damaged, although the city measures things by its own times and priorities, and soon set about the process of healing its many islands which lace to form the glittering web which circles the star called Sabil. Life, just as it always must, went on, and light still flashed from minaret to minaret each morning with the cries of the Dawn-Singers, even if many of the beauties of which they sang now lay ruined beneath. The Churches, too, had to heal themselves, and seek new acolytes after many deaths and betrayals. Here, tottering amid the smoking rubble, too young to fend for herself, was plain Isabel. It must have been one of the rare times in her life that she was noticed, that day when she was taken away with many others to join the depleted ranks of the Dawn Church.

The Dawn Church has its own island in Ghezirah, called Jerita, and Isabel may have been trained there in the simpler crafts of bringing light and darkness, although it is more likely that she would have attended a small, local academy, and been set to the crude, manual tasks of rebuilding one of the many minarets which had been destroyed, perhaps hauling a wheelbarrow or wielding a trowel. Still, amid the destruction that the War of the Lilies had visited on Ghezirah, every Church knew that to destroy the minarets which bore dawn across the skies would have been an act beyond folly. Thus, of all the Churches, that of the Dawn had probably suffered least, and could afford to be generous. Perhaps that was the reason that Isabel, for all her simple looks and lack of gifts, was apprenticed to become a Dawn-Singer as she grew toward womanhood. Or perhaps, as is still sometimes the way, she rose to such heights because no one had thought to notice her.

Always, first and foremost in the Dawn Church, there is the cleaning of mirrors: the great reflectors which gather Sabil's light far above Ghezirah's sheltering skies, and those below; the silver dishes of the great minarets which dwarf all but the highest mountains; the many, many lesser ones which bear light across the entire city each morning with the cries of the Dawn-Singers. But there is much else which the apprentices of the Dawn Church must study. There is the behaviour of the light itself, and the effects of lenses; also the many ways in which Sabil's light must be filtered before it can safely reach flesh and eyes, either alien or human. Then there are the mechanisms which govern the turning of all these mirrors, and the hidden engines which drive them. And there is the study of Sabil herself, who waxes and wanes even though her glare seems unchanging. Ghezirah, even at the recent end of the War of the Lilies, was a place of endless summer and tropical warmth, where the flowers never wilted, the trees kept their leaves for a lifetime, and the exact time when day and night would flood over the city with the cries of the Dawn-Singers was decreed in the chapels of the Dawn Church by the spinning of an atomic clock. But, in the work of the young apprentices who tended the minarets, first and always, there was the cleaning of the mirrors.

Isabel's lot was a hard one, but not unpleasant. Although she had already risen far in her Church, there were still many others like her. Each evening, after prayers and night-breakfast, and the study of the photon or the prism, Isabel and her fellow apprentices scattered to ascend the spiral stairs of their designated local minaret. Some would oil the many pistons and flywheels within, or perhaps tend to the needs of the Dawn-Singer herself, but most clambered on until they met the windy space where what probably seemed like the whole of Ghezirah lay spread glittering beneath them, curving upward into the night. There, all through the dark hours until the giant reflectors far above them inched again toward Sabil, Isabel pulled doeskin pouches over her hands and feet, unfolded rags, wrung out sponges, unwound ropes and harnesses, and saw with all the other apprentices to polishing the mirrors. Isabel must have done well, or at least not badly. Some of her friends fell from her minaret, leaving stripes of blood across the sharp edge of the lower planes which she herself had to clean. Others were banished back to their begging bowls. But, for the few remaining, the path ahead was to become a Dawn-Singer.

To this day, the ceremonies of induction of this and every other Church remain mostly secret. But now, if she hadn't done so before, Isabel would have traveled by tunnel or shuttle to the Dawn Church's island of Jerita, and touched the small heat of the clock which bore the unchanging day and night of eternal summer to all Ghezirah. There would have been songs of praise and sadness as she was presented to the senior acolytes of her Church. Then, after they had heard the whisper of deeper secrets, Isabel's fellow apprentices were all ritually blinded. Whatever the Eye of Sabil is, it must filter much of the star's power until just enough rays of a certain type remain to destroy vision, yet leave the eyes seemingly undamaged. The apprentices of the Dawn Church all actively seek this moment as a glimpse into the gaze of the Almighty, and it is hard to imagine how Isabel managed to avoid it. Perhaps she simply closed her eyes. More likely, she was forgotten in the crowd.

Thus Isabel, whose eyes were of a colour forever unrecorded, became a Dawn-Singer, although she was not blind, and—somehow—she was able to survive this new phase of her life undetected. She probably never imagined that she was unique. Being Isabel, and not entirely stupid, but certainly not bright, she probably gave the matter little deep thought. In this new world of the blind, where touch and taste and sound and mouselike scurryings of new apprentices were all that mattered, Isabel, with all her limited gifts, soon discovered the trick of learning how not to see.

She was given tutelage of a minaret on the island of Nashir, where the Floating Ocean hangs as a blue jewel up on the rising horizon. Nashir is a beautiful island, and a great seat of learning, but it was and is essentially a backwater. Isabel's minaret was small, too, bringing day and night to a cedar valley of considerable beauty but no particular significance, save the fact that to the west it over-looked the rosestone outer walls of the Cathedral of the Word. Before dawn, as she lay in her high room, Isabel would hear laughter and the rumble of footsteps as her mirror-polishing apprentices finished their duties, and would allow a few more privileged ones to imagine they had woken her with their entrance, and then help her with her ablutions and prayers. Always, she gazed through them. Almost always now, she saw literally nothing. She thought of these girls as sounds, names, scents, differing footsteps and touches. Borne up with their help onto her platform where, even atop this small minaret, the sense of air and space swam all around her, Isabel was strapped to her crucifix in solemn darkness, and heard the drip-tick of the modem which received the beat of Jerita's

atomic clock, and sensed the clean, clear waiting of the freshly polished mirrors around and above her as, with final whispers and
blessings, the apprentices departed to their quarters down by the
river, where, lulled by bird song, they would sleep through most of
the daylight their mistress would soon bring.

The drip-tick of the modem changed slightly. Isabel tensed herself, and began to sing. Among the mirrors' many other properties,
they amplified her voice, and carried it down the dark valley toward
her departing apprentices, and to the farmsteads, and across the
walls of the Cathedral of the Word. It was a thrilling, chilling
sound, which those who had morning duties were awakened by,
and those who did not had long ago learned to sleep through. Far
above her, in a rumble like distant thunder, the great mirrors
within Ghezirah's orbit poised themselves to turn to face the sun.
Another moment, and the modem's drip-tick changed again, and
with it Isabel's song, as, in dazzling pillars, Sabil's light bore down
toward every minaret. Isabel tensed in her crucifix and moved her
limbs in the ways she had learned; movements which drove the
pulleys and pistons that in turn caused the mirrors of her minaret to
fan their gathered rays across her valley. Thus, in song and light,
each day in Ghezirah is born, and Isabel remained no different to
any other Dawn-Singer, but for the one fact that, at the crucial
moment when first light flashed down to her, she had learned to
screw up her eyes.

A typical day, and her work was almost done then until the time
came to sing the different songs which called in the night. Sometimes, if there were technical difficulties, or clouds drifted over
from the Floating Ocean, or there was rain, Isabel would have to
reharness herself to her crucifix and struggle hard to keep her valley
alight. Sometimes, there were visitors or school parties, but mostly
now her time was her own. It wasn't unknown for Dawn-Singers to
plead with their apprentices to leave some small job undone each
night so they could have the pleasure of absorbing themselves in it
through the following day. But, for Isabel, inactivity was easy. She
had the knack of the near simple-minded of letting time pass
through her as easily as the light and the wind.

One morning, Isabel was inspecting some of the outer mirrors.
Such minor tasks, essentially checking that her apprentices were
performing their duties as they should, were part of her life. Any
blind Dawn-Singer worth her salt could tell from the feel of the air
coming off a particular mirror whether it had been correctly polished, and then set at the precise, necessary angle on its runners
and beds. Touching it, the smear of a single bare fingertip, would

have been sacrilege, and sight, in this place of dazzling glass, was of little use. Isabel, in the minaret brightness of her lonely days, rarely thought about looking, and when she did, what she saw was a world dimmed by the blotches which now swam before her eyes. In a few more months, years at the most, she would have been blinded by her work. But as it was, on this particular nondescript day, and just as she had suspected from a resistance which she had felt in the left arm of her crucifix, a mirror in the western quadrant was misaligned. Isabel studied it, feeling the wrongness of the air. It was Mirror 28, and the error was a matter of fractions of a second of a degree, and thus huge by her standards. The way Mirror 28 was, it scarcely reflected Sabil's light at all, and made the corner of her minaret where she stood seem relatively dim. Thus, as Isabel wondered whether to try to deal with the problem now or leave it for her apprentices, she regained a little more of her sight.

The valley spread beneath her was already shimmering in those distant times of warm and sudden mornings, and the silver river flashed back the light of her minaret. The few dotted houses were terracotta and white. Another perfect day, but for a slight dullness in the west caused by the particular faulty mirror. The effect, Isabel thought as she strained her aching eyes, was not unpleasing. The outer rosestone walls of the Cathedral of the Word, the main structure of which lay far beyond the hills of this valley, had a deep, pleasant glow to them. The shadows seemed fuller. Inside the walls there were paved gardens, trees, and fountains. Doves clattered, flowers bloomed, insects hummed, statues gestured. Here and there, for no obvious reason, were placed slatted, white boxes. Nothing and nobody down there seemed to have noticed that she had failed them today in her duties. Isabel smiled and inhaled the rich, pollen-scented air. It was a minor blemish, and she still felt proud of her work. Near the wall, beside a place where its stones dimpled in toward a gateway, there was a pillared space of open paving. This, too, was of rosestone. Isabel was about to shut her eyes so she could concentrate better on the scene when she heard, the sound carrying faint on the breeze, the unmistakable slap of feet on warm stone. She peered down again, leaning forward over Mirror 28, her unmemorable face captured in reflection as she saw a figure moving far below across the open paving. A young girl, by the look of her. Her hair was flashing gold-bands, as were her arms and ankles. She was dancing, circling, in some odd way which made no sense to Isabel, although she looked graceful in a way beyond anything Isabel could explain.

That night, after she had sung in the darkness, Isabel neglected to mention the fault with Mirror 28 to her apprentices. The next morning, breathing the same warm air at the same westerly corner of her minaret, she listened again to the shift and slap of feet. It was a long time before she opened her eyes, and when she did, her vision seemed clearer. The girl dancing on the rosestone paving had long, black hair, and she was dressed in the flashing silks which Isabel associated with alien lands and temples. Rings flashed from her fingers. A bindi glittered at her forehead. Isabel breathed, and watched, and marveled.

The next blazing day, the day after, Isabel watched again from the top of her minaret beside faulty Mirror 28. It was plainly some ritual. The girl was probably an apprentice, or perhaps a minor acolyte. She was learning whatever trade it was which was practised in the Cathedral of the Word. Isabel remembered, or tried to remember, her own origins. That swarming crowd. Then hunger, thirst. What would have happened if she had been taken instead to this place beyond the wall? Would she have ever been this graceful? Isabel already knew the answer, but still the question absorbed her. In her dreams, the hand which she held as the fighter plane swooped became the same oiled olive colour as that girl's flashing skin. And sometimes, before the thundering feet of her apprentices awakened her to another day of duty, Isabel almost felt as if she, too, was dancing.

One day, the air was different. The Floating Ocean which hung on the horizon was a place of which Isabel understood little, although it was nurtured in Sabil's reflected energies by a specialist Order of her Church. Sometimes, mostly, it was blue. Then it would glitter and grey. Boiling out from it like angry thoughts would come clouds and rain. At these times, as she wrestled on her crucifix, Isabel imagined shipwreck storms, heaving seas. At other times, the clouds which drifted from it would be light and white, although they also interferred with the light in more subtle and often more infuriating ways. But on this particular day, Isabel awoke to feel dampness on her skin, clammy but not unpleasant, and a sense that every sound and creak of this minaret with which she was now so familiar had changed. The voices of her apprentices, even as they clustered around her, were muffled, and their hair and flesh smelled damp and cold. The whole world, what little she glimpsed of it as she ascended the final staircase and was strapped to her crucifix, had turned grey. The wood at her back was slippery. The harnesses which she had cured and sweated and strained into the shapes of her limbs were loose. She knew that

most of the minaret's mirrors were clouding in condensation even
before the last of the murmuring senior apprentices reported the
fact and bowed out of her way.

The sodden air swallowed the first notes of her song. With the
mechanisms of the whole minaret all subtly changed, Isabel struggled as she had never struggled before to bring in the day. Sabil's
pillar was feeble, and the mirrors were far below their usual levels
of reflectivity. Still, it was for mornings such as this for which she
had been trained, and she caught this vague light and fanned it
across her valley even though she felt as if she was swimming
through oceans of clay. And her song, as she finally managed to
achieve balance and the clouding began to dissolve in the morning's heat, grew more joyous than ever in her triumph, such that
people in the valley scratched the sleep from their heads and
thought as they rarely thought, *Ah, there is the Dawn-Singer, bringing the day!* Despite the cold, white air, they probably went about
their ablutions whistling, confident that some things would never
change.

It was several more hours before Isabel was sure that the smaller
minds and mechanisms of the minaret had reached their usual
equilibrium, and could be trusted to run themselves. But the
world, as she climbed down from her crucifix, was still shrouded.
*Fog*—she had learned the word in her apprenticeship, although
she had thought of it as one of those mythical aberrations, like a
comet-strike. But here it was. She wandered the misted balconies
and gantries. The light here was diffuse, but ablaze. Soon, she
guessed, the power she had brought from her sun would burn this
moist, white world away. But in the west, there was a greater dimness, which was amplified today. Here, the air was almost as chill as
it had been before daybreak. Isabel bit her lip and ground her
palms. She cursed herself, to have allowed this to come about.
What would her old training mistress say! Too late now to attempt
to rectify the situation at Mirror 28, with the planes beaded wet and
the pistons dripping. She would have to speak to her apprentices
this evening, and do her best to pretend sternness. It was what
teachers generally did, she had noticed: when they had failed to
deal with something, they simply blamed their class. Isabel tried to
imagine the scene at the invisible west below. That dancing girl
beyond the walls of the Cathedral of the Word would surely find
this near-darkness a great inconvenience. The simple, the obvious
—the innocent—thing seemed to be to go down and apologise to
her.

Isabel descended the many stairways of her minaret. Stepping out into the world outside seemed odd to her now—the ground was so *low!*—but especially today, when, almost mimicking the effects of her fading sight, everything but her minaret, which blazed above her, was dim and blotched and silvered. She walked between the fields in the direction of the rosestone walls, and heard but didn't see the animals grazing. Brushing unthinkingly and near-blindly as now she habitually did against things, she followed close to the brambled hedges, and, by the time she felt the dim fiery glow of the wall coming up toward her, her hands and arms were scratched and wet. The stones of the wall were soaked, too. The air here was a damp presence. Conscious that she was entering the dim realm which her own inattention had made, Isabel felt her way along the wall until she came to the door. It looked old and little-used; the kind of door you might find in a story. She didn't know whether to feel surprise when she turned the cold and slippery iron hoop, and felt it give way.

Now, she was in the outer gardens of the Cathedral of the Word, and fully within the shade of faulty Mirror 28. It was darker here, certainly, but her senses and her sight soon adjusted, and Isabel decided that the effect wasn't unpleasant, in some indefinable and melancholy way. In this diffuse light, the trees were dark clouds. The pavements were black and shining. Some of the flowers hung closed, or were beaded with silver cobwebs. A few bees buzzed by her, but they seemed clumsy and half-asleep in this half-light as well. Then, of all things, there was a flicker of orange light; a glow which Isabel's half-ruined eyes refused to believe. But, as she walked toward it, it separated itself into several quivering spheres, bearing with them the smell of smoke, and the slap of bare feet on wet stone.

The open courtyard which Isabel had gazed down on from her minaret was impossible to scale as she stood at the edge of it on this dim and foggy day, although the surrounding pillars which marched off and vanished up into the mist seemed huge, lit by the flicker of the smoking braziers placed between them. Isabel moved forward. The dancer, for a long time, was a sound, a disturbance of the mist. Then, sudden as a ghost, she was there before her.

"*Ahlan wa sahlan . . .*" She bowed from parted knees, palms pressed together. She smelled sweetly of sweat and sandalwood. Her hair was long and black and glorious. "And who, pray, are you? And what are you doing here?"

Isabel, flustered in a way, which she had not felt in ages,

stumbled over her answer. The minaret over the wall . . . She pointed uselessly into the mist. This dimness—no, not the mist itself, but the lack of proper light . . . The dancer's kohled and oval eyes regarded her with what seemed like amusement. The bindi on her brow glittered similarly. Although the dancer was standing still, her shoulders rose and fell from her exertions. Her looped earrings tinked.

"So, you bring light from that tower?"

Isabel, who perhaps still hadn't made the matter as clear as she should have, nodded in dizzy relief that this strange creature was starting to understand her. "I'm so *sorry* it's so dark today. I've—I've heard your dancing from my tower, and I—thought . . . I thought that this oversight would be difficult for you."

"Difficult?" The girl cocked her head sideways like a bird to consider. The flames were still dancing. Their light flicked dark and orange across her arms. "No, I don't think so. In fact, I quite like it. My name's Genya, by the way. I'm a beekeeper. . . ." She gave a liquid laugh and stepped forward, back, half-fading. "Although, thanks to you, there are few enough bees today that need keeping."

"Beekeeper—but I thought these were the gardens of the Cathedral of the Word? I thought you were—"

"—Oh, I'm a *Librarian* as well. Or at least, a most senior apprentice. But some of us must also learn how to keep bees."

Isabel nodded. "Of course. For the honey . . ."

Again, Genya laughed. There seemed to be little Isabel could do which didn't cause her amusement. "Oh no! Never for *that!* We give the honey away to the poor at our main gates on moulid days. We keep bees because they teach us how to find the books. Do you want me to show you?"

Isabel was shown. That first day, the misty gardens were nothing but a puzzle to her. There were flowering bushes that she was told by Genya bore within each their cells whole libraries of information about wars fought and lost. There were stepped cryptlike places beyond creaky iron gates where, through other doors which puffed open once Genya made a gesture, lay bound books of the histories of things which had never happened in this or any other world. They were standing, Genya whispered, reaching up to take down a silvery thing encased in plastic, merely at the furthest shore of the greatest oceans of all possible knowledge. Yet some of these clear, bright, artificially lit catacombs were as big as all but the finest halls of the Dawn Church's own seats of learning.

"What is *that*, anyway?"

It was a rainbowed disk. After a small struggle, Genya opened the transparent box that contained it. "I think it contains music." Isabel had to gasp when Genya placed her fingertips upon the surface, so closely did it resemble a mirror. But Genya's fingers moved rapidly in a caressing, circling motion. Her eyes closed for a moment. She started humming. "Yes. It *is* music. An old, popular song about fools on hills. It's lovely. I wish I had a voice like you to sing it."

"You can *hear* it from that?"

Genya nodded. "It's something which is done to us Librarians. To our fingers. See . . ." She raised them toward Isabel's gaze. Close to the end, the flesh seemed raw, like fresh scar tissue. "We're given extra optic nerves. Small magnetic sensors . . . processors . . . other things . . ." She snapped the rainbow disk back into its case. "It makes life a lot easier." She tried to demonstrate the same trick with a brown ribbon of tape, the spool of which instantly took off on its own down the long corridor in which they were standing. She hummed, once they had caught up with it, another tune.

"It's all part of being a Librarian, having tickly fingers," Genya announced as she slotted the object back on its shelf. "By the way . . ." She turned back toward Isabel. "I was under the impression that there was a far worse excruciation for you Dawn-Singers. . . ." Genya leaned forward with a dancer's gaze, peering as no one ever had into the forgotten shade of Isabel's eyes. "You're supposed to be *blind*, aren't you? But it's plain to even the stupidest idiot that you're not. . . ."

Next dawn, the skies were clear again. Once more, the Floating Ocean was calm and distant and blue. Those in that valley who cared to listen to Isabel's song might have thought that day that it sounded slightly perfunctory. But ordinary daybreaks such as these were easy sport for Isabel now. She was even getting used to the different feel of the minaret that came from the fault in Mirror 28. Under blue skies that only a connoisseur or an acolyte would have noticed a slight darkening in the western quadrant, she hurried across the fields toward the rosestone walls of the Cathedral of the Word.

Even though their prosecutors were able to argue the facts convincingly the other way, neither Isabel not Genya ever thought that their acts in those long ago days of Ghezirah's endless summer amounted to betrayal. They knew that their respective Churches guarded their secrets with all the paranoid dread of the truly powerful, who are left with much to lose and little to gain. They knew, too, of the recent terrors of the War of the Lilies. But their lives had been small. Further up the same rosestone wall, if Isabel had cared to follow it beyond her valley, she would have eventually found that its fine old blocks were pockmarked with sprays of bullets; further still, the stone itself dissolved into shining heaps of dream-distorted lava, and the gardens still heaved with the burrowing teeth of trapmoles. Yet Nashir had suffered far less in the War of the Lilies than many of Ghezirah's islands. In the vast lattice of habitation that surrounded Sabil, there were still huge rents and floating swathes of spinning rubble. Seventeen years is little time to recover from a war, but peace and youth and endless summer are heady brews, and lessons doled out in the Church classrooms by the rap of a mistress's cane sometimes remain forever wrapped in chalkdust and boredom. Brilliant day after day in that backwater of a backwater, Isabel and Genya wandered deeper into the secrets of the Cathedral of the Word's cloisters and gardens. Day after day, they betrayed the secrets of their respective Churches.

The Cathedral and its environs are vast, and the farms and villages and towns and the several cities of Nashir which surround it are mostly there, in one way or another, to serve its needs. Beyond the ridge of Isabel's valley, standing at the lip of stepped gardens which went down and down so far that the light grew blue and hazed, they saw a distant sprawl of stone and glass spires on the rising horizon.

"Is that the Cathedral?"

Not for the first time that day, Genya laughed. "Oh no! It's just the local Lending Office. . . ." They walked on and down; waterfalls glittering beside them in the distant blaze of a far greater minaret than Isabel's. Another day, rising to the surface from the tunnels of a catacomb from which it had seemed they would never escape, Isabel saw yet another great and fine building. Again, she asked the same question. Again, Genya laughed. Still, within those grounds with their wild, white follies, and statues and shrines to Dewey, Bliss, and Ranganathan, there were many compensations.

As their daily journeys grew further, it became necessary to travel by speedier methods if Isabel was to return to her minaret in time to sing in the night. The catacombs of books were too vast for any Librarian to categorise even the most tightly defined subject without access to rapid transport. So, on the silk seats of caleches which buzzed on cushions of buried energy, they swept along corridors. The bookshelves flashed past them, the titles spinning too fast to read, until the spines themselves became indistinguishable and the individual globelights blurred into a single white stripe overhead. Isabel and Genya laughed and whooped as they urged their metal craft into yet greater feats of speed and manoeuvrability. The dusty wisdoms of lost ages cooled their faces.

They rarely saw anyone, and then only as faint figures tending some distant stack of books, or the trails of aircraft like scratches across the blue roof of the Ghezirahan sky. Genya's training, the dances and the indexing and—for an exercise, the sub-categorising of the lesser tenses of the verb meaning *to blink* in sixty-eight lost languages—came to her through messages even more remote than the tick of Isabel's modem. Sometimes, the statues spoke to her. Sometimes, the flowers gave off special scents, or the furred leaves of a bush communicated something in their touch to her. But, mostly, Genya learned from her bees.

One day, Isabel succumbed to Genya's repeated requests and led her to the uppermost reaches of her minaret. Genya laughed as she peered down from the spiralling stairways as they ascended. The drops, she claimed, leaning far across the worn, brass handrails, were dizzying. Isabel leaned over as well; she'd never thought to *look* at her minaret in this way. Seen from the inside, the place was like a huge, vertical tunnel, threaded with sunlight and dust and the slow tickings of vast machinery, diminishing down toward seeming infinity.

"Why is it, anyway, that you Dawn-Singers need to be blinded?" Genya asked as they climbed on, her voice by now somewhat breathless.

"I suppose it's because we become blind soon enough—a kind of mercy. That, and because we have access to such high places. We Dawn-Singers know how to combine lenses . . ." Isabel paused on a stairs for a moment as a new thought struck her, and Genya bumped into her back. "So perhaps the other Churches are worried about what, looking down, we might see. . . ."

"I'm surprised anyone ever gets to the top of this place without dying of exhaustion. Your apprentices must have legs like trees!" But they did reach the top, and Isabel felt the pride she always felt at her minaret's gathered heat and power, whilst Genya, when she had recovered, moved quickly from silvery balcony to balcony, exclaiming about the view. Isabel was little used to seeing anything up here, but she saw through her fading eyes many reflected images of her friend, darting mirror to mirror with her pretty silks trailing behind her like flocks of coloured birds. Isabel smiled. She felt happy, and the happiness was different to the happiness she felt each dawn. Chasing the reflections, she finally found the real Genya standing on the gantry above Mirror 28.

"It's darker here."

"Yes. This mirror has a fault in it."

"This must have been where you first saw me . . ." Genya chuckled. "I thought the light had changed. The colours were suddenly deeper. For a while, it even had the bees confused. Sometimes, the sunlight felt almost cool as I danced through it—more soothing. But I suppose that was your gaze. . . ."

They both stared down at the gardens of the Cathedral of the Word. They looked glorious, although the pillared space where Genya had danced seemed oddly vacant without her. Isabel rubbed her sore eyes as bigger blotches than usual swam before them. She said, "You've never told me about that dance."

"It's supposed to be a secret."

"But then, so are many things."

They stood there for a long time amid the minaret's shimmering light, far above the green valley and the winding, rosestone wall. Today felt different. Perhaps they were growing too old for these trysts. Perhaps things would have to change . . . The warm wind blew past them. The Floating Ocean glittered. The trees murmured. The river gleamed. Then, with a rising hum like a small machine coming to life, a bee which had risen the thermals to this great height blundered against Isabel's face. Somehow, it settled there. She felt its spiky legs, then the brush of Genya's fingers as she lifted the creature away.

"I'll show you the dance now, if you like."

"Here? But—"

"—just watch."

From her cupped hands, Genya laid the insect on the gapped, wooden boards. It sat there for a moment in the sunlight, slowly shuffling its wings. It looked stunned. "This one's a white-tail. Of course, she's a worker—and a *she*. They do all the work, just like in Ghezirah. Most likely she's been sent out this morning as a scout. Many of them never come back, but the ones that do, and if they've found some fine, new source of nectar, tell the hive about it when they return. . . ." Genya stooped. She rubbed her palms, and held them close to the insect and breathed their scent toward it, making a sound as she did so—a deep-centred hum. She stepped back. "Watch . . ." The bee preened her antennae and quivered her thorax and shuffled her wings. She wiggled back, and then forward, her small movements describing jerky figures of eight. "They use your minaret as a signpost . . ." Genya murmured as the bee continued dancing. Isabel squinted; there *was* something about its movements that reminded her of Genya on the rosestone paving. "That, and the pull and spin of all Ghezirah. It's called the waggly dance. Most kinds of social bees do it, and it's sacred to our Church as well."

Isabel chuckled, delighted. "The waggly dance?!"

"Well, there are many longer and more serious names for it."

"No, no—it's lovely . . . Can you tell where's she been?"

"Over the wall, of course. And she can't understand why there's hard ground up here, up where the sun should be. She thinks we're probably flowers, but no use for nectar-gathering."

"You can tell all of *that?*"

"What would be the point, otherwise, in her dancing? It's the same with us Librarians. Our dance is a ritual we use for signaling where a particular book is to be found."

Isabel smiled at her friend. The idea of someone dancing to show where a book lay amid the Cathedral of the Word's maze of tunnels, buildings, and catacombs seemed deliciously impractical, and quite typical of Genya. The way they were both standing now, Isabel could see their two figures clearly reflected in Mirror 28's useless upper convex. She was struck as she always was by Genya's effortless beauty—and then by her own plainness. Isabel was dull as a shadow, even down to the greyed leather jerkin and shorts she was wearing, her mousy hair which had been cropped with blind efficiency, and then held mostly back by a cracked rubber band. She could, in fact, almost have been Genya's shade. It was a pleasant thought—the two of them combined in the light that she brought to this valley each day—but at the same time, the reflection bothered Isabel. For a start, Mirror 28 poured darkness instead of light from her minaret. Even its name felt cold and steely, like a premonition. . . .

Isabel mouthed something. A phrase: *the fault in Mirror 28*. It was a saying which was to become popular throughout the Ten Thousand and One Worlds, signifying the small thing left undone from which many other larger consequences, often dire, will follow. . . .

"What was that?"

"Oh . . . Nothing . . ."

The bee, raised back into the air by Genya's hands, flew away. The two young women sat talking on the warm decking, exchanging other secrets. There were intelligent devices, Isabel learned, which roamed the aisles of the Cathedral of the Word, searching, scanning, reading, through dusty centuries in pursuit of some minor truth. They were friendly enough when you encountered them, even if they looked like animated coffins. Sometimes, though, if you asked them nicely, they would put aside their duties and let you climb on their backs and take you for a ride. . . .

The modem was ticking. Another day was passing. It was time for Genya to return beyond the walls of the Cathedral of the Word. Usually, the two young women were heedlessly quick with their farewells, but, on this blazing afternoon, Isabel felt herself hesitating, and Genya reached out, tracing with her ravaged and sensitive fingers the unmemorable outlines of her friend's face. Isabel did so too. Although her flesh then was no more remarkable than she was, she had acquired a blind person's way of using touch for sight.

"Tomorrow. . . ?"

"Yes?" They both stepped back from each other, embarrassed by this sudden intimacy.

"Will you dance for me—down on that paving? Now that I know what it's for, I'd love to watch you dance again."

Genya smiled. She gave the same formal bow which she had given when they had first met, then turned and began her long descent of the minaret's stairs. By the time she had reached the bottom, Isabel had already strapped herself into her crucifix and was saying her preliminary prayers as she prepared to sing out another day. Unstarry darkness beautiful as the dawn itself washed across all Ghezirah, and Isabel never saw her friend again.

Of the many secrets attributed to the Dawn Church, Isabel still knew relatively few. She didn't know, for example, that light, modulated in ways beyond anything she could feel with her human senses, could bear immense amounts of data. As well as singing in the dawn each day from her crucifix, she also heedlessly bore floods of information which passed near-instantly across the valley, and finally, flashing minaret to minaret, returned to the place where it had mostly originated, which was the gleaming island of Jerita, where all things pertaining to the Dawn Church must begin and end. Even before Isabel had noticed it herself, some part of the great Intelligence which governed the runnings of her Church had noted, much as a great conductor will notice the off-tuning of a single string in an orchestra, a certain weakness in the returning message from the remote but nevertheless important island of

Nashir where the Cathedral of the Word spread it vast roots and boughs. To the Intelligence, this particular dissonance could only be associated with one minaret, and then to a particular mirror, numbered 28. The Intelligence had many other concerns, but it began to monitor the functioning of that minaret more closely, noticing yet more subtle changes which could not be entirely ascribed to the varying weather or the increasing experience of a new acolyte. In due course, certain human members of the Church were also alerted, and various measures were put in hand to establish the cause of this inattention, the simplest of which involved a midday visit to the dormitories beside the river in Isabel's valley, where apprentices were awoken and quietly interrogated about the behaviour of their new mistress, then asked if they might be prepared to forgo sleep and study their mistress from some hidden spot using delicate instruments with which they would, of course, be provided.

The morning after Isabel had watched the bee's dance dawned bright and sweet as ever. The birds burst into song. The whole valley, to her fading eyes, was a green fire. Still, she was sure that, if she used her gaze cautiously, and looked to the side that was less ravaged, she would be able to watch Genya dance. Her breath quickened as she ascended the last stairway. She felt as if she was translucent, swimming through light. Then, of all things, and amplified by mechanisms which mimicked the human inner ear, the doorway far at the base of her minaret sounded the coded knock which signified the urgent needs of another member of her Church. In fact, there were two people waiting at Isabel's doorway. One bore a stern and sorrowful demeanour, whilst the other was a new acolyte, freshly blinded. Even before they had touched hands and faces, Isabel knew that this acolyte had come to replace her. Although she was standing on the solid ground of Ghezirah, she felt as if she was falling.

Unlike many other details of Isabel's life, the facts of her trial are relatively well recorded. Strangely, or perhaps not, the Church of the Word is less free in publishing its proceedings, although much can be adduced from secondary sources. The tone of the press reports, for example, is astonishingly fevered. Even before they had had the chance to admit their misdeeds, Isabel and Genya were both labeled as criminals and traitors. They were said to be lovers, too, in every possible sense apart from the true one. They were fool-hardy, dangerous—rabid urchins who had been rescued from the begging-bowl gutters of Ghezirah by their respective Churches, and had repaid that kindness with perfidy and deceit. Did people really feel so badly toward them? Did anyone ever really imagine that what they had done was any different to the innocent actions of the young throughout history? The facts may be plain, but such questions, from this distance of time, remain unanswerable. It should be remembered, though, that Ghezirah was still recovering from the War of the Lilies, and that the Churches, in this of all times, needed to reinforce the loyalty of their members. It was time for an example to be made—and for the peace to be shown for what it really was, which was shaky and incomplete and dangerous. For this role, Isabel and Genya were chosen.

As a rule, the Churches do not kill their errant acolytes. Instead, they continue to use them. Isabel, firstly, had her full sight, and then more, returned to her in lidless eyes of crystal that could never blink. Something was also done to her flesh that was akin to the operations that had been performed on Genya's fingertips. Finally, but this time in a great minaret on the Church's home island of Jerita, she was returned to her duties as a Dawn-Singer. But dawn for her now became a terrible thing, and the apprentices and clerks and lesser acolytes who lived and worked for their Church around the forested landscapes of the Windfare Hills returned from their night's labours to agonised screams. Still, Isabel strove to perform her duties, although the light was pure pain to the diamonds of her lidless eyes and the blaze of sunlight was molten lead to flesh that now felt the lightest breeze as a desert gale.

No one's mind, not even Isabel's, could sustain such torment indefinitely. As the years passed, it is probable that the portions of her brain that suffered most were slowly destroyed, even though the sensors in her scarred and shining flesh continued working. Isabel, in her decline, became a common sight amid the forests and court-yards of the lesser academies of the Windfare Hills; a stooped figure, wandering and muttering in the painful daylight which she had brought, wrapped in cloths and bandages despite the summer's endless warmth; an object lesson in betrayal, her glittering eyes always shaded, averted in pain. She was given alms. Everyone knew her story, and felt that they had suffered with her—or at least that she had suffered for them. She was treated mostly with sadness, kindness, sympathy. The nights, though, were Isabel's blessing. She wandered under the black skies almost at ease, brushing her fingers across the cooling stones of statues, listening to the sigh of the trees.

Perhaps she remembered Mirror 28, or that day of fog when she first met Genya. More likely, being Isabel, there was no conscious decision involved in the process of bringing, slowly, day by day and year by year, a little less light across to the stately rooftops and green hills of this portion of Jerita, other than a desire to reduce her own suffering. People, though, noted the new coolness of the air, the difference of the light amid these hills, and, just as Genya and Isabel had once done, they found it pleasantly melancholy. The Church's Intelligence, too, must have been aware in its own way of these happenings, although this was perhaps what it had always intended. People began to frequent the Windfare Hills because of these deeper shadows, the whisper of leaves from the seemingly dying trees blowing across lawns and down passageways. They lit fires in the afternoons to keep themselves warm, and found thicker clothes. It is likely that few had ever traveled beyond Ghezirah, or were even aware of the many worlds which glory in the phenomena called *seasons*. Only the plants, despite all the changes which had been wrought on them, understood. As Isabel, who had long had nothing to lose, one day took the final step of letting darkness continue to hang for many incredible moments over Windfare whilst all the rest of Jerita ignited with dawn, the trees clicked their branches and shed a few more leaves into the chill mists, and remembered. And waited.

This, mostly, is the story of Isabel of the Fall as it is commonly told. The days grew duller across the Windfare Hills. The nights lengthened. A ragged figure, failing and arthritic, Isabel finally came to discover, by accidentally thrusting her hand into the pillar of Sabil's light which poured into her minaret, that the blaze which had caused her so much pain could also bring a blissful end to all sensation. She knew by then that she was dying. And she knew that her ruined, blistered flesh—as she came to resemble an animated pile of the charcoal sticks of the leavings of autumnal fires—was the last of the warnings with which her Church had encumbered her. Limping and stinking, she wandered further afield across the Dawn Church's island of Jerita. Almost mythical already, she neglected her duties to the extent that her minaret, probably without her noticing in the continuing flicker of short and rainy days, was taken from her. The desire for these seasons had spread by now across Ghezirah. Soon, as acolytes of the Green Church learned how to reactivate the genes of plants that had once coped with such conditions, spring was to be found in Culgaith, and chill winter in Abuzcid. The spinning islands of Ghezirah were changed forever. And, at long last, in this world of cheerful sadness and melancholy joy that only the passing of seasons can bring, the terrors of the War of the Lilies became a memory.

One day, Isabel of the Fall was dragging herself and what re-mained of her memories across a place of gardens and fountains. A cool wind blew. The trees here were the colour of flame, but at the same time, she was almost sure that the enormous building that climbed ahead of her could only be the Cathedral of the Word. She looked around for Genya and grunted to herself—she was probably off playing hide and seek. Isabel staggered on, the old wrappings which had stuck to her burnt flesh dragging behind her. She looked, as many now remarked, like a crumpled leaf; the very spirit of this new season of autumn. She even smelled of decay and things burning. But she still had the sight which had been so ruth-lessly given to her, and the building ahead . . . the building ahead seemed to have no end to its spires. . . .

Cold rains rattled across the lakes. Slowly, day by day, Isabel approached the last great citadel of her Church, which truly did rise all the way to the skies, and then beyond them. The Intelli-gence which dwelt there had long been expecting her, and opened its gates, and refreshed the airs of its corridors and stairways which Isabel, with the instincts of a Dawn-Singer, had no need to be encouraged to climb. Day and darkness flashed through the arrowslit windows as she ascended. Foods and wines would appear at turns and landings, cool and bland for her wrecked palate. Sometimes, hissing silver things passed her, or paused to enquire if they could carry her, but Isabel remained true to the precepts and vanities of her Church, and disdained such easy ways of ascension. It was a long, hard climb. Sometimes, she heard Genya's husky breath beside her, her exclamations and laughter as she looked down and down into the huge wells which had opened beneath. Sometimes, she was sure she was alone. Sometimes, although her blackened face had lost all sensation and her eyes were made of crystal, Isabel of the Fall was sure she was crying. But still she climbed.

The roof that covers the islands of Ghezirah is usually accessed, by the rare humans and aliens who do such things, by the use of aircraft and hummingbird caleches. Still, it had seemed right to the forgotten architects of the Dawn Church that there should be one last tower and staircase that ascended all of the several miles to the top of Ghezirah's skies. By taking the way which always led *up*, and as the other towers and minarets fell far beneath her, Isabel found that way, that last spire, and followed it. Doorways opened. The Intelligence led her on. She never felt alone now, and even her pain fell behind her. Finally, though, she came to a doorway that would not open. It was a plain thing, round-lipped and with a

wheel at its centre which refused to turn. A light flashed above it.
Perhaps this was some kind of warning. Isabel considered. She sat
there for many days. Food appeared and disappeared. She could go
back down again, although she knew she would never survive the
journey. She could go on, but that light . . . Over to her left, she
saw eventually, was some sort of suit. A silvered hat, boots, a cape.
They looked grand, expensive. Surely not for her? But then she
remembered the food, the sense of a presence. She pulled them on
over her rags, or rather the things pulled themselves over her when
she approached them. Now, the wheel turned easily, even before
she had reached out to it. Beyond was disappointing; a tiny space
little more than the size of a wardrobe. But then there was a sound
of hissing, and a door similar to one that had puzzled her spun its
wheel, and opened. Isabel stepped out.

The great interior sphere of Ghezirah hung spinning. Everywhere within this glittering ball there were mirrors wide as oceans.
Everywhere, there was darkness and light. And Sabil hung at the
centre of it, pluming white; a living fire. Isabel gasped. She had
never seen anything so beautiful—not even Genya dancing. She
climbed upward along the gantries through stark shadows. Something of her Dawn-Singer's knowledge told her that these mirrors
were angled for night, and that, even in the unpredictable drift of
these new seasons, they would soon bring dawn across Ghezirah.
She came to the lip of one vast reflector, and considered it. At this
pre-dawn moment, bright though it was, its blaze was a mere
ember. Then, leaning over it as she had once leaned over Mirror
28 with Genya, Isabel did something she had never done before.
She touched the surface of the mirror. There was no sense left in
her ravaged hands, but, even through the gloves of her suit and
Sabil's glare and hard vacuum, it felt smooth, cool, perfect. The
mirror was vast—the size of small planet—and it curved in a near
endless parabola. Isabel understood that for such an object to move
at all, and then in one moment, it could not possibly be made of
glass, or any normal human substance. But at the same time, it
looked and felt solid. Without quite knowing what she was doing,
but sensing that the seconds before dawn were rapidly passing,
Isabel climbed onto the edge of the mirror. Instantly, borne by its
slippery energies, she was sliding, falling. The seconds passed. The
mirror caught her. Held her. She waited. She thought of the insects
that she had sponged from so many mirrors in her nights as an
apprentice, their bodies fried by the day's heat. But dawn was coming . . . For the last time, as all the mirrors moved in unison to bear

Sabil's energies toward the sleeping islands of Ghezirah below, Isabel spread her arms to welcome her sun. Joyously, as the light flashed to bear on her, she sang in the dawn.

In some versions of this tale, Isabel is said to have fallen toward Sabil, and thus to have gained her name. In others, she is called simply Isabel of the Autumn and her final climb beyond the sky remains unmentioned. In some, she is tragically beautiful, or beautifully ugly. The real truth remains lost, amid much else about her. But in the Dawn Church itself Isabel of the Fall is still revered, and amid its many mysteries it is said that one of Ghezirah's great internal reflectors still bears the imprint of her vaporised silhouette, which is the only blemish on all of its mirrors which the Church allows. And somewhere, if you know where to look amid all of Ghezirah's many islands, and at the right time of day and in the correct season, there is a certain wall in a certain small garden where Isabel's shape can be seen, pluming down from the minarets far above; traversing the hours brick to mossy brick as a small shadow.

As for Genya, she is often forgotten at the end of this story. She touches Isabel's face for a last time, smiles, bows, and vanishes down the stairways of the minaret toward oblivion. But the fact that she was also punished by her Church remains beyond doubt, and the punishment was as cruel and purposeful in its own way as that which was visited on Isabel. Genya retained all her senses, her special fingertips, even briefly her skills as a dancer; what her Church took from her was the ability to *understand*. She was then set the task of transcribing many manuscripts from one dead language to another, dictating, recording, endlessly reading and reciting with every input of her eyes and flesh. There were unrearth stories of princess and dragons, equations over which geniuses would have wept, but the meaning of them all passed through Genya unnoticed. Genya became a stupid but useful vessel, and she grew ancient and proficient and fat in a pillowed crypt in the far depths of the Cathedral of the Word, where the windows look out on the turning stars and new acolytes were taken to see her—the famous Genya who had once loved Isabel and betrayed her Church; now white and huge, busy and brainless as a maggot as she rummaged through endless torrents of words. But there are worse fates, and Genya lacked the wisdom to suffer. And she wasn't soulless—somewhere, deep within the rolls of fat and emptiness, all those spinning words, she was still Genya. When she died, muttering the last sentence of an epic which no other Librarian or machine could possibly have transcribed, that part of her passed on with the manuscript to echo and remain held forever somewhere amid all the vast cliff faces of books in the Cathedral of the Word. To this day, within pages such as these, Genya can still sometimes be found, beautiful as she once was, dancing barefoot across the warm, rosestone paving on an endless summer's morning in the time which was always long ago.

---

# The Summer Isles

## One

ON THIS AS ON ALMOST EVERY SUNDAY EVENING, I find a message from my acquaintance on the wall of the third cubical of the Gents beside Christ Church Meadow. It's two thumbnails dug into the sleek, green paint this week, which means the abandoned shed by the allotments past the rugby grounds in half an hour's time. A trail of other such marks run across the cubical wall; what amounts nowadays to my entire sexual life. Here— Oh, happy, dangerous days!—is the special triple-mark that meant a back room in the hotel of a sympathetic but understandably wary proprietor. He's gone now, of course, has Larry Black, like so many others. Quietly taken one night for the shocks and needles of the treatment centres in the Isle of Man.

I pull the chain, clunk back the lock, and step out into the sweet Jeyes Fluid air. Placed above me on the wall as I wash my hands, with what, if you didn't know this country, you would surely imagine to be ironic intent, hangs a photograph of John Arthur. He gazes warmly across his desk, looking younger than his forty-nine years despite his grey hair. The photograph is brass-framed, well-polished. Of course, no one has dared to deface it.

Outside along St Giles, twilight has descended, yet the warmth of this early summer day remains. A convoy of trucks lumbers around the cobbles, filled with bewildered-looking conscripts on their way to the sprawling camps in the southeast of England. A few of the newer or expensively refurbished pubs already boom with patriotic songs. I pause to relight my pipe as I pass St John's, then lean spluttering against a wall and cough up a surprising quantity of stringy phlegm, watched over by a small but disapproving gargoyle. Odd, disgusting habit—hawking and spitting. Something that, until recently, I'd only associated with old men.

There's still some life out on the playing fields. Undergrads are wandering. There are groups. Couples. Limbs entwine. Soft laughter flowers. The occasional cigarette flares. Glancing back at the towers of this city, laid in shadows of hazy gold against the last flush of the sun, it's all so impossibly beautiful. It looks, in fact, exactly like an Empire Alliance poster. GREATER BRITAIN AWAKE! I smile at the thought, and wonder for a moment if there isn't some trace of reality still left in the strange dream that we in this country now seem to be living. Turning, sliding my hand into my pocket to nurse the encouraging firmness of my anticipatory erection, I cross the bridge over the Cherwell as Old Tom begins his long, nightly chime.

Despite all the back-to-nature and eat-your-own greens propaganda that Home Secretary Mosley has been peddling, the shed at the far end of the allotments and the plots it once served remain abandoned, cupped as they are in a secret hollow, lost by the men who went to the War and never came back. I lever open the door and duck inside. Tools and seeds and sweet, dry manure. But no sign yet of my acquaintance as the floorboards creak beneath my feet. The darkness, even as my eyes grow accustomed to the gloom, becomes near absolute as night settles outside. A distant bell ripples a muffled shipwreck clang. The late train to London rattles by in the distance, dead on time.

My acquaintance is late. In fact, he should have been here first. As I pushed back the door, his younger arms should already have been around me. He trembles often as not when we first lock together, does my acquaintance. After all, he has so much more to lose. For, despite the darkness and the secrecy with which we pretend to cloak our meetings, I know exactly who my acquaintance is. I have studied the lights of his house shining through the privet that he trims so neatly each fortnight, and I have watched the welcoming faces of his wife and two daughters as they greet him at his door.

Checking, occasionally, the radium glow of my watch, I let a whole hour slide by as the residues of early hope and fear sour into disappointment, and then frank anxiety. But what, after all, do I know of the demands of being a father, a husband? Of working in some grim dead-end section of the Censor's Department of the Oxford City Post Office? At ten, I lever the shed door back open and step back out into the summer night, leaving my long-forgotten libido far behind me. The stars shine down implacably through the rugby Hs as I make my way back past lovers and drunks and dog walkers into the old alleys. I turn for a moment as I hear the whisper of footsteps. Could that be a figure, outlined against the mist of light that seeps from a doorway? But by the time I've blinked, it becomes nothing—an ageing man's fancy: the paranoias of love and fear.

Then quickly along Holywell, where an owl calls, and onward under the trees to my college and my quad, to the cool, waiting sheets of my room deep in the serene heart of this ancient city.

I open my eyes next morning to the sight of my scout Christlow bearing a tray containing a steaming pot of Assam, a rack of toast, my own special jar of marmalade. Even as the disappointments of the previous evening and the cold aches that have suddenly started to assail my body wash over me, I still have to smile to find myself here.

"Lovely morning, sir." Christlow drifts through diamonds of sunlight to place the tray astride my lap. The circled cross of the EA badge on his lapel winks knowingly at me. "Oh, by the way, sir. You asked me to remind you of your appointment today."

"Appointment?"

"At ten o'clock, you were seeing your doctor. Unless, of course, you've—"

"No. Yes." I nod in my pyjamas, what's left of my hair sticking up in a grey halo, a dribble of spilt tea warming my chin—all in all, a good approximation of an absent-minded don. "Thank you, Christlow, for reminding me."

In that scarily deferential way of his, Christlow almost bows, then retreats and closes the door. With a sound like distant thunder, his trolley trundles off down the oak-floored corridor. And yes, I truly had forgotten my appointment. The dust-spangled sunlight that threads my room now seems paler and my throat begins to ache as whispers of pain and uncertainty come into my head.

Walking along High an hour later, I have to squeeze my way through the queue outside the Regal for the day's first showing of

Olivier's *Henry V*. Many, like Christlow, wear EA badges. But all ages, all types, both sexes, every age and disability, are gathered. A mixture, most bizarrely of all, of gown and town—undergrads and workers—the two quite separate existences that Oxford so grudgingly contains.

Beyond the junction of Alfred Street I push through the little door beside the jeweller's and climb the stairs to the surgery. The receptionist looks up without smiling, then returns to stabbing a finger at her typewriter. The posters in this poky waiting room are like the ones you see everywhere nowadays. WITH YOUR HELP WE CAN WIN. NOW IS THE TIME. JOIN THE EMPIRE ALLIANCE—BE A PART OF THE MODERNIST REVOLUTION. There's a fetching painting of the towers and spires of this great, dreaming city aglow at sunset, much as I saw them yesterday. And, of course, there's John Arthur.

"Mr Brook. Doctor Parker will see you."

I push through the doorway, blinking. Doctor Parker is totally new to me. Fresh-faced, young and pinkly bald, he looks, in fact, almost totally new to himself. Of course, I have no one but myself to blame for taking my chances with the National Health Service. I could have availed myself of Doctor Reichard, who comes to our college every Wednesday to see to us dons, and is available at most other times, since, on the basis of a stipend granted by George I in 1715, these attendances comprise his sole professional duty. But my complaints—shortness of breath, this cough, the odd whispering that sometimes comes upon me, the growing ache in my bones—sound all too much like the simple ravages of age. And I nurse, also, a superstitious fear that my sexual leanings will be apparent to the trained medical eye.

"Sorry about this ah . . . I've only just got . . ." he says as he glances down at his page-a-day calendar. THURSDAY 13 JUNE 1940. The letters seem to glow, so brightly rainbowed at their edges that I wonder if this isn't some other new symptom. "You're the ah . . . the columnist, aren't you? What was it? The Fingers of History?"

"Figures of History."

"Of course. *Daily Sketch*, every Saturday. Used to find it handy at school." Then another thought strikes him. "And you knew him, didn't you? I mean, you knew John Arthur. . . ."

"That was a long time ago."

"But what's he *really* like?"

I open my mouth to give my usual non-committal reply. But it doesn't seem worth it.

"Here we are." He shuffles the X-rays into order, then leans over the file. "Um—*Griffin Brooke*. I thought it was Geoffrey, and Brook without the e?"

"It's a sort of pen name," I say, although in fact the *Oxford Calendar*, the door to my rooms—even the name tags Christlow sews into my gowns—also read Geoffrey Brook. Griffin Brooke, the names I was born with, now reside only in odd corners such as this, where, despite the potential for confusion, I find myself reluctant to give them up.

As my thoughts drift toward all the odd accidents in life that have brought me here—and how, indeed, Fingers of History would be a good description of some historical process or other—another part of me watches Doctor Parker as he then raises the cover of my file a few inches to peer sideways into it.

Something changes behind his eyes. But when he clears his throat and smoothes back down the papers and finally makes the effort to meet my gaze, I'm still certain that I'm fully prepared for the worst. What could be more terrible, after all, than growing old, or emphysema, bronchitis, tuberculosis. . . ?

"It seems," he begins, "that a tumour has been growing in your lungs . . . Outwardly, you're still in good enough health, but I really doubt if there's any point in an operation."

Not even any need for an operation! A stupid bubble of joy rises up from my stomach, then dissolves.

I lick my lips. "How long," I ask, "have I got?"

"You'll need to make plans. I'm so terribly sorry. . . ."

Thrust upon the gleaming linoleum rivers of the new NHS, I am kept so busy at first that there is little time left for anything resembling worry. There are further X-rays at the Radcliffe, thin screens behind which I must robe and disrobe for the benefit of cold-fingered but sympathetic men who wear half-moon glasses. Nurses provide me with over-sweet tea and McVitie's Digestives. Porters seek my opinion about Arsenal's chances in the FA Cup.

I feel almost heroic. And for a while I am almost grateful for the new impetus that my condition gives to a long-planned project of mine. A book not of history, but *about* history. One which examines, much as a scientist might examine the growth of a culture, the way that events unfold, and attempts to grapple with the forces that drive them. *The Fingers of History?* The odd way that inspiration sometimes arrives when you're least looking for it, I may even have stumbled upon a title; serious and relevant to the subject, yet punning at the same time on my own small moment of popular fame in the *Daily Sketch*.

After years of grappling with the sense of being an impostor, which has pervaded most of my life, I suddenly find that I am making good progress in writing the pivotal chapter about Napoleon. Was he a maker of history, or was he its servant? Of course, he was both—and yet it is often the little incidents, when history is approached from this angle, which stand large. Questions such as, what would have happened if his parents Carlo and Letizia had never met?—which normal historians would discount as ridiculous—suddenly become a way of casting a new light.

But one post-hospital afternoon a week or so later, as I huddle over my desk, and the warm air drifting through my open window brings the chant and the tread of Christlow and his fellow EA members parading on the ancient grass of our college quad, the whole process suddenly seems meaningless. Now, I can suddenly see the futility of all the pages I have written. I can see, too, the insignificant and easily filled space that my whole life will soon leave. A few clothes hanging in a wardrobe, an old suitcase beneath a bed, some marks on a toilet cubical wall. Who, after all, am I, and what possible difference does it make?

Pulling on my jacket, empty with fear, I head out into Oxford as evening floods in.

I was born in Lichfield—which, then as now, is a town that calls itself a city—in the year 1880. It's middle England, neither flat nor hilly, north or south. Barring Doctor Johnson being born and a messy siege in the Civil War, nothing much has ever happened there. My father worked for Lichfield Corporation before he died of a heart attack one evening whilst tending his allotment. He'd had a title that changed once or twice amid great glory and talk of more ambitious holidays, but he'd always been Assistant-this and Deputy-that—one of the great busy-but-unspecified ("Well, it's quite hard to explain what I do unless you happen to be in the same line yourself . . .") who now so dominate this country.

My mother and I were never that stretched; we had his pension and his life insurance, and she took on a job working at Hindley's Cake Shop, and brought home bits of icing and angelica for me when they changed the window display. By this time, I'd already decided I wanted to be "a teacher." Until I passed into Secondary School from Stowe Street Elementary, I was always one of the brightest in my class. Even a County Scholarship to Rugby seemed within reach. And from there, yes, I was already dreaming of the Magdalene Deer, sleek bodies bathing in the Cherwell at Parson's Pleasure.

My later years in school, though, were a slog. Partly from struggling to keep pace amongst cleverer lads, I fell ill with something that may or may not have been scarlet fever. On my long stay away from school, a boy called Martin Dawes would call in each afternoon to deliver school books and sit with me. Whilst up in my room, he would sometimes slip his hands beneath the waistband of my pyjamas and toss me off, as if that, too, was a message that needed to be delivered from school. Of course, I was deeply grateful. After I had recovered, locked in the upstairs toilet with its ever-open window as my mother shuffled about in the kitchen, I would dutifully try to incorporate women into my pink imaginings as, in the absence of Martin's attentions, I stimulated myself. But at some vital moment, their chests would always flatten and their groins would engorge as they stepped toward me, cropped and clean and shining.

That, in the personal history of what I term my pre-Francis days, is the sole extent of my sexual development. There was just me, my guilty semi-celibacy, and helping my mother look after her house, and watching the lads I'd known at school grow up, leave home, marry, start families. I had, by my early twenties, also come to accept my position as a Second Class Teacher for the Senior Standard Threes at Burntwood Charity. In the articles with which I began my short career in the *Daily Sketch* nearly thirty years later, I gave the impression that John Arthur was one of my brightest and most ambitious pupils there, a little comet trail across the pit-dusty Burntwood skies. Thanks to numerous flowery additions by the *Sketch*'s copy editor, I also stated that he was pale-skinned, quiet, good looking, intense, and that he possessed a slight West Country accent, this being the time before it had changed to the soft Yorkshire that we all know now—all traits which would have got him a good beating up in the playground—and that, "on summer evenings after school when the pit whistle had blown and the swallows were wheeling," he and I would walk up into "the hazy Staffordshire hills" and sit down and gaze down at "the spires of Lichfield, the pit wheels of Burntwood, and the smokestacks of Rugeley from the flowing purple heather." Now, after all these years of practice, this has become my party act. So, yes, John Arthur really is there in that classroom at Burntwood Charity with the smell of chalk dust and unwashed bodies. His hand is raised from the third row of desks to ask a more than usually pertinent question before I start to ramble on about one of my many pet subjects. That is how I recall him.

Too weary to stop, trailing cigarette smoke, memories, abstractions, I wander Oxford's new suburban streets, passing illuminated porches bearing individual nameplates; CHURCH HOUSE. DAWRIC. THE WILLOWS. It's quiet now, although scarcely past nine and only just getting fully dark. The houses have a sleepy look. Their curtains are drawn. Faintly, like the movement of ghosts, I can see the flicker of television screens in many darkened lounges.

A footstep scuffs in the street behind me, and the sound is so furtive and unexpected that I turn and look back, although there is nothing to see. I walk on more briskly. Beyond a patch of grass where BALL GAMES ARE PROHIBITED lies the home of my acquaintance, with its black-and-white gable, the privet, and the long strip of drive that, in these days of ever-growing prosperity, will probably soon be graced with a Morris Ladybird "people's car" instead of his Raleigh bicycle. But the windows of the house are darkened, uncurtained. And there is something odd about the look of them. . . .

My feet crunch on something sharper than gravel as I walk up the path to my acquaintance's front door. Many of the windows in the bay are shattered, there is a pervasive, summery smell of children's urine, and a fat, iron padlock has been fitted across the door's splintered frame. I see, last of all, the sign that the Oxford Constabulary has pasted across the bricks in the porch. TAKE NOTICE HEREBY . . . But this sky is incredibly dark and deep for summer, and I can't read further than the Crown-embossed heading. I slump down on the doorstep, scattering empty milk bottles, covering my face with my hands. Suddenly, it all comes to me. This. Death. Everything.

When I look up some time later, a figure is standing, watching me from the suburban night with her arms folded, head tilted, a steely glint of curlers. "I'm Mrs Stevens," she tells me, offering a softly companionable hand to help me up, then leading me past the hedge and the dustbins into the brightness of her kitchen next door. Slumped at the table, I watch her as she boils the kettle and warms the pot.

"I know," she says. "This must be a shock to you. . . ."

"They took them *all* away?"

"All of them. The pity of it really." She stirs her tea and passes me mine. "Them young girls."

"Nobody did anything to stop it?"

She gazes across at me, and licks the brown line of tea that's gathered on her small moustache. "I'll tell you what they were like, Mr Brook. In every way, I'd have said, they were a decent couple. Only odd thing I remember now is they sometimes used to leave the light on without drawing the curtains so you could see right in . . . The lassies were nice, though. Fed our cat for us when we went up to Harrogate last year. Knew them well yourself, did you?"

"He was just an acquaintance. But when they came to the house, was it the KSG or did—"

"—and you'd never have known, would you, to look at her?"

"*Her?* You mean. . . ?"

"Ah . . ." Mrs Stevens slaps her hand flat down on the table and leans forward, her brown eyes gleaming. "So you still don't know the truth of it? Her real name was something Polish. All Zs and Ks." She hurrumphs. "It's understandable that they *want* to come, isn't it? Just as long as they don't make themselves a burden, earn a decent living, talk like we do and don't bother our children and keep themselves to themselves."

"So what was the problem?"

"She was a Jew, wasn't she. All these years they've been living next door and acting all normal and hiding it from us." Mrs Stevens raises her shoulders and shudders theatrically. "To think of it. It's the *dishonesty*. And her nothing but a dirty little Jew."

## Two

Clouds sweep in across Oxford, thick and grey as wet cement. Rain brims over the low, surrounding hills and washes away the hope of what had promised to be another spectacular summer. In the whitewashed yard of the town prison on a hissing, grey dawn, two men are hanged for their part in an attempted mail robbery. In Honduras, the British prefix lost to revolution in 1919 is restored in a bloody coup. A car bomb in the Trans-Jordan kills fifteen German League of Nations soldiers. In India, as ever, there are uprisings and massacres, and I despair, as I work on my book, of ever making any sense of history. It seems, to quote Gibbon, little more than a register of cruelties, follies, and misfortunes.

In Britain, the Jews have always been small in number, and we're generally been "tolerant." Before the rise of Modernism, my acquaintance and his family probably had little more to fear from exposure than the occasional human turd stuffed through their letter box. After all, Jewishness isn't like homosexuality, madness, criminality, communism, militant Irishness: they can't exactly *help* being born with their grabby, disgusting ways, can they? Rather like the gypsies, you see, we didn't mind them *living*, but not here, not with us . . . In this as in so many other areas, all Modernism did when John Arthur came to power was take what people said to each other over the garden fence and turn it into Government policy.

I can well remember the *Homeland for British Jewry* newsreels: they were probably one of the defining moments of early Greater British history. There they were, the British Jews. Whole eager families of them helped by smiling Tommies as they climbed from landing craft and hauled their suitcases up onto the shingle of remote Scottish islands that had been empty but for a few sheep since the Clearances of a century before. And it was hard not to think how genuinely nice it would be to start afresh somewhere like that, to paint and make homely the grey blocks of those concrete houses, to learn the skills of shepherding, harvesting, fishing.

So many other things have happened since then that it has been easy to forget about the Jews. I remember a short piece on Pathé before Disney's *Snow White* in what must have been 1939. By then they looked rustic and sunburned, their hands callused by cold winters of weaving and dry-stone walling, their eyes bright from the wind off the sea. Since then, nothing. A blank, an empty space that I find hard to fill even in my imagination.

One morning, as thunder crackles and water streams and the whole college seems to shift and creak like a ship straining at its moorings, I'm still marooned in my rooms, ill and lost in the blind alley of my book, when Christlow arrives at eleven to do the cleaning.

"You know the Jews, Christlow," I chirp after clearing my throat.

"Jews sir? Yes sir. Although not personally."

He pauses in his dusting. The situation already has a forced air.

"I was wondering—it's part of my book, you see—what happened to the mixed families. Where a Jew married a gentile. . . ."

"I'm sure they were treated sympathetically, sir. Although for the life of me I can't imagine there were ever very many of them."

"Of course," I nod, and force my gaze back to my desk. Christlow resumes his dusting, his lips pursed in a silent whistle amid the rain-streaming shadows as he lifts the photos along the mantelpiece of my mother, my father—and a good-looking, dark-haired, young man.

"So you'll be alright, then, sir?" he asks when he's finished, picking up his box of rags and polishes. "Fine if I leave you now?"

"Thank you Christlow. As always," I add, laying it on thick for some reason, as if there's a deeper debt that he and I owe each other, "you've done a splendid job."

When he's gone and his footsteps have faded into the college's loose stirrings, I slide in the bolt, then cross to the gloom of my bedroom and drag my old suitcase from beneath the bed. I always keep its key in my pocket, and the hinges creak as I open them, rusty from disuse. Nothing inside has changed. The tin toys. The tennis slacks. The exercise book with the name FRANCIS EVELEIGH inscribed into the cardboard cover in thick, childish letters. A school badge. A Gillette safety razor—his first? A pistol wrapped inside an old rag. A decent-enough herringbone jacket. A single shoe. A steel hip flask. A soldier's pass for 14–26 September 1916, cross-stamped NO LONGER VALID. Various socks and old-fashioned collarless shirts and itchy-looking undies. A copy of Morris's *News from Nowhere*. And a Touring Map of the Scottish Highlands, folded so often that the sheets threaten to break apart as I touch them.

I grab a handful of his clothes and bury my face into them, smelling Oxford damp, Oxford stone, Four Square Ready-Rubbed, and Mansion House lavender floor polish. Little enough is left of Francis now. Still, that faint scent of his flesh like burnt lemon. A few dark strands of his hair . . .

What a joke I have become. My sole claim to fame is having dimly known a great man when he was still a child, and my sole claim to happiness lies almost as far back; a miracle that happened for a few days nearly thirty years ago. I suppose I've convinced myself since that homosexuals cannot really love—it's easier that way. And yet at the same time, in all the years since, Francis had always been with me.

"It really doesn't matter, Griff," I hear him say as his fingers touch my neck. He smells not of lemons now, but of the rainy oak he's been standing beneath as he watches my window from the quad. But he hasn't aged. He hasn't changed.

"No, it doesn't matter at all," he whispers as he turns me round to kiss me. "Not any of this. That's the secret of everything."

I smile to find him near me, and still shudder at the cool touch of his hands. In the moment before the thunder crackles closer over Oxford and I open my eyes, all pain is gone.

Eric Svendsen, with his suspiciously foreign name, his long nose, his thick glasses, seems an unlikely survivor of my kind. He puts it down to something that he has on Oxford's Deputy Chief Constable, although I would have thought that would have made him a prime candidate for a hit-and-run car accident.

We meet at a park bench the next afternoon, during a break in the rain.

"Do you think they'll let them stay together?" I ask as he tosses bread from a brown paper bag to the feathered carpet of ducks that have gathered around us. "Will they send him to the Isle of Man, the girls and the mother to the Western Isles?"

Giving me a pitying look, Eric shakes his head. "It doesn't work like that, my friend. Oh, they'll get it out of him. He'll tell them anything—lies or the truth. People always blab on so when you threaten them . . . I shouldn't worry," he adds, seeing the expression on my face. "If something was going to happen to you, it would have happened already. Being who you are, I'm sure you'll be safe."

"I'm not who I am. I'm not anybody."

"Then you're doubly lucky."

"I keep asking myself what the point is. I mean—why?"

"I think you've forgotten what it's like, my friend."

"What?"

"Being the way we are—bent, queer. The guilt. The stupid scenes. You remember those leaflets, the promises of help, that we could be cured. Don't tell me you didn't secretly get hold of one." He sighs. "If we could just press some button—pull out something inside us—don't you think we'd all do it? Wouldn't you take that chance, if you were given it? Isn't John Arthur right in that respect —and wouldn't the Jews feel the same?"

But to change would mean re-living my life—becoming something other than what I am. Losing Francis. So I shake my head. And I've heard the stories of what happens to my kind. The drugs. The electrodes. The dirty pictures. Swimming in pools of your own piss and vomit. *That* kind of treatment that was available even before Modernism made it compulsory. "It isn't John Arthur," I say. "It's all of us. It's Britain . . ."

Eric chuckles. "I suppose you'll be alone now, won't you?"

"Alone?"

"Without companionship. Without a cock to suck."

I glance across the bench, wondering if Eric's propositioning me. But his eyes behind his glasses are as far away as ever; fish in some distant sea. Sex for him, I suspect, has always been essentially a spectator sport. That's why he fits in so well. That's why he's survived. He doesn't want a real body against him. All he needs is the sharp, hot memories of those he's betrayed. Crucified flesh. Blood-curdled semen.

"Look," I say, "I just thought you might have some information about what happens to . . . to the Jews—and to people like us. Surely somebody has to?"

"All I know is what I read in the papers, my friend. And what I see in the newsreels." His gaze travels across the silvered lawns. "I understand how it is. We're only human, after all. It's always sad when you lose someone. . . ."

He stands up, shaking the last of his bread crumbs over the ducks, and I watch as he walks off, splashing a shortcut across the lawns and then around the sodden nets of the empty tennis courts. I can't help wondering if there will be a black, official KSG Rover waiting for me somewhere soon. The polite request and the arm hooked around my elbow and the people passing by too busy going about their lives to notice. The drive to a dark clearing in a wood, the cold barrel to the forehead . . . I can't help feeling selfishly afraid. But as I make my way down Holywell past the old city walls, the clouds in the west begin to thin, and the wind picks and plays with rents of blue sky as the sun flickers through. Dawdling along the narrow, unpredictable streets that wind around the backs of the colleges giving glimpses of kitchen dustbins and Wren towers, the light brightens. And Oxford. Oxford! All the years that I longed to see myself like this amid these quads and buildings, the twin shining rivers, the whispering corridors of learning.

Working on my book each evening after school in the front parlour, as my mother nodded over her knitting in her chair behind me, I always knew that the dream was impossibly far away. But nourishing my one great work, I never even bothered to think of setting some more realistic target and perhaps submitting an essay on local history to the *Lichfield Mercury* or *Staffordshire Life*. It was all or nothing—and perhaps in my heart of hearts I was happy enough with nothing. One evening, I remember, the work at the parlour table was going particularly well and the hours slid by until I cracked my weary fingers and turned around to my mother to comment on the faint but foul smell that I had noticed. She sat unusually still in the dimness of the room behind me. Her head was lolling, her fingers were clenched around the knitting needles and her ball of wool had rolled from her lap in her final spasm.

## Three

Now that the rain has ended and the sun has come out, all of Britain seems to drift, held aloft on wafts of dandelion and vanilla, the dazzling boom of bandstand brass. Each morning, the *Express*, the *New Cross*, and the *Mail* vie for punning headlines and pictures of Modernist maidens in fountains, ice cream-smeared babies, fainting guardsmen. With or without me, life seems intent on going on—but I find that I remain remarkably active in any case: with Christlow's help, for example, I can manage to be fully dressed, my lungs coughed-out, my tablets taken, my limbs unstiffened, my eyes fully focused, my heartbeat and my breathing made almost regular by half past eight or nine at the latest. And thus aroused, thus fortified, I have taken a surprising number of trips out this August. This, after all, is my last chance to see anything, and I can easily afford to squander my savings by going First Class. But still, as I queue at the Oxford City Post Office for the appropriate cross-county passes that will get me to Lichfield, I can't help but wonder if the woman behind the spittle-frosted glass knew my acquaintance, and who emptied his desk upstairs in the Censor's Office, who scratched his name off the tea club. . . .

Next morning, climbing aboard the *Sir Galahad* after it slides into Oxford Station, its streamlined snout oozing steam and the sense of far-away, I stumble past four senior officers of the KSG, the Knights of Saint George, as I make my way down the carriage in search of my reserved seat. They all look sleek, plump—seals basking on a sunny shore, washed by the warm waves of the future. A mother and daughter are opposite my place in the no-smoking section further along. The morning sun pours over their blonde hair and their innocent, blue eyes rest on me as I slump down. I feel I must look strange and sinister, already a harbinger of death, yet their manner is welcoming, and we begin to talk as the train pulls out in that absent, careless manner that strangers sometimes have. The husband, the little girl's father, is a Black Watch major who's risen through the Army ranks on merit in the way that only happens in real conflicts, and is currently on active service on the ever-troublesome India-Afghanistan border. The mother tells me she sleeps with his and John Arthur's photograph beneath her pillow. I smile as their faces shine back at me and then gaze out of the window, watching the telegraph lines rise and fall and the world flash by, carrying me on toward Lichfield.

∗       ∗       ∗

Living in what I still thought of my mother's house back in the years before the War, alone and celibate, I still entertained thoughts of writing my book. But, after many botched attempts, I began to wonder if something else was missing. History, after all, is ever changing, and must always be viewed from the perspective of the present. I was still as neutral in politics as I imagined myself to have become sexually, yet in my efforts to take myself seriously as a historian, I decided that politics probably lay at the cutting edge of current affairs, and I joined the local Fabian Society. It was probably a good job that I dipped my toe into the waters of political debate without any high ideals. Still, I can see with hindsight that it was an interesting time for British left-wing politics. The younger and generally rowdier element (of which Francis Eveleigh was undoubtedly a member) were busily undermining the cosy nineteenth century libertarianism of William Morris—the Morris, that is, who existed before he was reinvented by Modernism. But it was all naively innocent. Francis, for example, worked six days a week behind the counter of the John Menzies bookstall at Lichfield station, lived in digs, lifted his little finger when he drank tea, was secretive about his background, and spoke with a suspiciously upper-class accent. Still, I was drawn to him. I liked his youth, his enthusiasm, his good looks.

He and I began meeting occasionally after he had finished work at the station bookstall, and we would take quiet walks across the flat, Staffordshire countryside. When we were alone, there was a lot less of the usual posturing and political debate, but nevertheless, the prospect of a war in Europe soon began to dominate our conversation. Francis, although supposedly a pacifist, was fascinated by the whole idea of conflict. In a white shirt, his collar loose, he would walk ahead of me as we wandered at evening along misty canal towpaths and across muddy spring fields. His body was slight and bony, yet filled with energy. He grew his hair a little longer than was then fashionable, and I loved to watch, as he walked ahead of me, the soft nest of curls that tapered toward the back of his neck.

"You understand, Griff," he said to me once as we stood to catch our breath amid the cows beneath a dripping tree. "I can work these things out when we walk together."

My heart ached. I could only smile back at him.

The idea of our taking a cycling trip to Scotland seemed to evolve naturally, gradually from this process. That was probably a good thing, for if I had planned that Francis and I could be on our own, sharing thoughts, ideas, and boarding-house rooms for a whole fortnight, I am sure that love and terror would have prevented it from ever happening. But somehow, I found that we were checking maps and timetables on the basis of a vague hypothesis —playing with the whole idea, really—until suddenly we were talking proper dates and actual bookings and the thing had miraculously come about. And I was to pay. That, too, slipped easily under the yawning bridge of my uncertainties. Thank God, the idea of two men traveling together on holiday raised few suspicions in the summer of 1914. Francis, bless him, probably had a far clearer idea of where he was leading me, and what was to come. But for all of that, for absolutely everything about him, I am eternally grateful.

We ate in the dining carriage as the train pulled out of Birmingham, studying our maps. Yet we went to our shared sleeping compartment quite early, I recall, filled with that soothed, tired feeling that only the start of a long railway journey brings. In that narrow compartment, I tried to busy myself with sorting the contents of my suitcase on the lower bunk as Francis undressed beside me. Trembling, alone after he had headed up the corridor to wash, looking down at the half-erection that, absurdly, was trying to nudge its way out of my pyjamas, I cursed myself for my stupidity in ever falling for the idea of this holiday. I pushed passed him when he returned, and pulled down a window in the corridor and watched the fields burn with sunset as the telegraph wires rose and fell, rose and fell. By the time I finally got back to the compartment, the landscape had become a grainy patchwork and Francis was up in the top bunk, reading *News from Nowhere*. Muttering about how tired I felt, I climbed in below.

I stared up at the shape his body made against the bars of the bunk. It truly was soothing, this motion of the carriage, the steel clatter of the wheels. Eventually, when Francis turned off his light and wished me good night, I truly felt ready for sleep and when, about half an hour later, he began to shift down from his bunk, I simply imagined that he was heading off on a final trip to the toilets. Instead, he climbed in beside me.

His pyjama shirt was already undone. He smelled faintly of soap and toothpowder, and beneath that of the warmth of this own flesh, like burnt lemon.

"This is what you want, Griff, isn't it. . . ?" he said. Then he put his arms around me, and he kissed me, and nothing was ever the same.

*       *       *

*Clatter, tee, tee* . . . even here, on the way to Lichfield, that same sense of passing. Then as now, the onward rush of a train. Stations beside canal bridges. Stations in farmyards. Stations piled with empty milk churns and mailbags in the middle of pretty nowhere. And posters, posters. Posters of the seaside and posters of the country. Posters of towns. THE LAKE DISTRICT FOR REST AND QUIET IMAGININGS. TAKE THE SUNDAY SPECIAL AND VISIT LAMBOURN DOWNS, where a smiling couple are picnicking with their two pretty daughters as coloured kites dance against a cloudless sky. . . .

Francis loved the place names as we journeyed across Scotland. Mellon Udrigle. Plockton. Grey Dog. Poolewe. Smearisary. The Summer Isles. When he wasn't reading the newspapers he got hold of every day to keep track of the repercussions of the assassination of an obscure Archduke, he'd run his finger along some impossibly contoured and winding route that the pedals of our basket-fronted Northampton Humbers were supposed to carry us down, chosen entirely to include as many of those wonderful names as possible.

Alone together in those yellow-lit boarding-house rooms with their great, empty wardrobes, riding the creaking seas of hollowed-out double beds, his chin cupped in his hand and bare feet in the air, laughing at something, humming to himself, twiddling his toes, Francis would study his maps and his newspapers. Then he'd lay a hand across me and pull me closer with a touch that was both warmly sexual and at the same time had nothing to do with sex at all. "This is real history, Griff," he said to me once when I expressed amazement that anyone should care about what was happening in the Balkans. "How can you pretend to be a historian and then let all this pass you by?"

I remember that Francis and I were in a pub on the evening of August 4th, 1914, when Asquith had announced that Britain would be at war with Germany from midnight. I knew that he was going to enlist, and I could see that he was elated. It was no use arguing. And I, too, was excited by the prospect of this new future that lay ahead of us—that night, it was impossible not to be. Suddenly, after years of trying, we British could love each other and hate the Germans. Politics and diplomacy seemed trivial compared to the raw certainties of war. Soon, we were dancing in the crowd. Francis even kissed me. That August night, nobody cared. We were all one mass of hope and humanity.

On our journey south from the Highlands, without access to a sleeping carriage now that everyone wanted to travel, I did my best to talk seriously to Francis. I needed to fix as much of him in my mind as I could. But he was teasing about his past. *Yes, I went to school but it was just a place. How do you think I learned? Do I have a* brother?—*well, you tell me. Go on, you know what I'm like, so guess* . . . It was a game we'd played before, but this time it was harsher, more hurtful. As we waited on swarming platforms and changed trains and searched for seats and stood in crowded corridors, I ended up telling Francis about myself instead.

"So, Griff," he smiled as we leaned against a window by our cases and the sleepers raced by. "You want to be a Professor? Have you ever even *been* to Oxford? Or would that spoil the dream?"

The train rocked us on, and Lichfield, despite my willing it not to, arrived soon enough. Francis and I parted outside the station without saying very much or even shaking hands, and I walked off toward what I still thought of as my mother's house almost looking forward to being alone. In Saint Martin's Square, a brass band was playing. Men, jolly as a works outing, talking and laughing freely in the way that we British so seldom do, queued up to enlist in the Staffordshire Regiment. They beckoned me to join them, but there was no bitterness when I smiled and shook my head, such was our country's optimism.

Walking once again along the strangely shrunken streets of my home town, heavier now with the burdens of age and illness, looking over the low front wall of the house where I lived most of my life, I note the pebbledash that the new owner has added to the rendering, the replacement window frames. Hindley's Cake Shop is still there with what look like the same cakes displayed in the window, although the butcher's shop above which Francis used to live has become a gent's outfitters, and the window of his room now bears the words FORMAL DRESS HIRE.

I take the bus in search of Burntwood Charity. But there's no sign of the school where I started my career—or even of the road that led to it with fields on the far side, or of the pit wheels. The whole place consists of nothing but houses and a vast new "comprehensive" school. Quite remarkably when you come to think about it, John Arthur remains uncommemorated. I visit the Town Library, another old haunt, but, just as in Oxford, the Lichfield census data and the voting lists and the rating and the parish records and pretty much every kind of document covering the period between the 1900s and the start of the thirties have been destroyed. Here, in fact, the scythes have cut even deeper. Even the *records* of the records are gone, along with the spaces they were supposed to occupy. It's as if whole decades have vanished entirely.

The War in Britain was a strange affair, like a fever. People were more sociable, strangers would talk to each other, and even I went out more often; to the theatre or to the music hall, or to one of the new cinematographs. At school, I taught my lads about the many historic acts of German aggression, and had them compose outraged letters to the Kaiser about the Zeppelin bombings of Great Yarmouth.

Francis wrote me the occasional letter at first after he volunteered. *Griff, you'd hardly know me now . . .* I could almost see him trying on his new soldierly identity. The letters were filled at first with catalogues of acquaintances and military stupidities as he was posted around various training camps and temporary barracks in southern England. They grew shorter and blander once he reached France and the rapidly solidifying Western Front. I was like the millions of puzzled relatives and loved ones who were the recipients of such letters. I put his terseness down to a shortage of time, and then to the military censors. But soon, by early 1915, Francis stopped writing to me altogether.

Two years passed. I only learned about Francis by chance when, queuing for a copy of the *Post* from the John Menzies bookstall on the platform at Lichfield station, I suddenly thought I heard his name being spoken. I knew what had happened straight away, just from the voices, although none of them had known him well. I'd heard its echo many times before from teachers and children at school, and people you passed in the street talking about a son, a husband, a brother. Like so many others, Francis Eveleigh had died in the Somme Offensive.

Pushed numbly into action, prodding and probing at the facts of Francis's life in a way that I had resisted when he was still alive, I was able to discover that his parents lived in a large house set in arable countryside just outside Louth in Lincolnshire. Standing outside in my muddy shoes on a cold day, as quizzical light fanned from their hall, I introduced myself to the maid as "a friend from Lichfield," and was ushered into the drawing room where Mr and Mrs Eveleigh stood still as china figures on either side of the unlit fire, as if they had been waiting there for a long time. Mr Eveleigh managed a bank, whilst his wife (Francis's eyes and pale skin, his full, dark hair that she always tied back in a bun) oscillated between various bridge clubs and civic societies. They were solid, dependable, and I was flattered and charmed that they were prepared to have anything to do with me. There was no hint, of course, that Francis and I had been lovers—or even that he'd had any kind of sexual life. But there was always a sense, somewhere amid all the weekends I was invited to the Eveleighs' house, of a shared, deeper fondness.

The light was always grey at the Eveleighs' house, and a chill came to whatever part of your body that was turned from the fire. Sitting in the dining room, as the clocks ticked and the fire spat, through interminable meals of boiled cabbage, boiled potatoes, and boiled bacon, it wasn't hard to see why Francis had gone away. But I found it easy enough to fit in, and there was always the pleasure of being able to sleep in Francis's childhood bed, which still bore the imprint of his body, to slide open drawers that contained the starched uniforms of the various cheap public schools he had been forced to attend and bury my face in their folds.

Mr Eveleigh talked endlessly about politics and the War. He'd ask me about the Jews; whether I didn't think they were involved in a conspiracy to set one half of Europe against the other. I think he even mentioned "dumping the buggers on some remote Scottish island and leaving them to get on with it." He asked if I agreed that the average working man was fundamentally lazy. He doubted whether every Tom, Dick, and Harry should be given the vote, and thought Lloyd George was just a Welsh windbag—what this country really needed was a true, strong leader. . . .

The last time I saw the Eveleighs was just after the French Capitulation. I remember that my train journey up through Peterborough and Lincoln took place in an atmosphere as feverish as it had been when Francis and I journeyed back from Scotland four years before—but also very different. Strangers were talking to strangers again, but their voices were confused, their faces were hard and angry. There were rumours already of Lloyd George's resignation and of a General Election, although, as all the major parties had supported the War, no one had any clear idea of what the campaign would be about. I bought one of the few papers that were left at a newsagent's and stared at the headline. WAR OVER. ALLIES DEFEATED. It was 6 August 1918; a date, it seemed to me, that would never look right in the cold pages of history.

The Eveleighs' front door was open—which seemed like final confirmation that everything had changed. People were milling. Clients from the Bank. Friends from the bridge circle. Farmers and neighbours. Time passed. Voices grew louder, then began to fade. I was tired and had a headache by the time I found myself alone with Mr and Mrs Eveleigh. Still, Mr Eveleigh insisted on spreading out a map of Belgium and France, then asking me to explain exactly who was to blame for this mess. No doubt making less sense than I imagined, I told him that the economies of all the nations had been seriously weakened, that the Bolshevik's treaty with Germany had been a capitulation, and the promised American reinforcements had been too few, and had come too late. Once the Germans made a break in the Allied lines, the certainties of trench warfare had crumbled; tactics were suddenly about communications, swiftness, surprise. With Paris succumbing and the British and Colonial Forces clustered chaotically around Cherbourg and Dieppe, there was nothing left to do but surrender to the Germans.

"We can't leave it like this." Mr Eveleigh said, swaying as he poured himself yet another whisky. "There'll have to be another war. . . ."

Later, Mrs Eveleigh showed me up to my room. "You might as well have these," she said, handing me a child's exercise book with Francis's name on the cover, a couple of battered tin toys. "Oh, and there's something else." I sat on the bed and waited as she carried in a cardboard box with a War Office stamp on it. She lifted it open, filling the room with some faint other smell. Mud? Death? It was certainly unpleasant. The box proved to be half-empty. There was that cheap edition of *News from Nowhere*. A pair of thick, standard-issue, grey-green military socks. More odd was the pistol. It seemed well kept and, more surprising still, a yellowed paper containing a dozen of what looked like live bullets. Mrs Eveleigh just gazed down at me as I sat on the bed and handled the thing.

"Keep that too," she said, something new and harsh in her voice. "I don't want it."

She was standing closer now. Like me, and in her own quiet way, I think she had passed into that grey hinterland that lies beyond an excess of drink. I glanced around at the familiar wallpaper, the twee pictures, expecting her to turn and leave. But she just stood there in front of me, her hands knotting and unknotting across the long line of buttons that ran down her black dress.

"I only feel as though I've lost him now," she said. "Before I knew we'd thrown away the War, it was always as if some part of him might still come back to me."

I nodded, staring up at this twisted image of Francis as a middle-aged woman. Her eyes were lost in shadow; a shade deeper than black.

"And I wonder, even now, if he ever knew a woman." She took a step closer so that our knees touched. I was looking right up at her now, the folds of her chin, the rapid rise and fall of her breasts. "I never knew what he was like," she said.

"He was . . ." I tensed my hands, feeling enclosed, threatened. But something snapped. "I loved him, Mrs Eveleigh. I just loved him. . . ."

She took a step back and nodded severely. I had truly thought for a moment that we could somehow share our Francislessness. But, instead, I heard the sigh of her dress as she left the room, the soft clunk of the door closing.

The Eveleighs never wrote to me after that.

I never saw them again.

With half an hour to kill and the return train to Oxford delayed, I buy a *Lichfield Mercury* from the same John Menzies bookstall at the station and then share the waiting room with three members of the Young Empire Alliance. They're little more than lads, really, and yet they affect maturity and ease as they smoke their Pall Malls and stretch out in long-trousered "boy-scout" uniforms. Two of them begin to hum a tune under their breath, alternately kicking each side of my bench in rhythm. A woman in a floral hat appears at the window, and I shoot her a despairing glance before she decides not to come in. I do my best to study the paper, the SITS VAC, where a Decent Widow is looking for a Clean Anglo-Saxon Couple to take care of her and her Nice House. The Classified columns, where various Modernist and EA self-education courses and camps are on offer, along with supposedly War Office-endorsed photographs of the Mons Archers. The photo on the back page, beside a column giving advice to Young Mr and Mrs Modern on setting up home, is of an elderly woman hunched in the stocks on a village green. She has been put there, the caption jokily informs us, as a "show of local outrage." Similar submissions from other readers are invited.

"I was wondering . . ." The best-looking of the YEA youths smiles. "Where's an old bastard like you going?"

"Oxford," I croak.

"Not one of them fucking eggheads, are you?"

"Well, as a matter of fact. . ."

"Tell you what . . ." He stands up. His face his tanned. His brown hair is cut so short that it would feel like velvet if you stroked it. He comes close to me and leans down. "The problem is . . ." A soft rain of his spittle touches my cheek. "I'm all out of cunting matches. Light my fag for me?"

He keeps his eyes on mine as I fumble in my coat pocket. His friends watch on, grinning. His irises are an intense, cloudless blue. He squints slightly as the match flares, and he holds my hand to guide it toward the tip of his cigarette. Moments later, my train arrives, and I leave the waiting room a sweaty wreck, still bearing an uncomfortable erection.

My journey, though, is far from over. Summer heat has buckled the main-line rails, and I end up stranded on the sun-bleached platform of a remote rural station with the faint promise of an eventual Oxford connection. There, I talk to the station master, a round-faced man whose body bulges gently from the gaps between the buttons of his uniform like rising dough.

"You know," I say, clearing my throat, taking the kind of risk that the nearness of death encourages, "I've always wondered what happened to the people who were sent north. The newspapers about five years back always used to speak of the Jews. I mean . . ." I hesitate, searching without success for a better word, "their relocation."

His eyes narrow as he looks at me, but the station is empty, and the rails stretch down through Leicestershire and Nottinghamshire amid nodding scoops of cow parsley and wild fennel. The air seems joined to the sky. We are safe here, alone. At other times, in other, happier places, I suspect that this station master and I might be engaged in some other kind of transaction. That is why we choose to trust each other.

"It's quieter here now," he says. "But three, four years ago, a lot of freight trains went past. Long things, they were, with slatted, wooden sides, like the farmers use for market—only always at night. One of them pulled up, and this soldier got me out of bed to send a message down the line. A bad smell came off the trucks and I could hear movement inside. I thought it was just animals. But there were voices. And you could see their eyes . . . children's fingers poking out of the slats. . . ."

The station master stands and shuffles through the tin heat toward his little station house. He returns with something in his hands.

"I found this," he says, unfolding it, holding it out to me. "On the platform afterward."

It's a travel poster, almost like the ones for Skegness and Bar-mouth that are smiling down at us. A family striding down a winding road that leads to a glittering sea. The father is grinning, beckoning us to join him whilst his wife holds the hands of their two daughters, who are chattering and skipping excitedly, their pigtails dancing in mid-air. Set within the ocean, more hinted at than revealed, yet clearly the focus of the picture, lie a scatter of small islands. Looked at closely, they blur to just a few, clever brush strokes, but they suggest hills and meadows, wooded glades, white beaches, and pretty shingle-roofed and whitewashed houses; a warm and happy place to live. The caption reads: RELOCATE TO THE SUMMER ISLES.

The promised train does eventually arrive, and the stationmaster and I make our farewells, briefly touching hands, a soft pressure of the flesh that I will soon be losing. I gaze out of the carriage as the train rattles on, close to tears. Oxfordshire comes. Then Oxford. Along Park End and George Street, the city is warm, summer-quiet, at peace with itself now it has lost the unwanted distraction of students, and smells sweetly of dusty book shops, old stone, dog shit, grass clippings.

"Something for you, sir." Christlow says, nearly falling over himself to intercept me as I limp across the quad. I take the letter he's waving and climb the old oak stairs to my rooms, then stare at the crested envelope as I lean against the door, wondering if I should play a game with myself for a while and let it rest, wondering just how dangerous a letter can be . . . But already my hands are tearing at the wax seal, dragging out the one thick sheet of paper that lies inside.

Beneath a lion and unicorn, it reads:

## WHITEHALL
## FROM THE OFFICE OF THE PRIME MINISTER

8 August, 1940

G B—

I know it's been a *long* time, but I honestly haven't forgotten.

You may have heard that there's going to be a "National Celebration" in London before and around 21st October, Trafalgar Day. It probably still seems a long way off, but I'd really like to see you there. I promise it'll be nothing formal.

I really do hope you can make it. My staff will send you the details.

*All the very best as ever,*

J A

Later that evening, I build a small fire in the grate of my rooms and feed it with the pages of my book. Everything, after all, ends this way. Napoleon, Peter the Great, Bismarck . . . all the *Figures of History*. The pages curl. Glowing fragments of paper dance up the chimney. Soon, there's barely anything left to burn. It's all over so quickly, and what is left of my life, as I open up my old suitcase and cradle Francis's old pistol in my hands, feels simpler already.

## Four

My college principal Cumbernald comes to my rooms one evening, stretching out in one of the chairs facing the fireplace and companionably beckons me to join him. He's a tall man, is Cumbernald. He radiates smooth affluence and, like most inferior academics, has pushed his way into administration. Yet he has risen ridiculously far, ridiculously fast. It's almost nice, as the sunlight gleams on his bald head, to think that I'm probably going to bugger up his plans for the next academic year by dying.

"About Michaelmas Term," he begins, crossing his legs to reveal a surprisingly brown length of shin. "I was thinking of giving you the old decline and fall for a change. Bit of a problem with Roberts, you see. Evidently wrote a book back in the twenties about the economics of the Roman Empire. Argued that the colonies were a drain on Rome. *Then* he keeps drawing comparisons with Britain. Even crops up in his student's essays—although of course we can't expect the dear things to know any better unless we teach them, can we?"

"I'd be surprised if Roberts's book was still available."

"But that's not the point, is it? Remember *Hobson. . . ?* And *Brooking?* Gone, of course. History changes. . . ."

"By the way," I say, interrupting him as he pushes on, "you'll have to do without me for the first week or so of Michaelmas."

"Oh?"

"I have a personal invitation to the Trafalgar Day celebrations from John Arthur."

I reach for the gold embossed wad of papers that arrived soon after that letter. Cumbernald studies them. He swallows audibly. "I'm sure that we can manage without you for a week of so . . ." He smiles at me. "But you're looking a bit peaky, Brook, if you don't mind me saying so. And Eileen and the children and I, well, we have a chalet at this place outside Ross on Wye. It's very clean, very friendly, very smart. All very *modern*. We're always saying there's room enough to fit in at least one *interesting* guest. So I was wondering. . . ."

❊     ❊     ❊

*Eggs and Bacon, Eggs and Bacon, Apple and Custard, Apple and Custard, Cheese and Biscuits, Cheese and Biscuits, Fish and Chips, Fish and Chips . . .*

Cumbernald's two daughters are making piston-movements with their elbows, going faster and faster, pretending the Daimler's a train as we bowl along the A40 toward Wales and Gloucester. Christine's the eldest at eleven; a plump pre-adolescent who's designated "clever" and "reads a lot." Barbara's seven, thinner, more self-assured, and "sporty." Cumbernald clicks on the radio, and he and his wife Eileen argue about whether they want to listen to the Light or the Third Programme. Snatches of Vera Lynn, static, and Tchaikovsky roar out from the loudspeakers—it's like the avant-garde "European" music they'd be so quick to condemn—whilst Christine and Barbara grow alarmingly green and listless.

It seems later than it really is when we finally arrive at Penrhos Park. The lodge, clad with logs like some fairy-tale woodsman's cottage, is set in a pine-shaded clearing. Cumbernald prepares the dinner out-of-doors using a crude iron device filled with charcoal whilst Eileen unpacks and the children disappear into the pines. Looking over the forest crown, I see the smoke of other cooking fires rising like Indian signals. As it gets darker, Eileen sets a lantern on the outdoor table, and we watch the moths flutter into oblivion on the hot glass.

"You look a better man already," Cumbernald says, wineglass in his lap, looking pleasingly ridiculous in sandals, baggy shorts. "This is *some* place, though, isn't it, eh? A real breath of England."

It's suddenly night-quiet. With the faint stirring of the pines, the distant hoot of an owl, it wouldn't take much imagination to catch the growl of a bear, the rooting chuff of a wild boar, the howl of wolves—the return of all the beasts of old to the vast Wood of Albion. Then I hear a thin shriek. The sound is so strange here, yet so familiar, that it takes me a moment to realise that it's simply the passing of a train.

"It's just a goods line," Cumbernald explains. "Never quite worked out where it's from or to. But I shouldn't worry, old chap. That's the latest I've ever heard one go by. They won't disturb your sleep. I was thinking we could go down to the Sun Area this morning, by the way. That okay with you?"

"Oh? Yes. Fine. . . ."

There's eggs and bacon in the morning, which the girls have

already been down to buy from the site shop so that Eileen, back in
her traditional role now that the cooking's indoors, can prepare
them. The sound of their sizzling mingles in my head with the
clack and roar of the trains that fractured my night.

The Sun Area is lavishly signposted, yet still requires a long
trek past high hedges and long walls, then a queue at a turnstile.
The swing doors beyond lead to a hot, wooden tunnel lined with
benches: some kind of changing area. Eileen Cumbernald
removes her halter top and hangs it on a numbered peg. She isn't
wearing a bra. Cumbernald, contrarily, first removes his shorts and
his baggy y-fronts before taking off his sandals. The children, by
some instantaneous process, are already naked, and scamper off to
be swallowed by the bright square of light at the far end.

Cumbernald really *is* brown. Eileen, too; although I can see
that she's not as blonde as she pretends to be. I undo a few token
buttons of my shirt, wondering how easy it would be to wake up if
I pinched myself. *The most amazing dream. I was with the college
principal and his wife. They took all their clothes off, then asked me
to do the same. . . .* Having somehow divested myself of my clothes,
and hobbled into the amazing sunlight, I promise to keep an eye
on the children, and sit beside the lake with a copy of something
called *Future Past* whilst Cumbernald and Eileen go off to rustle
up a team for volleyball. Out in the distance, white sails are turning. A woman breast-feeds her child on the towel next to mine,
engaging me in alarming snatches of conversation. A young Adonis
strides at the water's edge. There's barely any hair on his body.
Amid all this display, his genitals are disappointing—a small after-
thought—but then it really is true what they say; people in the
nude are impossibly decent. We should all go around like this. I
can see it now—*Naturism—The Answer to the World's Troubles.*
The only trouble is, I have a feeling that it was a title I drew the line
at when I was stocking up for my researches on John Arthur in
Blackwells.

I squint at the book I'm supposed to be reading. "Chapter Five.
The Greatness of the British Heritage—Truth or Myth?" But I can
feel the air passing over me—it's strangely exhilarating—and I lie
back on the towel and let the dreary pages splay in the sand. I'm
part of the water, the air, the shouts, and the cries . . . Noon comes
and goes. The afternoon glides by. I swim. I eat ice cream and a
Melton Mowbray pork pie. I drink gallons of Vimto. By evening,
as we grab our few belongings and head back up the slope, my
skin is itchy and my prick, I can't help noticing, looks a bit like one

of Cumbernald's barbecued sausages; cooked on just the one side.

That night, I shiver and roast, glazed in minty unguents. And the trains are busy again, banging back and forth, clanking chains and couplings, hissing brakes as they trundle back and forth. Then a creak of springs comes through the lodge's thin walls as the Cumbernald's indulge in their own bit of coupling. And there are children's cries, too; the clatter of the showers from which they emerge like drowned figures with their hair lank, thinly naked as they walk on to be swallowed by the light. . . .

At three o'clock, feeling stiff and nauseous, I pad through the dim parlour and open the patio doors. Silvery night lies over the trees in the clearing and I can hear the breath, like a great animal sighing, of a train that must be waiting almost directly behind the lodge. Barefoot, wrapped in my crumpled sheet, I wander toward it.

The huge engine sighs in impatience, then the wheels slip as they begin to take up the tension and move again, hauling the vast burden of wagons that lie behind. They are open-backed, covered in mottled camouflage, although it's easy enough to make out the huge bodies of the Lancaster bombers as they clack past. *Eggs and Bacon, Eggs and Bacon, Apple and Custard, Apple and Custard, Cheese and Biscuits, Cheese and Biscuits, Fish and Chips, Fish and Chips.*

I shuffle back to the lodge trailing my shroud, and lie down to stare up at the grey, swirling ceiling of my bedroom, wondering if I could truly perform the act that my thoughts, like the grinding of some unstoppable engine, keep returning: the one deed that would make my life mean something, and repay the debt that I owe to my acquaintance, and to Larry Black, and to all the others, the pleading fingers pushed through the slats of a railway carriage, those lost, smiling families heading down the road to be swallowed in the brightness of the Summer Isles. I even owe that same debt to Francis, although the reasons are much harder to explain.

*Bang bang.* Scurrying KSG officers. The salty drift of cordite and smoke. I'm Charlotte Corday as she plunges her knife into Marat, I'm Gavrilo Princip and the Archduke Ferdinand, I'm John Wilkes Booth and Lincoln . . . I'm *The Fingers of History*.

*Bang bang.* Long after the stillness of the forest has reasserted itself, I can still hear the sound of that train.

The commonly accepted truths about John Arthur's upbringing are that he was born John Arthur of William and Mary Arthur on 21 October 1890 in a suitably pretty cottage (now open to the public)

in Cornwall. Mary Arthur died in childbirth, whilst William Arthur
and his son ended up traveling through Britain. In the popular
imagination, John Arthur never lived in a house before the age of
about twelve. He slept in barns, beneath hay ricks, under the stars.
He sat on milestones gazing into the future. In the more far-fetched
books I've encountered on my researches, you find pictures of
John Arthur hand-prints in stones, John Arthur hawthorns that
lean against the prevailing wind.

A small link with Burntwood is generally made along the lines
of: "William Arthur set about learning his new trade as a miner in a
pit (now disused) in Southern Staffordshire, where John also briefly
attended school before heading north to the South Yorkshire village
of Raughton." The famous pit at Raughton has also closed—the
miners' sons and daughters now work behind the counters of gift
shops, museums, pubs, and guest houses. But here, for all I know, is
where a boy called John Arthur really did spend his adolescence,
and where his father died in a pit accident.

At the age of fifteen, John Arthur supposedly went down the pit
himself. At eighteen, he was working the roads. At twenty, he went
to night school in Nottingham. At twenty-three, the War inter-
vened. He was wounded first in Flanders in 1915, and then again at
the Somme. Back at the Front by mid 1917, promoted corporal, he
famously won the George Cross at Ypres, yet somehow survived
that and the confusion of defeat.

By the agreed figures, John Arthur would have been twenty-
seven by then. As an ex-corporal, a leader of small groups of men
used to the harsh decisions and horrors of war, he would have been
well equipped to make his mark in the strange and violent world of
1920s' fringe politics. In Italy, Il Duce was already in power, building Romanesque temples and thumping his chest from balconies,
whilst John Arthur was still trying to make his voice heard in the
corners of East End bars and complaining about the injustice of
the Treaty of Versailles. But for Britain, as South Africa plunged
into civil war and the Russians expanded across Afghanistan toward
the Indian border, there were only other losses to face, and then
one final, crushing humiliation. In 1923, the Irish Republicans defeated the British forces, street by street in Dublin, then savaged
them as they withdrew north.

Nothing seemed to have much value then. I, too, queued outside the grocers for £10 then £50 and then £100 worth of rotten
cabbage as General Election followed General Election and Mac-
Donald succeeded Baldwin and then Baldwin took over again.

India was in famine. There were street battles and demonstrations. When Churchill took power during the Third General Strike of 1924–5 and succeeded in defeating the miners and the train drivers, then issued a "Guaranteed Pound" that people somehow actually believed in, it seemed as though the worst of Britain's post-War nightmare might soon be over. But money was still short. The Communists and the Fascists didn't go away. Neither did the reparations payments, the feeling of defeat, the whole sense of national crisis, which Churchill was often so good at exploiting. In this new world order, Britain was a third-rate nation; a little island off a big continent, just like Tierra del Fuego, Ceylon, Madagascar.

I saw John Arthur once during that time, although I know that's a privilege so many people claim nowadays. I was working by then as a teacher at Lichfield Grammar, although we had to subsist on credits and half pay. I was aware of the various bus stops and bushes that the lonely men of Lichfield would sometimes frequent, but I also knew about police entrapment, the shaming articles in the *Lichfield Mercury* that were so often followed by the suicide of those named, the long prison terms, and the beating and truncheon-buggerings that generally accompanied a night in the cells. Of course, I could have tried to honour Francis's memory by seeking someone I cared about, but instead, as the twenties progressed from the time of the £500 haddock into Churchill's empty pontificating, I became a regular weekend visitor to London. From Francis, I had taken the turn that many inverts take once love has failed them, which is to remove the holy power from sex by making it a means of humiliation, parody, comedy, degradation.

Once, wandering near midnight in an area of East End dockland houses that the police had long given up policing, I crossed toward the gaslit clamour of an end-of-terrace pub. Just half an hour before, I had been on all fours on a fire-blackened wasteground, half-choking as a fist twisted the back of my collar whilst an unlubricated cock was forced into me. The pub was called the Cottage Spring. Dry-throated, I made my way toward the bar, then had to give up as I was pushed and shouldered. There was a sense, I suddenly realised, that something was about to happen here.

Those were restless, anxious nights in the East End. Yet, so obsessed was I with my own sexual pursuits that I hadn't realised the many other kinds of risk I was taking. No one had noticed me when I came in, but I was sure that they would notice me now if I tried to leave. I glanced at the man nearest me and saw that his lips were moving. A whispered name, barely audible at first, but becoming clearer, was filling the air. He clambered up on the bar, then, did this man they were all calling for. His face looked pale and his hands were stained with mud or blood, yet he managed to keep an easy dignity as he balanced there with the dusty rows of glasses behind him. He raised his arms and smiled as he looked down at his people. Although he had changed much in the eleven years since I had last seen him, it was that smile that finally made me certain. I was as sure that this man—this John Arthur they were calling for—was in fact Francis Eveleigh.

I didn't wave my arms and cry out. I didn't even try to meet his eyes. Instead, I backed slowly toward a large pillar at the far end of the bar as others pushed forward to get nearer him. I hid myself from his gaze.

He's refined his technique in all the years since, has John Arthur. Nevertheless, his performance on that night was essentially the same as those since outside 10 Downing Street, and on the nation's television screens. That initial pause. The sharing, self-mocking smile that tells us that he still doesn't understand why it has to be *him*. By then, you're expecting nothing more than a calming chat, but suddenly, one of his anecdotes will twist around to some moment of national humiliation. Perhaps the forced scuttling of the fleet at Scarpa Flow in 1919, the refusal of MacDonald's petition to join the League of Nations, or Ireland. There was always Ireland. John Arthur, more clearly in control now, will gaze sadly at his audience. Truly, his eyes say, if only we could only laugh and play like innocent children. . . .

When his voice rises, it is imperceptible because it always lies in the wake of the passion of his audience. He seems so calm, in fact, so reluctant, that you find yourself filled with a kind of longing. Exactly what was said on that night matters as little as his recent speeches at the Olympics, or to Fordingham's gloriously ill-fated Everest Expedition. All I know is that, despite my shock and fear, I was moved in the way that good, popular music sometimes moves me. And that, when John Arthur had finished speaking and had stepped down from the bar, the men were happy to drift into the darkness toward whatever passed for their homes. For many years, I have clung to that image of John Arthur as the queller rather than the creator of violence. It's part of what has kept me sane.

I found myself momentarily rooted behind my pillar when the crowd began to thin in the Cottage Spring. Francis's hand was resting on the shoulder of a plumper, slightly older man who is now our Deputy Prime Minister, William Arkwright, and he was also talking to his then second-in-command Peter Harrison, who was executed for treason in 1938. I was surprised, as he stood there, to realise how much I still longed to hold him. Then, with that unnamed sense of being watched, he cast his eyes across the fallen tables and chairs in my direction. I just stood there with my hands in the pockets of my grubby coat, looking like the ageing mess I knew I was. For a moment, John Arthur's eyes bore the trace of a smile as they met mine, a shade of what could only be recognition. Then he looked away.

*Eggs and Bacon, Eggs and Bacon . . .*
Back from Penrhos Park to Oxford, and the days flash by. Golden Week nears. The stones and the fields glow with anticipation. The older University hands, us fellows and dons, doctors and vicars, MAs in abstruse subjects, best-selling authors, sexual molesters, surreptitious alcoholics, athletes, and aesthetes, caw and flap at each other in own black gowns as the punts still move and slow, move and slow beneath Magdalene Bridge.

Resuming my occasional traipses over to the Radcliffe, new X-rays reveal that the vast, cancerous network that runs through my body has stopped growing. It's still there, still almost certainly lethal, but, to all intents and purposes, the thing's biding its time. Waiting, just as I am, whilst the days slip by into the maw of history.

"Couldn't help noticing, sir," Christlow says, preparatory to spitting on his cloth and wiping the small mirror above my bookshelves one morning, "that you've had an Invitation." He actually says, *Han Hinvitation* on the traditional working class assumption that anything posh has an extra "h" in it.

"That's right," I turn from the A-Z Map of Central London I've been studying.

"Matter of fact," Christlow continues, still rubbing the mirror, "I'll be off down in London myself for the period of the celebrations. In my own minor, small capacity. So we may bump into each other. . . ."

"I'll certainly keep an eye out," I say. But London's a big place.

He puts down his rag, and we find ourselves gazing at each other. I'd never realised before how much Christlow looks like Mussolini: Modernism was probably always his destiny. He clears his throat. He's probably about to ask me why I'm always hanging around now when he's cleaning my rooms, and why I've put another lock on that old suitcase. But he simply gathers up his things as if in some sudden hurry and closes the door, leaving me to my thoughts, my dreams, my desk, my studies.

I open the window and take in a great, shivering breath of Oxford air. It has a cooler feel to it this morning. The limes are dripping, sycamore seeds are spinning, soft autumn bathes the towers and rooftops and domes with light. And the bells are ringing, filling my head, my eyes, my lungs, my heart. Oh, Oxford! Oxford! I cannot bear to leave you.

But history beckons.

My moment has come.

## Five

The narrator in William Morris's *News from Nowhere* awakes in London to find that summer has at last arrived. The air smells sweeter. The Thames runs cleaner, and the buildings along its banks have been transformed into glorious works of art. The people wear bright costumes, and smile at each other as they go about their everyday tasks. There is no poverty. Children camp in the Kensington Woods. The Houses of Parliament have been turned into a vegetable market.

A full century and a half before Morris predicted, his dream of Nowhere has come true. Truly, I think as I sip gin and gaze down from an airship droning high above the stately parks and teeming streets and the sun-flecked river, this city has never looked lovelier. The Adelphi Theatre. Cleopatra's Needle. The sightseeing boats that thread their wakes across the Thames . . . The engines of the *Queen of Air and Darkness* rise in pitch as she sinks down through the skies and across the flashing lakes and lidos of Hyde Park. Eventually, after much tilting and squealing of airbags, she is safely moored to a huge gantry, and I and a dozen or so other minor dignitaries are escorted along a wobbling tunnel to the lift that bears us dizzily to the ground.

It would be rude not to smile and wave for the lenses of the Pathé News camera that follow the progression of our open-top bus. Who knows, a darker thought nudges me, this image of the killer's face may be the one that makes it into history. We turn along Oxford Street into the wide, new architecture of Charing Cross Road. Then Trafalgar Square, from where the Victory Spire at the end of Park Lane looks like some Jules Verne rocket, or a new secret weapon. Compared with all of this, the great government offices along Whitehall are solid and sombre. To our right lies

Downing Street, and, even as I watch, the gates slide open on electronic hinges, and out rolls a black Rover 3 Litre with Austin police patrol cars ahead and behind. There are no bells, no flashing lights. As the cars turn up Whitehall, I glimpse John Arthur's face, absorbed in thought as he stares from the Rover's plain, unsmoked glass, and my heart freezes.

A loud-hailer calls out incoherent instructions as we disembark outside the New Dorchester's entrance on the South Bank. Reeve-Ellis, the Under Secretary who's in charge of us, lays a hand on my shoulder and steers me through the doors and across the vast main atrium where bare-breasted caryatids raise their arms to support the arches of the glass-domed roof.

"Two days before the big day now, Brook," he murmurs in that dry voice of his. "About time we had that little chat. . . ."

He leads me to a door marked NO ADMITTANCE, where plump Police constable T3308 jumps up from his chair, his holstered pistol swinging between his legs like a cock. My skin prickles, but all that lies beyond is a long corridor bustling with the click of typewriters and the slam of filing cabinets. " 'Fraid everything's a mess here," Reeve-Ellis says as he removes his jacket in his temporary office and shrugs on a baggy, grey cardigan. His little moustache bristles as he attempts a smile. I know already that Reeve-Ellis is a Balliol man, 1909 intake, and was working in the Cabinet Office when Lloyd George resigned. So he's seen it all, has toiled under every shade of administration.

"I've been meaning to ask," I begin. "Exactly how—"

"—You'll be in the VIP seats for the afternoon parade up the Mall. Have to miss the end of *that*, though, I'm afraid, if we're going to get you across to Downing Street in time."

"So there'll be—what?—about twenty or so people in the gardens at Number Ten. And I suppose some . . . staff?"

"That's about right. It's an informal occasion."

"What if it rains?"

"We're a lucky country, Brook. It won't rain." He smiles again. "As I say, keep a space in your diary for six o'clock, Monday. Don't worry about protocol or what suit to wear—JA's the least bothered person about that kind of thing you could possibly imagine."

"I do have a new suit, actually," I say. "It was delivered to me this morning from Hawkes on Saville Row." Hand-tailored, the thing cost me a fortune, and feels quite different to any clothing I've ever worn. Just as I requested, the jacket has been tailored with an especially strong and deep inner left-side pocket, to accommodate the pistol that currently lies hidden in the aged lining of the old suitcase I have brought with me.

I thought I'd already been through all the possible stages of grieving for my Francis when I discovered that he was alive again. I'd been angry. Almost suicidally miserable. Eventually, I'd come to imagine that my life was no longer under his shadow. But just knowing how I looked to him as I stood in that pub made me realise that everything about my life was still Francis, Francis, Francis. What, otherwise, was I doing in London in the first place, if not trying to wipe out my love for him?

Even in 1925, this John Arthur that he'd become was no longer a totally obscure figure, and I was soon saved the trouble of having to delve through *National Rights!* and *The Spitalfields Chronicle* to follow his activities. His was one of several names to emerge into the wider acres of political debate on the back of Churchill's use of right-wing groups to help break the long succession of strikes. But John Arthur was always ahead of the rest. With his accent, his manners, he seemed both educated *and* working class. In an age of lost certainties, he made good copy. And he had a knack of simply stating the obvious—that Britain was poor, that we were shamed by the loss of Ireland and Empire—that most politicians seem to lack. Unlike William Arkwright, Peter Harrison, and the soon-to-be rising star of Jim Toller, John Arthur was never openly racist or intolerant. His carefully cultured background, the wanderings, the War record, the thuggery and unemployment of the East End, presented, like the rest of the man, so many facets that you could select the one you preferred and ignore the rest.

In the winter of 1927, John Arthur stood at a by-election in Nottinghamshire as the first-ever Empire Alliance candidate. I can well remember the moment when I picked up my newspaper from the doormat on the morning after his maiden speech in Parliament. Appropriately enough, I think it was the *Sketch* that ran a smaller by-line asking WHO IS GEOFFREY BROOK? that quoted an aside in his speech about how he'd been much influenced by a teacher named Geoffrey Brook in Burntwood, Lichfield. After all, I was a distant memory to him; there was no reason why he should exactly remember my name.

Over the next few days, when the press discovered my address, I had my own small moment of fame. They called me Geoffrey, and it seemed churlish to correct them when they were so nearly right. Would it have made any difference if I had announced that, whilst

I knew little enough about this man who called himself John Arthur, he reminded me markedly of someone else with whom I had once had a homosexual affaire? Other than betraying a trust and guaranteeing my death in some freak accident, I doubt it.

The next year, 1928, whilst John Arthur was joined by another ten EA MPs at the spring General Election, and Churchill continued about the dogged business of keeping himself in power, the editor of the *Daily Sketch* approached me about writing a weekly column. At last, I felt like someone who mattered. Churchill, meanwhile, lasted until October, 1929 and the Wall Street Crash. Ramsey MacDonald then became Prime Minister of a Government of National Unity whilst Oswald Mosley struggled to reunite Labour before giving up and joining the EA six months later, thus forcing yet another General Election. This time, John Arthur traveled from constituency to constituency by Vickers aeroplane, and such was the dangerous glamour of the EA by then that even his fat deputy William Arkwright with his trademark Homburg hat became a vote winner. Uniformed EA members marched in the streets of all the big towns, noting names as people emerged from polling stations. The EA won seventy seats. Amid an atmosphere of increasing crisis—unemployment, means tests, riots and starvation, open revolt in India, popular support for Unionist terrorist attacks in Ireland—John Arthur refused new Prime Minister Neville Chamberlain's offer of a post in his Cabinet.

Chamberlain's "get tough" policy in India over the next few months only served to increase the bloodshed, and the rest of the Empire was also starting to fray. A new Egyptian Government nationalised the Suez Canal. Welsh and Scottish Nationalists began to talk of independence. The country was in a state of collapse. Chamberlain was probably right in imagining that Britain would be torn apart by another pointless General Election. He was running out of options, but there remained one figure that the great mass of the public seemed to believe in. Not really a *politician* at all, and head of an organisation that had never properly disowned violence. But controllable, surely; a useful figurehead to keep the prols happy and the bully boys at bay whilst the real brains got on with sorting out the mess that the country was in. It was thus without fuss or bloodshed, in a deal in which he seemingly played no part, that John Arthur was finally summoned to Number 10 and offered the only Cabinet post that he had said he would ever consider accepting.

Just after six o'clock on the chilly evening of November 10,

1932, John Arthur emerged from that famous black door to the clink of flashbulbs. In those days, traffic was still allowed along Downing Street, and he had to check left and right before he crossed over and raised his arms, smiling slightly as he looked about him. He said that he would be heading off to Buckingham Palace in a few minutes, where he planned to seek King George's advice about forming Greater Britain's first Modernist Government.

The flags and the bunting are going up as I'm chauffeur-driven across London to meet the King and Queen next morning. Tomorrow is the eve of Trafalgar Day, and there's a Thanksgiving Service at Westminster Abbey. Already the advertisements on the sides of buses for Idris Table Waters have been replaced with cheery messages to our Leader. GREATER BRITAIN THANKS YOU. HERE'S TO THE FUTURE.

My black Daimler sweeps with a stream of others around Hyde Park Corner and through the towering gates to pull up beside the steel flagpoles in front of New Buckingham Palace. I wade through a dizzy sense of unreality past the guardsmen in their busbies. I'm giving Monday's suit a trial-airing, and have even placed *News from Nowhere* in the inner pocket to give a similar weight and feel to the pistol.

Dresses rustle as the queue shuffles forward. His Highness the Duke of York stammers slightly as he greets me. I bow. Then his wife the Duchess, and their two plain daughters. A moment later I'm standing before King Edward and Queen Wallis. I glance discreetly to both sides as I bow. It would be easy for me to reach inside my jacket at this point. Click back the hammer as I pull the pistol out. Two shots, minimum, thudding into the chest at close range. Within moments, this whole Palace would implode in shatters of glass and steel, drawn up through the skies in a hissing gale, back toward fairyland where it belongs.

The guests wander out through pillared archways into the afternoon's gracious warmth. There's a stir when the silver trays of sweet Merrydown wine emerge for the loyal toast. The gardens, as I explore them, still feel a little like Green Park of old. The stepped orchards and monumental statues don't quite fit. The roses that amazingly still bud and flower on the trellises in this bright October sunlight look too red, too raw. You can almost smell the paint, and hear the bellowing voice of the Queen of Hearts. *No! No! Sentence first—verdict afterward.* Looking around for something more filling than smoked salmon sandwiches, light-headed as my belly growls and premonitions of pain begin to dance around me, I recognise a famous face.

"Personally, I can't stand fiddling around with plates and standing up at the same time," he says affably. "Strikes me as a foreign habit."

Deputy Prime Minister Arkwright looks small and ordinary in the flesh, almost exactly like his pictures, even without the pipe and the Homburg. In fact, he really hasn't changed that much from the man I glimpsed standing with John Arthur all those years ago at the Cottage Spring. He was probably born cherubically plump, going-on-fifty.

"Hmm. Oxford," he says when I tell him who I am. "You know, I still wish I'd had a university education. And you know John from way back?"

"I taught him briefly when he was a child," I reply, conscious of the rainbowed sun gleaming on Arkwright's blood-threaded cheeks, the strange intensity, even as he chomps cocktail sausages, of his gaze. William Arkwright's the EA's comic turn. He's frequently seen on the arms of busty actresses. But he's Deputy Prime Minister *and* Home Secretary. He's the second most famous face in the country, even if he trails the first by a long way. He can hardly have come this far by accident.

"John's always so quiet about his past—not that you'd believe it if you read the press." Arkwright chews another handful of sausages. "Of course, no one gives a bugger about *my* upbringing. It's called charisma, I suppose. Some of us have to make do with hard work."

"Did you ever think you'd get this far?"

Arkwright tilts his head as the water clatters over the green, brass dolphins behind us. "I'm permanently amazed, Mr Brook. Although I know I don't look it. . . ."

I nod. I'd never realised how difficult it is to talk to someone famous, that sense of knowing them even though you don't, and the way Arkwright's looking at me as if there really is something shared between us . . . Then I realise what's happening—and immediately wish I hadn't. It's there in his eyes. It's in that smile of his and the way he studies me. After all these years, I've finally met someone else who knows the truth about John Arthur.

"What do you think of John Arthur, Mr Brook? I know it's been a long time, but do you like him personally?"

"He has my . . . admiration."

"Admiration." Deputy Prime Minister William Arkwright smiles at me. "I suppose that's about as much as any of us can hope.

. . ." Then he pretends to see someone else he recognises over my shoulder, and waddles away.

Much of what happened after John Arthur became Prime Minister seemed so *traditional* that at first even the sceptics were reassured: the marches, the brass bands, the jamborees, the improvement of the roads and the railways. The arrests certainly came. The few remaining communist and socialist MPs were immediately deprived of their seats—after the years of riots, strikes, and disturbances, that only seemed like a sensible precaution. Left-wing newspapers like the *Manchester Guardian* suffered firebomb attacks. The Jews and the Irish were the subject of intimidation. Homosexuals were still routinely beaten up. In many ways, in fact, little had changed.

At this time, Britain was still supposedly a democracy. But John Arthur plainly had little time for the fripperies of a discredited political system. In his first weeks in power, he passed a short Enabling Act that effectively meant he could rule by decree. In a country without any written constitution, that was all that was needed.

It was a time of whispers. In schools, there were Modernist masters who would report any colleagues to the EA-dominated Local Education Authorities. Anxious to keep our jobs, the rest of us never quite seemed to realise that we had crossed the line from the truth and had began to peddle lies. Despite the thrill of the fresh, new vision that was gripping Greater Britain, as we now called our country, there was an atmosphere of almost perpetual crisis. When I was summoned to the Headmaster's study midway through the 2B's Tuesday morning lesson one day in 1932, all the usual suspicions went through my mind. Poor results, perhaps, in the new Basic Grade exams? My sucking off that foundry worker outside the Bull at Shenstone last Saturday evening? Some new twist of the national curriculum that I had failed to absorb? The *Daily Sketch* and I had already parted company. Once again, I was a nobody, nearing retirement, and easily discarded. And behind that, behind it all, was the fearsome burden of what I knew about John Arthur.

"Take a pew, take a pew . . ." The headmaster smiled at me with alarming warmth as I slumped down. "I've received a letter this morning." He rubbed the thick vellum between his fingers as if he still didn't believe it. "From the Vice Chancellor at Oxford, in fact. It seems that they're seeking to widen their, ah, *remit*. Trying to get in some fresh educational blood. Your name, Brook, has been mentioned. . . ."

Back at the New Dorchester, surrounded by bakelite angels, deep fur rugs, soft leather chairs, a huge television set, and an ornate stained-glass frieze depicting Saint George Resting in a Forest, quite unable to rest, I put on my coat and head out into the sprawling London night. The traffic roars by as I cross Westminster Bridge and the strung lights twinkle along the Embankment. People are *running*, amazingly enough, dressed up like athletes in shorts and vests, and there are accordionists and street vendors, floating restaurants, arm-in-arm lovers, wandering tourists. The newshordings for the final edition *Evening Standard* proclaim FRANCE AND BRITAIN CLASH OVER EGYPT. You can almost feel the news heating up as the summer cools.

Fairgrounds have been set up in all the parks, and the sickly smell of candy floss spills across all of London. Children, their faces shining with sugar, grease, and excitement nag their parents for a last ride on one of the vast machines. I find a shooting gallery and aim and shoot, aim and shoot whilst the couple beside me smear their mouths across each other's faces. *Bang Bang.* Gratifyingly, several of the tin ducks sink down, and my hand hardly seems to be trembling. Further out beyond the tents and the rides lies a great bonfire. Two Spitfires swoop out of the night, agitating the sparks and trailing ribbons of smoke whilst lads stripped to the gleaming waist climb over each other to make trembling pyramids, marshalled by absurd middle-aged men in khaki shorts and broad-brimmed hats, and I'm enjoying the comedy and pondering the question of what else goes on in those lines of tents, when I sense that I'm being stared at from across the ring. It's Christlow, his face slippery with firelight as he marshals the next shining cluster of Modernist youth. But his eyes flick away from mine when I attempt to smile at him. He looks around as if in panic, then stumbles from sight into the trembling heat.

Everything seems tired now. Lads are yelling fuck-this and fuck-that at each other and the toilet tents have turned nasty. As I limp back along the safe, tramp- and pervert-free streets in search of a taxi, all London is suddenly, dangerously quiet, and seems to be waiting. The night staff at the New Dorchester are out with mops and vacuum cleaners in some of the communal spaces, doing their night duties, and everything in my room is immaculate, unchanged. Saint George is still at prayer in his forest of glass. The sheets of my huge bed are drum-taut. I sleepwalk over to the tall, ash-and-ebony cabinet and pour out a drink from the first bottle that comes to hand, to help down the tablets. Now, I notice, my hand really is shaking. I reach to the line of buttons and make the lights dim. Saint George fades, the forest darkens.

I lift my old case out from the wardrobe, sliding my hand into the flabby lining and feeling for the gnarled stock of the pistol, conscious of the weight of the metal, the pull of history, gravity, fate. Then—as now seems as good a time as any—I begin to load it. Five bullets are left out of the ten I started with, and they look newer and cleaner than I imagined. I tested the others against a dead tree stump late one evening in Readon Woods when the very stars seemed to shrink back in surprise that the damn things still worked. Now, each remaining one makes a tiny but purposeful click in the cylinder.

It was a cool day when I first arrived at Oxford, with the year's first frost covering the allotments. The sky was pale, English blue and beneath it lay everything that I had ever dreamed of or expected. The bells, the bicycles. Christlow. Worn stone steps. Faded luxury. Casement windows. The college principal Cumbernald taking me for lunch at the White Horse, jammed between Blackwells and Trinity, as if he really had every reason to welcome me. But by the time we'd opted—yes, why not?—for a third pint of Pedigree, I didn't even feel like an impostor. I felt as if I was gliding at last into the warm currents of a stream along which my life had always been destined to carry me.

I remember that the news vendors were selling a Special Extra Early edition of the *Oxford Evening News* as we walked back along High. Cumbernald bought a copy and we stood and read it together. Other people were doing the same, forming excited clusters, nearly blocking the street. A British Expeditionary Force had landed north of Dublin, and a task-force fleet led by HMS *Hood* had accepted the surrender of Belfast. All in all, it was a fine day to be British.

More fine days were to follow. There was easy victory in Ireland. The commemorative Victory Tower went up and up in London. I, meanwhile, shivered pleasurably at Christmas to the soaring music of the choir at Kings. And for these new and nervous students, who entered my rooms clutching essays and reading lists, I became what I had always been, which was a teacher. There were gatherings, panelled rooms, mulled wine in winter, mint teas and

Japanese wallpapers in the spring, cool soft air off the river on long walks alone. Greater British forces aided Franco's victory over the communists in Spain. The Cyprus Adventure came and went. We retook Rhodesia. I brought myself an expensive new gramophone.

The rest of the world found it easier to regard John Arthur as a kind of Fascist straight man to Mussolini. France, Germany, and the Lowlands were too busy forming themselves into a Free Trade Community whilst the USA under Roosevelt, when it wasn't worrying about the threat in the Far East from a resurgent Japan, remained doggedly isolationist. In the Middle East, Britain's canny re-alignment of Egypt's King Farouk in the Modernist mould, and his conquest of Palestine with the help of British military advisors, were seen as no more than par for the course in that troubled region. After all, Britain was behaving no more aggressively than she had throughout most of history. Even now that the whole of Kent has been turned into a military camp as a precaution against some imagined Franco-German threat, the world still remains determined to think the best of us.

Meanwhile, I grew to love Oxford almost as much in reality as in the dream. Eighties Week. The Encaenia Procession. Midnight chimes. The rainy climate. The bulldogs in their bowler hats checking college gardens for inebriate sleepers. The Roofs and Towers Climbing Society.

History went on. The Jews were relocated. Gypsies and tramps were forcibly "housed." Homosexuals were invited to come forward for treatment. Of course, I was panicked for a while by *that*—but by then I had my acquaintance, our discreet messages on the cubical wall at the Gents beside Christ Church Meadow, our casual buggerings when he'd do it to me first and then I'd sometimes do it to him—my soft and easy life. I had my desk, my work, my bed. I had my books, the tea rooms, the gables, the cupolas, the stares of the Magdalene deer, the chestnuts in flower, music from the windows of buildings turned ghostly in the sunlight, young voices in the crystalline dusk, and the scent of ancient earth from the quads.

I was dazed. I was dazzled. Without even trying, I had learned how to forget.

## Six

I am dragged back toward morning by sleek sheets, a clean sense of spaciousness that cannot possibly be Oxford, and an anguished howling. My head buzzes, the light ripples. London, of course.

London. The New Dorchester . . . I fumble for my tablets on the bedside table as the sirens moan, and I'm blinking and rubbing my eyes when the door to my room swings open.

"Sorry about this, Brook." Reeve-Ellis leans in. He's already dressed, and has PC T3308 in tow. "Frightful cock-up to have an air raid practise on this of all days. You know what these bongo-bongo players are like—probably think it's the Great White God coming down to impregnate their daughters. There's a good man. Just pop on that dressing gown. . . ."

It's pandemonium along the corridors. People are flapping by in odd assortments of clothing with pillow creases on their cheeks and electrified hair. Reeve-Ellis steers me down the main stairs, then on through crowds in the main atrium. "A lot easier if we go this way," he says, and he, PC T3308, and I struggle against the flow until we reach an eddy beside the hotel souvenir shop where another PC— he's K2910 according to his shoulder badge—is standing guard at the same door marked NO ADMITTANCE that I was led into two days before. PC K2910 follows us as we go in. The howl of the siren, the sound of people moving, suddenly grows faint. This early in the offices beyond, there are no phones ringing, no typewriters clicking.

"Along here," Reeve-Ellis says, shoving his hands into his cardigan pockets. PC K2910 keeps just behind me. PC T3308 strides ahead and opens another door marked EMERGENCY EXIT ONLY that leads to a damp and dimly lit concrete tunnel. It slams shut behind us. Here, at last, the New Dorchester's carpets and luxury give out. The passage slopes down. Water drips from tiny stalactites on the roof. The air smells gassy and damp.

We reach a gated lift that clanks us down past coils of pipework to some kind of railway platform. An earthy breeze touches our faces as we wait and the rails begin to sing before an automatic train slides in, wheezing and clicking with all the vacant purpose of a toy, hauling a line of empty mail hoppers with pull-down wooden seats. PC K2910 clambers in first, then helps Reeve-Ellis. I try taking a step back, wondering about escape.

"Might as well just get in, sir," PC T3308 says, offering a large, nail-bitten hand. Hunched in our train as we slide into the tunnel, I'm conscious of my slippered feet, my pyjamas beneath the dressing gown. Grey wires along the walls rise and fall, rise and fall. I study the two policemen squatting opposite me in what light there is. PC T3308 is bigger and older, with the jowelled, meaty face and body of an old-fashioned copper. PC K2910 is freckled, redheaded, thin; he seems too young, in fact, to be a policeman at all.

We disembark at another mail station, and travel upward in another gated lift. Then, suddenly, the walls are almost new—painted the same municipal green that covered the walls of the Gents by Christ Church Meadow. PC T3308 grips my arm. There are doors leading into offices, but the place seems empty, abandoned, and we're still deep underground.

"It's in here." Reeve-Ellis opens a door to an office where there are three chairs and a desk, one battered-looking, tin filing cabinet, and fat pipes running across the ceiling.

"You may as well sit down, Brook." Reeve-Ellis points to the chair on the far side of the desk as PC K2910 locks the door behind us, and I notice as my body settles into it that it gives off a sour, unfortunate smell. The air is warm in here, almost swimmingly hot.

"Whatever all of this is," I say, "you should know that I've no close friends or relatives. And I have terminal cancer—you can look it up in my NHS records."

"I'm afraid," Reeve-Ellis says, "that it doesn't work like that."

PC T3308 leans across and lifts my right hand from the arm rest, splaying it palm-up at the edge of the desk. He sits down on it, his fat-trousered bottom pushed virtually in my face. I hear the rasp of a belt buckle, and something jingles. I imagine that they'll start asking me questions at any moment, long before they do anything that might actually cause me pain.

"If this is—" I begin just as, with small a grunt of effort, PC K3308 brings the truncheon down across the fingers of my right hand.

Alone now, I can hear Reeve-Ellis voice as he talks to someone on the telephone in a nearby room. *Yes. No. Not yet. Just as you say* . . . I can tell from the sound of his voice that he's speaking to a superior.

I'm cradling my right hand. It's the most precious thing in the entire world. My index finger is bent back at approximately forty-five degrees just above the first joint, and it's swelling and discolouring as I watch. The first and middle fingers are swelling rapidly too, although they could simply be torn and bruised rather than broken.

This is terrible—as bad as I could have imagined. Yet I've had plenty of opportunity lately to get used to pain. The thing about torture isn't the pain, I decide between bouts of shivering. It's the simple sense of wrongness.

The keys jingle. Reeve-Ellis and the two PCs reenter the room.

"I won't piss you about, Brook," Reeve-Ellis says. "I'm no expert, anyway, at this kind of thing. . . ."

PC K2910 extracts his note pad and pencil. With that freckled, narrow face of his, he still looks far too young. PC 3308 leans back against the wall and nibbles at his nails. A sick tremor runs through me.

"Perhaps you could begin," Reeve-Ellis continues, "by telling us exactly why you're here. What all of this is about . . ."

"*You* brought me here. I'm supposed to be an honoured guest, and then you . . ."

But almost before I've started, Reeve-Ellis is sighing in weary irritation. He's nodding to PC K2910 to find the keys to let him out of the room again. Once he's gone, the two PC's glance at each other, and come around to me from opposite sides of the desk. They hook their hands beneath my armpits.

"I didn't think this was the sort of thing the London Constabulary specialised in," I say. "I always imagined this was all left to the KSG nowadays."

"Oh, we don't need those fancy boys, sir. Piss-poor at anything from what I've heard. Now, if you'll just stand up. . . ."

I try to grab the chair's armrest with the fingers of my good hand, but soon I'm standing upright and the PCs are moving me toward the old, grey filing cabinet in the corner of the room. I feel the agonising pull of my tendons as they hold my damaged right hand over the open drawer. Then PC T3308 raises his boot and kicks it shut.

"These things have a pattern," Reeve-Ellis says, sitting in front of me again. "You have to accept that, Brook. What you must realise is that there's only one outcome. Which is you telling me everything."

A soft click, and there on the table, although stretched and blotched to my eyes as if in some decadent non-realist painting, lies the pistol that I inherited in some other life, some other world, from Francis.

"If you could just tell me how and why you got this thing, and what it was doing in your suitcase."

"It's a relic," I say. "It belonged to a friend of mine who died in the War."

"Can you tell me his name?"

A hesitate. A billow of black agony enfolds me. "Francis Eveleigh. As I say, he's dead."

"Where did he live?"

I tell him the name of the street in Lichfield, and then—what could it matter now?—that of Francis's parent's house in Louth. "It came back with his effects when he died at the Somme."

"And the bullets?"

"They came with the effects as well."

"So it all came to you . . ." Reeve-Ellis strokes his chin. "This gun, these bullets, as a memento of this Eveleigh fellow? And you've kept them with you ever since?"

"Yes."

"Ever used the gun?"

"No . . . well, once. I wanted to make sure that it still worked."

"Did it?"

"I'm no expert. It seemed to fire."

"I see. And what did you intend to do with it?"

"What do you think?"

Reeve-Ellis frowns. "I thought we'd got past that stage, old man."

"I intended to kill John Arthur."

Reeve-Ellis nods. He seems unimpressed. Behind him, PC K2910 frowns, licks his pencil, makes a note. Somewhere, a phone is ringing.

"It was Christlow," I say, "wasn't it?"

"Who?"

"Christlow, my scout. He told you about the gun."

"We seem to be forgetting here exactly who is asking the questions." Reeve-Ellis smiles. I sense that the two PCs behind him are loosening their stance. Perhaps all this will soon be ending. Then he stands up and nods to them as he leaves the room, even though I'm screaming that I've already told him everything.

But there are more questions, the nightmare of my hand in the filing cabinet again. Pain's a strange thing. There are moments when it seems there has never been anything else in the whole universe, and others when it lies almost outside you. I think of Christ on his cross, of Torquemada, and Matthew Hopkins. All those lives. And even now. Even now. In Japan. In Spain. In Russia. In Britain. I'm not lost at all. Not alone. A million twisted ghosts are with me.

I flinch as the lock slides and the door opens. Alone this time, Reeve-Ellis sits down.

"I was once John Arthur's lover," I swallow back a lump of vomit. "I bet you didn't know that?"

Reeve-Ellis frowns at me. A loose scab breaks open as the flesh on my hand parts and widens. The sensation is quite disgusting.

"I was asked to show you these," he says, laying down a brown manila envelope and sliding out four grainy enlargements of faces and upper bodies, all apparently naked. Three are white-lit against a white cloth background; the forth—a man, I realise when I've sorted out the approximate details of these gaunt, near-bald, blotched, and virtually sexless figures—is standing against a wall. They are each holding, in spider-thin hands, a longer version of the kind of slot-in numbers that churches use for hymns. My vision blurs. A large part of me doesn't want to recognise these people.

"How do I know," I say, "that they're still alive?"

"You don't."

I gaze back at the photographs. Eyes that fix the camera without seeing, as if they can fill up with so many sights that light is no longer absorbed. My acquaintance, he looks younger, older, beyond time, with the thin bridge of his nose, the ridges of his cheeks, the taut drumlike skin, the sores. His wife, his children, are elfin, fairy people, blasted through into nothingness by the light that pours around them. . . .

"These people—"

"—I was just asked to show you, Brook. I don't know who they are, what they mean to you."

The lock on the door slides back. Both PCs stand close to the wall without a word, watching me and Reeve-Ellis.

"Are you proud of this?" I say to them all. "Is this how you wanted the Summer Isles?"

"Just concentrate on telling us everything, old man." Reeve-Ellis looks weary, defensive, frustrated. In spite of everything, I still have this feverish sense that there's some part of this equation that I haven't yet glimpsed. "Do you really think you could get even *this* close to John Arthur with a pistol unless someone wanted you to? Still, it must have been fun while it lasted, playing your stupid, little game."

He picks up the photos, taps them together and slides them back into the envelope. PCs T3308 and K2910 move toward me, grip me beneath my arms, and bear me toward the filing cabinet once again.

When I've told them more than I imagined I ever knew. When I've told them about Francis Eveleigh and about my acquaintance and about poor Larry Black at the Crown and Cushion and Eric

282 BREATHMOSS AND OTHER EXHALATIONS

Svendsen who deserves it anyway and all the children I used to teach who I know are grown up by now and culpable as all we British are yet at the same time totally blameless. When I've told them about that time in the twenties when I saw Eveleigh again at the Cottage Spring, except he was now really John Arthur. When I've told them everything, I'm suddenly aware of the sticky creak of the chair I'm in, and of the waiting emptiness that seems to flood around me.

"Well . . ." Reeve-Ellis says. "I suppose we had to get there eventually." He takes PC K2910's notebook. The way he stuffs it into his pocket, I know he's going to destroy it. The two PCs are careful this time. They lift me up almost gently and, amazingly, my limbs still work as we stagger out along the corridor. We come to a door marked MAINTENANCE ONLY, where PC K2910 fiddles with the bolts and swings it open into a shock of night air. I can hear the murmur of traffic as PC T3308 leads me into the darkness, but the sound is distant, shielded on all sides by brick and glass and concrete. The patch of sky is the same shape and colour as a cooling television screen—there's even one small dotlike star in the middle. I'd always imagined that my life would end in a prettier place. A remote clearing in some wood in the Home counties, the cry of a fox and the smell of leaves and moss . . .

I glance back. Reeve-Ellis stands in the lighted doorway, hands stuffed into his cardigan as he leans against the frame. It really is quiet here. The whole of this pre-Trafalgar Day, and the celebratory service I was expecting to attend at Westminster Abbey, has gone by. PC T3308 lets go of me and I sag to my knees, still struggling to protect the precious burden of my hand. I hear the creak of leather as he reaches to release the flap of his holster as somewhere, faintly, dimly, deep within the offices, a phone starts ringing. His breathing quickens.

"Wait!" Reeve-Ellis calls across the courtyard, and his footsteps recede. The night falls apart, pulses, regathers as I breathe the rotten air that my own body is making, trying to wish away this moment, this pain. Eventually, the phone stops. Somewhere across London, a train whistle screams. I think of a rocking sleeper carriage. A man's arms around me, his lips against mine. The gorgeous, shameless openness . . .

Reeve-Ellis's footsteps return, the lines of his body reshape against the bright doorway.

"There's been," he calls, "a change of plan. . . ."

\*        \*        \*

Reeve-Ellis drives a Triumph Imperial, a big, old car from the pre-Modernist early thirties with rusty wings and a vegetable smell inside given off by the cracked, leather seats. It creaks and rattles as he drives, indicating fitfully, jerking from side to side along the London streets.

"Who was that phone call from?"

"After what you've been through, old man . . ." he says, stabbing at the brake as a taxi pushes ahead of us. "You really don't want to know. Believe me. Just count yourself as bloody lucky. . . ."

The brightening sky shines greyish-pink on the Thames as we cross Westminster Bridge. At the New Dorchester, the remnants of a fancy dress party are lingering. A Black Knight is clanking around in the remains of his armour whilst Robin Hood is arguing mildly about some aspect of room service with Reception. We fit in here, Reeve-Ellis and I. He's come as what he is, and I'm something from the War—or perhaps the last guest at *The Masque of the Red Death*.

Reeve-Ellis punches the button for the lift.

"The message," he says as the lighted numbers rise, "is that you carry on as before."

"What?"

"Today, old man. You still get to see John Arthur . . ."

We arrive at my floor. My bed has been made, but otherwise nothing has changed since I left here a day ago. The nymphs still cavort across the ceiling. Saint George is still at prayer in his forest.

"Get some rest," Reeve-Ellis advises after summoning the hotel's resident nurse and doctor on the phone. "Watch the parades on television. I'll make sure someone fixes you up and sees that you're ready in time. . . ."

"Those people—the photographs you showed me."

"I don't know."

"And what about you? Aren't you afraid?"

"Of what, old man?"

"This . . ." I gesture wildly about me, nearly falling. "Hell."

"If there is a hell," Reeve-Ellis says, reaching to grasp the handle of the door, "you and me, old man—we'd probably hardly notice any difference. We'd just get on with doing the only things we know how. . . ." Then he closes the door, leaving me alone in my plush room at the New Dorchester. My wristwatch on the bed-side table has stopped ticking, but the electric clock on the wall tells me it's just after six in the morning. I make the effort to slide back the wardrobe doors with my left hand and check my suitcase. The scents of Oxford still waft from inside, and everything has been left so neatly that it's almost a surprise to find that the pistol really is missing. Clambering to my feet, I swallow a handful of my tablets and study the label on the bottle, although the handwriting is indecipherable. But how would my body react if I took the whole lot? Would that be enough to do it? And the anti-inflammatories, I could take all of those, too. I gaze at the stained-glass frieze of Saint George. There's dragon's blood, I notice now, on his praying, gauntleted hands. I've been left alone—so perhaps they're expecting this of me; a bid at suicide. But then wouldn't I have been killed already? I throw the bottle across the room with my clumsy left hand. Somehow, it actually hits the frieze, but it bounces off with a dull clunk, raining tablets. Weeping, I scuttle across the floor, picking them up, and collapse on my huge bed.

Beyond my windows, a barge sounds its horn. Lozenges of light ripple and dance with the nymphs on the ceiling. I'd press the button on the headboard that makes the doors slide back, were I able to reach it. I'd like to smell the Thames on what feels like this last of all days, I'd love to hear it innocently lapping. Here in London, it has fostered trade, cholera, prosperity, and the muse of a thousand poets. There were bonfires upon it in the reign of Queen Elizabeth, so hard did it freeze. . . .

I see myself in front of a class of students once again, speaking these words. Francis Eveleigh is there—he's a young boy, no more than ten, and for some reason his arm is in a sling. And Cumbernald, and Christlow, and Reeve-Ellis, and my acquaintance, and the many other faces that have filled my life. I smile down at them as they sit with their scabbed elbows and knees, their grubbily cherubic faces, the looming playtime forgotten for a while as they listen. These, I know, are my only moments of greatness. So listen, just listen. All I want to do is to tell you one last tale.

## Seven

Monday, 21 October 1940. Trafalgar Day. John Arthur's fiftieth birthday, his silver jubilee. At nine, and under clearing skies even though the forecasts had remained doubtful, the church bells begin to ring out all across the country. There had been talk of rain coming in from the North Sea, driven down over Lincolnshire and across the Fens toward London. But that was just a tease. After a glorious summer of seemingly endless celebrations, no one ever doubted the perfect autumn day this would turn out to be.

By eight o'clock, as the hotel doctor sets and splints my hand

and the nurse gags my mouth with a stick to stop me biting my tongue in my agony, trestle tables are being laid in village halls and on dew-damp greens from Mablethorpe to Montgomery, from Treviscoe to Nairn. Balloons are being inflated and jellies turned out onto plates. Guardsmen are polishing their buckles and blancoing their straps whilst grooms feed and brush their shining mounts. We British are still unsurpassed at doing this sort of thing.

The doctor's manner is brisk—so unsurprised that there doesn't seem to be any point in asking whether he's used to dealing with this sort of thing. And I'm too busy weeping, anyway, until he gives me one last, blissfully large injection. Floating, white as angels, the nurse and a hotel steward remain on hand to help me with the tricky process of bathing and dressing. Then I'm placed before my television set, which is already glowing, giving off a smell of warm bakelite and electricity, and my head is supported and my arm is rested. I drift in and out the rest of the morning on the monochrome visions that come out at me. Already, the ghosts of Empire are moving from Horse Guards Parade, past Admiralty Arch, and along the Mall. Fizzing out at me in shades of grey, they turn at Palace Gardens and march back along the far side of the Mall. The Forth Infantry. The Gurkhas. The Northamptonshire (Youth) Branch of the Empire Alliance. Bowler-hatted veterans from the War. The Metropolitan Police. The Knights of Saint George.

As noon passes, the King arrives in a white uniform. Pointedly, a gap still remains between him and Deputy Prime Minister Arkwright. It's typical of John Arthur to delay his entrance on this of all days. I can well imagine, in fact, what a delicious luxury it must be to sit in the book-lined calm of his Downing Street study, working quietly through papers whilst the yearning sea-roar of a whole nation and Empire drifts through the sash windows. It's hard to imagine a greater moment of power. Where to after this, Francis? Oh, *Francis*—despite everything, I almost feel as if I can almost understand. . . .

Then he arrives. John Arthur, wearing a plain, grey suit, settles into his seat beside the King, and every eye, every camera, and with it, the attention of the whole world, shifts to watch him. The latter part of the parade is more military. It's hard not to be impressed by grey-black tanks of such shining bulk that they leave burning trails behind them on the television, and artillery, and bombers swooping low; the sound of their engines reaching me first overhead, trembling the warm air through my balcony windows. But through everything, even in the long minutes when he's not on the screen, my thoughts remain fixed on that one distant figure. I keep asking how it's possible for one man to change anything. And would I have killed him? I don't know. I don't know. Already, that dream seems as lost and remote as the Summer Isles that Francis and I never got around to visiting.

The procession finally ends at half past four with a final massive *boom*, and gouts of cordite and tank exhaust. The air in my room is cooler now, and the sky outside my balcony doors is already darkening.

"Here's the suit, sir, is it. . . ?"

The process of dressing me is more like armouring a knight of old; it would be easier if we had pulleys and winches. But still we get there, these hotel people and I, moving along shifting avenues of pain as the light from the television plays over us. Then triumphal music cuts short and John Arthur sits at his desk in his Downing Street study. His eyes are black pools in the moment before the dancing electrons settle in the camera; his silver hair dazzles like wet sand.

"As most of you probably know by now," he begins, arms on the desk, a small sheaf of papers in front of him, "today is a special day for me personally. As well as celebrating Admiral Nelson's famous victory at Trafalgar with all the majesty our nation can muster, I must also celebrate my own fiftieth birthday . . ."

A nostalgic and a personal note, then, to begin with. It must be said, though, that John Arthur doesn't look fifty. He doesn't look any age at all. The chauffeur touches my good arm, my good shoulder, but I'm still looking back at the screen as he steers me out into the corridor, trying like the rest of the world to trap a little of John Arthur's light. Outside in the grey, London dusk, I sink down into the soft hide of yet another Daimler as the New Dorchester slides away. Despite everything, I feel a gathering sense of excitement as, warmly beside me, John Arthur's voice murmurs on the car radio.

"There are signs—indeed, alarming signs—that in Britain itself, this very island, we must prepare for troubles to come. I heard only this morning that Presidents De Gaulle and Von Papen have signed a treaty that draws even closer links between their economies and also those of the Low Countries, uniting their military forces into what is effectively one vast European army . . ."

The French-and-German threat has been a favourite theme in the popular press, but now John Arthur is giving it his own approval. I stare at my chauffeur's close-cropped neck as we drone across the empty tarmac of Westminster Bridge, wondering; does he hear those guns, the same grinding engine of history that fills my bones? Much though we British relish the threat of war, there is always a strange sense of shifting values when a fresh enemy is declared. And our main ally in this can only be Stalin's Russia, with Spain, perhaps Italy. Such a conflict would drag in America and the Colonies, China, expansionist Japan. . . .

We drive along Whitehall as the speech ends in a typically wistful finale. All this talk of war seems like a dream as we pass into Downing Street. The old Whip's Office is now the National Headquarters of the Empire Alliance, and the traffic and the tourists are kept back by those iron gates, but little else has changed here with the advent of Modernism. A London constable still stands guard at the polished, black door of Number 10, just as he has done since Peel introduced them. He doesn't even wear a gun. Inside, the air smells disappointingly municipal—a bit like Oxford—of beeswax and floor polish and fried bread and half-smoked cigars; slightly of damp, even. There are voices. Other people are wandering. I look around, and glimpse one or two of the other nobodies I've come to recognise during my stay at the New Dorchester. I really am back on the tracks of the itinerary that had always been intended for me —6 o'clock, PM meets and greets—it's as if the pistol, this hand, never happened. I wander through to an elegant room of wood panels and mirrors, then out into the Downing Street gardens.

Seen from the back, with its tall widows, pillars, its wrought iron, and its domes, Number 10 looks a small, stately home tucked into a quiet side street in the heart of London. The transformation from that terraced front is so much like all the other shams of Modernist Britain that I have to remind myself that the building has been this way since the 1730s. The willows in the garden slump limp and grey, the rose bushes are crumpled fists of paper. Paraffin lamps are carried out, shining on the guests as they move amid the mossy urns and statutes, glinting over the mirror-black waters of the ornamental pool. As they mill and chatter in the hushed tones of visitors to a consecrated building, I follow the gravel path leading to the deeper darkness beside the garden's outer wall.

A small stir arises, followed by lightening blasts of flashbulbs, and a grey-haired man of slightly less-than-average height moves easily amid his people; one to the next, shaking hands. Their voices reach me as wordless calls; cries, murmurs, exclamations. John Arthur's shirt looks incredibly white. The lanterns seem to brighten as he passes them. I imagine my last moment of history as I step toward him from these deeper shadows and he smiles with that warmth of recognition that politicians have. Then the feel and the sound of the gun. *Bang bang.* Blood flowering blackly within the white of his shirt. His eyes fixed on mine, knowing and unknowing as he falls back.

John Arthur seems to glance in my direction as I stand hidden against the dark mass of the ilex tree. Already, discreet KSG minders are shepherding some of the guests back into the house. The garden slowly empties and the voices grow fewer and quieter as damp darkness thickens. I've seen almost all I want to see as John Arthur, arms behind his back now, white cuffs showing, looking a little tired, prepares to follow them. Then he turns and glances back. He takes a step toward the darker reaches of the garden. And I, feeling some impelling force behind me in the night, take a step forward. It's almost as if I'm still being pushed into this moment by the fingers of history.

We meet at the very edge of what remains of the light.

"It *is* you, isn't it?" John Arthur shakes his head. His voice, his whole posture, belong to a far younger man. His hands flutter white, then his eyes flicker down to my sling.

"That was done yesterday," I say, my voice more unsteady than I'd intended. "Your people did it to me when they took away the gun."

"No," he shakes his head, his gaze fixing mine so firmly that a tremor runs through me. "It wasn't *my* people, Griff. You were arrested without my authority. . . ."

*Griff.* A blackbird sings briefly from a bush, but otherwise there is earthy darkness, an implacable sense of silence.

"I heard that you were ill and I wanted to see you. That was all. No one told me about . . ." He runs his hand back through his sleek, grey hair. It's a fair impression of distress. "No one told me about the gun. As soon as I heard you'd been arrested, I ordered your immediate release."

I study him. What am I supposed to say?

"Haven't got long to talk now Griff," John Arthur points toward the house with his thumb. "They'll soon want me back in there."

"I thought you made your own decisions."

He laughs at that. Then he shrugs and shoves his hands into the pockets of his suit. It's a typical gesture of his; we've all seen it a million times. "But, look, I've been thinking about you these last few months . . ." We are standing barely a pace apart now, yet he looks grainy and grey with the great house now glowing behind him. Still less that real. "I'd like for us to talk this evening, have a drink. We could go somewhere, Griff. Just you and me. I could shake this for a while. . . ."

With that, he turns and walks back toward the house. There are many stars kindled overhead now; the night will be crisp and clear. Shadows that I hadn't noticed before separate from the trees and the ancient walls and move toward me. I almost want to run.

John Arthur is silent as he drives swiftly along Horse Guards Parade and then on through clear, barricaded side streets. No one turns to stare. The speeding, blank-windowed official car is, after all, commonplace in Modernist Britain.

"You enjoyed the show?"

"The *show?*" I look over at him.

"Of course." He pushes the car faster. "You were here to kill me. . . ."

Drunk and jolly Tommies squat aside the lions as we pass Trafalgar Square. Everywhere, flags are being waved, people are leaning dangerously from windows. There will be deaths tonight. There will be conceptions. On through Covent Garden and across the Strand, then past the Inns of Court. A taxi draws up beside us as we queue to get into Cheapside. Two women in evening clothes are talking animatedly in the back.

"Tell me this, though, Griff," he says, his fingers clenching and unclenching the wheel's stitched leather. "Whatever made you think the world would change if there was no John Arthur?"

"Who would replace you? Jim Toller's too young—and nobody trusts him. People like Smith and Mosley are second-rate politicians. I suppose there was Harrison, but then he was conveniently executed. And we've all been laughing at William Arkwright for years. . . ."

"You shouldn't underestimate Bill. I've kept him close to me because he's the one person I can least trust. You're wrong about it all, in fact, Griff. The military, the bloody establishment. They all want rid of me. Why do you think I made that speech this evening? Why do you think this country has to fight? They're afraid, Griff. All of them are afraid. . . ."

Soon, we are in Whitechapel. He makes a turn and the tyres squeal across the wet cobbles, then rumble to the kerb of a dead end beside a scrap of wasteground. Clinging to my dignity, not waiting him to come and help me, I climb slowly out. It's cold and dark here. The ground is sticky with litter and the air has a faintly seasidey smell of coal smoke and river silt. John Arthur opens the rear door and takes a hat from the back seat—an ordinary-looking trilby—then a dark overcoat, which he pulls on, raising the collar.

"There," he says, turning with his arms outstretched, "who would recognise me?" The transformation is, of course, complete.

My walk is slow and laboured as we head past the terraced houses, and John Arthur helps me by snaking his arm around my back to support some of my weight, giving me a little lift as we step over a pothole and up onto the loose beginnings of a pavement. In odd, flashing moments, he feels almost like Francis. His breathing and the way he walks is almost the same, and his skin, beneath everything, still smells faintly of burnt lemon.

Soon, we're drawing close to the sidings, tracks, and cliff-face brick warehouses of the docks, where local people have gathered for a view of the fireworks above the Thames. Mothers in slippers with scarves wrapped over their curlers. Men with fags behind their ears and the stubble of a day off work peppering their chins. They *ohh* and *ahh* as the sky crackles and the colours shine in gutters and ignite the myriad warehouse windows. No one notices John Arthur as we slip between them. He's just a slight, middle-aged man helping his invalid father.

A little away from the crowd, tea chests lie heaped beside a wall. I slump down even though the air is sour here, and John Arthur sits beside me. In shadow, he risks taking off his hat, gestures toward the crowd. "They all seem so happy," he says. "A few drinks, a bed, food, some flesh to hold, some bloody fireworks . . ."

"They worship you."

"*Do* they? You tell me, Griff. You're the historian." He looks at me challengingly then, does this ex-lover of mine—does this John Arthur, and something chill and terrible runs down my spine. Now, powerless as I am, I'm sure that I was right to try to kill him. "It's not enough, is it? After what we went through. I thought it might be enough when I first visited Dublin after the victory. And then again when word came through from Rhodesia." He shakes his head as sulphurous plumes of red smoke drift over London. "You don't know what the War was like, Griff. No one does who wasn't there. . . ."

He's leaning forward now, eyes fixed on nowhere as the flashes of light catch and die over the planes of his face, the silver of his hair, his elbows resting on his knees as he grips the rim of his hat, turning it over and over.

"It was all so easy when I enlisted," he says. "There were men chatting with each other on the train that took us down to this big park north of Birmingham. Suddenly we were all the same— bosses and labourers . . . I was a rifleman, Griff. Third best shot in the training battalion when the Lee Enfields finally arrived. Went to France in December as part of Kitchener's First Army . . . and don't believe any of the bloody rubbish about King and Regiment and Country, Griff. You fight for the bloke who's standing next to you. You put up with all the mud and the lice and the officers and the regimental bullshit for their sake."

"It must have been terrible."

"It wasn't terrible. Don't give me that. It wasn't terrible at all. I've never laughed more in my life, or felt more wanted, more as if I belonged. The rain. The rats. The mud. It was all like some stupid practical joke. And it was quiet a lot of the time and there were empty fields where you could lie down in the evening and stare up at a perfect sky. Then down to the town, most us of half-drunk already, and the fat, white mademoiselles spitting on their fingers and saying *laver vous*. Yes, Griff, I did that too. And I had friends, mates, encounters. There were places. Nobody cared. . . ." He stares down, his silvered head bowed as the rockets whoosh and wheel, scrawling out the sky.

"We were sent to the Somme in June, 1916. It was supposed to be the big push that would win the War, but we knew that we were just covering a French cock-up. I lay awake that last night. We all knew we were going over the top in the morning. Not that they told you, but you could tell from the guns. I couldn't sleep. Boom, boom, and the stink of the trenches. Boom, boom, boom. Then the big guns stopped, and that silence was the worst thing of all. We were moved up to the front line. Thousands, thousands of us. And there was silence, just men breathing and the shuffle of our feet on the duckboards and the creak and jingle of our packs. And for the first time, I knew that I'd lost it. I felt terribly afraid.

"The whistle went and men started to climb out of the trenches. A lot of them just fell back and I thought they were being clumsy until I realised they'd been already shot. And I just stood there. It was the worst moment of my life but I knew I couldn't go back, so I started to climb up out of that trench. My mates were already running around the pool of a big shell hole ahead, but I was just wandering in a nightmare, looking for somewhere to hide . . .

"I don't know when I got hit, Griff—or how long it took. But there was this heat across my side as I slid down into this long hollow. I knew it wasn't that bad . . . I should have gone on, Griff.

I could have climbed out of that ditch and gone on. But I didn't. I just crouched there the whole day. Boom, boom—I could hear the shells whistling over. The bullets rattling. But I was alone with my fear, Griff. Quite alone.

"Darkness came and the flares went up. Men with stretchers found me and hauled me out, and I looked enough of a mess to be convincing as I was taken back to the field dressing station. I was given some water and a jab of morphine and quinine and carried across the fields to a big river barge just as dawn was coming. You could still smell the coal that they'd cleared out of the barge beneath all the other stench, and you could hear the water laughing around the sides as we pulled away from the jetty.

"A few men were crying and moaning. A lot were comatose or simply asleep. There was a man with his head half-blown off on the stretcher nearest to me. He couldn't possibly live, his brains were coming out, and then he started this terrible moaning. He was trying to speak, but his jaw was so wrecked I couldn't understand what he was saying. Something K and something M. His limbs were jerking and this noise he was making just went on and on. It was a sound out of hell. Then I looked at him again with the top of his skull ripped off like an egg, and I realised what he was saying. He was saying kill me . . .

"I managed to stand up, and he seemed to quieten for a moment then, and looked back up at me from his ruined face with his one good eye. I took strength from that, and I understood that what he wanted was what you'd do for any mate of yours in the same position. He had a pistol on his belt, but I knew that it was too late to use it here. And I was still lost, still afraid. In fact, it seemed as if it was *his* strength that enabled me to take the blanket from by his feet and push it down over his face and hold it there. Of course, he began to fight and buck after a while—it takes longer than you'd imagine to kill a man—but eventually he stopped struggling, And I was glad that I still had this one soldierly act left in me. I knew that he'd died a hero's death, this man. This soldier.

"Perhaps it was that or the drugs I'd been given which made me do what I did next. I don't know. I felt for the waxed envelope that they'd tied to his tunic at the dressing station. His name was John Arthur, and he was a private in the Staffordshires like me, although from a different battalion. And it struck me that John Arthur was a good name for a soldier, a good name for a man. I'd always hated being Francis Eveleigh, anyway. It was all done for that moment, in the foul air of that barge with the water laughing beside me, swapping names just to see how it felt to become him. And straight away, you know, as I lay down again on my pallet and the fever began to take a bigger hold, it felt better. . . ."

John Arthur is silent for a moment as the sky above London foams with light, pushing at us like a wind.

"Didn't anyone ever suspect?"

"The rest of my platoon had been wiped out. So had John Arthur's. And I caught pneumonia, you see, Griff, so I was shipped back to England. By the time I was finally ready for active again, I could have been anyone for all the difference it made. So I went back to the front as S4538 Rifleman Arthur, D Company 7th Service Battalion, The Rifle Brigade, and I knew from the first time I heard the guns that this time it would be better, this time I wouldn't feel any fear. I was even made corporal, and I won the George Cross . . . but that's common knowledge."

"What was it like when the War ended?"

"I went up to Raughton, which was John Arthur's last address before enlisting. I found out that the Yorkshire accent I'd copied from one of the cooks was all wrong, but that didn't matter. We were like ghosts. Nobody seemed to belong anywhere then. The place was just a pit village and the address was a cheap boarding house. One or two people told me they remembered him, but I never really knew if they did. He'd been slightly older than me, but seemed to have made little impression of the world. His father had been an itinerant who'd started out in the West Country and had died in a mining accident . . .

"But I knew I had to do something more with this new life John Arthur had given me. Do you understand that, Griff? So I jumped on a cattle truck, took the train down to London. It was cold that winter and there was the flu epidemic. Each morning under the bridges and in the shop fronts, a few extra bodies didn't wake up. And the men in suits and the women in hats who'd never done anything but complain about the rationing just wrinkled their noses and stepped over them. And there were queers like you, Griff, who'd get a man to do anything for the price of a meal. And fat cats and Jews. And the bright, young things. And the colonels who were back from the War, jingling with medals and a big pension.

"But I still remembered I was John Arthur. And I began to meet people who understood that there was nothing left in all the lies that had once kept this country afloat. And you saw what it was like, Griff, that night fifteen years ago. You saw how easy it is to *be* John Arthur. He was always waiting there. Even now, he's leading me on."

The big display is reaching its climax. Even here, what must be two miles off, there's a sweet-sour reek of gunpowder as the flares blossom overhead. John Arthur puts his trilby hat on, straightens it, checks that his coat collar is still up and offers me his hand again. "Come on, Griff, I'll buy you that drink. . . ."

I let him help me up, and an elderly woman in a hairnet and a housecoat glances across the road. Her hand goes up to her mouth for a moment, childlike in wonder. Is it? But no, no . . . it couldn't be. Relieved, she looks back toward the crackling sky.

John Arthur breathes easily beside me, helping me along as I wonder what I should say, what horrors I could tell him that he doesn't know already, what questions should I ask. But it's like all those letters that I never wrote to him. It's like all the promises of love that, even in that brief, glorious time when Francis and I were alone, were never given. It's like my unwritten book. It's like my whole life.

The sky is on fire now. The houses look flash-lit, pushed back into skeletons of their real selves. I stumble as renewed pain shoots through me. Our two linked shadows leap, burned and frozen ahead into the pavement, and it seems that we're at the lip of a vast wave that will soon break through everything, dissolving, destroying. Then, with one last, final bellow, the display ends and we move on through the East End, the ordinary East End of London in this night of the 21st of October 1940 beneath a bruised sky, in shocked, blotchy darkness.

A public house juts at the triangular meeting of the two streets facing toward the Mudchute and the Isle of Dogs. The sign is un-illuminated, painted in dark colours. If I didn't know this place already, I probably wouldn't be able to make out the words COTTAGE SPRING. The room inside is smaller than the place I remember stumbling into fifteen years before. But I recognise the counter that John Arthur leapt onto, and the pattern of the mirror, now cracked, that lies behind it; there, even, is the fat pillar in the corner that I once hid behind.

There's a moment of bizarre normality as John Arthur takes off his hat, lowers his coat collar, and walks up to the bar. Two cloth-capped men are playing darts, whilst three underage lads sit nursing their pints, and an old man stares at his evening glass of stout. They're some of the few who couldn't be bothered to see tonight's fireworks, or even watch them at home on telly, and it's amusing to observe their reactions as they realise who's just come in. There's puzzlement, doubt—like that old woman by the docks —followed by that standard British reluctance to make a fuss.

"I'll buy everyone their next round," John Arthur says, speaking with that soft Yorkshire accent: the very image of himself, and suddenly, they're all clustered around him, breathless and eager like children at a fete when Father Christmas finally arrives. John Arthur signs beer mats, he laughs and shares a joke. He really is John Arthur now, and these are his people. The old man downs the rest of his stout, spilling most of it down his shirt, and quavers that he's like another. The lads ask for halves of ginger beer, which John Arthur laughingly changes to the pints of Fullers' that they were on before.

Outside, word of who's here must have got out, for there are children's and women's voices, the shadows of raised hands and heads shifting across the frosted windows. And I'm just standing here, tired and in pain. Drained of anger. Drained of hope. Soon to be drained of life. I shuffle closer to that pillar at the end of the bar, in need once more of its reassuring anonymity. John Arthur's forgotten about me anyway. *These* are his people. *This* is where he belongs. I'm just a name from the past that he couldn't remember well enough to get right when he made his speech to the Parliament that he later dissolved. A phone begins to ring at the back of the pub, unanswered. Somewhere, a car engine is racing.

The voices of the men are easier now. Yes, they realise, he really is just as everyone says; an ordinary bloke you could share a drink with. John Arthur looks across as the roar of an approaching car fills the street. He seems to notice me now almost as he did all those years ago. It's as if nothing has ever changed. But this time, somehow, his smile is more genuine, and as he walks over with his arms a little apart, I can't help but smile back at him.

There comes a sharp sound of banging, and the thought passes, too quickly to be fully formed, that the fireworks have resumed. Then, one by one, the frosted windows of the Cottage Spring begin to fall in. They burst into shining veils, and splinters of wood fly out as the room explodes in a reflecting spray of collapsing mirrors. The men at the bar are jerked, thrown back, lifted. The glass is like a great, watery tide, rolling and rising. John Arthur pirouettes as the last window explodes and the shining air flowers silver and red around him, then the pillar I'm beside splatters and streams before everything stops and fills with sudden, terrible silence.

As I look down at this shattered place and these broken dolls lying on the crimsoned linoleum, there comes a sudden crash as the last of the big mirrors falls, and faint, at the very edge of everything, are the sounds of crying, fumbling, moaning, weeping. Then the roar, once again, of that car. Gears smash as it turns, and I wait for more bullets, but instead something large and metallic flies through a gaping window. A thick, round-cornered box with a single wire protruding, it hits an upended table and skids hissing through the sparkling wreckage to settle beside Francis's body.

Then the car pulls away with a screech of tyres in the last moment before the world erupts into darkness.

## Eight

Every morning now, I awake not knowing who or where I am; filled with a vague sense of horror and helplessness. I do not even know if I am human, or have any real identity of my own. For a moment then, I am under the rubble again and Francis is beside me. His hand is in mine, and flutters like an insect in the moment that he dies. My life seems to float out in both directions from that point. It's like unwrapping a complex present; tearing away at silvery ribbons of the future and the past, although I know that it's all just some trick—a party game—and that I will be left clutching nothing but tangled paper, empty air.

I ungum my eyes and look out at the world, accepting the strange fact of my continued existence. But it remains a slow process even though this beamed ceiling is familiar to me; fraught with a sense of aftermath. I am Brook, yes, I am Geoffrey Brook. I am a lecturer, a teacher—in fact, a true Professor of History now. And Oxford, yes, Oxford.

I feel for my glass, my tablets, which lie a long way beyond the Chinese pheasants cavorting on my eiderdown. I sense that it is early, still dark outside my window, although a strange light seems to wash up from the quad and there is a chill to the air beyond the crackling heat of my fire. Somewhere across the rooftops and towers, a bell, distant yet clear, begins to chime the hour. When silence and equilibrium return, I slide inch by inch across the sheets until my feet drop off the edge of the bed. I am old, I think. I am old. Perhaps that is the last shock I have been waiting for.

Bunioned, barefoot, trying not to exhaust myself by coughing, I stumble through the cavorting firelight toward my window, dribbling fingers of condensation as I wipe the mullions with my wrecked and arthritic right hand and gaze at the strange whiteness. It has snowed again in the night. Of course. This is Oxford and it has snowed again in the night . . . I have to close my eyes, then, as a twinge of pain and the rawness in my throat sets off another ugly memory.

I remember everything now. I am here. I am alive. This is the last day of the year of 1940. John Arthur is dead.

I'm still leaning there, still staring from my college window in a drugged half-doze, when the breakfast trolley rumbles toward my door. The knock sounds hesitant, mistimed, yet still I'm somehow expecting Christlow as the handle turns and the chill outer air touches my skin. But it's Allenby.

"Good morning, Professor. Terrible lot of snow in the night as you've doubtless seen. Got a nice fire going for you earlier whilst you were still asleep." He slips my padded silk dressing gown from the hook near the fire where it's been warming. His breath is cool on my neck as he helps me into it; like the sense of the snow. He bends down to sheathe my feet in lambskin slippers. He's young and good-looking, is Allenby. He says all the right things; he doesn't even wear an EA badge. But he still seems like a barely competent actor, forever trying and failing to find the essential meaning of his role.

"You've got that appointment, by the way."

"Appointment?"

"Twelve o'clock at the George Hotel. Miss Flood is coming up from your publishers in London."

Then he lays the morning's papers out before me. Sheet upon warm rustling sheet that smell crisply of ink and freshly felled wood; all that history in the making. I'm tempted to ask Allenby to take the damn things away, but I know that would seem ungrateful. And there's something—I remember now—something that still pricks my interest, although as yet I can't quite recall what.

I reach out toward the table, using my right hand like a scoop to push the *Times* into the better grip of my left. PM ANNOUNCES IMMEDIATE INQUIRY INTO SCANDAL OF JEWISH HOMELAND. RAF AIRLIFTS AID. The photograph beneath shows a group of people huddled outside a rough hut. They are skeleton-thin, clothed in rags. I raise it closer to my eyes, so close that their faces become collections of printed dots.

My college Daimler slides through the slush along High, Catte, and Broad. We park at the corner of George Street and the Cornmarket, where my driver helps me out onto the oystered ice of the pavement and leads me into the Ivy Restaurant. The colours, that the snow and the cold have bleached out of Oxford, all seem to have fled into these rooms. The ceilings are pink, the walls lean with gilded mirrors, there are flowers at every table. As is often the case now, rumour of my arrival has spread before me, and I must wait and smile and raise a trembling hand in acknowledgement as the dining room erupts into applause. But the moment isn't over-played as I shuffle toward the best table by the window where Miss Flood awaits me.

Her bracelets jangle as she sips her wine. Her fingers are restless as she picks at a bread roll, missing the chains of cigarettes that, since I succumbed to a coughing fit at one of our early meetings, she refrains from smoking in my presence.

"I was speaking to Publicity only yesterday, Geoffrey," she tells me. "And you're definitely the flagship of our spring list."

"That's good to know . . ." I wheeze. "I received your letter with the, er, galleys only the day before yesterday."

"Try not to think of them as *galleys* or *proofs*, Geoffrey. Think of them as . . ." Miss Flood waves her hand, clutching an imaginary cigarette. "Complimentary reading material." She smiles.

I nod. What she means is that she wants to keep me well away from the tricky business of correcting my own scholarly inaccuracies, my ungrammatical turns of phrase.

Miss Flood delves into her briefcase and shows me a glossy mock-up of the dust jacket. The first print run is thirty thousand, with the presses ready to roll with another thirty thousand after that. You'll never know from the look of this book that Miss Flood's other major authors write do-it-yourselfs and who-dunnits. I really can't complain.

"As to the title," she says, tapping the celluloid with a scarlet fingernail, "you'll see that we've stuck with our original idea. That, er, *other* suggestion that you made. Good though it was, I'm afraid that it didn't quite *click* with out marketing people. *Fingers* of History was too close, if you see what I mean. There are a lot of people out there who still remember your work and who'd love to have a hard-back copy of your best articles . . ."

## FIGURES OF HISTORY
### Geoffrey Brook

"Oh, and we've finally cleared up the copyright business. Being who you are, Geoffrey, I really didn't think that the people at the *Sketch* would resist. But we'll need to hurry you," Miss Flood says more quietly, slipping in the words when she imagines that I'm not really conscious as I gaze out of the window at the snow-softened spires, domes, towers of this city. Balliol, All Souls, Queens . . . the litany of my dreams . . . "If we're going to squeeze in that new extra chapter you were talking about."

"I've decided," I squeak, "what I want to write about. It fits in with research I was doing into the history of the Jews." *Jews* . . . my voice sounds even lighter than ever as I end the sentence, and I'm sure that the restaurant conversations fade around me. "What with all the fuss there's been in the papers these last few days about the Highlands . . ." Something sticks and crunches in my throat. "I was thinking . . . thinking that the time is right to remind people. . . ."

"Geoffrey, that sounds *fascinating*." Pause. "Although everyone's hungry to hear more about your links with John Arthur."

"Of course."

"Not that I want to steer you in any particular direction."

My eyes are watering. My nose is starting to run. I fumble to find a clean corner on my handkerchief as I begin to cough and the chime of bells and the clatter of lunch-time cutlery, the waitresses's whispering and the taste of the wine and the smell of the cooking and clangour in the kitchens and whispers in ancient corridors and the scent of old stone and fresh snow, the dreaming towers of these rabbit-hole rooms—the sense of all Oxford—fractures around me.

*Geoffrey Brook was born in Staffordshire, Lichfield, in 1880. He has devoted most of his life to teaching history, firstly in and around the city of his birth, where he influenced the young John Arthur, and later in his life at one of the most distinguished and ancient Oxford colleges . . .*

Running my pen through the word *ancient*, scratching a question mark over *distinguished*, I close the file of publicity material as my college Daimler hisses slowly along High. Already, it's getting dark and the lights in the shop windows are glowing. Prices have gone up a lot recently—taxes, as well—and you'd think that people would have had enough of shopping after the frenzied weeks before Christmas. But the windows offer BIGGEST EVER SALE and HUGE POST-XMAS DISCOUNTS, even though it won't be twelfth night until Sunday.

My college tower looms and the chill air bites as I dismiss my driver and wade unaided across the snowy quad. Wheezing, I slump down into one of the leather armchairs beside the fire in my room and drag my telephone, a new privilege, onto my lap and stab and turn, stab and turn, dialing out a number from the back page of the *Times*, willing all the ghosts of history to give me strength, and trying to picture a bustling newsroom filled with the same clean, purposeful smell as the papers Allenby brings me. . . .

But today's New Year's Eve, and there are no newspapers tomorrow. The telephone just rings and rings.

The world already knew that John Arthur was dead by the time I was hauled out from the rubble of the Cottage Spring. I could hear it in the crowds sobbing howls as the masonry slid and crumbled, and in the fireman's angry voices.

One of the beer-drinking lads survived for two nights at Barts inside an iron lung. Another remains alive to this day, though a mindless cripple. There were also many deaths and disablements amid the onlookers who'd gathered in the street outside. Only I, Geoffrey Brook, protected by that pillar—and, perhaps, in some strange way, by the fact that I was already close to death—truly survived. I suffered a gash along my cheek which required five stitches, a dislocated shoulder, two septic lungfuls of plaster. Of course, I had my bad right hand already, although that fact often feels as lost to me as it is to the rest of the world.

Even as I was carried to the ambulance, the flashbulbs were popping, the television lights were glaring. Three days later, as I was propped up in my hospital bed, smoothed and groomed, sweetly drugged, the new Prime Minister William Arkwright called at my hospital room. The flashbulbs of the many newsmen he'd brought with him popped and crackled as he shook my good left hand and grinned around his pipe. He already seemed bigger than the man I'd met in the gardens of New Buckingham Palace. "And it's Professor Brook from now on," he said as he picked up his trademark Homburg hat from my bed. "Did I mention that just now? No matter—it'll be in all tomorrow's papers."

John Arthur's death is already as much a part of his myth as everything that happened during his life. This time, unlike the fire at Old Buckingham Palace—and unless Jim Toller and the several senior officers of the KSG commit suicide in their cells—there will even be a trial. The national mood is predominately one of sadness and disillusion. EA badges are less frequently worn, and KSG officers suffer children's jibes as they walk the streets, implicated as they all are by association in the death of our great leader. And the British economy, it seems, is far weaker than we ever imagined, damaged by ten years of over-expenditure. Conscription is being phased out, and negotiations with France and Germany about mutual disarmament will commence in February. There is even talk—oblique, as yet—of giving India and Ireland a semblance of Home Rule, and fresh elections for a new People's Assembly.

All the rest, that last glorious summer of hope and expansion, already feels like a dream. After all, the world is becoming an increasingly dangerous place—Japan has attacked China, Stalin has annexed eastern Poland—and it's obvious that the countries of Western Europe must draw together if they are not to be swept away by Communism and a commercially belligerent America. John Arthur's threats toward France and Germany, his canny alliance with Stalin, have simply given us a top seat at the table in the negotiations to come.

I found his picture had vanished from the Gents beside Christ Church Meadow when I made my recent farewell visit there, although the nail marks that I and my acquaintance made in the third cubical remain. Somehow, as I touched their soft indentations, they spoke to me of nothing but hope and human decency.

The Cumbernald's house shines out amid a spray of car headlights as I arrive that evening.

"All terribly kitsch, I know," Eric Cumbernald assures me as I hobble past the flashing fairy lights in the front porch. "Everyone's waiting for you. . . ."

Within moments, I'm surrounded, touched, smiled at, reminded of previous meetings, and promises of lunch. Grateful for the armour of my tablets, I shuffle across the carpets toward the largest and most inviting looking chair. Cumbernald brings me a sweet sherry and a Spode plate with a sausage roll and the crowd around me thins as it becomes apparent that I'm not responding to their questions. From being a living link to John Arthur, I'm demoted to being an old relic, to be touched for luck, then forgotten. Music plays. The fire flickers. The Christmas decorations turn and sway. There are many hours to go yet before midnight and the coming of 1941.

Eileen Cumbernald sits for a while on the arm of my chair, brown as ever in a low-backed dress. Her husband Eric's impending promotion to Vice Chancellor of Oxford University has left her totally unchanged.

"I *so* enjoyed that time we spent together at Penrhos," she tells me. "You really *must* come down with us again next year. . . ."

I have to smile. It's funny, how people choose to ignore my obvious physical decline. I suppose that they imagine it's only natural. In fact, it would be wrong for me to appear too hale and hearty after surviving an explosion that killed John Arthur.

"You're even *more* like dead Uncle Freddie now!" Barbara

Cumbernald declares delightedly as she imprisons me in her hot arms whilst Christine hangs back a little, looking just as pale and hot as her sister, but more clearly the eldest now. "Will you tell us one of your funny stories?"

"Why don't you both tell *me* a story instead?" I suggest. "Tell me what you know about John Arthur."

"John Arthur," Barbara intones, her arms still around me, smelling of wine and sweat and toffee, "died a hero's death as we as a Nation celebrated Trafalgar Day. Bad people who wanted to—" But at this point, Christine begins to tickle her, and they collapse on the floor in a squealing heap.

Will the Cumbernalds stay in this house on Raglan Street, I wonder, in the wake of Eric's promotion and the knighthood that will almost certainly follow? With the billiard room and the conservatory, the hugely expensive kitchen I got a glimpse of, they've clearly got things here exactly as they want them. But they will move, of course, ever-upward toward some semi-stately home. They'll continue to swim the warm English currents until age and frailty finally catch up with them. They'll probably even accept death with good grace—just like me, they'll have no cause to complain about the way history and these Summer Isles have treated them.

Me, I really am a full Professor now. And MA, Modern History, from my own college, too. As Cumbernald has carefully explained, my Master's can be seen as either honorary or de facto depending upon the angle from which you choose to view it. The thing often switches back and forth even in my own befuddled mind—a strange state of existence which I suspect that the scientists you used to hear about a few years ago would recognise from their studies of the hints and glimmers that apparently make up our universe. We're barely there, it seems, if you look closely enough; just energies and particles that don't belong in a particular time or place. Stare at the world too hard, breathe at it from the wrong direction, and it falls apart. Explodes.

Christlow was found drowned on a muddy bank of the Thames down by the Isle of Dogs the morning after the Cottage Spring. A presumed suicide, there were whispers on the Oxford grapevine of evidence found in his rooms of preferences that should never be entertained by a man who works with children.

I don't doubt, in fact, that he was following me. Where and how it began, and whether he always knew of my sexual dalliances, I will never know. But I'm also sure that he found the pistol in the suitcase beneath my bed. No doubt he imagined he was doing no more than his patriotic duty by reporting this fact, and my movements. But here the picture grows fuzzy, unscientific, unhistoric. . . .

My thoughts always come back to the man who has most plainly benefited from John Arthur's death. More that ever now, it's clear that we all underestimated William Arkwright. He's a consummate survivor, a dealer and a fixer, a betrayer: a *politician* in the sense that John Arthur—who lived, for all his faults, by the heart, by the flame and the fire—never was. It must have been plain to Arkwright, long before it was to the rest of us, that Modernism was in crisis, seduced by its own myth, in danger of launching itself into economic catastrophe and a disastrous European war. So perhaps Arkwright finally persuaded the relics of an establishment that is now resurgent that enough was enough. As even the arrest of Jim Toller and his senior KSG colleagues acknowledges, John Arthur's death was executed too professionally to be the work of mere fanatics.

From this, I soon find myself taking the kind of wild flights that, even when I was spinning through the most dangerously speculative pages of my long-projected book, I would never have considered undertaking. History—the only kind of history, anyway, that anyone ever cares about—is always reducible to solid facts that can be learnt by students in hour-long lessons and then regurgitated in exams, or used to add colour to television dramas, or as the embroidery in escapist novels. But what could have been more convenient than to have some dying madman kill John Arthur, alone and unaided? So I wasn't arrested. I remained an idea to be toyed with—or at least not discarded until the last appropriate moment. Even as I wandered the gardens of New Buckingham Palace, it was still quite possible that I would be allowed access to John Arthur with my gun. After all, there was no particular reason why I shouldn't succeed, other than the question mark that hung over my own character. And whom should I meet there amid the terraced fountains, but none other than William Arkwright?

It was then, I think, that I was finally weighed in the balance and found lacking. Arkwright ordered that I be arrested by his own officials, perfunctorily questioned to make sure I wasn't hiding anything, then shot whilst more reliable contingencies were put in hand. Only some chance enquiry from John Arthur's office about my whereabouts—that midnight phone call echoing in that shaft between the buildings—saved my life.

Did John Arthur know that an assassination attempt was likely?

Was it I who led him to his killers at the Cottage Spring? But no, no. All of this is too fantastic—worse than those dreadful Modernist books that I forced myself to read. The fact is that I will never know. Perhaps in years to come when the truth is no longer potent, some hack or scholar will come up with a theory that questions the role of Jim Toller's KSG in John Arthur's death. They may even stumble across the strange fact that another figure, an obscure, populist academic named Brook, was arrested in possession of a gun. Odder still, this Brook character was then released and was with John Arthur at the time of his death—survived, even, the bullets and the explosion. I cannot imagine what threads they will draw out from these odd facts. By their nature, the true conspiracies are the ones that are least likely to be unearthed in the future. The truth, at the end of the day, remains forever silent. We are only left with history.

"*There* you are, Brook!" Cumbernald looms from the ceiling decorations and lays his hand on my shoulder. "Can't just drift off like this, you know. There's a phone call for you. A Miss *Flood*."

My knees pop and crack like tiny fireworks as he helps me up. His right arm supports me as he leads down the corridor. "You can take it here in my study," he says, pushing open the door, watching for a few moments as I settle down on a new leather chair to make sure that I know how to operate this fancy-looking phone of his.

"*Geoffrey*, there you are!" Miss Flood sounds excited. "I got your number here from that creepy chap who works for you at the college."

"*Allenby?*"

"Whatever. I've marvellous news, Geoffrey . . ."

I wait as Miss Flood burbles on, studying the ample bookshelves that cover these study walls (mostly do-it-yourselves and who-dunnits, a few biographies and thin histories; a small space where my own forthcoming work will fit in easily), doing my best to banish the sense of gloomy premonition that still comes over me when people announce they have news.

". . . so Arkwright's own Private Secretary asked if it wasn't too much of a presumption. I mean, as if we'd really *mind*. Of course, we'll have to redo the dust jacket to give his name due prominence . . ."

"You mean Arkwright is—"

"—Yes, going to write an Introduction to your book! I know, I know. I still haven't got over it either. I haven't even started to *think* what this'll do to the print runs! Of course, it means that you, Geoffrey, can relax. You won't have to write *a thing more . . .*"

Part of me drops away as I gaze down at the receiver. There are two ways, I decide, to gain a person's silence and compliance. You either take away their lives and scrub out their identity. Or you give them everything.

"So that's it, then?"

"Marvellous! And Happy New Year. Oh, Geoffrey . . . not that it matters now as far as the book's concerned, but I do have a contact for that research you were talking about. Someone in the Government who's coordinating the Jewish relief effort."

I cradle the phone between my shoulder and chin, searching the leather and ash expanse of Eric Cumbernald's desktop for something resembling a pen or a pencil. I begin to write out the number and the name that Miss Flood dictates in my left-handed scrawl, then stop half way and put down the phone without wishing her goodbye.

"Everything okay in there?" Cumbernald asks. His eyes travel down to my bit of paper. "If you want to make another call . . ."

"I don't think I'll bother."

"In that case . . ." he slides back a cabinet front to reveal a television screen surrounded by nests of equipment, "there's something I'd very much like to show you."

I crumple the note as the comforting smell of warming valves slowly fills the room. The name Miss Flood's given me of the Home Office official who's overseeing the operation to provide food, medical treatment, and shelter to the Jews is Reeve-Ellis. The television screen snows. Then there are ghostly figures that make me think of my acquaintance and his family, huddled in their crude huts or blanketed in the hurricane wilderness. Of course, the Government has come to their rescue now. The terrible situation has been proclaimed by Ministry of Information Press Release, and the newspapers have lapped it up unquestioningly. Soon, it will be dealt with, and—a little sadder, a little wiser, a little less trustful— we Britons will watch the results on the BBC News. This Jewish Scandal has come at just the right time. It shows Arkwright as a man of honesty who is prepared to deal with the aberrations that so blackened Modernism's reputation in the rest of the world. It may even get us back into the League of Nations. In a few months—or years, perhaps, depending upon political contingencies—a similarly narrow spotlight will fall upon the treatment camps in the Isle of Man. But, even if my acquaintance and his family have survived, angel of death that I am, I realise I must never try to contact them.

Cumbernald places a large, silver disk on a spinning turntable. "I had the cine-recording transcribed to video," he explains, as I watch the jumpy white outlines of Eileen, Christine, Barbara, and myself sitting outside the summer lodge in Penrhos Park on the television screen. Behind it all is a crackle and a rumble. *Eggs and bacon, Eggs and bacon. Apple and custard . . .*

"Been thinking, by the way," he says, leaning against a bookshelf as he admires his camerawork. "About who should replace me as principal at college. We need someone with *reputation*, don't you think? Someone with an agile mind . . . and I don't really think you'll be surprised, Brook, when I tell you that your name was the first that came to mind."

"I'm far too old," I mutter, still gazing at the screen as Christine and Barbara run up to me, their tongues stuck out like gorgeous gargoyles, their whole futures ahead of them. "Far too ill. . . ."

"Such a pity," Cumberland says, refolding his arms, adding just the right note of regret, "even if it were true." But he doesn't push it. In fact, he sounds relieved.

"Anyway," he stoops down, preparing to lift the needle from the record as the matchstick figures dance and shift, grey on white. "Time we got back into the throng, old man." Christine and Barbara dissolve into a flash of light, then shrink down through a pin dot into the blackness. "It's nearly midnight."

The lights are off now in the main room as the bells of Big Ben begin their famous chime. *Bong*—and there it is. *Bong*—a New Year is beginning. Lips and hands press against my own with the rustle of tweed and rayon, the dig of jewelry, wafts of perfume. Afterward, as I'm sipping the sweet, fizzy alcohol and thinking of getting back to my tablets, my rooms, the doorbell sounds along the hall. I'm already on my way toward it in the hope that it's my driver come to rescue me when I realise that eager hands are assisting my passage, eager voices are urging me on. The doorbell sounds again. It's clearly some neighbour out first-footing with a piece of shortbread, a lump of coal. And who better than I, the famous Geoffrey Brook, to greet them?

The Cumbernald's front door swings inward, and I'm expecting a figure, perhaps even the dark, handsome stranger of tradition, to be standing on the doorstep. But the doorway remains empty, and I, pushed on, seem to travel into blackness and terrible, empty, cold.

## Nine

I've been reading—or rereading, I'm really not sure now—that stained copy of William Morris's *News from Nowhere*. The curled pages, brittle with dried mud and the dusty air of nearly half a century, speak of nothing that resembles the vision of Greater Britain that came to pass. Morris hated big industry, he hated all big things, he hated terror and injustice. How, then, was his name pulled so deeply into the currents of Modernism that Blackwells are even now trying to get rid of discounted piles of *The Waters of the Wondrous Isles?* All that Morris and Modernism ever shared was a preparedness to dream, and a love of a bright, clean, glorious past that never was. But perhaps that was enough; perhaps the dream, any dream, is always the seed from which nightmares will follow.

John Arthur is fading. His memory is twisted and pulled to suit whatever meaning people choose to give it as easily as were Morris's unread pages. It's almost as if I'm the only person left in this nation who grieves for him, or who still wishes to understand. And that last, fatal night when we were together follows me even now. All the questions I should have asked, the challenges I should have made. Either I loved, I suppose, the incarnation of something evil, or John Arthur was a puppet like me, jerked by the whims of some incomprehensible greater will. Between these two horrors, I keep trying to find some middle way, a decent path that anyone might wander along in their life and find themselves unexpectedly and irrevocably lost. Francis was no monster, for all that I know that he used me much more than he loved me in the brief time that we were truly together.

So I keep thinking instead of Mrs Stevens, my acquaintance's neighbour, who offered me tea and the bright warmth of her kitchen, and of Cumbernald, and of the woman behind the counter in the Post Office, and the doctors and the policemen, and, yes, of Christlow, and even Reeve-Ellis, and the faces you see looking out from train windows, and the children you see playing in the street. And my own face in the mirror is there, too, although haggard as death now, the stranger-corpse that will soon be all that is left of me. Francis belongs there, with us. He didn't close the cell doors himself, he didn't pull the ropes, touch the wires, kick shut the drawers of filing cabinets.

We all did that for him.

*     *     *

For a few short days of our Scottish holiday, Francis and I lived in a ramshackle stone cottage. The place had a rough, slate floor like something carried in by the tide, thick walls with tiny windows that overlooked the beach. In storms, in winter, the thin, turf roof would have leaked the sea and the wind and the rain. But the weather was like honey when we were there. The sea was like wine. Alone, miles from the world, we swam naked and caught translucent shrimps from the pools beyond the dunes.

Time stopped. The whole universe turned around us. Francis's skin was browned and bleached to lacy tidemarks by the sea and the sun, and he tasted like the shrimps; briny salt and sweet. Lying one night amid the blankets of our rough cot, my skin stiff from the sun and the soles of my feet gritty, some twist of emptiness made me reach out and open my eyes. Francis had gone from beside me, was standing naked at the open cottage doorway, looking out at the pale sea, the star-shot night.

"You see over there. . . ?" he said, sensing from the change in my breathing that I was awake. "Right over there, Griff, toward the horizon. . . ?"

I propped myself up, following his gaze out along the white shingle path, the low wall, the pale dunes that edged into the luminous ripple of the waves. Perhaps he was right. Perhaps there was something out there, the shining, grey backs of a shoal of islands that daylight made the air too brilliant to see.

"I think we should go there, Griff," he said, his shoulders and limbs rimed with starlight. "Remember? That lovely name. . . ?"

"There won't be anything to see," I laughed, lying back in the blankets. "There'll be no ferry."

But I could see those islands more clearly now as I closed my eyes again and the darkness began to take me. Heathered hills rolling down to dark green copses of pine. Sheep-dotted lowlands. The summer-sparkling rim of the sea. I could even smell a uniquely milky scent of summer grass and flowers carried to me on the soft breeze off the Atlantic. Yes, I thought, we will go there.

But the weather had changed in the morning when we awoke. Low, grey clouds lay across the dunes and met with the sea. So we never did get to visit the Summer Isles, and Francis pushed quickly down the track as we left our cottage beneath a sky that threatened nothing but rain, cycling fast as he always cycled, forever heading on. I even feared that I, teetering with my older legs as I bumped along with my heavy suitcase strapped behind me, would never catch up. It was then, I think, as he crested the top of the first hill and vanished from sight, freewheeling eagerly down toward the farm on the headland where we would hand in the keys, that I finally lost my Francis. It was then that he was swallowed by history, and that everything else that was to happen began.

Well-anchored in my wheelchair on this steamship's juddering deck, I gaze at those famous white cliffs, as grey on this late January morning as is the sea, the sky, these circling gulls. The air is bitter and cold, filled with the groan of engines and the smoke and salt they churn in their wake. There will be no last glimpse of England —I realise that now—just this gradual fading.

Like so many other things I have done in my life, my departure has proved surprisingly easy. I could detect no resistance as my driver ferried me about Oxford and I withdrew my funds and made my travel arrangements. In any event, the number of stamps and passes required to leave this country are greatly reduced. Back in Oxford, I suppose, Allenby will have found my note by now, and passed it on to Cumbernald as he tidies his desk and prepares to leave. My letter, posted to London the day before, will probably also be waiting for Miss Flood. Of course, there will be concern about my semi-mysterious disappearance, but that will soon be followed by weary, head-shaking amusement at the thought that I still had this one last act in me.

Thus I travel, ill, wealthy, and alone. My precise plans, as the maps and the possibilities widen in my mind, remain vague. Long journeys hold no fears for me now: if you are rich enough, there are always people who will give you what you think you need. All I know is that I want to end my days somewhere far from England where the climate is dry and warm, where there are lizards on the walls and the stars are different. From Calais, I shall continue east and south for as far as this body will take me. First Class, and preferably by train. Preferably by sleeper.

Three thousand copies of this book have been printed by the Maple-Vail Book Manufacturing Group, Binghamton, NY, for Golden Gryphon Press, Urbana. IL. The typeset is Electra with Bordeaux display, printed on 55# Sebago. Typesetting by The Composing Room, Inc., Kimberly, WI.